SOMETHING IN
DISGUISE

SOMETHING
IN DISGUISE

Elizabeth Jane Howard

NEW YORK

The Viking Press

Published in 1970 by The Viking Press, Inc.
625 Madison Avenue, New York, N. Y. 10022

SBN 670-65656-9

Library of Congress catalog card number: 75-94846

Printed in U.S.A.

For my brother, Colin Howard

CONTENTS

PART ONE

―――――――――••✠••―――――――――

April

ONE

··✥··

WEDDING

WHEN Oliver saw his sister in her bridesmaid's dress he laughed so much he could hardly stand.

'I've never looked my best in pink.

'Oh shut *up*, it's not as funny as all that.'

'You look like a sort of elongated Shirley Temple. Or a chimpanzee at a Zoo tea-party: yes—more like that, because of your little hairy arms peeping out from all that dimity, or whatever it is—'

'Organza,' she said crossly; 'and it's quite pale on my arms.'

'What is? Your fur? Don't worry about that. Lots of men love hairy women, and if they turn out not to, you could always fall back on another chimpanzee in a sailor suit. Turn round.'

'What for?' she asked when she had done so.

'Just wanted to see if the back was as funny as the front.'

'Is it?'

'Not quite, because one misses your face. Do keep that expression for the wedding photographs.'

'You are being beastly. *Anyone* would look awful in it. *You* would.'

'Let me pop it on. I bet I could bring tears to your eyes. The tragic transvestite: a sort of leitmotif for Colin Wilson. Come on, Lizzie. I'll go mincing down to Daddo, and send his old blood coursing through his veins—'

'Get dressed, you fool. The whole day's going to be quite awful enough without you doing a thing to make it worse. It is poor old Alice's day, after all.'

'I haven't had any breakfast.'

11

'Well you won't get any now. You'll get buffet lunch in—' she looked at her man's watch strapped by black leather round her wrist —'just over an hour and a half.'

'You'll have to take that watch off. You might as well be carrying a tommy-gun. I promise I'll be nice to Alice. I *like* Alice. I like *Alice*,' he added going to the door. 'And May. And you. I shall always remember the first time I saw you like this.'

'You're not going to see me like it any other time. Really be nice to Alice.'

'Really being nice would entail a kind of Rochester wedding. Finding that Leslie had a mad wife shut up in one of his building estates—'

'Who's Shirley Temple?' Recognizing *Jane Eyre* reminded her that she didn't know that one.

'An infant prodigy who looked her best in pink. Honestly, you don't know *anything*.' He slammed her door so that it burst open. She shut it, and turned sadly to the pointed satin court shoes that had been half-heartedly dyed to match. They'd be too uncomfortable to wear in ordinary life anyway.

∗ ∗ ∗

Alice sat in front of her stepmother's dressing-table wondering whether she could improve her hair. She couldn't, she decided: it had been back-combed with such obsessional care by the local hairdresser, that any interference with it now would probably be disastrous. 'My wedding morning,' she thought, and tried to feel momentous and festive—somehow more worthy. It was April; the sky was overcast in slate, and livid green trees waved wildly in the gusty wind. Ordinarily, by now she would be feeding the dogs which Daddy would not have in the house, and cleaning out their horrible kennels that smelled like animal public lavatories however often you cleaned them. It wasn't at all a nice day from the weather point of view. 'I'm leaving home,' she thought; but even that seemed a bit hopeless as they'd only lived there for two years and she'd never liked it anyway. Daddy had bought the house when he married May: it was large and ugly, and Alice knew that secretly May didn't like it either—she was always too cold, she said. 'I *want* to leave,' she thought more vehemently. Then she thought what a good man Leslie obviously was, and that she would miss May who'd been much nicer to her than her other stepmother—nicer even than her own mother who'd always seemed to be what Daddy called failing. He loathed ill health.

She opened her dressing-gown to see whether her skin had subsided from pink to white after her bath. May had insisted on her using this room with its bathroom attached; had insisted also upon giving her the last remaining bath salts, had offered to help her dress, or keep out of the way—in fact was behaving with effortless, model kindness. It was amazing that anyone could be so practical about feelings when they weren't at all about things. 'Weren't at all *what*, Alice?' Daddy would say, with his pale bulging eyes fixed upon her (when she was little she had thought he did it to bully, when she was a young girl she had thought it was because he was stupid—now she thought it was a bit of both); 'Practical, Daddy,' she would always have replied in a small uninteresting voice used only on him. Oliver and Elizabeth hated him. It was only affection for their own mother, May, that prevented them from being rather horrible to poor old Daddy. As it was, Oliver called him Daddo— in quotes—and gave him earnest, frightfully unsuitable Christmas presents which he then kept asking about. He'd made him a Friend of Covent Garden, for instance, and given him a whole book of photographs of ballet dancers and books about pygmies and Kalahari Bushmen which said how wonderful and civilized they were when Oliver must know perfectly well that Daddy thought black men and ballet dancers were the *end* ... Elizabeth was not so bad, but she thought that everything her brother did was all right, and they were always having private jokes together and May just laughed at them and said, do be serious for a moment, not really wanting them to be at all.

I must be. I'm getting married. I must get dressed. She got up from the dressing-table and slipped off her multi-coloured Japanese kimono. All her underclothes were new. Her skin had now reverted

13

to milky-whiteness. She was tall, big-boned and an old-fashioned shape. She had, indeed, the heavy brows, beautiful eyes, slightly Roman nose and square jaw that were typical of du Maurier. Modern underclothes did not suit her—the gaps were not alluring, but faintly embarrassing—they embarrassed *her*, at any rate. She suffered intermittently from hay fever, mastitis and acne, and anti-histamine, unboned bras and calamine lotion fought an uneasy battle with the anxieties of her nervous, gentle temperament. Today it was the mastitis that was giving her trouble; her brassière was too tight, but it was the one she had worn for fitting her dress—she couldn't change it now. All the dressing and undressing in marriage must be so difficult—if one hated doing it even in shops when trying on clothes, what would it be like in a bedroom with a man, an audience of one? And the *same* one at that? Not that she meant... Poor Alice had an unfortunate capacity for confounding herself—even when alone, even with what could fairly be described as innocently random thoughts: she conducted a great deal of her spare and private time (and there had been a good deal of that because she was rather shy) with some anonymous, jeering creature who seemed only to exist in order to trap her with some inconsistency, some banal or lewd or plain dotty remark which it waited for her to make. *She* was the last person in the world to want hundreds of men watching her take off her clothes ... Sneering, incredulous silence.

She walked over to her wedding dress which hung stiffly with the long sleeves sticking out, not looking as though it could fit anyone. The trouble with satin—even cut on the cross—was that it fitted you as long as you didn't move at all; the moment you did, great rifts and creases and undercurrents of strain determined themselves: this had happened at every fitting, and an angry woman in mildewed black, who combined a strong odour of Cheddar cheese with the capacity to talk with her mouth bristling with pins, had stuck more pins into the dress (and Alice) with no lasting effect.

The veil would conceal a certain amount. It had been carefully arranged in an open hat-box which now lay on May's bed, but on approaching the box, she discovered that it was entirely full of her cat, Claude, who lay in it like a huge fur paperweight. She mentioned his name and he opened his lemony eyes just enough to be able to see her, stretched out a colossal paw and yawned. He was an uneasy combination of black and white: on his face this gave him an asymmetrical and almost treasonable appearance. His pads were the bright pink of waterproof Elastoplast, and between them, the thick, white fur was stained pale green. He'd been hunting, she told him as she lifted him off her veil, and he purred like the distant rumble of a starting lorry. He was heartless, greedy and conceited, but the thought of going to Cornwall (the honeymoon) without him made her feel really sad. She had not liked to ask Leslie whether he could live with them in Bristol, and, indeed, it had crossed her mind that even if Leslie agreed, Claude might not. His standard of living in Surrey was exceptionally high—even for a cat—as apart from two large meals a day that he ate primly out of a soup plate, he procured other, more savage snacks such as grass snakes and rabbits, that he demolished on the scullery floor at times convenient to himself. Enough of him, she thought, putting him tenderly on the bed. He got up at once, shook his head—his ear canker rattled like castanets—and chose a better position eight inches from where she had put him. Her veil was quite crushed and spattered with his hairs —he moulted continuously in all his prodigious spare time. 'What on *earth* am I doing?' she thought as she hung the veil on the back of a chair. 'Starting a new life without Daddy, I suppose.'

There was a whimsical fanfare of tapping on the door, and before she could answer, Leslie's sister, Rosemary, came in. She was dressed from head to foot in pink organza: it was she who had chosen the bridesmaids' dresses. Pink, she had said, was her colour, and it certainly provided a contrast to the dark, wiry curls and the mole on the left side of her face. She was older than Leslie, unmarried, and with a robust contempt for all Englishmen. When younger, she had been an air hostess, and so was able to back up this contempt with many a passing romantic interlude in which men, generically described by her as continental, invariably demonstrated their superior approach to ladies. She regarded her brother's marriage to Alice with almost hysterical indulgence, and had arranged so much of the wedding that Alice felt quite frightened of her.

'Here I am!' she exclaimed. Her nails were far too long, thought Alice as Rosemary twitched the wedding dress off its hanger.

'In view of the time, I think we ought to pop this on—why—whatever *has* happened to your veil? That awful cat!'

Alice, inserting her arms into the tight, satin sleeves (it was rather like trying to put back champagne bottles into their straw casings), mumbled something defensive about Claude and at once, without warning, her eyes filled with tears. Rosemary, like many obtrusive people, was quick to observe any such physical manifestations of dismay and to rush into the breach she had made for the purpose. She would get the veil ironed; Sellotape was wonderful for removing hairs; Alice must cheer up—it would not do for her to meet Leslie at the altar with red eyes. But at least she went, leaving Alice to struggle with the tiny round satin buttons—like boiled cods' eyes —that fastened the sleeves at her wrists. 'Something borrowed,' she thought miserably. She would far rather borrow Claude's hairs than anything else she could think of. If only May would come; would stop being tactful, and come, and just stay with her until it was all over ...

* * *

May, wearing an anonymous macintosh over her wedding clothes, was mixing the dogs' food in the scullery. Biscuits—like small pieces of rock—a tin of animal meat and last night's cabbage lay in a chipped enamel bowl, and she was stirring it with a wooden spoon. It smelled awful and did not look enough, but she did not notice either of these things because she was trying to think about the Absolute—a concept as amorphous and slippery as a distant fish and one that she feared was for ever beyond her intellectual grasp. 'The Whole,' she repeated dreamily: at this point, as usual, the concept altered from being some kind of glacial peak to an orange-coloured sphere—a furry and at the same time citrus ball; but these visual translations interrupted real understanding of the idea—were nothing, she felt, but childish cul-de-sacs, the wrong turning in this cerebral maze. She tried again. 'God,' she thought, and instantly

an ancient man—a benign King Lear and at the same time Father
Christmas in a temper—was sitting on a spiky, glittering chair.
'Absolute Being': the chair wedged itself on the glacial peak. She
sighed, and a bit of cabbage fell out of the bowl. A very interesting
man she had met recently had told her to live in the present. She
picked up the piece of cabbage and put it back into the bowl. The
trouble with the present was the way it went on and on and on, and
she found it so easy to live in that when the man had suggested to
her that she wasn't doing it the right way, she had felt sure he was
right.

It was so easy to be a vegetable, she thought, staring humbly into
the bowl, and somehow or other the amount more that was
expected of one must be achievable by slow degrees: it was not
necessary to jump straight from a cabbage to God. It was worse than
that really; babies, for instance were all right; even children—'little
children'—were spiritually acceptable; but somewhere along the
line leading to adolescence people got demoted from being children
to being vegetables, and often wicked vegetables at that. The
Christian world blamed a good deal of this on to carnal knowledge.
This seemed, to her, to be an over-simplification, because even she
could think of a lot of dreary and comparatively unevolved people
whose carnal knowledge seemed to her nil ... Anyway, this interesting man had said that sex was a good thing—if properly approached
—but he had added that hardly anybody understood how to
approach it properly. The only time she had thought about sex had
been the gigantic months after Clifford had been killed, when
underneath or inside her misery had continued her aching un-
attended body that simply went on wanting him, that seemed no
more able to recognize his death than some poor people could
recognize that a limb that itched and twitched was no longer there
because it had been cut off. Several of her friends had lost their
men in the war, but she quickly discovered that the plane on which
such losses were touched upon was the empty-chair-beside-the-fire
one: the empty body in the bed was never admitted in the social
annals of bereavement. She hadn't 'approached' sex before Clifford,
and she hadn't approached it with him. He and it had arrived

together; she had loved him almost at once and remarked—breathlessly soon afterwards—how lucky it was that when you loved someone there was so much to do about it. They had had four years of interrupted, but otherwise splendid pleasure, but always with the war lying in wait—at first, hardly mattering, seeming distant and unreal and vaguely wicked as a child's view of death. After Oliver was born there were a few more months when Clifford —doing navigation courses at a Naval Training Establishment— worked harder, but was still able to get home more often than not. Home was then a two-roomed flat at the top of a non-converted house in Brighton. They were poor—a sub-lieutenant's pay and her fifty pounds a year was all they had—but Clifford had a second-hand bicycle for getting to work, she became extraordinarily good at vegetable curries and, as Clifford had pointed out, a baby was one of the cheapest luxuries currently available. Then the war had pounced: a fine spring afternoon, and he had come back early— she heard his step on the linoleum stairs and ran to meet him trembling with unexpected delight ... Next morning he left her at five, a full lieutenant newly appointed to a frigate. She had sat in the tiny blacked-out kitchen staring at his half-drunk cup of tea and wondering how on earth she could bear it. To be in love, to say goodbye for an unknown amount of time (weeks? months? years? she would not imagine further) only to know that *he* was to be put professionally in danger somewhere, and that, worse, this was fast becoming the accepted, general situation, was the beginning of the war for her. She had sat in the kitchen hating men for devising, allowing, lending themselves to this monstrous stratagem, which seemed to her then as evil and pointless and heartless as the origins of chess. Even *he*— she had sensed his professional excitement, his pride in that wretched piece of gold lace, his complete acceptance that the Admiralty could, at a moment's notice, break up his private life and send him anywhere to fight and perhaps be killed ...

He *hadn't* been killed for nearly another three years after that morning: the war had played cat and mouse with her: after three years of sharpening her courage by a succession of these partings, of stretching her anxiety and loneliness to breaking point in the months between them, of informing her fears (it was impossible not to discover a good deal of the horrors and hazards of convoy work in the North Atlantic and that was Clifford's life), it pounced again. He never saw his daughter: he never even *saw* her, she had used to reiterate—a straw of grievance which she clung to for months because even some kind of grievance seemed to help a bit—with the days, at least. So, like thousands of women and hundreds who had been deeply in love, she settled down to the problems of bringing up two children without their father or enough money ... When they were up, and before, she hoped, they had begun to think of her as a responsibility, she had married again.

Reminiscence was not thought: it couldn't be, because it was so easy. Another interesting point the interesting man had made was that anything worthwhile was difficult; he had not actually said that if you stumbled upon some natural talent, the talent would turn out to be inferior or unnecessary, but she suspected, in her own case, at least, that this was probably so. Obedience to natural laws, he had said, was essential, *if only you could find out what they were.* Obedience and your own talents turning out to be no good had a ring of truth about it: the people who ran institutions seemed always primarily concerned with the dangers of spiritual/temporal pride in their subjects; look at nuns and the Foreign Office ...

'Oh madam! Whatever are you doing in here on a day like this!' It was Oliver doing his imitation of the horrible housekeeper who had ruled the colonel's life until May had come into it.

'I'll do it,' he continued, looking into the bowl; 'you haven't got enough there to keep a lovesick Pekinese—let alone those two great witless sods in the kennels. Give me another tin of what's-his-name and go and be gracious somewhere.'

'Thank you darling. Have you seen Alice?'

'No. Should I have?'

'I just wondered if she was all right.'

'Why don't you go and see, then? It'd be a kindness: that ghastly Rosemary's been at her, and guess what she's up to now?'

May shook her head as she struggled out of the macintosh.

'She's made Liz iron Alice's veil. Came to her and said she

couldn't find any of the servants to do it. "There aren't any, my dear," I said. "What, in a great house like this!" she said. (Christ, this stuff smells like Portuguese lavatories!) "There's Mrs Green who does for us three times a week, but she's sulking because of the caterers so she's not doing for us today." So then she went mincing off to Liz who says that ironing is dangerous because her dress is too tight under the arms. She really does look awful in it, but she's ironing just the same. We may not have servants, I told Rosemary, but the house is fraught with splendid little women. Rosemary said something about Alice being a bit weepy.'

May looked concerned: 'I'll go and see her. Where's—'

'My stepfather is bullying the caterers. You look much less awful than Liz, I must say. Who *usually* does this filthy job?'

'Alice used to. From now on it'll be me.'

'Make Daddo do it.'

'Oliver—don't call him that. Just for today. It upsets him. He's afraid you're laughing at him.'

'His fears are absolutely grounded, *I'm* afraid.' Then he looked at her again and said, 'You know what I think?' He had lit two cigarettes and put one in her mouth. 'I think you should get out. After two years of this you must know it can only get worse.'

'Please darling, shut up.'

'Right. Sorry. I just want you to know,' he added in a quavering manner, 'that vulgar and pretentious though it is, you can always make your home with me.'

'Good,' she said in a more comfortable voice, and went.

* * *

Herbert Browne-Lacey, May's husband, Alice's father and the step-father of Oliver and Elizabeth, had given up the caterers in despair (the fellows didn't seem to understand a word he said to them, as though he was talking Dutch or Hindi) and was now stalking up and down the side of the lawn which was banked by rhododendrons beginning to flower. He was in full morning dress and walked slowly, holding his grey top hat behind his back in both hands: the

wind was very uncertain. His feelings were sharply divided: naturally any father would feel so at the marriage of his only daughter.
He was glad that she was getting married in some ways, and sorry
in others. He would miss her; he thought of innumerable things:
the way she made his middle-morning beef tea; her ironing the
newspaper if May got hold of it first (women were the devil with
newspapers and it was absolutely unnecessary for them to read them
anyway) how good she was with the dogs (the long, wet walks,
kennel-cleaning and feeding), her housewifely activities (the house
had twenty-five rooms but Alice had helped to make it possible to
do with the one char), and as for boots and the odd medal (he
touched his left breast and there was a reassuring clink), why, she
was jolly nearly up to his old batman's standards. Of course she
was marrying a prosperous, steady young man. Leslie Mount was
clearly going far; the only thing that worried the colonel was
whether he had a sense of direction. Money wasn't everything ...
He began to think about money. The wedding was costing far
more than he had meant it to: on the other hand, he would no longer
be responsible for Alice. When he had told Leslie that Alice was
worth her weight in gold he had felt that he was simply being
appropriately sentimental: now, he began to wonder whether there
wasn't some truth in the remark. May, bless her, of course, was so
confoundedly unworldly: not always impractical—she made damn
good curries of left-overs, not hot enough, but damn good—but
she had her head in the clouds too much of the time to recognize the
value of money. She did things and bought things quite often that
were totally unnecessary. Totally unnecessary, he repeated, working
himself into one of his minor righteous rages. And those children
of hers were totally out of hand. *They* were responsible for her worst
extravagances: it would have been much better to put the boy into
the army than to send him to a fiendishly expensive university, and
as for the girl, what was the point of having her taught domestic
science—again, at fiendish expense—if the result was simply that
she sent all the housekeeping bills soaring with her fancy cooking?
Money between husband and wife should be shared, in his opinion,
and this meant that May had absolutely no right to squander that

inheritance from her relative in Canada—an estimable old lady who had died about a year before the colonel had married May. He had forced her to buy this house with some of the money, because any fool could see that property was going to go up, but after that, he had got nowhere. She had insisted upon having her own bank account and cheque books, and could therefore scribble and fritter away any amount of capital without reference to himself. The only times when the colonel could contemplate being French—or something equally outlandish—were when he thought about the marriage laws: there was no nonsense about women being independent *there*. His rather protuberant and bright blue eyes blazed whenever he thought about the Married Woman's Property Act. Well at least he made her pay her share of the household accounts: she couldn't have it both ways. But the wedding presented difficulties. He had managed, by playing on Leslie's father's snobbery and patriotism, to wrest from him a certain share of the—in his view—totally unreasonable and iniquitous expenses of this jamboree. He was, after all, a gentleman, a soldier and he had served his country, and he had made these three points delicately clear to Mr Mount who was clearly no gentleman, but had the grace to recognize this fact, and who had been reduced to explaining and apologizing for his flat feet (a plebeian complaint if ever there was one, nobody at Sandhurst had ever had flat feet, by God!) which had precluded his serving his country in any way but building ordnance factories. There was a world of difference between that sort of job and being in Whitehall.

But the fact was that those factory-building fellows had made the money, and simple chaps like himself, fighting for their country, hadn't. Mr Mount had offered to pay half the cost of the reception, and the colonel had accepted this, because, after all, Alice *had* no relatives that they ever saw apart from himself, whereas the Mount contingent was positively pouring from Bristol or wherever it was they came from, so Mr Mount paying half was really the least he could do. The border was looking very ragged. Alice hadn't seemed to put her heart into it these last months although he had pointed out again and again that if you wanted a decent herbaceous border you had to work hard on it in the spring. He sighed and his waistcoat creaked: he had had the suit twenty-six years after all—bought it to get married to Alice's mother, and although his tailor had adjusted it several times to accommodate the effects of time, no more adjustments were possible. Few men, however, could rely upon their figures when they were in their sixties as well as he could. The upkeep of this place was a terrible strain to him: it was so damn difficult to get anyone to do anything these days. He pulled a pleasant gold half-hunter out of his watch pocket—twenty to twelve —must be getting a move on. The watch had been left to Alice by her godfather, but it was no earthly use to a girl ... He turned towards the house and began shouting for his wife.

*　　*　　*

The church was Victorian neo-gothic: varnished oak, brass plaques and candlesticks, atrocious windows the colours of patent medicines, soup, syrup and Sanatogen foisted upon the building by families who had feared society considerably more than they can ever have feared God; hassocks like small dark-red ambushes lurked awk-wardly on the cold stone floor; battered prayer books slid about the pew desks, and tired little musty draughts met the guests as they were ushered in. The organ, whose range seemed to be between petulance and exhaustion, kept up the semblance of holy joy about as much as a businessman wearing a paper hat at a party pretends to be a child. Even the beautiful white lilac and iris could not combat the dis-comforting ugliness of the place. 'Poor God,' thought May. 'If He is really present here, and many places like this, it must be like being a kind of international M.P. A hideous place with boring people not meaning what they say, except when they come to some private grievance.'

The organ came to an end, took an audibly bronchial breath and began on what was recognizably some Bach. Alice had entered the church on her father's arm, followed by Rosemary and Elizabeth. Heads turned and turned back to the chancel steps where the vicar stood waiting for them. 'He's a wonderful looking man,' thought Gertie Mount wistfully. A kind of cross between William Powell and Sir Aubrey Smith, she decided, as the colonel glided past her and came to a majestic halt and Leslie materialized out of the gloom beside his bride. Alice handed her bouquet to Rosemary, who received it with operatic humility, and the marriage service began. Mr Mount, whose clothes seemed to him to be slowly strangling him at all key points, glanced surreptitiously at the wife. She might start at any moment, but he had a nice big clean one handy: he groped in his right-hand trouser pocket, forgot about his morning coat and dropped his prayer book. He stooped to retrieve it, but the pews were so narrow that he hit his bottom—a hard but springy blow—on the edge of the seat. This had the effect of knocking him forwards, his jaw came in contact with the pew desk and his false teeth gave an ominous lurch. He now seemed to be wedged, and was only rescued by his teenage daughter, Sandra, who hauled him to his feet and handed him her prayer book with a minutely crushing smile. She was, in his opinion, well on the way to becoming over-educated, and terrified him. He turned to Gertie for comfort: she'd begun, and he felt (more warily) for the hanky.

The vicar was asking the couple if they knew any impediment to their marriage. His voice and manner, Oliver thought, gave one the feeling that he could not possibly be real—might at any moment, in a Lewis Carroll manner, turn into a sheep or a lesser playing card: that would be an impediment, all right. He didn't believe in marriage himself.

Leslie was looking forward to the bit where he had his say, which he had practised privately on a corner of the golf course at home. So keen was he about getting on with the job that he interrupted the vicar after the first question and said 'I will' with immense resolution, but the vicar was accustomed to amateurs and simply raised his voice a semi-tone. Leslie's final asseveration was far more subdued. 'Will *what?*' muttered his Great-Aunt Lottie peevishly. She seldom had what Mrs Mount called a grip on things, and Mrs Mount had been against bringing her all this way, but Mr Mount had said that it would be an outing for her. Gertie felt in her bag for the tin of Allenbury's Blackcurrant Pastilles, and nearly ruined her glove getting one out and thrusting it into Auntie's mumbling hairy jaws.

The colonel waited until the padre had asked the question that usually applied to fathers, nodded briskly and stepped smartly back to the front pew beside May. His actions, to Gertie, showed that of course he had the proper respect, but he was a plain man with no nonsense about him. She was sure he had a heart of gold.

'Going, going, gone!' thought Alice wildly. Leslie's hand was soft and dry, her own, damp and icy. Enunciating with care, he was plighting his troth: it did not sound like his usual voice, but then these were not things that people usually said to each other. In a moment it was going to be her turn ...

'I *hope* she's secretly terrifically in love,' thought Elizabeth hopelessly as she listened to Alice's clear, unexpectedly childish tones repeating her share of the phrases after the vicar. But how could you be, with Leslie?

'With my body I thee worship,' Sandra repeated derisively to herself: the whole thing was unbelievably old-fashioned. *She* would get married in a registry office or America or a ship, in white leather, and go away in a helicopter. And she certainly wouldn't marry anyone as old as Leslie.

Rosemary watched the ring being put on Alice's finger and felt a lump in her throat: a lot of her men friends had said she was too emotional, but there it was. *She* felt like crying, and those two, standing there, seemed quite unmoved: that was British phlegm for you. If *she* had been standing where Alice was, her eyes would be full of great, unshed tears.

The vicar, gathering speed, was pronouncing them man and wife. He's like an old horse, Oliver thought, on the last lap to the stable, or, in this case, the registry. His stomach was rumbling uncontrollably and he had the nasty feeling that it was just the sort of sound most suited to the acoustics of this church.

End of the first lap, thought the colonel, rising to his feet. He had managed, during the service, to count the guests—roughly, anyway— and on the whole he felt he had been sensible to put away two of the cold salmon trout that the caterers had been laying out. Those fellows always produced too much food because then they could charge you for it. So he had simply taken away two of the dishes and put them in the larder ...

Where Claude, who never had very much to do in the mornings,
smelt it. He had known for ages how to open the larder door, but
had not advertised the fact, largely because there was hardly ever
anything there worth eating; but he was extremely fond of fish.
He inserted a huge capable paw round the lower edge of the door
and heaved for several minutes: when the gap was wide enough
he levered it open with his shoulder and part of his head. The fish
lay on a silver platter on the marble shelf, skinned and garnished.
He knocked pieces of lemon and cucumber contemptuously aside,
settled himself into his best eating position and began to feast. He
tried both fish—equally delicious—and when he could eat no more,
he jumped heavily off the shelf with a prawn in his mouth which
he took to the scullery for further examination.

TWO

···⚕···

FLIGHT

ELIZABETH, back into her comfortable blue jeans and one of Oliver's old shirts, had taken the two salmon trout from the larder and laid them on the vast kitchen table. Her assignment was to patch up one of the fish for supper, so that the colonel need never know of Claude's depredations. Alice, before she had left, had begged both Elizabeth and May to look after him; of course they had both promised, and Alice was scarcely out of sight before May discovered the larder crime.

Taking pieces from one fish and transposing them to another was like a frightful jigsaw with none of the pieces ready made. On top of this, the fish had been overcooked so that the flakes broke whenever she tried to wedge them into position. 'I'll have to cover the whole lot with mayonnaise,' she thought despairingly. Well—at least she knew how to make good mayonnaise: at *least* she knew that.

'Isn't it nasty having the whole house to ourselves?'

It was only Oliver.

'How do you mean?'

'I mean that anywhere as large and hideous *and* otherwise un-distinguished as this is only bearable when it's heavily populated.' He sat on the kitchen table. 'It must have been built by someone who made a packet out of shells or gas masks in the First World War. Do you know what the first gas masks were made of?'

'Of course I don't. What?'

'Pieces of Harris tweed soaked in something or other, with bits of tape to tie round the back of the head. What fascinates me about that is that it should have been *Harris* tweed: so hairy—a kind of counter-irritant.'

A minute later, he said,

'Listen, ducks, what are you going to do?'

Elizabeth had been separating two eggs into pudding basins.

'How do you mean?'

'Don't be so *stupid*, Liz.'

'I'm *not* being stupid—I just don't know what you mean.' She seized a gin bottle filled with olive oil.

'I said: what are you going to *do*?'

'Make mayonnaise.' She selected a fork and began to beat the eggs: her eyes were pricking. 'That's one thing I *can* do.' The feeling that she was dull, and that Oliver, whom she loved, was brilliant and would therefore suddenly realize this one day and abandon her, recurred for what seemed like the millionth time. How did he *know* about First-World-War gas masks? she thought. Why didn't she know *anything* surprising like that?

'I'll pour—you beat.' She wasn't very bright, but from her first moments, May had, so to speak, let him in on looking after her. She wasn't very bright, and needed him.

'You're not stupid,' he said, taking the oil bottle. 'Goodness me, how weddings make women cry. Cheer up: think of spending a fortnight in Cornwall with Leslie.'

She smiled: she would have giggled if she'd felt better.

'A pink chiffon nightdress and all the lights out and twin beds.'

'He's taken his golf clubs,' she said, entering the game.

'They can't talk about what they did last week, because they didn't have one.'

'They can discuss the wedding. To tide them over.'

'He can tell her about his future: and how he can't stand dishonesty—he's funny that way—but he's all for plain speaking. That cuts down nearly anyone's conversation.'

'But on honeymoons,' said Elizabeth hesitantly, 'don't you spend a lot of time making love to the person?'

'That's a frightfully old-fashioned way of putting it. Besides, golf takes much longer: if he plays two rounds a day, he won't have all that time.'

'Steady: don't put any more in till I tell you.'

'What happens if I put in too much?'

'It separates and I have to start all over again with another yolk.'

'Listen: what I meant just now was, you don't want to just stay here, do you?

'I mean, there's a serious danger that Daddo will just push you into being another Alice,' he went on when she didn't reply.

'I know.'

'We can't have *you* escaping to Southport or Ostend in five years' time for a gay fortnight with a girl friend and meeting someone like Leslie: if you had to choose between dog kennels and Daddo or the equivalent of Leslie you might easily choose Leslie. Seriously, Liz, you'd be better off in London.'

'Where?'

'With me.'

She flushed with delight. 'Oh—Oliver!'

'We'll live on our wits—Edwardian for sharp practice.'

'How would we?'

'My wits then,' he said with careless affection. 'Awful people are always offering me jobs.'

'Aren't you *in* a job?'

'The accountants' office? Honestly, Liz, I couldn't stand it. I left last week.'

'Does May know?'

'*She* knows, but *he* doesn't. We've agreed not to tell him. He'd think I was going to the dogs more than ever. It's funny how keen he is on girls going to *his* blasted dogs, when he can't stand young whipper-snappers like *me* going to them.'

'What are you going to *do*?'

'I don't know: that's what's so nice. After all those years of educational regimentation I want a breather. I shall probably marry an heiress,' he added carelessly.

'You mightn't love her. I mean—you couldn't just marry her because of that.'

'Oh, couldn't I! Well—until we find her—we could always advertise as an unmarried couple willing to wash up, or something like that.'

There was a pause while she beat industriously (the sauce was now the colour of Devonshire cream) and wondered what she ought to do. Then she said, 'It's all right now: pour a thin, steady stream.'

He said, 'I know what's the trouble. You're worrying about May.'

She hadn't been, she'd started to imagine life in London with Oliver: concerts, cinemas, cooking up delicious suppers for his friends, all charming, funny, *brilliant* people like Oliver—people he'd met at Oxford ... 'Don't .go: Elizabeth will you knock up something to eat?' 'I say, Elizabeth, is this what you call knocking something up? It's fabulous!' (no, wrong word—a bit cheap and unintellectual) 'It's the best pasta I've ever eaten in my life'...

But she'd been going to end up thinking about May: May stuck here for the rest of her life, in this awful red-brick fumed-oak stained-glass barracks—every room looking like a Hall on Speech Day—even the garden filled with the worst things like rhododendrons, laurels, standard roses with grotesque flowers, hedges of cupressus, a copper beech and a monkey puzzle, cotoneaster and an art nouveau sundial; all this instead of the cosy little house in Lincoln Street where they had lived the moment Great-Aunt Edith had kicked the bucket in Montreal ... Aloud, she said, 'It's not just the house: it's *him.*'

'Daddo?'

She nodded. 'He gives me the creeps. He ought just to be poor and funny, but he isn't.'

'Well he *is* funny: he's a pompous old fool.'

'You're not a woman: you wouldn't understand.'

There was enough mayonnaise; she seasoned it and began spreading it over the fish with a palette knife.

'If she's lonely enough, she might leave him. If you stay here, she never will.'

'I could come back for week-ends,' she said anxiously.

He pushed his hand through her silky brown hair.

'I'm not my sister's keeper.'

'What are you *doing*?'

'Getting the oil off my hands.'

The next conversation about Elizabeth's future was at dinner.

*   *   *

The dining-room was, of course, large; a rectangular room whose ceiling was too high for its other dimensions. A red-and-blue Turkey carpet very nearly reached the caramel-coloured parquet surround. The colonel had bought the carpet, together with a gigantic Victorian sideboard, a stained oak pseudo-Jacobean table and eight supremely uncomfortable and rickety chairs, in a local sale. The windows were also large, but so heavily leaded that they gave the room the air of a rather liberal prison: the top of the centre one was embellished in a key pattern of blue and red stained glass. There were four immense pictures (also bought by the colonel in another sale): one of a dead hare bleeding beside a bunch of grapes on a table; a huge upright of a Highland stag standing on some heather; a brace of moony spaniels with pheasants in their mouths; and a rather ambitious one of a salmon leaping a weir. These were hung upon panelling of highly varnished pitch pine: they were not glazed, and so, as Oliver said, wherever you sat at table there was no way of escaping at least one of them. It was twenty-five to eight, and the colonel was doling out sparse portions of the salmon trout. 'What's all this?' he said when he saw the mayonnaise.

Oliver answered immediately, 'It is a sauce made of egg yolks and olive oil and flavoured with black pepper and vinegar called mayonnaise. It was invented by a French general's chef at the siege of Mahon—hence its name; how *interesting* that you should never have encountered it before.'

The colonel put down his servers and glared steadily at his stepson. May said, 'Herbert didn't mean that, did you dear? He meant—'

'What's it doing *here*?' finished Oliver. 'Ah, well Liz made it, with a bit of help from me. We thought you'd like a sauce with a military background.'

There was an incompatible silence while the colonel served the fish and handed plates to May for new potatoes and peas.

Then he said, 'I'm all for plain English cooking, myself.'

May shot a reproachful glance at Oliver which he did not miss, and said, 'Anyway, these are the first of our own peas.'

The colonel stabbed one with his fork. 'Far too small: Hoggett is always premature. If I've told him once, I've told him a hundred times—'

'They taste delicious,' said Elizabeth. (I can't *bear* this: meal after meal of trying to make things right—of keeping them dull so that they won't go wrong.)

'Are these our own potatoes?' asked Oliver politely.

'We don't grow enough potatoes to have new ones,' said Elizabeth quickly. Oliver knew perfectly well that one of the colonel's petty tyrannies was to force an arthritic old gardener to go through the motions of keeping up an enormous kitchen garden. This meant that the colonel resented bought vegetables and prohibited the use of their own until they were so old as to be almost uneatable. He *knew* that, so why didn't he shut up? She glared at him, and his grey eyes immediately fixed upon hers with an empty innocent stare.

'... hope Alice was pleased, anyway.' May was saying to her husband.

'Tremendous palaver—just to get a girl married: still it all went off quite smoothly. The Mounts seemed impressed with the house.'

'I'm not surprised,' said Oliver.

The colonel took his napkin out of a cracked and yellowing ivory ring, wiped a moustache of much the same colour and turned to Oliver.

'Oh. And why, may I ask, are you not surprised?'

'I only meant that as they are in the building business, they would so to speak, look at it with a professional eye. It must have cost a packet to build—even in nineteen-twenty.'

Elizabeth was stacking the plates which she then carried to the sideboard, where waited a trifle, left by the caterers. She brought this, placed it doubtfully in front of her mother, and went for clean plates. The colonel had decided to accept Oliver's speech about the house at face value, and so he had merely grunted. Now he said, 'Ah! Trifle!'

There was a silence while they all looked at the trifle. 'Caterers' Revenge,' thought Elizabeth, as her mother began gingerly spooning it on to the plates. She knew what it would be like. Sponge cake made of dried egg smeared with the kind of raspberry jam where the very pips seem to be made of wood, smothered in packet custard laced with sherry flavouring. The top was embellished with angelica, mock cream and crystallized violets whose dye was bleeding carbon-paper mauve on to the cream.

'A classic example of plain English cooking,' said Oliver smoothly.

'When is he going to *leave*?' thought the colonel. 'Insufferable beggar.'

'What time is your train, Oliver?'

He looked at his mother and felt reproved. 'The last one is ten thirty-eight.' He cleared his throat, feeling suddenly nervous—something of a traitor. 'Liz and I thought—I wondered whether it might not be a good thing for her to come up with me for a bit. Look around, and perhaps get herself a job.'

May was clearly taken aback, but she managed to look calmly at her daughter, and asked—really wanting to know, 'What do you think, darling?   Would you like to go to London?'

'I think I might quite like to.' Her eyes were on her mother's face; she frightfully wanted to find out what May really felt, but now, with Oliver doing it all so treacherously in front of him, she was afraid she wouldn't find out. May might awfully mind her going away, and not be able to say so. 'It would be leaving you with rather a lot.'

'Nonsense.' Even the colonel had found the trifle heavy going, and was again wiping his moustache. 'You must stop treating your mother as though she is a chronic invalid: she's perfectly capable of looking after herself. And on those few occasions when she is not, what am I for? Eh?' He glared round the table, looking, Oliver thought, about as jocular and useless as the Metro-Goldwyn-Mayer lion.

'Is there room in the flat at Lincoln Street?' May, who had given herself hardly any trifle, now stopped pretending to eat it.

'She can have the second-best bedroom and a fair share of all mod. cons. She can look after me when I get home exhausted from work: very good practice for both of us.'

May opened her mouth and shut it again.

The colonel took a tin of Dutch cigars from one of his capacious pockets, opened it, and offered one to Oliver. There were—as usual —two in the tin. Oliver refused. The colonel, pleased about this, lit one for himself, and said, 'Ah—the office. And how is the job, Oliver? Going well, I trust?'

Oliver said, 'As well as can be expected.'

'I could come home for week-ends.' Elizabeth was the kind of girl who blushed if other people told lies, and deflection was her form of apology.

'There comes a time,' the colonel said, 'when all young people have to leave the nest and try their wings.'

'Well, that's settled, then.' Oliver got up from the table. 'Liz joins the chicks in Chelsea. If you'll excuse me, I must go and pack. What about you, Liz?'

'Are you going to*night* darling?'

Elizabeth halted in her tracks: if only Oliver hadn't done all this at dinner; if only she could have *talked* to her mother; if only she didn't feel so guilty about wanting to go so badly ... But May got briskly to her feet and said,

'In that case, I had better come and help you pack.'

The colonel was left in the dining-room alone. He took a second tin of cigars from another pocket, extracted one, and put it in the first tin. It would be a relief to get rid of both young Seymours: have May to himself: with Alice gone, it was better to have May to himself.

*   *   *

Barely three hours later, Elizabeth sat opposite Oliver in the train. Most of the reading lights in the compartment did not work, but in any case, she did not want to read. Oliver had gone to sleep: she stared without seeing anything out of the dirty window and tried to think, but she was feeling so much that it was very difficult.

Escape was the first thing she felt: a sense of freedom, but funnily, of *safety* as well; as though she had been locked up or ill-used—like girls in ordinary Victorian novels, and detective or spy stories since. Why? Nobody had ever been unkind to her; it was her fault that she could not feel at ease with her stepfather who had only ever been dull, pompous, and *obvious* really with her. Too like himself to be true—something like that. Before she had met him, she had thought that what people said about Colonel Blimp and ex-army men, particularly those who had served in India, was a sort of coarse shorthand to save them having to know or describe anybody. She couldn't think that now. It was almost as though he was a jolly good character actor toeing the popular line. Perhaps it was the house that was so ugly and nasty as to be sinister. May had said when she married him, 'He's not meant to be your father, darling, because you had a perfectly good one; he's just meant to be my husband: it would be stupid of me to try and provide you with a new father at your age. Of course I hope you like him, but you needn't feel you've got to.' But how could she—how *could* she ever have thought that she would be happy with him? And in that house? She had bought it because he wanted it. The moment she had married, Elizabeth had realized how much she was meant to be married to somebody; she wasn't at all the kind of woman to manage life on her own. And just when Oliver and she might have started looking after *her* for a change, she'd made it impossible for them. Their family life had become a kind of conspiracy; jokes, habits, any kind of fun or thinking things awful and become furtive and uncomfortable. Apart from the blissful feeling of escape (and as she was so selfish she couldn't help feeling that), she felt really worried about May. While Alice had been there, she had provided a kind of buffer for all of them. Alice was used to her father; she had become devoted to May, she had never stopped doing things for other people, or at least for her father, which stopped other people having to do them for him.

She had never got to know Alice: they had always been so anxiously, fumblingly *nice* to each other, had early set such a high standard of you-through-the-swing-doors-first courtesy that neither had never found out what the other really liked or wanted. Alice had once shown her some poetry—short, rhyming verses about nature going on whatever she was feeling: they were very dull, imbued with a kind of sugary discontent; nature-was-pretty-and-Alice-was-sad stuff. She had read them very slowly to look as though she cared, and said they were jolly good in a hushed voice to show that words were inadequate to express her feelings. And Alice had said how bad they were very fast a good many times, laughing casually and getting very pink. But really the poems, which Elizabeth could see had been meant to be a confidence, had simply put another barrier of nervous dishonesty between them. Practically their only point of contact had been Claude. She had found Alice, changed into her new pale-blue going-away suit, with Claude overflowing in her arms: Alice was crying and Claude was licking his lips and staring hopefully at the floor so perhaps they were *both* minding. Elizabeth had promised to be nice to him, and now, except for concealing the larder crime, here she was escaping. At least if I'm not famous for being intelligent, I ought to concentrate on being reliable and nice. But she had a feeling that people's natures just went on regardless of their talents; you weren't any nicer because you were stupid. Oliver, except for his dastardly behaviour to Herbert (she called him Herbert to herself and nothing to his face), was just as *nice* as she was, and although she didn't always agree with him he was far more interesting because he knew so much and could talk about it. She had tried reading books about *things*, like soil erosion and monotremes and the Moorish influence in Spain, but none of these subjects ever seemed to fit into day-to-day conversation. She had tried asking May what she ought to do about this (just after she failed Oxford and before the domestic science school), but May had said most unhelpfully that hardly anybody she knew thought. Oliver did, she retorted; he was brilliantly clever—a Second and he hardly seemed to work at all! But May had just said, 'Yes darling, I expect he is' rather absently, like someone agreeing with a boring question so that they could stop talking about it. Much though she adored her mother, Elizabeth had wondered then whether it was because she was a bit old-fashioned *and* a woman (a pretty hopeless combination when you came to consider it) that made her not set the store by intelligence that she should. She wouldn't have married Herbert if she'd cared about an intellectual life. She certainly hadn't married him for money, and at her age sex appeal was out of the question—so what was it? It was like being stuck with someone for ever who said at least one awful, obvious thing a day, like a calendar where you tore off Tuesday but couldn't help reading what it said. The most outstanding feature of her mother was how nice she was to absolutely everybody, so possibly she regarded Herbert as a challenge; perhaps, also, she was the only person who could see that secretly, deep down, Herbert was a very good man. Dull people often were, unless that was what their friends said about them to make up for their dullness. I do hope I get less dull, she thought. Living with Oliver ought to help that. She looked at him. He lay, or lounged, opposite her, legs crossed so that she could see a blue vein between his socks and his trousers. His head was thrown back, his eyes shut, a lock of his pale-brown hair was lying over his bulging forehead. Even asleep, he managed to look plunged in thought. He was wearing a very old but nice tweed suit that had belonged to their father: his only civvy suit, May had said, so he had got a good one—to last. He had lovely eyelashes that curled upwards very thickly: he said girls always remarked on them. She supposed she would be meeting his girls at Lincoln Street. I can always go home at week-ends to keep out of his way, she thought; I'll be terrifically tactful and not surprised at anything. Anyway, I *should* go home: I would hate her to feel abandoned. She started to think of her mother carrying the heavy supper trays from the dining-room all along the passage—two baize doors that were meant to stay open but never did—to the kitchen. And then doing all the things that had to be done before anybody could have an evening there, let alone go to bed. Usually Alice and she had done a good deal of it; mostly Alice, she admitted honestly. Putting all the horrible food away so that they were certain to be faced with the left-overs next day, feeding Claude, turning out lights and getting more coal for the fire in the colonel's den (wouldn't you know he'd call it that) where they sat in the evening. There was only one really comfortable chair, and you bet, he took it. Filling hot-water bottles, turning down the beds, drawing bedroom curtains: Herbert liked everything to go on as though there was a large resident staff: oh lord, and now it was just May to be that ... She shouldn't have come or gone or whatever she'd done ...

Oliver opened his eyes.

'Dearest Liz. You look as though you've got indigestion; remorse, I bet. Cheer up. It was all my fault: that's why I did it at dinner. If we'd given them too much notice, I was afraid of Daddo working on May to stop you: he's going to wake up tomorrow and kick himself for letting all that free labour go. Cheer up: think of spending two weeks in Cornwall with Leslie.'

'I have. I am.'

They smiled at each other; then she laughed.

* * *

Leslie had just said, 'Excuse me, dear', and gone to the magnificent peach-tiled bathroom that was part of their suite. A bedroom and the sitting-room—where they were now sitting—was the rest of it. They had arrived at the hotel rather late for dinner in the dining-room, and so Leslie had ordered supper in their suite. The head waiter had been able to let them have consommé—hot or cold—cold chicken and mixed salad, pêche melba and cheese. Leslie had ordered a bottle of sparkling burgundy with this repast, and brandy and crème-de-menthe afterwards. (Alice had had hot consommé and crème-de-menthe, Leslie had had three brandies—he had told the waiter to leave the bottle when he had brought the weak but bitter coffee.) Hours seemed to have gone by since then, and they were still sitting at the small round table with the pink-silk-shaded lamp on it. At the beginning of the meal they had not said much: each of them had made a few desultory remarks about the wedding which the other had instantly agreed with. But when his second brandy was inside him, Leslie had become more expansive. He thought the time had come for a little plain speaking. He was funny that way, but he couldn't stand dishonesty. He looked at her for approbation of this curious and unusual trait. Alice looked seriously back.

'What I want you to know,' Leslie went on, 'is—well it's a bit difficult to put it in the right way. I'm forty-two as I think I told you—'

'Yes.'

'Well—it wouldn't be reasonable to expect me to be completely inexperienced at my age—now would it?'

'No.'

'I'm not—you see. Not at all inexperienced: quite the reverse— you might say. I've been—intimate—with quite a number of women. I've never known them *well*,' he added hastily, 'you understand what I mean, don't you Alice?'

'Yes.'

'I mean, naturally, they weren't the sort of women you'd expect me to have known well. That wasn't their function if you take me. But it *does* mean that I know a good deal about a certain side of life. That's necessary for men. For women—of course—it's different. I don't suppose—well I wouldn't expect you to know anything at all about that.' He finished his brandy and looked at her expectantly.

'No.'

'Of course not.' He seemed at once to be both uplifted and disheartened by this. 'But naturally I've got about a good deal. The war—Belgium—you get all kinds of women there—' He poured some more brandy: his forehead was gleaming. He started to tell her about Belgian women ...

*   *   *

By the time May had cleared up the supper, wedged the larder door so that Claude could not possibly open it, opened him a tin of cat food that, naturally enough, he did not feel inclined to eat although he had made it plain that he was unable to be certain about this until the food was on his soup plate, put on a kettle for hot-water bottles (the house was never really warm and May felt that she got colder there week by week), turned off some passage lights that her children had left on, and conducted a tired and abortive hunt for her spectacles, all she wanted to do was to go to bed. But Herbert, she knew, would be waiting for her. Usually Alice had played backgammon with him after dinner while she pretended to do *The Times* crossword puzzle or got on with her patchwork, but from now on there was no Alice, and Herbert needed her company. Perhaps they could just have a cosy post mortem on the wedding, which now seemed an age away.

The colonel stood with his back to the small coal fire and was gazing reproachfully at the door through which she came.

'What on *earth* have you been doing?'

'Just clearing up supper.'

'Why don't you leave that sort of thing for Mrs what's-her-name?'

May cast herself into the one comfortable chair. 'She may not come tomorrow. Tomorrow isn't her day.'

'She didn't come today, did she?'

'No. Today was supposed to be her day, but she wouldn't come because of the caterers. In any case there is far too much for her to do.'

The colonel grunted. 'The woman's getting above herself. Why don't you fire her, and get somebody else?'

May kicked off her shoes. 'Because there isn't anybody else. Who would come, I mean. We're not on a bus route, so it means nearly two miles walking or on a bicycle. People won't do that nowadays. We've plenty of room: we ought to have somebody living in—a couple.'

The colonel looked wounded: then he stalked slowly over to his filing cabinet, took an immense bunch of keys from a pocket made shapeless by them and unlocked a drawer. He was going to mix his nightcap: a small whisky and soda. They both spoke at once. Then the colonel said, 'I beg your pardon, my dear. What did you say?'

'Just that I thought I'd like a whisky tonight: a small one.'

She knew that he had strong views about what women should, or should not, drink: he particularly disliked her drinking whisky.

'Are you *sure*?' He surveyed her with as broad-minded dis-approval as he could muster.

'Just tonight, darling. It's been such a day.'

He mixed her a small weak drink in silence, handed it to her, made himself one, looked disparagingly at the bottle which was only about a quarter full, put it away and locked up the cabinet. All this seemed to take a very long time, and May resisted the impulse to gulp her drink. Then, when the colonel had made his way, as it were, blindly to her chair, discovered that she was in it, and remained standing (it was *his* chair she was lounging in, and nothing else would do), he said, 'You must realize, my dear, that we cannot possibly afford a couple living in. The expenses of this house are— ah—stretched to their fullest extent; their fullest extent. A couple would land us with heavy expenses that with the best will in the world they could not justify.'

'Perhaps we ought to sell the house then, and find something smaller.' She had finished her whisky, and now wanted a cigarette, but as she only had ten a week and had already smoked two that day she knew there were none left.

'My dear May! You surely cannot mean what you say!'

'Well I did—actually.'

'Part with our *home*!'

'Only to get another one, dear.'

'You speak as though homes are a mere matter of exchange and barter.'

'Well they are really, aren't they? I mean, we bought this one.'

The colonel sat suddenly down on quite an uncomfortable chair. He was speechless, absolutely speechless, he repeated to himself. To justify this situation, he said nothing, he simply stared at her.

'Darling, don't look so appalled! It just seemed to me that with Alice gone, and my two in London, perhaps we don't need all these rooms'—she pretended to count—'what is it? Nine bedrooms we aren't using.'

As he still kept silent, she added, 'Not counting all the other rooms.'

41

He perceptibly found his voice. 'My dear May, this house was an absolute bargain—dirt cheap—an absolute bargain—'

'Goodness,' May thought as she stopped listening, 'you couldn't call it that. Or perhaps I've been poor too many years to think that spending eleven thousand pounds on *anything* would be a bargain. *My* eleven thousand pounds,' she also thought, and then felt thoroughly ashamed of herself ...

' ... simple chap,' the colonel was saying, 'can't be said to have expensive tastes—moderation in all things—but all my life—serving my country and all that—*all* my life, I've looked forward to settling down—in a simple way—my own piece of land—a comfortable home—somewhere that I can call my own—chopping and changing difficult for a feller my age—'

The upshot of what, at their time of life, amounted to a scene was that she was forced to recognize what he said the house meant to him. Her private dream of a cottage in the country and the half of Lincoln Street that was now let being their homes vanished for ever that evening. If she would leave the management of the house to him—not upset her head about it—*he* would keep the whole thing within bounds of their income. She thought at one moment that he was trying to get her to sell the London house (because Oliver and now Elizabeth were to live in it rent free) but, strangely, he seemed most anxious that she should keep it. What it was necessary to review, he said, was their remaining free capital. Here she sensed danger: she did not want to have to discuss Elizabeth's allowance or anything that she gave Oliver with him, or indeed with anyone. She was awfully tired, she said at this point. They would both be the better for a spot of Bedfordshire, he said. But the most incongruous aspect of the whole argument or discussion or whatever one could call it was that he had been really upset; eyes moist, stuttering slightly, repeating phrases more than usual: she honestly hadn't realized that this house meant so much to him. He said, too, that he wanted to be alone with her—to have her to himself. She did not trust him enough about things: if she would leave it all to him everything would work out. He had blown his nose for a long time on one of the handkerchiefs she had given him for his birthday and this had touched her much more than anything he had actually *said* (which had left her not so much unmoved as indefinably depressed). It was the house that depressed her, but now she would just have to make the best of it.

*　*　*

Elizabeth lay in the dark in bed in the tiny top-floor back bedroom at Lincoln Street. The room had no curtains, because May had sent them to the cleaners and Oliver hadn't bothered to put them up when they came back, so light from a street lamp patterned the ceiling and some of the walls. The bed was familiar and uncomfortable—she had had it as a child; indeed, for a short time—the blissful period after Aunt Edith died and before May married Herbert—this had been her room. Now the basement and ground floor were let and they only had the first and top floors. It was wonderful to be here—with Oliver. She wondered what *sort* of sharp practice he had in mind ...

*　*　*

Alice lay very still on her back in the dark. The twin bed beside her was empty. Leslie had passed out (there was no other word for it) in the sitting-room. After a time, she had lifted his legs—unbelievably heavy—on to the other end of the sofa from his head: it hadn't seemed to make any difference to him. He was clearly alive because his breathing was so noisy. She had stood looking down on him for a bit without thinking or feeling anything very much. Any fear or excitement that had lurked in wait for the end of this day had long since gone. By the time he had finished telling her how many women he had known, he had drunk nearly all the brandy. She had left the pink silk lamp lit in case he woke up and wondered where he was, and retired for the night. No problem about undressing, she had thought with bitter exhaustion. She wished one could stop being a virgin without noticing it ...

THREE

MARKING TIME

B Y the end of a week in Lincoln Street, Elizabeth was thankful that she had found some sort of job. Living with Oliver, though tremendously exciting, disconcerted her: it was like having a very exhausting holiday, or the last week in someone's life, or before they were going to be caught by the police, or one's birthday every day; really she didn't know *how* to describe it. To begin with nothing ever happened when she expected it to; meals, getting up, parties, conversations, all occurred with consistent irregularity. The first day had been lovely. They had got up very late and had boiled eggs and warm croissants that Oliver had fetched from a shop, and strong coffee and then a kipper each because she had found them in the fridge and they found that eating was making them hungrier; and Oliver had had two very intelligent conversations with friends on the telephone—one about Mozart and one about the Liberal Party. Then Oliver had said, 'How much money have you got?' and they had looked at her cheque book and it didn't say because she was bad about her counterfoils, so she had rung up and the bank said eleven pounds thirteen and fourpence. 'Oh well,' Oliver had said, 'we've no need to worry.' And he had stretched out his legs—he was wearing black espadrilles over purple socks. She had suggested that she should clean up the house, it was pretty awful, really, but he had said no, no; he was going to cut her hair and then they'd go to the cinema. He'd tied a tablecloth round her neck and cut her the most expert fringe. 'Now you look much more as though you're lying in wait. For something or other,' he had added. They'd cashed a cheque for five pounds and gone to *Mondo Cane* in Tottenham Court Road —a simply extraordinary film, but Oliver laughed at it quite a lot.

Then they had walked to Soho, and Oliver had made her buy fresh ravioli and a pair of black fishnet tights.

'Why?' she had said both times. 'We might have a party in which case it would come in handy,' he said about the ravioli; and, 'I haven't been through your clothes yet, but what*ever* you've got will look better with tights.' Then it had begun to rain, and Oliver bundled her into a taxi. Awful extravagance. She mentioned then that she thought she ought to think about getting a job, and he stopped the cab and bought an *Evening Standard.* 'I'll look through it in the bath for you,' he had said.

While he was doing this, she set about the living-room. There was so much dust in it that everything *was* actually dust-coloured. The room had been painted entirely white, but the walls and wood-work were now, as Oliver had remarked, the colours of old cricket trousers. 'I take refuge in calling it *warm* white,' he had said: 'but really redecoration does so go with being pregnant or homosexual or in love, and my emotional life never seems to reach any such peak—just tidy it up, love. That chest of drawers is for tidying things into.' He had disappeared into the bathroom for about an hour and a half where she heard him having conversations on the telephone—a frightfully angry one about D. H. Lawrence and some much friendlier ones to people called Annabel and Sukie. She cleaned away—with a carpet sweeper that didn't really work, until she found that it was entwined and choked with fantastically long auburn hairs, and a duster that was so dirty she used one of her handkerchiefs.

The party had been a success in the end, but it took a long time to start. Sukie and Annabel arrived in a Mini each. Neither of them had auburn hair. They wore clothes like string vests and feather boas and striped plastic boots, so Elizabeth was glad about her tights. Apart from their striking appearance they seemed awfully intelligent and knew all Oliver's other friends and whom they were talking about. A lot of them had been to Oxford, and some of them had gone to Spain together—apart from innumerable parties like these where they all knew all the records they were playing—and she felt rather out of it. She tried to be helpful about the food and what drink there was. Sukie had brought a bottle of Scotch, and Annabel a nearly full bottle of Cointreau which a friend of Oliver's insisted on mixing with Coca-Cola and soda. 'It's absolutely *foul*, Sebastian.' But Oliver had said nonsense; all drinks were foul till you got used to them. Afterwards she found that Sebastian had mixed them up like that—with Oliver's approval—to make them last. The Gauloises ran out after the pubs had shut, but somebody produced some sort of sticky wodge in a cold-cream jar that he said was hashish, and one or two people tried a spot of that on Annabel's nail file. By then, everybody was very friendly and there was a competition to gauge what hashish was most like. Stuff from between tremendously wide floorboards, Elizabeth had thought aloud, and all the people who had said worse than school jam and scrapings off the lids of chutney bottles agreed with her, so warmly that she blushed with her sudden notoriety. Thereafter, whenever she had said anything, people stopped talking and listened kindly for another *mot*, but she never said anything else that was any good. Nothing seemed to happen to anyone as a result of the hashish, except for someone called Roland who was sick, but he said that that was something he had for lunch. By then they were drinking Maxwell House in the whisky-Cointreau-Coke glasses, the gramophone had been changed from jazz to Monteverdi which Oliver said could be played at a mutter (people had banged on the wall and finally rung up), and a—to her—incomprehensible, but frightfully interesting argument had broken out about the time-lag of influence that philosophers had upon politics and religion. Kiyckerkgard, Neecher, Marks, Plato (at least she'd heard of *him*) were being bandied about and words like subjective and relative were in constant use. It seemed generally agreed that it was all right for things to be relative, but not at all all right for them to be subjective. She noticed that nearly everyone could squash anyone else by calling them that. She felt terribly sleepy by then and was quite glad when Annabel said she must get out of her eyelashes they were weighing her down so, and they went upstairs. They stayed in Elizabeth's bedroom, talking about eye make-up and really good second-hand clothes' shops and what it would be like to marry an Asian or African, and Annabel said how much simpler everything would be if everybody was sort of fawn-coloured, but this would probably take a million years and *they* wouldn't live to see it; and it was very cosy being with Annabel in such eugenically difficult times ... Then Annabel told her about how frightful it had been being an au pair girl in Lyons, and they talked a bit about careers, and that was when Annabel told her about this marvellous new agency. 'You just go to them and say you want a job: it doesn't matter a bit if you think you can't do anything: *they* think of that. They specialize in being a last resort for people who want someone; they say their clients are so broken down by the lack of butlers and people to arrange flowers and do typing for them that they're glad to have *anyone*. I've been exercising a cheetah for the last ten days. Fifteen bob an hour—you can get danger money for exotics, so I never do dogs and any of that domestic jazz. Daddy doesn't mind what I do as long as I don't get overdrawn.'

By the time they joined the others Elizabeth felt that Annabel was almost certainly going to be her best friend.

The conversation had changed when they got back to what it would be like nowadays being a modern master-criminal. Pretty easy, most people seemed to think, but rather dull. That was one thing where a class structure was invaluable, Oliver said: the aristocracy of the underworld ought to steal huge sums of money from people like mad, but never hurt anyone. It would only be the working classes who hit old ladies over the head and took their handbags with pensions. He was instantly accused of being a ghastly snob by someone called Tom who was reading sociology. The conversation got boring again. She went to sleep.

She woke hours later, to find Oliver carrying her upstairs. He took off her clothes, wrapped her in his dressing-gown and levered her into bed. 'Your fringe is a wow.' Sleep again.

Next day Oliver was terribly gloomy. She knew that brilliant people were far more moody than the other kind, and made him a specially good brunch, but he wouldn't eat it. He said that the party had been kid's stuff, old ropes, a nasty little canapé de vieux: he was getting nowhere; he was damned if he wanted to be reduced to writing a novel at *his* age ...

'Is that what you were thinking of doing?'

'It's bound to cross the mind. If you don't *know* anything and can't write poetry or a decent play, there's not much left, is there?'

'I suppose not,' she said respectfully. She was sitting carefully on the end of his bed trying not to move her legs which people who were *in* bed always called kicking.

'I'm too old, really, anyway. I don't want to *be* a novelist, you see. Just to write one adolescent best-seller. You have to be under eighteen for that. Even you are too old.'

'Was the *Evening Standard* no good?'

'There was nothing in it for you. I wasn't looking for me. *The Times* is the one I look in for me. It's different for girls: you just need a job; I need a career.'

'What's the time?'

'Twenty past two. I would like something like being Churchill's private secretary: I seem to have missed everything. It's this damned narrow social life I lead. It's a pity May didn't have me taught to play the trumpet or to be a dentist or something obviously rewarding like that ...'

'Have a lovely hot bath.' She was beginning to know some things about him.

'Good idea. You run it. No cold—just hot: I'm practising for when I go to Japan.'

'I know what,' he said an hour and a half later. 'I say, you *have* made this room nice ...'

She was so pleased that she looked round it to notice what he had noticed; the *Encounters* all upright, which made them look distinguished instead of merely untidy, everything clean, or clean*er*, and she had hung the curtains back from the cleaners since last December ...

'You haven't listened to a word I was saying!'

'Sorry!'

'I think the best thing is for me to marry a very rich girl—very rich indeed. Then my natural talents will have time to develop naturally. Also, have you noticed how everybody nowadays who is supposed to have initiative always turns out to have some capital as well? And, it's much easier to develop integrity if you've got something to lose ...'

'What about the girl?'

'Eh?' He looked at her. 'Oh, she'll love me all right, don't worry.'

'But supposing you don't—'

'That doesn't matter,' he said, almost irritably. 'Rich girls are used to a pretty low standard of marriage. She'll adore *me*, and I'll be considerate and nice to her, and she'll be thankful I don't turn out to be an utter swine. That's what they usually marry—a swine in a sheepskin car coat who takes her out in a borrowed E-type.'

She said nothing. She was shocked and hoped he was joking.

* * *

Annabel's agency was above a greengrocer in Walton Street. It took her nearly a week to find this out because whenever she rang up Annabel, a woman who sounded as though she had been born in Knightsbridge on a horse said that Annabel was out and she had simply no id*eah* when she would be in. She laughed a lot after she said this, which was very loudly, and Elizabeth found it tremendously difficult simply to say 'Goodbye' to somebody who was in the middle of laughing like that, and not frightfully easy even just after they had stopped. So she didn't ring up much, and the curious days and nights with Oliver went by; but in the end Annabel *was* in, and she got the agency's address, put on her tidiest clothes and went to see them.

It was run by two ladies called Lady Dione Havergal-Smythe and Mrs Potts. Both seemed rather surprising people to find running an agency: Lady Dione looked about fifteen—even in dark glasses— and Mrs Potts, who was the perfectly ordinary age of about fifty— old, anyway—turned out to be Hungarian. The agency consisted of two small rooms: one in which customers or clients waited to see Lady Dione and Mrs Potts and one where they saw them. There were two telephones which rang very nearly as often as they could, so that any sustained conversation was difficult. In between two calls

Elizabeth was invited to sit down which she started to do, until she realized, perilously near the point of no return, that the chair indicated was minutely occupied by a Yorkshire terrier.

'Put her on the floor, would you very kindly?' Lady Dione's voice was unexpectedly deep and authoritative, and Elizabeth felt that the kindness referred to the dog rather than to herself.

Mrs Potts was talking fluent Italian (Elizabeth, who didn't know her nationality at this point, thought that she must *be* Italian as the peevishly caressing inflections continued). Lady Dione's telephone rang again—she listened for about half a minute and then said, 'Good God! No.'

'And what can we do for *you*?' she asked, as though she was quite ready to repeat her earlier remark after Elizabeth had told her.

'I've come about a job. Annabel Peeling told me that you had them. Jobs, I mean.'

'Oh! People nearly always come to us wanting people to *do* jobs.' Lady Dione seized a very expensive-looking leather address book.

'Do give me your name. And address. And things like that.'

Elizabeth did this.

Lady Dione pushed her dark glasses on to the top of her head and said earnestly, 'What would you *like* to do? I mean—somebody wants almost anything.' Her eyes were like Siberian topazes, Elizabeth thought: her only piece of jewellery was them so she jolly well knew what they looked like. Knowing that was a bit like Oliver, she thought: but she had to be left a brooch to know anything, and that was the only thing she'd ever been left, so that showed you ...

'I can cook a bit,' she said.

'Gosh! Can you really? I mean not just *sole Véronique* and chocolate mousse?'

Elizabeth shook her head.

'Hetty! (Mrs Potts, she's Hungarian.) Miss—'(she consulted her book) 'Seymour can cook!'

Mrs Potts had stopped having her Italian conversation, and was having another in some unknown mid-European language.

'How marvellous!' she said, with only a trace of an accent (pre-war B.B.C.). 'Wait for me, Di. We must spread her very thin!'

'We must wait for Hetty.' Lady Dione took a small cigar out of her lizard handbag.

'I must say that when you said Annabel had sent you, my heart sank. That girl thinks of nothing but money and is quite ungifted. If you live on your connections—as opposed to your attractions—under the age of twenty, you are in for the most ghastly middle age.'

Mrs Potts finished her conversation, and having replaced her receiver, took it off again.

'Oh—all right,' Lady Dione did the same.

'Now. You can get three guineas for cooking for up to six, and more for more. I take it you just want to do dinners?'

'What are your qualifications?' Mrs Potts's voice, though chameleon to the point of virtuosity, had a certain edge which those non-committal creatures do not, in their neutral moments, seem to possess.

Elizabeth took a deep breath.

'I spent a year at Esprit Manger, six months Cordon Bleu, and three months with Mme Germaine. Orange,' she added.

Lady Dione and Mrs Potts looked at each other in a way that made Elizabeth feel quite important. Then Lady Dione said:

'How many evenings would you like to work? Don't do more than you feel like,' she added earnestly.

Elizabeth thought. 'About four?'

'That's simply marvellous of you.' She turned eagerly to Mrs Potts. 'What do you think Hetty? I mean there are just scads of people who—'

'I think we shall be able to suit you, Miss Seymour,' Mrs Potts interrupted smoothly. 'Perhaps we could call you later in the day?'

The moment Elizabeth got to her feet, the Yorkshire terrier leapt, with one neat spring, into the chair, where it gazed up at her with burning, reproachful eyes.

'We have your telephone number, Miss Seymour?'

Elizabeth nodded. Mrs Potts had met her eye some minutes ago, and continued Elizabeth found now, implacably to meet it. Elizabeth wondered rather uncomfortably whether Mrs Potts was perhaps a

Lesbian, but then she thought no you couldn't be Hungarian *and* a Lesbian, it would be too much of a coincidence getting two minorities in one person ...

'Right then—sweet of you to come.' Lady Dione's dark glasses were back into position. 'And do remember,' she called as Elizabeth reached the door, 'that if you don't *like* anyone we send you to, you needn't ever go again.'

'You can report to us,' confirmed Mrs Potts—with a smile as sugary and firm as Brighton Rock.

*　　*　　*

When she got home, she found Oliver lying on the sitting-room floor poring over an enormous sheet of paper.

'I've had a brilliant idea—a new board game based on the Battle of Britain. I'm going to call it "Dogfight": it'll make a fortune—you'll see,' he remarked. 'Get me your nail scissors, there's a duck, and I would love a Welsh rarebit.'

So she wrote to May, whom she knew would be really interested to hear about her new job, and waited to tell Oliver when he felt more like it.

*　　*　　*

Lady Dione rang up a few days later to say would she mind awfully doing a dinner that very night? No. Right: had she got a pencil? She'd get one. She was to go to some people called Hawthorne in Bryanston Square. 'They're quite young from the sound of her voice,' Lady Dione had said, 'just married, and she can only cook one thing she learned from Cordon Bleu. She wants you there at five thirty; dinner for six, and she'll have bought all the food. Right? Right. And the best of British luck to you,' she added, more amiably than people usually make that remark.

'Do you want me to fetch you?' asked Oliver, who was now entering into the spirit of the thing. 'I can easily borrow Sukie's car by taking her out first. Haven't been out for days.' The game was now permanently on the sitting-room floor, and he had spent hours making friends play test games which they always lost because he was still inventing the rules. But Sukie, who had spent nearly two terms at an art school, had painted him an **art** nouveau board and they'd spent many a happy hour making tiny little models of aeroplanes, people and bombs out of glitter wax, bits of matchboxes and tinfoil.

'It would be lovely, if it won't be too late for you: probably after eleven.'

'My darling Liz, you must stop worrying so about *time*.'

'Yes, I must.' She wanted to get on with clearing up the house, having a hot bath and eating a couple of boiled eggs before going to Bryanston Square. She nearly always had boiled eggs before any sort of adventure and she didn't want to be late for this one. 'I'll try not to worry about it,' she repeated, and escaped.

* * *

Mrs Hawthorne opened the door to her at Bryanston Square. She was tall and thin, and fashionable to the point of prettiness: she wore a Thai silk trouser suit, pearl encrusted sandals and such an enormously thick dark pigtail draped over one shoulder that Elizabeth guessed it must be false.

'Hullo!' she said. 'You must be Miss Seymour.' She was carrying a small, white, elegantly clipped poodle who began yapping uncontrollably the moment Elizabeth stepped inside the flat. Mrs Hawthorne shut the door saying without any conviction, 'Shut up Snowdrop—shut *up*!

'I'll put her in the bedroom: hang on a minute.'

While she was doing this, Elizabeth waited in the hall. It was a very expensive flat: very thick pale-blue carpet, and a tank full of tropical fish; William Morris wallpaper, the kind she knew you jolly well had to like in the first place, since if you cleaned it with pieces of bread it would last for ever.

'Now. Where shall we put your coat?'

Elizabeth felt she could not be expected to know the answer to that; however, she took it off and looked obliging.

'I suppose you'd better shove it in the coat cupboard.' Mrs Hawthorne made this sound so like a concession, that it was almost offensive.

'I'll take you to the kitchen.'

'You'd better, if you want any dinner,' thought Elizabeth, wondering how Mrs Hawthorne managed to make quite ordinary sounding remarks sound so rude.

The kitchen was small, but spotless, all steel and Formica and what passed with the uninitiated as teak. It looked as though it was an Ideal Home kitchen, and not as though anybody had actually ever used it.

'All the food's in the fridge.' She opened the door of a gigantic Lec. 'Potted shrimps for first course, cold duck, and stuff to go with it, and then strawberries and cream. That was absolutely all I could *get*. Oh yes—some cheese. All right? You'll find knives and things in drawers. The dining-room's through there.' She pointed to a hatch. 'I must go and cope with Snowdrop: she can't stand strangers and she loathes being shut up.'

'What was the point of *having* me?' Elizabeth muttered as she unpacked her overall. The mixture of there being virtually no cooking to do, and Mrs Hawthorne's unfriendly behaviour, was most disconcerting. 'I must be fairly stupid to mind being disconcerted so much; Oliver wouldn't,' she thought as she took the food out of the fridge. Horrible frozen peas—the worst kind: and who in their senses would put new potatoes in the freezing compartment? The duck had that wizened, false look that nearly all shopcooked birds seem to get; the strawberries turned out to be green on their hidden sides; but the potted shrimps were comfortingly just themselves as they always are. She found a huge white loaf—like a giant's Sorbo sponge—in the bread bin and that was that. There did not seem to be any butter, or coffee. The kitchen, indeed, contained one small packet of Indian tea, a jar of lump sugar and tins of grapefruit juice and Aristodog. Nothing else. It was twenty to six: she went in search of Mrs Hawthorne.

She heard her talking on the telephone and knocked rather timidly on the door. Mrs Hawthorne told her to come in, but the moment that she did so, the poodle rushed at her in a cacophonous frenzy. Mrs Hawthorne, who was lying on a white satin eiderdown (the room was unmistakably the bedroom) said, 'Oh lord! Hang on a minute, Boffy darling, I'm being interrupted,' heaved herself off the bed and collected the poodle.

'I'm sorry to bother you, but there doesn't seem to be any coffee — or butter for the toast and the vegetables ...'

'Oh—really!'

'I could go out and get them, if you like. I don't think all the shops will be shut.'

'Oh well—do that then. That's marvellous.' She turned back, with the poodle in her arms, to the telephone. 'Boffy? Still there darling? A domestic crisis ... '

'Er—the only thing is, I'm afraid I haven't brought any, so could you possibly let me have some money?'

'Oh God—hang on again darling, there seems to be another one. Another *crisis*—well, she's new . . .' She put the receiver down and indicated with her head. 'Over there.'

There was a small lilac silk purse the same colour as her suit. Elizabeth picked it up and opened it.

'No—bring it to me: I'll do it.

'Damn! I only seem to have a pound note.'

Elizabeth opened her mouth to say something about most shops having change, but she didn't because she knew she was going to croak or squeak which was what always humiliatingly happened to her voice when she was angry and nearly in tears.

'You'll have to take it, won't you? Don't be long.'

She ripped her coat out of the coat cupboard and marched out of the flat. The lift was being used so she went on marching—down the stairs. She had never met anyone so *young* and so horrible in her life. For a moment she thought of not going back; but then she realized that she couldn't let the agency down like that, on her first job too: they'd probably never give her another one. Mr Hawthorne must be horrible as well; or else terribly stupid. Perhaps the moment you earned your living, people *were* horrible to you. No wonder poor Oliver hadn't been able to stand the accountants' office if this was true. Then she remembered May and how she'd behaved to the few people who'd ever worked for her. Of course it was nonsense: there was probably nobody as nasty as Mrs Hawthorne in the whole of north-west London. It was only for one evening; she'd do her best, earn her three guineas and get the hell out. By the time she reached Edgware Road, where she knew there was a large self-service grocer, she was planning to tell Oliver all about it. Mr and Mrs Hawthorne drinking tinned grapefruit juice and eating bowls of Aristodog for breakfast, because what *else* they did for that meal she could not see. Perhaps feral-type vitamins really brought out the beast in people.

In the grocer she bought butter, coffee and a couple of lemons for the shrimps, and cashed out at a register operated by a young black man. He took her pound impassively, but when she smiled at him, and apologized for not having anything smaller, he smiled so beautifully at her that she felt warmed by it. In the middle of his smile he yawned, put up an elegant hand which hardly hid his mouth and then laughed. 'All work makes you tired,' he said putting change on to her palm. 'Work is a terrible thing.' He put the lemons into a bag then the butter into a bag, and then the coffee into a third bag. 'You have no basket?' ''Fraid not.' He stooped and came up with a carrier. 'I give you family hold-all bag.' There were people queueing behind her, but he placed each of the three small bags carefully in the carrier and then held it to see if the parcels were well disposed therein. The woman behind her looked sour and began to mutter. He put the carrier back on to the counter, arranged the string handles for her and inclined his head. 'Ready for you now. Easy—and nice.'

She thanked him, and saw his face shut down again as the sour woman plonked her stuff on the counter and thrust her money at him saying, 'We haven't got all night, you know.'

She walked back worrying about how people nearly always seemed to be horrible to one another—just in ordinary life—so naturally there would be wars.

Mr Hawthorne opened the door to her this time. His face was a uniform pale pink, and he was very nearly bald, but he was clearly quite young in spite of this, in the same way that you could tell about pigs. In one hand he carried a cocktail shaker which he was agitating steadily all the time he opened and shut the door. 'Good evening,' he said. 'And what shall we do with your coat?'

'Last time, we seemed to think it had better go into the coat cupboard.'

'Of course.' Her accent had thrown him. Filthy snob. Anyway, she needn't be *sorry* for him.

The rest of the evening was more of a cold war against the kitchen than against the people. (She didn't see much of the guests, whose voices sounded very much like their hosts', but she reflected that nobody who wittingly went to dinner with the Hawthornes could be very nice.) The problems were much more that there was neither a bread knife nor a potato peeler anywhere to be found, and come to that, not even a sharp knife of any description. The horrible, new, spongy bread was a nightmare to cut; the potatoes were the joke kind of new that would not scrape; she found, also, that she was expected to carve the duck. Laying the dining-room table when you didn't know where anything was, and it had been made impossible for you to ask, took simply ages. Luckily, Mr Hawthorne came out to the kitchen to decant some claret, so she was able to ask him when they wanted to eat and where they wanted their coffee served. Twice the poodle escaped in order to come and yelp at her and snap round her ankles. She came to the conclusion that it was slightly off its head, as indeed she would be if she had to live cheek by jowl with Mrs Hawthorne. When she took the coffee in, they had obviously been talking about her ('... hasn't had to *cook* a thing—' Mrs Hawthorne was saying as she brought in the tray), and their efforts at covering this up were rudely ineffective. When she was washing up, Mr Hawthorne came into the kitchen and said, 'Are we expected to pay *you*?'

No, she said, the agency: *they* would pay her.

'Because really it seems a ridiculous sum, considering how little you have had to do.'

'I was asked to come here to cook dinner. The fact that Mrs Hawthorne had bought pre-cooked food is nothing to do with me.'

'Naturally, I can *see that*,' he said, as though he was making an enormous concession because she was so very stupid. 'It doesn't take very much intelligence to *see that*. But the fact remains that you didn't have to do anything except boil a few potatoes, which I take it most of us could manage if we were really pushed to it, and you're trying to charge us four guineas.'

Elizabeth, her heart thumping, put down the (only, and wringing-wet) drying-up cloth. 'The agency are charging you, Mr Hawthorne: they engaged me on your behalf. I think you'd better take the matter up with them. My brother is collecting me in ten minutes so I must finish the washing up now.' And in case he could hear her heart thumping, she turned on the cold tap very hard which splashed them both so suddenly and so much that he retreated without saying another word.

She dried the rest of the things on her apron, wiped the draining board, turned out the kitchen lights and collected her coat. She couldn't bear to wait in the flat for Oliver, who, in any case, might be late, as watches never went very successfully on him.

He *was* late; not very, but enough to make her feel abandoned as well as miserable. He and Sukie drew up with a flourish: they looked very gay, with Sukie wearing a pink velvet yachting cap on her straight, ashy hair.

'Pop in, sorry if we're late, how was it?'

Sukie was thoughtfully in the back, so she climbed in beside Oliver just as tears began to spurt from her eyes.

'Darling Liz! Here!' He seized the remains of a packet of popcorn and started to feed her. 'It's almost impossible to cry if your mouth is absolutely full. Unless you're about two, when it all slides out like a slimy blind. Poor Liz!' He put his arm round her and gave her a hug and such a weighty kiss on the cheek nearest him that all the popcorn had to change sides, and she nearly laughed.

She told them about it, and Sukie said things like, 'The bastards!' 'Fantastic scum!' and what a good thing they were *both* so ghastly, married couples often weren't, and Oliver said he had a good mind to join the agency and get hired by them; one evening with *him* as their cook and they'd change their tune. The rest of the drive home cheered Elizabeth up completely, because Oliver thought of such awful things to do while being their cook: 'Casserole of poodle was probably a fine Siege-of-Paris dish; of course I'd say that I only cooked live food: the meal would start with their beastly tropical fish *en gelée*, and end with me advancing on lovely Mrs Hawthorne with my meat chopper asking him how he would like her done.'

They all had hot buttered rum when they got back to Lincoln Street, because Sukie had found a very pretty silver flask of her father's that she was stealing to put scent in, and it seemed a waste not to use up the rum. After it, Elizabeth suddenly felt so tired that she was being turned to dormouse stone on the spot, so Oliver told her to go to bed. Sukie must have stayed the night, because when Elizabeth woke at about six, as she always did when things were worrying her, and went down to get a drink of water, the scarlet Mini was still parked outside the house. But by the time she and Oliver got up there was no sign of Sukie, and the Mini had gone. When she mentioned tentatively to him how nice Sukie was, his face closed and he said shortly, 'She's all right. A bit dim, though. A little of her goes a long way.' 'Goodness!' she thought, 'If he thinks that about Sukie, it's jolly nice to have *me* all the time.'

FOUR

···❖···

A NEW LIFE

'AND now it'll go on for ever and ever,' thought Alice. It seemed impossible that somebody could turn out to be so different all the time; surely they must sometimes have been it before—and she had simply never noticed? And it was no good saying that love was blind, because she was far from sure what love was—now. It was obviously her own fault for expecting a miracle, but she had thought that the reason that people made so much fuss about (going to bed with someone) was because it was the only certain way of having an intimate friend. All that (sex) would only be possible if you felt really close to the person all the time when they weren't (making love to you). He wasn't unkind to her: she simply felt miserably shy with him—in fact, exactly as she felt with everyone else, only now, with him, there were more, and more awful opportunities for feeling shy. For the hundredth time she went back to her meeting with Leslie: on a beach in Sitges. He and some friends were playing with a large rubber ball which had fallen near her and bounced off her back. He had come to apologize and she had sat up. She had been wearing a navy one-piece bathing suit and a huge pink straw hat (she always had to be careful of the sun on her skin). He had lingered, asked her if she would like to join in the game: she had shaken her head, smiling too much to conceal how nervous she felt and also not to seem rude. It was very kind of him to ask her. Then, a bit later, they had met in the sea, and he had asked her whether she was enjoying herself and she had said yes, although she hadn't been, much. Holidays were always difficult if you were on your own. How had he known that? He could tell. He was bronzed which made his eyes look bluer, more piercingly kind. She had had drinks with him and

60

his friend (who'd been best man at the wedding), and then lunch.

After that, they had met every day until her holiday time was up. He had proposed to her their last evening among the floodlights, red gravel and green hillocks of the miniature golf course. She had admired him; she was deeply flattered by his attentions to her (nobody had ever treated her like that in her life; or anything like that when she came to think of it, which during the holiday she unceasingly did); he was all masculine steadiness and assurance and she imagined that he understood her. She was nearly twenty-six and nobody had ever proposed to her before, or for that matter got anywhere near it. She had said yes, and then found she was trembling so much that he had given her a brandy before walking her home to her hotel. On the way back, he'd found a dark archway and kissed her in an exploring kind of way. Distaste and gratitude and the odd tremor of nervous curiosity. 'You're shy— you're very tense,' he'd murmured. 'Don't worry, I'll always be kind to you.' Gratitude had welled over everything else: indeed, now, when she remembered his voice saying that, she was back to her nearest point of loving him, of knowing now, that then she had thought it was the beginning of love. Perhaps if they'd gone back to Sitges for their honeymoon it would have been better? But he had said it was too early in the year; they wouldn't be able to bathe, and the golf course in Cornwall was a very good one. And the hotel, he had assured her, would be first class—nothing on the cheap and much more reliable food. She had had a couple of lessons at golf, but she was absolutely no good and uninterested in the game: so then she'd walked around with him for a day or two, and then, because she felt tired nearly all the time, she'd simply stopped walking round. 'Have a nice rest,' he had said: he seemed very much in favour of that. So she'd tried, but lying down in the afternoon simply made her feel restless and a bit guilty. (Daddy would have roared with laughter at a healthy woman mollycoddling herself.) So she used to go for walks on the cliffs above the sea, making sure that she got back to the hotel before Leslie returned from his afternoon round. Once she wrote a poem about a seagull and being lonely, and this made her feel much better for a day or two. When, at tea, she told Leslie that she had been for a walk and watched this seagull he said he was glad she had been amusing herself, so she didn't tell him about the poem. He frequently asked her if she was happy and she knew that he felt sure she was, so of course she said yes. She supposed the sex part of marriage got better as you got used to it. It couldn't possibly go on being like it was in Cornwall, because otherwise people surely wouldn't stay married even the amount that they did. Once she had rung up home, and May had fortunately answered (she'd picked the afternoon when Daddy would be having his rest) and apparently Claude was perfectly all right except that he'd given the window cleaner an awful fright by jumping on to the top of a sash window while it was open and being cleaned so that it slammed down on the man's arms and nearly knocked him off his ladder. He was marvellously agile for his weight and age, Alice thought, and he'd always liked giving people surprises. His canker was worse, and when May had managed to get a few drops in his ears, he'd gone on shaking them out for hours over all kinds of things ... Her father was fine, May had volunteered, adding, 'He keeps buying things for the lawn. You know how the moment he's stopped worrying about the Budget, he starts on the lawn.' She had not said anything about herself, and Alice afterwards felt ashamed of having forgotten to ask.

The fortnight in Cornwall had got used up: now she was packing to go. She wondered how much she would remember it when she was old. Four kinds of meals every day. Breakfast with Leslie in the dining-room: stewed prunes or corn flakes, bacon and egg or sausages and tomato, tea or coffee, rubbery toast, not enough butter and Cooper's Oxford marmalade. Leslie read the *Express* and she had *The Times*, which impressed him. In between reading their papers, people looked out of the windows and wondered aloud about the weather, which was showery enough to keep them wondering. Lunch in the Golf Club, a room which gave the impression of being a Tudor swimming bath, as it was immense, very low-ceilinged, with oak panelling and incredible clashing echoes: people laughed like horrible giants about their morning game, and a fork dropped was like the clash of spears in a Roman epic film.

Tea in the television lounge at the hotel; deep chairs and little rocking tables covered with scalding silver jugs and teapots (she liked China and he liked Indian), mercilessly dainty sandwiches and very small, evil, shining cakes. Dinner in a short silk dress—a bit shivery but everyone wore them; thick or clear, turbot or sole, chicken, or veal, crème caramel or ice cream and cheese. A drink in the bar with coffee, perhaps a bit more television—and bed. Leslie always let her go to the bathroom first; she undressed in there. The worst part was lying in bed waiting for him to come out in his pyjamas, because sometimes he climbed into her bed and sometimes he didn't, and whichever he did seemed wrong. Afterwards she would lie awake in the dark blaming herself variously for not having the right instincts, not being attractive enough, for not, perhaps, recognizing that this was what women had to do in return for being clothed and fed and looked after all their lives. This last was the worst, and she tried strenuously not to believe it, at the same time feeling that as it was the most despairing likelihood it was probably true. It would be better for there to be something wrong with *her* than for it to be awful for everyone—all women, at least. She was docile, passive, even brave when he hurt her, which he did a good deal at first; she tried to be affectionate, to conceal her senses of isolation and embarrassment and inadequacy, but in the end she decided that he did not seem to notice her much. One night he gently touched her breasts—which were large and painfully tender—and murmured something about them being lovely: she felt her whole body begin to respond, as though sealed eyelids had opened for the first time inside her, but then he had crushed himself upon her and the feeling vanished. She only had it once, and even by the end of two weeks she began to wonder if she had imagined it.

She had finished the packing—Leslie's and her own. Leslie was downstairs paying the bill, and just as she closed the last case, there was a knock on the door.

'Porter, madam.' He was old and short and very broad, and came sideways through the door out of habit. His ears stuck out and he leered like a horrid old version of Punch.

'Just the four. And I hope you've enjoyed your *stay*, madam.'

'I hope I have.' It came out before she could stop it, and, blushing, she stalked angrily out of the room, slipped on one of the brass studs that nailed the carpet down and nearly tripped.

'Oops-a-daisy,' he said in his mechanically fruity old voice. In the lift, he fixed his eyes on a point just below her stomach and remained unwinking and motionless as they descended. If he'd moved or said anything, she could have told him to stop staring at her, but he'd had far too much practice: the lift cage simply became charged with unclean thoughts.

In the reception hall he turned into a bustling, obsequious crab—treating all their luggage as though it was desperately heavy and very fragile—filled with atom bombs. Leslie gave him a pound.

They had lunch on the train. There was a small, brilliant slug in her watercress: she thought it looked very pretty, but it made her not want the watercress and when Leslie discovered she wasn't fancying it, he gave her an immensely knowing smile and said he wondered whether there might not be—you know—a little stranger on the way. He hadn't seen the slug. After lunch, Leslie went to sleep and she did some of *The Times* crossword—she still felt privileged to have this newspaper all to herself, instead of yesterday's scrumpled up by Daddy and with all the easiest clues done. London: Paddington station. It was very hot; the air under the glass-domed roof was thick with dust and illuminated by majestic shafts of sunlight—cosmic revelation falling upon the paltry antics of arrival and departure.

'Come *on*, dear. You're daydreaming!'

She wondered how quickly he would descend from admiring her for constantly doing something which was to him so incomprehensible, into irritation at having to keep on prodding her into life on his terms. Getting used to people cut both ways. They were going to the Station Hotel—have a gin and tonic while they waited for the Bristol train. In the bar she remembered that May had said that Elizabeth had gone to stay with Oliver in London. 'I could ring her up,' she thought suddenly, feeling urgent and homesick. So she told Leslie, who was having an argument with a man at the bar about underfloor heating, and the woman at the desk put her in a telephone booth and got the number.

Oliver answered. There was a lot of talking in the background. '*Who*? Hold on a sec while I turn the gramophone off.'

'My dear Alice. No—she's out. She's cooking dinner for some Christian Scientists in Pimlico. Me? Oh—I'm doing a spot of reviewing: *Julius Caesar* on L.P.s for a friend's magazine. Just a little job. How are you? Was it foul in Cornwall? The weather, I mean,' he added.

'A bit changeable. I'm at Paddington.' She could not think of anything interesting to say. There was a short pause, then she said, 'We're off to Bristol on the six forty-eight.'

Another short pause. 'I see,' he said.

'How's May?'

'I don't know, really. She keeps saying she's coming up, and then she doesn't seem to make it. I'll give her your love.'

'And to Elizabeth.'

'Of course. Come and see us if you're in London.'

'I will. Goodbye.'

He said goodbye at once: she imagined him starting his gramophone again; immediately devoting his brilliant, critical attention to the schemes of the Roman senate. If he hadn't been so brilliant, she would have been hopelessly in love with him. He was so attractive, so entertaining; he had such an air of constantly finding life easy and amusing, of being able to do anything if only he felt like it, that even things like going with him to return the empties to the pub turned into a sort of holiday venture. But he was far, far too clever for her: also she was two years older than he was, and anyway, almost as soon as she met him, he became a kind of relation. And this last, she thought, going to pay for her telephone call, did not seem to make knowing people or being able to talk to them any easier. She thought of the Mount family—now all turned at one stroke into relations—waiting in Bristol for her to get on with them ... Her mother-in-law at least was kind.

Mrs Mount *was* kind. As they did not arrive until nearly ten o'clock, she was sure they must be very tired and hungry, in spite of them having had, as they had told her they would, dinner on the train. There was an immense cold collation laid out in the Mounts' gloomy dining-room: ham, tongue, spiced loaf, potato salad, beet-root, pickles and radishes, tinned fruit, home-made caraway seed cake and bakewell tarts and some pastel coloured junkets. There was tea, coffee, whisky and pale ale. Mr Mount said it was quite a feast, whereupon Mrs Mount described it as just a snack. Rosemary, dressed in ski pants and smoking through an exceptionally long holder, rolled her eyes knowingly at Alice and said that she was sure Alice knew what parents were. Sandra, wearing white tights, an imitation lizard skin tunic and silver plastic boots, said nothing at all. She was so staggered by her own appearance that she was entirely taken up with looking at herself in various mirrors, or watching the others seeing her for the first time and willing them to be amazed. But, '*You* look smart, Sandra,' Leslie said kindly, spoiling it all. It was just as well he was so frightfully stupid and tasteless; it knocked out any possibility of incest, which otherwise rather appealed to her as the simplest and wickedest way of shocking everyone at once.

Alice, who was really tired and had eaten a large dinner on the train to fortify herself against this homecoming to her in-laws' house, looked frantically at the plate that Mrs Mount had heaped up for her. She said that she was not very hungry and looked to Leslie for support, but he quelled her by saying that he could always fancy Mother's food, however much he had eaten elsewhere. The room was very hot: her hay fever had started with the country air and the anti-histamine pills always made her feel stupid, but some, at least, of the food on her plate had to be eaten; some questions—about Cornwall, the hotel, her family's health and so on—answered. Leslie was soon engaged upon business gossip with his father while Mrs Mount told her which shops were reliable in Whiteladies Road, Rosemary told her about a hairdresser whose favourite client she was—he was Italian and need she say more? Sandra stared at her and asked her whether she had ever learned judo or been to America. Halfway through the meal, there was a scratch on the door which Mrs Mount then opened, and a huge, heavy dog waddled in. It lay down at once between two electric fires and immediately began to snore. At intervals, and in comparative silence, it emitted offensive, and seemingly endless smells. Mrs Mount, Alice discovered, was the sort of person who, when she found that you did not eat what was put in front of you, simply gave you a huge plate of something else. This did not strike Alice as especially kind, but obviously Mrs Mount thought it was: she knew everybody knew that she was kind and she was the sort of person who always said things and always did them, too.

At last she felt that she could perhaps go up to their room and unpack. Mrs Mount said she'd pop up and show her the way: Rosemary said she would come too—she longed to see Alice's nightgowns. Sandra followed in their wake—partly because she had been sent to bed and it was the easiest way of pretending she wanted to go up anyway. Before they left, Mrs Mount put Alice's plates of largely unfinished food in front of the dog who gulped up everything without otherwise moving at all—it was a kind of living Hoover, Alice thought with weary disgust.

The room—the guest room as Mrs Mount explained, no good putting Alice in Leslie's old bed—had been done up specially for Alice. New paper, new curtains and bedspread: Rosemary had chosen it, as Mrs Mount was a weeny bit old-fashioned. Two walls were ochre-coloured and two were a rather muddy turquoise. The carpet was a mixture of these colours—speckled like a thrush but not in nearly such good taste. The room contained a three-piece suite and a small double bed covered with a slippery old-gold eiderdown which Alice knew would be possessed of reptilian agility in the night. On the dressing-table was a colour photograph of a very fat little boy leaning against a lamp-post. 'Leslie when he was little,' said Mrs Mount, 'a present for *you*, dear. For years I've been saying it was high time he got married. He was such a lovely little boy.'

Sandra made retching noises, and that was the end of *her*, since Mrs Mount, in an entirely different tone of voice, ordered her to bed that minute. She went—kicking her boots against the skirting board before she remembered that they were her new birthday boots—bought with Great-Aunt Lottie's money.

Rosemary, with unspeakable energy, had started to unpack one of Alice's suitcases. Alice hated this so much that she wanted to scream, but instead she smiled and protested inside. Mrs Mount, laughing indulgently, said *she* knew when she was in the way, she'd be popping off, and leave the girls together. This she did.

'At last!' cried Rosemary. 'Old people never know when they're not wanted, do they? Now! Let's put our feet up, and tell me all about it.'

Alice went on unpacking, or tried to, but at the same moment as she realized that she couldn't think of anything to say to Rosemary— something that would make her shut up or go away—the back of her neck felt icy cold and she couldn't see anything properly. She heard herself asking for the bathroom, and the next thing she knew was that she was alone in it, having been violently sick. She sat down on the edge of the bath, shivering, and too weak even to wash her face. She noticed that she had bolted the door, and then heard Rosemary's voice.

'Are you all right? Alice!'

'I just want to go to bed.' Then, with a further effort, she said 'Please leave me alone, Rosemary.' It was amazing that she had bolted the door. Her face was wet with tears and sweat—like a bit of Kipling. She did not care what Rosemary did now: she would not come out until Rosemary had gone. The worst of it was that although she wished that she was not there, in Mrs Mount's bathroom in Clifton, Bristol, she could not really think where she wanted to be. Not in Surrey, certainly: look at the lengths she'd gone to to get away from there. Before that, there had been furnished rooms: in Earl's Court, in Stanmore, in Finchley, in Stoke Newington. Before that, the house in Westdown Road, Seaford, that had belonged to her first stepmother—twenty years ago, she could hardly remember it; she'd been six, and they'd just come back from India. No—India had been two years earlier; she must have been four then. All she could remember about India was the spicy smell of her Indian nurse, the wailing at her mother's death, delicious fruit drinks and an old man who seemed always to be watering the garden of their bungalow. Coming back to England it had been funny not having to wear a hat, and people's feet made an awful lot of noise so that she'd been afraid of being trampled on, which she'd never felt with Indian people. She couldn't want to be in India if that was all she could remember of it. The trouble was that all these places had Daddy looming over them so much that it had made them nearly the same. In fact, everything she could remember seemed to be years and years of being alone; the only child; being nearly always bored and sometimes frightened; being in the way, or at least out of place; wondering what to do with herself and hearing other people openly speculate about this problem—punctuated by terrifying occasions when she was suddenly dispatched without warning to some new school, or to some acquaintances of Daddy's: agonizing afternoons of answering a battery of dispassionate questions, choking on bread and butter, having to drink milk, or tea with horrible sugar in it, and Daddy coming to fetch her talking in a kind of public genial voice which he never did at home … The schools were worse, though, because they went on for longer and sometimes she had even had to live in them. By the time she was sent off in this manner she had become used to hours and even days alone, and to live in a regimented but alien crowd was torture to her. Introspective children who are neither pretty nor very clever are simply a baffling nuisance to overworked staff; the children immediately recognized her as easy prey for bullying, and in the end too dull even to be worth those attentions. She longed for a friend, but had no idea how to make one; she blushed very easily, and her asthma ruined every summer term; school food brought out the worst of her acne; and the difficulty she found in communicating—with anyone at all—made her seem far more obstinate even than she was. May was the first person whom she had really not been in some measure afraid of, and by then she was twenty-three. Oliver and Elizabeth had seemed so wonderfully lucky and glamorous that to become related to them was an almost celestial privilege. At first she had planned that Elizabeth would become her greatest friend and Oliver might become—anything. She had actually shown some of her poems to Elizabeth, but watching Elizabeth read them, she'd seen pretty quickly that poetry didn't mean much to her: she'd been impressed, of course, but she hadn't understood it. Her feelings about both of them—Oliver and Elizabeth—had soon settled to a kind of fearful admiration, and she had turned, with some relief, to May. At first she had thought that Daddy's third marriage was going to release her from unpaid bondage into the freedom of a job and money of her own. But when Daddy had insisted on May buying that enormous house, she had realized that for someone not used to looking after Daddy anywhere, let alone in a mansion, the combination would be too much for any one person, and certainly for May, who was not really a practical person at all. So she had stayed at home to help, until she had slowly begun to feel that Daddy really wanted her to make a life of her own. He had even offered to send her on a cruise to meet people. She had refused that point blank; the thought of being stuck on a ship with a lot of strangers getting on with one another seemed like being the only prisoner in a social concentration camp. She had compromised with Spain, once she had found that May thought she ought to have a proper holiday: Sitges and Leslie had been the result, and here she was. So it was idiotic to say that being here was worse than being anywhere else, really—it was just strange, and goodness knows she was used to strange places. She got up from the edge of the bath and washed her face in cold water, and then making sure that she was leaving the bathroom as she expected Mrs Mount would wish to find it, she went back to the bedroom. Rosemary was nowhere to be seen. She undressed behind the door, in case Leslie should come in, and climbed into bed. She had been right about the eiderdown. If only Claude was here, he would pin it down. The last thing she thought of before going to sleep were the lovely times when she would wake in the night with a feeling of claustrophobia and a dead weight on her chest, open her eyes to find two luminous orbs a few inches from her face and hear the grumbling mutter of his purr starting up as he realized he'd made her uncomfortable enough to wake her up. Perhaps *he* felt lonely, too.

* * *

Alice and Leslie were only staying with the rest of the Mounts until they could move into their new home. This was a luxury bungalow built by the Mounts on a new housing estate beyond Clifton. Leslie had shown Alice the plans, but she found them so difficult to understand that she was completely unprepared for the—nearly completed—article when she saw it. Leslie took her the next morning, after a huge Mount breakfast (the Mounts went to work on nearly everything you could think of to be on the safe side). The point about the bungalow, Leslie explained, was that they were building forty-nine others that were structurally the same, which brought down the costs quite a bit, but, on the other hand, as this one was to be theirs, he had added a number of features to it which would certainly make it a one-off job with a distinction of its own. What sort of features, Alice had asked, really not knowing what features of a building might be. Spanish-style touches, Leslie had answered. She glanced at his profile—he looked complacent and mysterious.

The housing site was a large one, and the sense of devastation which any building enterprise brings to the surrounding land was probably at its worst, since all the bungalows had been begun, and many of them were in varying stages of completion. From the distance they looked like white mini-bricks put on a ploughed field; as they got nearer, Alice saw that the third-of-an-acre plots had been marked out with barbed wire and chestnut palings. Here and there were drunken remnants of the original hedges that had marked the fields. A concrete mixer was working; scaffolding was being noisily disassembled; there was a bonfire burning what looked like giant's rubbish; and the perky cackle of transistor radios filled up the cracks of silence between the crashes, thuds, hammering and tip-up lorries changing gear as they were ponderously manoeuvred in the rutty, makeshift roads. A great many men were standing about watching the man loosening the bolts on the scaffolding with a ring spanner, and several men were vociferously directing a lorry loaded with tiles which seemed to have got stuck.

Leslie drove to one end, or corner, of this battlefield where one of the most finished of the bungalows crouched.

'Here we are,' he shouted.

Getting out of the car, Alice stepped immediately into a heap of very wet sharpsand. 'Look out!' cried Leslie, as people usually do after you haven't. She stood on one leg and took off her other shoe: the sand was like damp sugar; several men had stopped watching a man unloading tiles from a wheelbarrow and were watching her. Leslie came up and held her arm. 'Bad luck!'

'Never mind. Let's go and see the house.'

At this moment a small man in a hat turned up at a kind of fast hobbling walk—like someone pretending to run in a comedy.

'Good morning, Timpson.'

'*Good* morning, sir.'

'This is the new Mrs Mount.' Leslie said this as though there were dozens of them.

'*Good* morning, madam.' He had a ferrety little face and all his gestures were exaggerated by dishonesty. Now, he looked at his hand, wiped it on his trousers and held it out to Alice with an expression of such humility that it was almost aggressive. His hand wasn't in the least dirty.

'Mr Timpson is our foreman. I've brought my wife to see our new home.'

'Definitely.' He held his hand out again—this time as though warding off a blow. 'Don't tell me. I know. All ladies are impatient. I'll tell you frankly—it's a miracle what we've performed in the time. Forty-seven—no I'm telling a lie—forty-eight weeks ago this place was just a field with animals in it. Now—and have we had our troubles—you wouldn't recognize the place. Fifty lovely homes in the twinkling of an eye.'

They were walking up what Alice supposed would eventually be the path to her front door. When they reached it, Mr Timpson clapped a hand to his head: this seized up any other movement he had been on the point of making. 'Don't move, sir! Isn't there a lovely little old custom that slipped our memory?'

Leslie and Alice stopped too, and looked at him.

'I may be wrong,' cried Timpson: he was now mincing sideways up to Leslie, 'but,' he put a hand shielding his mouth from Alice and spoke even louder, 'don't we carry the bride over the threshold the first time she enters her domain? Correct me if I'm wrong.' He clapped his hand over his mouth and looked roguishly ashamed.

'Quite right,' said Leslie, and turned to Alice.

Alice, as we have said, was a big girl: she was quite simply the wrong size to be carried at all—except by Tarzan, or in an emergency like the house being on fire. But Leslie, though not much taller than she, was stocky and determined. He picked her up and carried her, her handbag thumping painfully against his thighs as he staggered into the bungalow.

'Easy does it,' cried Mr Timpson having seen that it hadn't. He had also seen one of her suspenders as her skirt had got rucked up, and Alice loathed him more than ever. She was blushing and didn't know where to look so as to avoid Mr Timpson's horrid little eyes, so she looked down, straight on to the enormous bottom of a man in blue dungarees who was hitting what looked to her like random bits of floorboard with a tiny hammer.

'Move for the lady, George,' said Mr Timpson in a voice which bordered on being quite different from any he had used before.

Alice looked at Leslie to see if she could tell what he thought about Mr Timpson, but she couldn't. In fact, Leslie couldn't have minded him, she thought resentfully as they got back into the car half an hour later, since Mr Timpson had been allowed to accompany them throughout their tour of the bungalow, which was not very large, and except for workmen and loose doors and tools and things was empty. She had seen it all in about five minutes, but Leslie and Mr Timpson stood interminably in each room talking about sub-contractors, the Government, the Electricity Board, fibreglass insulation and Marley tiles. Mr Timpson always agreed with Leslie, so perhaps that was why they talked so much, Alice thought. The Spanish-style features turned out to be the threat of a good deal of wrought iron, tiles on the floors, which she thought would be slippery and cold, and an all-black bathroom, which did not strike her, among other things, as particularly Spanish. There was also an eye-level grill in the kitchen. There were two bedrooms, one large and one small, a large sitting-room, a sort of study, a small dining-room with a hatch through to the kitchen, one bathroom and two lavatories. Her future home. In the car, Leslie asked her what she thought of it, and she said she was sure it was going to be very nice.

FIVE

THE GARDEN OF ENGLAND

MAY woke first, as she always did (the alarm-clock was beside her
bed as Herbert was a light sleeper until, he said, about six-thirty
in the morning: it was most important to him to get those vital
two hours of real rest). For this reason, May never slept very well
for the hour or so before the alarm went off, as she had to quell
it at its first buzz, or, as Herbert pointed out, it defeated its object.
He liked to sleep until the strong Indian tea was actually steaming
in a huge cup at his bedside. Usually she stopped the clock before
it had a chance, but on this particular morning she woke with such
a feeling of excitement that she forgot. Today was probably going to
be one that she would remember all her life. Herbert was going to
London, to see his stockbroker, lunch at his club and look in at
Lords, and *she*, nefariously—she hadn't dared tell him—was having
a very interesting man to lunch; possibly, she thought, one of the
most interesting men in England—if not the world. He was not
coming alone; dear, kind Lavinia was bringing him; but then,
without Lavinia she would never have heard about, let alone met
Dr Sedum. Lavinia was a second cousin—somebody she had
vaguely known as a child, and then met again when they were
grown-up and going to parties together. They had never *seemed*
to have much in common and after Lavinia had married a Texan
millionaire and she had married Clifford their ways had entirely and
naturally parted. Lavinia's husband was now dead and so she had
returned to England, an older and richer woman . . .

The alarm went off, and May clutched at it, and then turned
fearfully to see whether it had woken Herbert. It didn't seem to
have done.

She put on an old cardigan and then her dressing-gown. The house was always its coldest early in the morning, and anyway, she was a cold person. The floors of the wide, dark passages were polished oak, which, as Herbert had pointed out, obviated the need for carpets. The staircase was also oak—no carpet there, either, which made it slippery and a nightmare to negotiate with heavy trays. The hall, with its huge, heavily-leaded window—too large to curtain—was somehow always freezing, even in summer, and dark, too, because here the oak·had crept up the walls to a height of about nine feet, making any ordinary furniture look ridiculous. There was also a tremendous stone fireplace in which one could have roasted an ox; and, as Oliver had pointed out, nothing less would have done either to warm the place or to defeat the joyless odour of furniture polish. 'It really is a monstrous house,' she thought, and recognized this to be what Dr Sedum had described in one of his 'talks' as a mechanical pattern reaction—something to be avoided if one was to evolve. But later on in the same talk he had said that we were all liars because we were incapable of responding consistently to our environment, and then she didn't know what to think. When she had asked Lavinia after the Time, as meetings were called in the League, Lavinia had said that one could not start at all, until one had perceived the Paradox. She had only been to one Time, and when Lavinia had said that she must not try to walk before she could fly, she realized that she had a long way to go.

The moment she got into the kitchen, Claude hoisted himself wearily out of the vegetable trug by the Aga and set about his usual process of tripping her up until she had provided him with his early morning milk. This morning, she gave in to him at once; she wanted nothing to interfere with the clockwork routine which was to conclude with Herbert catching his train to London. She had told him she was having a cousin to lunch several days ago, but he had been deep in some gardening manual, and she had not been sure whether he had heard.

Two hours later she waved to Herbert as he lurched down the drive in the old Wolseley. Alice had washed the car once a week before she had married, but it was one more of those things which May simply didn't seem to get time to do. A final wave—he would not have seen her, but he liked all his expeditions to be taken seriously—and she heaved at the huge iron-studded front door until it shut with a prison-like click. There was a terrific amount to do before Dr Sedum and Lavinia arrived, but she was so exhausted with anxiety and the feeling that she was doing something exciting and momentous behind Herbert's back that she fled to the kitchen for a cup of coffee and a cigarette (Herbert did not like her to smoke in the mornings). 'I'll make a list,' she thought. She always resorted to lists: they proved that she had a great deal to do, and to some extent, as she crossed things off, they proved that she was doing them. Mrs Green was coming this morning: she began with a list for Mrs Green. She had decided to entertain her guests entirely in what was called the morning room: by dint of transporting most of the electric fires (the ones that were in working order, anyway) she could manage to get it tolerably cosy by one o'clock. There was a reasonable round table there; it wobbled rather on its pedestal if one cut bread or made any other emphatic movements of that nature, but was otherwise suitable for lunch. The room was sternly bare: Herbert had not put much furniture there as he did not use it, but she could collect bits and pieces from other rooms. Anyway, Dr Sedum probably appreciated austerity as long as it did not make him *too* uncomfortable. Lunch was to consist of roast spring chicken, new potatoes and peas (safe food, surely, for such an occasion) and crème caramel, which she had got very good at as Herbert had been used to it in India. Mrs Green could do the vegetables and clean the room; she would prepare the chicken, make the room as warm and nice as possible and put on her blue suit. She wrote 'half past twelve' at the bottom of the lists and set about every-thing.

By twelve she thought she had done everything, but the list had mysteriously disappeared, so it was impossible to be sure. The room looked much better, and was noticeably warmer than the rest of the house, although she had only been able to plug in two heaters because that was all the plugs there were. Mrs Green had polished the food trolley and altogether entered into the spirit of the occasion; they had lugged two heavy armchairs in and laid the round table. She had picked some lilac from the garden and arranged it in the scullery while Mrs Green kindly did the dogs' food. A lot of earwigs fell out of the lilac, but Claude was at hand to dispatch them which, with a good deal of unnecessary strategy, he did. It was a lovely day, cold but sunny, no sign of rain which was an excellent thing, because rain sometimes stopped Herbert going to Lord's, and then he came home earlier rather grumpy.

Her blue suit had been her best for so long now that even putting it on induced a mechanical sense of festivity. With it she wore a jersey made by Alice in a paler blue which toned very nicely. It was awful to feel pleased that Alice was not here, but really, it was a blessing; with Elizabeth she could have been quite frank—simply told her to beat it, she wanted a private lunch—but with Alice this would have been pretty well impossible. Alice would have been hurt, would have had to be included in lunch, and then the whole thing would have been spoiled, since people in the League were not allowed to talk about it to people outside. Of course, *she* wasn't actually in it yet, but she knew that they were considering her; the lunch was probably a kind of *test* ...

She saw them arriving from her bedroom window in Lavinia's Bentley, and it was such a long way down to the front door that she was a bit breathless by the time she succeeded in getting it open.

'May! How nice!' Her cousin managed to make this sound like some graceful coincidence. Dr Sedum—an enormously tall man— loomed gently behind her: he was smiling in a temperate sort of way.

'It's lovely to see you. Do come in.'

'Of course, you've met Dr Sedum.'

'Yes.' May found she was getting breathless again. 'It's most awfully good of you to come.' She wasn't quite sure whether to shake hands, but Dr Sedum spread his out in a gesture denying all goodness, so she thought probably better not. She led the way to the far end of the hall, through the oak door, down the wide passage (she'd put the lights on) and through a baize door, after which a narrower passage culminated in the morning room.

'You certainly have room to turn round here,' exclaimed Lavinia, walking to the bay window where the round table was set. 'Isn't it frightfully difficult to get enough staff?'

'I expect it would be, but we don't try. Wouldn't you like to take off your coats?'

'And have some sherry?' she added, moments later. She felt tentative about this, not knowing whether the kind of person Dr Sedum was drank.

'That would be delightful.' She had forgotten how very quietly he spoke; so quietly, that it was impossible to hear, unless one gave him one's whole attention and watched his face. She had bought a bottle of Bristol Cream in case drink was the thing. Dr Sedum now produced a gold cigarette case and offered her a cigarette.

'You look surprised,' said Lavinia as she accepted her sherry. 'We are not supposed to deny ourselves the good things in life.' She sat in one of the arm-chairs and turned expectantly to Dr Sedum, who shook his head benevolently.

'That would be too easy. There would be an entirely false sense of achievement. The interest begins when one can say to oneself: I am smoking a cigarette, I am drinking sherry, and have a clear understanding of the *senses* that those activities bring.'

May, who had taken a sip of sherry and a puff of her cigarette and thought 'how nice' on each occasion put down her glass with the small thrill of humility and excitement that she had so often felt before when she did not understand something that seemed crystal clear to other people. 'Oh please explain to me,' she said.

Dr Sedum shook his head again: his large, round, pale blue eyes were fixed upon her face. 'On our way here, we stopped to ask the way. A man, wheeling a bicycle—an ordinary man—replied, "I'm a stranger here myself." '

May waited for him to say more, but he didn't. Instead he drank some sherry, still watching her as she gazed at him. Even sitting down, he seemed to tower above her, but his smile made her feel that if anyone could help her understand anything it would be he.

It was rather difficult to drink her sherry after that, so she was glad when Lavinia said:

'I think it's so brave of you to embark on a house this size these days.'

'Oh—it wasn't me who was brave. It was Herbert: my husband. He simply insisted that I—that we buy it. It's ridiculous really; Alice, my stepdaughter, is married, and my two are in London leading their own lives so we rattle about here like two peas in a pod, I don't mean a pod—you know what I mean.'

She stopped. Lavinia had a fringe—just like when she was small, she noticed; only then the rest of her hair had been cropped very short, had been thick and silky, and now it hung in rather greasy strands over the collar of her velveteen dress. Dr Sedum had almost no hair: none at all on the top of his head, which was smooth and the same texture as a close-up photograph of a wax pear. There were also coarse, reddish tufts at the sides just above his ears. It was extraordinary how, when you *knew* about people, their appearance took on an entirely different meaning.

Dr Sedum had finished his sherry, but as he was probably the only person she had ever met with a clear understanding of how to drink it, one expected him to finish first. She offered more; it was accepted, and she wondered when the serious talking would begin. Not until she'd got lunch actually on the table by the feel of things. She filled up Lavinia's glass, and then her own. There was an astonishingly long silence at the end of which Dr Sedum and Lavinia smiled at each other, and Dr Sedum said,

'That was good; very good.'

'I think Harvey's are a very reliable brand.'

A low rumbling broke from Dr Sedum, that, as she got used to it, May recognized as his compassionate chuckle: she had heard him use it when people asked questions at the one Time she had been to. She felt herself beginning to blush.

'I'm sorry—I thought you meant the sherry. I think I'd better get lunch now.'

'I won't offer to help you.' Lavinia made this sound like a really imaginative and generous concession.

Which May thought, as she started the journey to the kitchen, it was, on the whole, because it would have been frightfully rude to leave someone like Dr Sedum all by himself.

∗   ∗   ∗

The colonel lowered himself into a chair at his favourite corner table. He was feeling quite peckish, and looking forward no end to a damn good lunch. Henry, the head waiter, limped forward:

'Would you care for anything to drink, Colonel?'

'Oh yes, Henry, I should certainly care. A large pink gin.'

'With soda, sir?'

'With soda.'

It was early, and the dining-room was almost empty: very few people lunched before one, and at these times, Henry always gave any early member his personal attention. His reputation in the club stood very high; Henry was 'wonderful'. This simply meant that he remembered what each of them liked to drink and smiled obsequiously at all the monotonous badinage that went on and on and on about it. 'Henry must have seen a lot: he must know a thing or two,' was another thing people far too often said about him. In fact he hardly ever saw anything: men behave differently in their clubs, but they all manage to behave differently in the same way: and all Henry ever saw was a lot of Old Head Boys having a (bit of a) spree. His varicose veins were awful, and he only stayed because he had first pick of the batches of fresh and buxom Irish girls who streamed across the Channel to earn their living and lose their virginity. The staff said he was a terror with the girls: the girls giggled and whispered about him in their attic bedrooms at the top of the building, and told one another fearful lies about his disgusting and manly ways, and the junior waiters held tremulously revolutionary meetings about him in their local. The older waitresses treated him like any other member, as though he was rather mad and failing in health. The Kitchen loathed him, though this held them together as nothing else could do, and the committee regarded him as a tradition.

While Henry was seeing to his drink, the colonel picked up the business-like typewritten menu. Potted shrimps, fresh asparagus, *pâté maison* and *œufs en gelée*: damn difficult to choose. A young waitress with rippling red hair, and a real figure, came to clear away the spare place.

'Good morning.'

'Good morning, sir.'

'Haven't seen you before. What's your name?'

'My name is Maureen, sir.'

She wore high-heeled shoes and definitely naughty stockings.

'From Oiled Oiland are you?'

'From Dublin, sir.'

She had bent to pick up the mitred napkin and put it on her tray. 'There is something about a starched apron stretched across a decent pair of breasts that brings out the worst in me,' he thought, delighted with himself.

He watched her walk languorously across to the sideboard with her tray: good from the back, too. He turned to the second course. Salmon trout, game pie, roast saddle of lamb, grilled kidneys and bacon ...

'Here you are, sir. No ice for you, isn't it, sir.' It was Henry with the drink. 'I'll send Doris to you for your order.' Two members had entered the dining-room and stood waiting for their table and to tell Henry that he didn't look a day older.

The colonel sipped his drink and felt in his inner breast pocket for his spectacles. He was wearing a lemon yellow carnation, that looked very well against his fine, black-and-white houndstooth check. Now he could see the menu with no trouble at all, and by God, it made a nice change from poor old May's efforts: all one wanted was good, simple food, produced at regular intervals with no fuss. He decided upon potted shrimps and game pie. Doris, standing by the sideboard, realized that he'd decided and padded over to him. She wore sensible, low-heeled shoes with double straps, thick, fawn cotton stockings and a very great deal of uncompromisingly heavy make-up. Her uniform made her look as though she'd be a wonderful old girl in an emergency.

'Ready to order, sir, are you?'

'Why not, Doris, why not? Tell me—what is your opinion of the game pie?'

'It's very nice, sir.'

'Then I'll risk it. Now, as we both know perfectly well what garden peas are, what other vegetable would you recommend?'

'I'd have the broccoli, sir—it's fresh.' She'd told him at least fifty times that the peas were frozen, but he'd got it into his head that they were tinned and there was no shifting him.

'And what to start with, sir?'

'A few potted shrimps would do.'

'Thank you, sir. I'll send the wine waiter.'

When he had ordered his usual, half a bottle of club claret, he started to review his morning's work. 'Lawyers all the morning— you know how it is,' he murmured to himself, in case he met any members he knew who would ask him what he was doing with himself these days. He didn't—not even the member who had suggested this particular firm to him as very decent chaps. It had been a ticklish business. Because what he'd wanted to know didn't sound right, somehow, as something to walk in and ask a total stranger about. He'd had to sort of lead up to it—hedge the whole thing a bit. He'd been wanting to make his will, he said, and old so-and-so had put him on to *you*. They'd had a brief talk—well, exchanged a few remarks about their supposedly mutual friend (whom he had only met twice) at the end of which he decided that the lawyer barely knew who they were talking about. So much the better: he didn't like the idea of his private affairs getting about, and although these chaps were supposed to be discreet—how could you tell? Well—about his will. He didn't, of course, want to leave his wife in a jam, and although he was in the best of health, it was as well to be on the safe side. The lawyer (his name was Mr Pinkney) who had been trained for years to agree with this view, agreed with it. He'd have to make a list of his securities and so forth: there would be a pension of course, but apart from that ... but the thing was, that their house, their home in Surrey, happened to be in her name—so legally he supposed it was hers anyway, whether he kicked the bucket or not? And he fixed the lawyer with a look of piercing, frank anxiety. Yes, of course, the house (freehold or leasehold? Freehold? So much the better) was certainly the property of his wife—he'd be very happy to look at the deeds of course, but from what the colonel was telling him there would seem to be no doubt upon this point. The colonel relaxed almost theatrically—that is to say that if you had been up to a hundred yards away from him at the time you would have seen that that was what he was doing. It depended, Mr Pinkney went on rather more warmly (nice old chap—simply didn't know the first thing about business; you got it again and again with these retired servicemen), on the size of the colonel's estate. One might reach a position where, if things were not carefully arranged, his wife might not have sufficient income to *live* in the house in which case, although it was a realizable asset, she might be placed in some temporary embarrassment ... She wouldn't *want* to live in the place without him, the colonel said: far too big for her—she'd be lonely in it. That reminded him of another, small point: supposing *she* were to die—would the house then naturally belong to him? Trifling point, but as he was here, he might as well clear up everything he could. Had his wife made a will, Mr Pinkney inquired? He believed she had made one years ago—before she married him. All wills made prior to marriage became invalid upon that ceremony, and it was necessary to make fresh ones. Of course, if Mrs Browne-Lacey did *not* make another will, her estate would naturally go to her husband—and vice versa. Unless, of course, there were children on either side by previous marriages? What would happen then? asked the colonel—a trifle sharply (Mr Pinkney must understand that all this legal jaw was quite difficult for a plain, simple, ordinary man to follow), he hadn't quite grasped what Mr Pinkney was driving at about children ...

Mr Pinkney had explained. Having established that there were no children of the present marriage, nor likely to be, he had gone carefully into the respective situations of Alice and of Oliver and Elizabeth. The colonel had thanked him heartily for making everything so clear, had got to his feet saying that the whole matter needed thinking about, but that he would be in touch when he had done his sums, and had finished by giving Mr Pinkney one of his handshakes (Oliver had once described them as Tarzan pretending to be a Freemason).

By now he was well into the game pie and wondering whether he would have room for cheese. There was no need to worry about *Alice*; she would never cause any trouble, and in any case, as he had explained to Mr Pinkney, she had married a man of substance. The trouble, which he had *not* mentioned to Mr Pinkney, was clearly May's children. She was besotted with them, and really he wouldn't put it past her either to leave them so much of her estate that the house had to be sold to realize the cash for them, or, and possibly worse, to leave them the actual house. And it was now clear that if she *didn't* make another will, they—in fact he meant Oliver—would start kicking up if they didn't get what they thought was a fair share of the great-aunt's money. Elizabeth would almost certainly get married, but who knew what the feller might turn out to be like? One of those grasping fellers with a legal mind, or else one of those damn pacifist wallahs who wouldn't use birth-control. It really wasn't fair at his time of life that he should have to sit here worrying whether he would have a roof over his head. He wouldn't have cheese—just a brandy with his coffee. Lucky to be able to afford *that*.

*   *   *

'One of them is cherry brandy and the other's orange curaçao.' May looked from Dr Sedum to Lavinia. She looked both anxious and triumphant; she was very proud of herself for remembering the two miniature bottles she'd given the children in their stockings at Christmas, but she was worried lest both drinks might prove too *frivolous* for Dr Sedum. The coffee—made the way that Elizabeth had taught her—now stood on the trolley. It *was* such a pity there was no brandy, but she'd said that once—before she'd remembered the miniatures.

'Which are *you* going to drink?' inquired Dr Sedum.

'Oh neither. I don't like it—them. At least, sometimes I do, but

85

not today.' (It was frightful the way she caught herself out telling a lie to Dr Sedum—it showed what she was like. 'I expect I only noticed it because he was here, and really I tell thousands of lies without noticing'.)

Dr Sedum turned to Lavinia: she did not mind which she drank. Impartiality—in Dr Sedum's case, a touch roguish—seemed to be the code; May, without meaning to, suddenly imagined Oliver being there, but dismissed him at once. Oliver wouldn't really understand Dr Sedum, who was simply trying to ...

' ... enter into the spirit of the thing.' He was smiling again.

'I'm afraid there isn't much spirit in two miniatures.' May heard herself saying this as though someone else had said it.

The drinks were poured, and people lit cigarettes. Now, perhaps Dr Sedum would talk. He did.

At the time, she knew that it was absolutely fascinating—although of course, very difficult. Afterwards, they had got to their feet, put on their coats, stood silently eyeing one another (a kind of mystical weighing up, she had felt, although *she* was naturally not up to this process; she knew she wasn't fit, as they so obviously were, to weigh anyone) and then walked quietly to the Bentley, where Dr Sedum most *humanly* had wound a rather ugly woollen muffler round his throat before getting into the front seat beside Lavinia—all without a single (unnecessary) word; oh yes, as they drove off, he raised his hand in a manner which reminded her, before she could stop herself, of the queen mother. Then, after they had gone, almost at once, as she turned to the huge prison front door, she had started trying to sum up all those breathtaking things he had been saying. About one's identity and not actually having one—it being all a desperate egocentric invention. Only, on the other hand, everybody had what he described as a true personality buried out of sight of conscious understanding. How did one find it then, she had asked? A very good question, he had answered. The trouble with very good questions seemed to be that their very quality guaranteed their not being answered. There would be a pause, and then—he had so much to give—he would say something quite different. There were certain people, he had said, who were searching for something very difficult to find, who did not *want* or expect the search to be an easy one. Not for them the panacea of some universal dogma and a set of rules, penalties and rewards. There were a few people who understood that there could be no rules, no penalties and no rewards. A rule only manifested itself after one had broken it: the person paying a penalty was the last one to discover what it was, and to be aware of a reward was to understand a failure in oneself. There was no such thing as cause and effect, simply a chain joined upon itself and one had the choice of being a bead upon the chain, or the chain itself. What happened when one became one of those things? But this, alas, turned out to be another good question. It was not possible either to take or to give anything to anyone: the hysteria of that kind of practical morality had to be discarded. People were not able either to give or to take—they simply were; the problem was how to discover *what* they were. It was sometimes necessary to demonstrate the impracticability of giving and taking by going through these motions: many people embarking upon the precious and mysterious search had to be initiated in this manner. One could not understand the emptiness of any gesture until one had made it. Then he had talked about the Unconscious Self and Emotion—not as she, May, and indeed most people defined that word, but something that none of us were, initially at least, capable of feeling (that was when she realized that it had a capital E); indeed, most people went through their lives without being aware of its existence; 'Like me,' she had thought—she was indeed, she felt, like most people in every respect. What did one do with this Emotion when one got hold of it? A good question: one had then to make it continuous. It sounded awfully tiring, she had thought, and then felt thoroughly ashamed of herself for being so feeble. While she was thinking this, Dr Sedum had gone on speaking, but so quietly that she hadn't been able to hear, let alone understand what he had said. Then he suddenly rose, and suggested looking at the house. She had thought that he meant he wanted to go to the lavatory, but she had turned out to be embarrassingly wrong. He had wanted to see the whole house, and so, uncomfortably, she had showed both him and Lavinia. 'Some white elephant,' Lavinia had remarked at the end of their tour. 'Oliver, my son, said a real white elephant couldn't possibly be more trouble and would be far more interesting.' Neither of them had smiled, and she had realized that darling Oliver would seem incurably frivolous to them. Back in the morning room, Dr Sedum had murmured that it was always easier to set out on a journey lightly appointed, and then, Lavinia having reminded him that *he* had an appointment in London, they all got up from the chairs they had returned to. That was roughly it. But she couldn't pretend to herself that she under*stood* much of it. They had said that they would get in touch with her very soon, so at least she hadn't been rejected out of hand. That was something. She walked dreamily back to the morning room in order to set about the frightful task of returning it to its usual state of barren, under-furnished drabness. She was immensely *interested*, she repeated to herself, but not yet actually *enlightened*.

*　　*　　*

Hilda had one of those awful beds that squeaked. As he leaned forward to pull on his socks, the colonel shifted his weight to allow for or avoid the noise, and failed. He'd got one sock on before he realized that it was inside out. Damn, he thought. It was extraordinary how everything invariably combined to irritate him after one of these sessions. He would set about them feeling quite jolly and serene: ring up Hilda, who seemed always to be free and always glad to see him—'Pop along' to her place (remember to ring her flat bell in the rhythm of 'Colonel Bogey' it always made her laugh) and there you were; Bob's your uncle, all that kind of thing. Hilda was the good old-fashioned sort; properly dressed to start with, but nippy enough getting out of it all—or whatever combination of all you fancied—and then there was a nice cup of tea and Bourbon biscuits afterwards ... here she was, with the tray, before he'd even got his *socks* on, dammit.

'Here we are, then.' She put the tray down on a small bamboo table by the window, and with her back to him, peered into the dressing-table mirror to make sure that none of her mascara had smudged. She knew it hadn't, but men never liked you to watch them dressing. She had slipped into her embroidered kimono affair that a very nice regular had brought her all the way back from the Far East ... which reminded her that she was just in time to adjust the hands on the cuckoo clock to stop the poor little chap from coming out and shouting cuckoo four times for four o'clock. A very nice gentleman had brought it all the way back from Switzerland: her flat was full of these foreign tokens, each one with its own story if truth would out.

'How's the tea coming along?'

'It should be perfect now.' If only he'd get up off the bed, she could fold it up and return everything to normal. 'Come and have it in this nice chair.'

When he was well into his second biscuit, she filled up his cup and said, 'Bogey!'

'What is it?'

She'd been dreading this moment ever since he'd rung up.

'I'm afraid everything has got a weeny bit dearer.'

He put his cup down in slow motion and turned to stare at her.

'How do you mean "everything"?'

His pale blue eyes bulged like glass marbles: he knew perfectly well what she meant. Oh well! If he was going to dig his toes in, she would have to put her foot down.

'I mean things like tea and biscuits—' (he started to push his cup away) 'and the rent, Bogey dear.'

'Same for all of us. Cost of living only goes *up*: never comes *down*.'

'Don't I know it.'

'Oh, I don't suppose you do. Women never have any head for the practical aspects of life. Leave that to the men.'

There was a brief unsatisfactory silence while she told herself there was no sense in losing her temper, and he wondered what devil in him made him come and see her at all. Something pretty primitive and deep-down and uncontrollable. Her figure wasn't what it was.

'Well there it is, I'm afraid.'

'There *what* is?'

'It's another thirty bob: on top of the usual. I can't help it, Bogey—I've kept it down as long as I could.'

'I thought you were *fond* of me.'

'It has nothing to do with how I feel.'

'I looked on you as much more than a—'

She stared at a biscuit. Eventually, he said,

'Some prices may be going up, but you're not getting any younger, you know.'

Her hands held on to each other for comfort, but because of the kimono sleeves he couldn't see them. He got heavily to his feet, feeling in his pockets, counted out the notes and then slowly sorted four half crowns which he put on top of them on his biscuit plate.

'There y'are m'dear: all present and correct.' Unwilling jocularity, or perhaps he was sorry about what he had just said and didn't know how to make amends. He walked slowly to the door, opened it, and said,

'Seriously, Hilda, chaps like me—living on a pension and all that —you don't want to price yourself out of the market, do you, old girl?'

She shut the door after him and went to the bathroom to fetch poor little Siegfried—she always had to put him out of the room when she had customers, or else he chirped and sang all through everything. She took off his cover, dear little chap, he put his head on one side and made an experimental cheep. As she picked up his cage and carried it carefully back to the room, she realized she was crying: a tear splashed through the bars on to Siegfried's cage sand, making an enormous blob like ink in advertisements. She knew she wasn't getting any younger.

*   *   *

May heard the Wolseley coming up the drive and hurried to the front door. The house was—not exactly frightening—but more and more depressing to be alone in: towards the end of a day, one could easily feel quite frightened at how depressed one had become, and things like turning on the wireless often made it worse. She missed

Alice: if only the dogs were allowed into the house, or if Claude was less self-contained and spoke more—really, Lincoln Street with Oliver and Elizabeth had been so cosy ...

'There y'are m'dear, all present and correct.' He put his old Burberry on the carved eagle's shoulders of a lectern and bent to kiss her cheek and pat her shoulder as he always did.

'Did you have a pleasant day?'

She had to ask him again, as he seemed not to have heard her.

'Fair to middling.'

After the shepherd's pie and tinned figs, which they consumed in his den, he suggested that he make her some coffee. So she loaded and fetched the tray with all the apparatus—test tubes and spirit lamps, filters and, of course, the actual coffee. As the muddy brown liquid churned up and down, he asked,

'Did that cousin of yours make it for lunch?'

'Yes! Oh yes. She brought a friend with her: it was very interesting.'

There! Now there was hardly any concealment: although she knew that there was, really: the very idea of Dr Sedum and what he stood for would make Herbert simply furious. At the thought of Herbert thinking her underhand, she blushed.

Herbert said he was too tired to play backgammon and had the notion that a spot of early Bedfordshire would do no harm. She knew that she would not sleep so soon after the coffee, so she said she would watch the television for a bit. She switched on the vision without sound to see whether it would be funny, or she would like it, but this seemed to clear the way for the only thought she had been trying not to have, and having ever since Dr Sedum and Lavinia had left: that if she had not married Herbert she would now be living in London with darling Oliver and Elizabeth (if they wanted her to, of course) within easy reach of Great Possibilities (Dr Sedum and his Ideas); and finally, and perhaps worst of all, that she seemed to have less and less in common with Herbert who was (quite honestly) both exacting and dull. Oh, this was really *shocking* of her! She turned up the sound on the television to drown her guilty protestations ... a *good* man ... deep depression sweeping southwards ... simple and straightforward ... unusually heavy frosts for the time of year ... A *good* man.

PART TWO

August

ONE

·⋯·✤·⋯·

FIRST SIGHT

By the beginning of August, Elizabeth had cooked fifty-two dinners: Oliver, on the other hand, had gone to eleven interviews and had actually taken two of the jobs, but neither of them had turned out to be right. One of them had been in a very new book shop that concentrated upon selling poetry and giving customers cardboard cups of Nescafé, and he had quite quickly had a row with the shop's manager: 'In one morning, he said the Tibetans were probably better off under Chinese rule; all Americans were suffering from vitamin deficiencies from eating so much frozen food; and the French were the only people with literary taste. I'll Robbe-Grillet you, I said, and that was that.' The other job had been as a courier, taking a lot of nice, middle-aged women to the Costa Brava, which he said he could not go on doing because they simply hated it when they got there, and group dysentery and dis-illusionment wore him to a thread. 'Dogfight' had not yet been sold, although Sukie had driven him patiently all over the suburbs to places where stony-faced men bought and manufactured games. He had had to write out the rules in frightful legal jargon so that nobody could understand them, at least, certainly neither Elizabeth nor Sukie could, and Sukie said he'd simply managed to make the game sound complicated and boring. He quarrelled with Sukie rather a lot, and alternated bouts of depression with fractious, manic energy. Elizabeth would come home weary from clearing up some dinner party to find that he had made a great Indian feast by collecting dishes from the nearest curry restaurant. Or he would take her out and make her spend far more of her earnings buying clothes for herself than she felt she could afford. For about three weeks he gambled, with, she felt, horrifying success: he spent these sudden gains on a pair of wine coolers he bought in an auction at Sotheby's.

'How much did they cost?' she yelped just after she had fallen over them in the narrow hall.

'Forty-two pounds.' He switched on the hall light. 'Aren't they a marvellous sight?'

'What *are* they?'

'Wine coolers. How vulgar of you to ask how much something that you don't know what it is costs.'

She gazed at the fluted tubs of some impassively dark wood delicately inlaid with brass. The lids were fluted as well, and crowned by a handle made of a carved, rather angry crouching swan. She touched one of them. 'That part is nice.'

'See?' He lifted a lid. 'They've got their linings. What did you *think* they would be for?'

She frowned. 'Well, I suppose some Indian could keep the ashes of his best elephant in one of them. What on earth made you spend all that money?'

'You remember David Broadstairs? Well, he's starting an antique business on a Thames barge. He asked me to keep my eyes open for anything nice, so I have—I did. He'll sell them for me at the most enormous profit, you'll see.' Then he added sadly, 'He's got a terrifically rich sister, but she looks like an old-fashioned Channel swimmer and she couldn't even pass her "O" levels. I do think God's sense of justice goes too far at times. I'm off to see our mother in Surrey now.'

'You never told me!'

'I've told you the moment I saw you after I knew. She sounds as though she needs a visit.' He kissed her lightly on a bit of cheekbone, and was gone. She opened the door after him and called:

'When will you be back?'

'Late tonight, probably—why do you want to know?'

'People ringing up—you *fool*.' He whipped round in the street and charged straight at her so that she had to clutch him not to fall over.

'Let's get this clear: *you're* the fool: *I'm* the whiz kid: you're younger than me: I'm far heavier and stronger and my sense of chivalry died when I saw matron at school during a fire practice. O.K.?'

'O.K.' She was nearly in tears at being called a fool but she was laughing. She scratched what looked like some egg off his corduroy jacket, and a lot came off under her nail, but the mark looked exactly the same.

'Why can't I go with you?'

'Because it's nicer for May if we spread her children out.' He kissed her. 'You smell like a delicious clean cow. If Sukie rings, tell her I'm out with Shirley MacLaine: no—tell her, and I mean this, tell her I've gone away with Ginny Mole: she'll believe *that* all right, and it'll be more likely to choke her off.'

Then he really did go.

Back in the silent, empty little house, Elizabeth made herself a large mug of iced Nescafé, kicked off her sandals and lay on the battered old sofa wondering whether she ought to read a serious book as she was having some free time by herself. London in August wasn't very nice: or perhaps nowhere felt so good if Oliver wasn't there. She ought, as he pointed out, to make some friends of her own, but somehow, what with her job (and she had to have that because between them they needed more money than May socked them) *and* Oliver and his friends and life, there never seemed to be any time. But she had to face it: the job wasn't getting her anywhere —just as Oliver not getting a job wasn't getting *him* anywhere: the trouble was that Oliver didn't mind—after the courier job he'd said that he simply wasn't one of life's travellers, and that Stevenson's remark was a horrible mixture of austerity and showing off; personally, he, Oliver, was one of life's arrivers and wasn't going to let his life degenerate into a hopeful mystery tour. She hadn't liked to ask who Stevenson was (either a friend of Oliver's, or else someone dead and famous, because whichever he was she'd get snubbed) ... Well, she couldn't read a book, because she had awful leather patches to put on the elbows of Oliver's tweed jacket: she'd promised to do the sewing if he got the leather, thinking he'd never get it, but he did, at once. 'And what's more, it's very distinguished.'

'What *is* it?' And she had gazed with discomfort at the strip of stiff, wrinkled hide that still had tufts of dark and pale fur attached to it.

'The hind leg of a man-eating tiger. Annabel's father shot it in Bengal and had it made into one of those *snarling* rugs, but he doesn't take much notice of it nowadays, so Annabel cut off this bit for me. If he *does* notice, she'll say it got moth.

'He was a frightful tiger—full of cheap bangles and beads: just get on with your sewing and *don't* get soppy about the wrong things,' he added. 'You can't be sad about *every*one who's dead.'

Now, she'd no sooner started getting on with it, when the telephone rang, and a voice that was clearly Sukie trying to pretend to be someone else, asked for Mr Oliver Seymour.

Elizabeth explained that he was out, and the person—Sukie—rang off before she could say when he'd be back. A moment later, it rang again and Sukie, sounding pretty desperate, said, 'I know it's you. Are you *sure* he's out?'

'Yes, of course I am. All day.'

'When, when will he be back?'

'He wasn't quite sure.' The trouble with loyalty was that it always seemed to include a good deal of hard-heartedness to whoever you weren't being loyal to. There was a pause, then Sukie said,

'The awful thing is, I think Oliver's tired of me: I can't *bear* to think it, but I can't help thinking it.'

'Oh—poor Sukie!'

'What do you think?'

'Well—'

'Is there someone else, do you know?'

'I don't—'

'Because he keeps on talking about one of the most boring people I've ever met in my life and I couldn't help wondering.'

'Sukie, I really don't—'

'Has he mentioned someone called Ginny to you?'

'Only just.'

'Well he never stops mentioning her to me. She's one of the most boring people I've ever met in my life.'

There was another pause, during which it was quite clear to Elizabeth that Sukie was crying. Unable to stand this, she said,

'As a matter of fact, Oliver has gone to see his mother—our mother.'

'Honestly?'

'Honestly: he told me just before he left. Probably back tonight.'

'Really and truly? You swear you're not making this up?'

'Sukie, I absolutely promise.'

'Oh! Elizabeth! Do you think that means there is some hope for me?'

Before she could stop herself, Elizabeth had said, 'No I don't. Oh look here, Sukie, you'd better come round: it'd be much better than talking on the telephone.'

So Sukie came round in a flash, and they had a long talk about Life and not being possessive and whether young marriages turned out well on the whole or not and what jealousy did to people's character and how much being brilliant had to do with being cold, and whether young, and particularly young *brilliant* men ever really knew what they wanted and when neither of them could think of any more ways of discussing Oliver, Elizabeth made some more iced Nescafé and then Sukie helped her wash her hair. Sukie was very good at this, rinsing Elizabeth's hair until it squeaked, and saying kindly that if Elizabeth took more trouble with it, it could be one of her best features, and that hundreds of people spent thousands of pounds having artificial red-gold lights put into their hair. It was just one more of those days when knowledge of soil erosion, monotremes and the Moorish influence in Spain (or indeed anywhere else) would not have proved of the slightest use ...

About four o'clock they were just looking through an evening paper in case there was a film worth seeing, when the telephone rang.

'Is that by any chance Miss Elizabeth Seymour?'

'Yes.'

'You won't remember me. I was a guest at a dinner party cooked by you in Eaton Square last week. Artichokes vinaigrette, trout with almonds and cream cheese tarts: that one.'

'Oh yes; I remember.' There had been eight people in all, so that meant he could be any one of the three male guests.

'I was the tall, nearly bald one with thick glasses. The thing is, I'm in rather a mess. I wonder if you could help me out?'

Elizabeth waited.

'I've suddenly been presented with the necessity of having dinner at home without staff of any kind. I wondered if, by any chance, you happen to be free to help me out?'

'How did you find me? I usually work through an agency.'

'So I was told. But they seem to be permanently engaged: so I rang the Mountjoys—the Mountjoys of Eaton Square—and they gave me your number. I'm really rather desperate or I wouldn't have gone to such lengths. I've never liked the telephone.'

'Well—I usually do work through the agency, and they would expect—'

'Oh, I'll pay them anything they expect, and I'm quite prepared to pay you more. I have a rather vulgar attitude to money in fact. I've found it's the best attitude to have. So don't worry about that aspect.'

'How many people do you want me to cook for? I *am* free, as a matter of fact,' she added hurriedly.

'Oh, what a relief! Just for two. A Mrs Cole and myself: I've ordered some of that very thick steak and some sort of pâté to go with it. Mrs Cole is something of a carnivore.'

'Do you want any kind of savoury or pudding?'

'A savoury would be delicious. Could I leave that to you? Have you got a pencil to write down my address?'

'No: hang on a minute.' She couldn't find one, but Sukie kindly produced her eyeliner and an advertising page of the *Evening Standard*. The address turned out to be in Pelham Place (walking distance from Lincoln Street, jolly good thing), but when he produced his telephone number, the eyeliner broke, and she had to repeat it aloud while Sukie kindly arranged bunches of matches on the carpet.

'And what's your name, please?' she remembered to ask before he rang off.

'John Cole. Tremendously in keeping with my appearance, I'm afraid you'll find. Goodbye.'

'What on earth could he mean by that?' Elizabeth said as she put the receiver down.

'By what?' Sukie was cramming the unused matches back in the box. 'You must admit I'm a marvellous secretary: full of resources.'

'Saying his name was John Cole and it was tremendously in keeping with his appearance.'

'No idea. It's a pretty dull name.'

'That's it, then. He said he was nearly bald and wore thick glasses.'

'Poor old thing,' said Sukie absently. Then she turned the awe-inspiring contents of her handbag on to the hearth-rug and found a pencil.

*   *   *

Elizabeth walked to Pelham Place. Sukie had offered to drive her, but she felt like walking, and also her hair wasn't quite dry. She had managed to get Sukie to go, on the grounds that it would be rather obvious for Oliver to find her in Lincoln Street, supposing he got back before Elizabeth did. The talk with Sukie had left her feeling far more contented with her lot or life than she had been feeling before Sukie rang up. It was much luckier to be Oliver's sister than one of his mistresses: to begin with, he was far kinder to her than he seemed to be to people like Annabel or Sukie, and to go on with, whatever he was, he couldn't really stop being it, which made the whole situation feel far more secure and free.

She arrived at the house at Pelham Place at about seven o'clock. It was one of those stucco, non-committal houses where you couldn't be sure what kind of person might live. A long time after she had rung the bell, she realized that the front door was open—and walked in. She could hear a gramophone, and a bath running: the kitchen, with luck, would be on the ground floor, and if not, certainly in the basement. The gramophone was playing Mozart: one up to him, she thought, but she had got fairly professional in her expectations of her employers. Few of them had turned out as awful as those first ones in Bryanston Square, but, on the other hand, none of them had struck her as people one was sorry not to be having dinner *with* (instead of actually cooking their dinners). The kitchen *was* in the basement, but so was the dining-room, so *that* was all right. It was a comforting mixture of Formica and Elizabeth David —hygienic, but well-equipped. The dining-room had rather old-fashioned Cole's wallpaper (perhaps *he* made it) and the traditional amount of damp—or mildew. She unpacked the materials for the savoury, put on her overall, and started looking for everything else.

John Cole materialized in that kind of twilight that you never notice until somebody else brings your attention to it. He was holding two glasses in his hands. 'Do you like champagne?' is what he eventually said. He *was* very tall, and his spectacles winked in the reflection from the street lamp outside the basement window.

'Now I would.' Elizabeth took the glass and drank gratefully.

'Your overall is so dazzling that I can't see your face in this Stygian light.' He switched on some lights. 'I hope you are managing to find everything. My resident couple left rather suddenly. This afternoon in fact. Would you like some more of that?'

'Well—a little more. It's very good.'

'Ostentation combined with stinginess have given champagne an unfairly bad name.' He had opened the huge fridge and extracted an unopened bottle. 'Chuck me that cloth, would you? Have you ever drunk decent champagne at a wedding, for instance?' He was untwisting the wire from the neck of the bottle.

'Sorry, I thought when you said "more" that we'd be finishing a bottle.'

'That's all right. *I'm* not stingy—ostentatious, but not stingy. And I wanted some more myself. Hold it out.'

He drew the cork and filled her glass to the brim. After he had replaced the bottle in the fridge, he leant against one of the teak draining boards and said, 'Would it be all right with you if I stay and drink with you while you do your stuff? I've had a pig of a day,

and if I go and sit upstairs by myself I shall fall asleep.' There was
the briefest pause, then, before she had replied, he added, 'I *could*
say that I'd be a help if you couldn't find anything, but that would
be a complete lie. I haven't really the faintest idea where anything
is.' Another slight pause, before he said, 'But if you hate people
being about when you are at work, I should quite understand.'

Elizabeth said, 'Oh no! It's—it's much better having someone to
talk to. Do stay.'

'I will.' She found she was looking at him exactly when he began
to smile: this made him look more different from when he wasn't
smiling than anyone she had ever seen. She smiled briefly back—
even across the room she had to look up at him: he was extraordinarily tall. For a second, the whole evening suddenly seemed
festive and momentous, as though something very good was certainly going to happen. Amazed by this, she continued to look at
him, or rather in his direction, but seeing only herself now. '*You're*
the fool,' Oliver had said only a few hours ago, and a feeling like
that simply showed how right he was. She saw herself—a pair of
little white dwarfs reflected in his glasses—and then she saw him
again, shoulders slightly hunched, head a little to one side, at the
end of his smile—'staring casually,' she thought, if that made sense.
Her forehead felt burning under her fringe. She got her pad with
pencil attached out of her bag, and started to write out the menu
in full in order to check off her materials.

'What time would you like to have dinner?'

They both looked at their watches.

'I should think in the neighbourhood of half-past eight. The
trouble is that I can't be sure when my guest will arrive.'

'And of course you will want time for a drink before dinner.'

'No.'

She glanced at him, surprised, and then told herself that it was
none of her business: but then, it was, a bit.

'I don't think I can start to cook your steak until your guest has
actually arrived—'

'There's some caviare to start with. Here.' He opened the fridge
and indicated the largest pot of caviare that she had ever seen.

'Right. Do you like onion and egg and chopped parsley—all that sort of thing?'

'None of that sort of thing. Mrs Cole and I eat it in porridge bowls with spoons: I say, you're lagging behind a bit with that champagne: if it's too warm chuck it away; the hallmark here is seasoned vulgarity.'

'Mrs Cole and I.' Of course, he had mentioned a Mrs Cole earlier. She was fitting greaseproof paper round the small soufflé dish she had brought: it did seem a curious way of referring either to your wife or your mother—but that really *was* none of her business ...

'Is Mrs Cole your wife?' (How could I. Don't tell me, I don't want to know.)

'Mrs Cole is my wife.'

(Oh. Is she indeed: well I don't see why you had to be so secretive about it.) 'Oh.'

'To be exact, she *was* my wife: she isn't any more; we're divorced.'

(Well that's something. *What?* in that case why did you ever say she was your wife and why on *earth* are you taking all this trouble to have her to dinner?) 'Oh.'

'Do *you* like caviare?'

'I've never had enough to be sure: by itself, I mean. It's nearly always *on* things. Now I'd better lay the table. Is the silver in the dining-room?'

'Let's go and see. It's possible, I suppose, that Colonel Grzimek has walked off with it; or motored, which was more his style. Isn't it odd,' he went on as he opened the dining-room door for her, 'how one always speaks of servants in the past tense the moment they have left? There's a nasty streak of egocentricity there, all right.

'I maligned the colonel. There is the silver: all of it, by the look of things.'

He was towering over the sideboard on which there was a large rosewood canteen systematically stuffed with spoons and forks.

Elizabeth, suddenly remembering Daddo, couldn't help beginning to laugh and then going on. He looked at her while she did this with approval and interest.

'What an extraordinarily involuntary noise that is. The idea of a colonel being a butler amuses you? Well, he almost certainly wasn't one. He was Romanian (there I go again, no doubt he still is), and it was his way of showing me that he was too good for the job. There is something comfortingly international about military rank. He also said his wife was an ex-opera singer. He almost certainly wasn't married to her, and she showed no signs of even retrospective musicality, but she was a damn good cook. She did everything. She cleaned *his* shoes, while he cleaned mine.' By now he was sitting in the carver at the head of the table, while Elizabeth laid a place in front of him.

'Where shall I put Mrs Cole?'

'A very good question. It's no good putting her at the other end, because she won't stay there. There, I should think, would be as safe a compromise as any.'

'If they were so good, why did they leave?'

'I wanted them to come out to the villa and the colonel said that somebody had insulted him in Monaco in 1936 and there had been a little trouble; and then he said *I* was insulting him and after that he sulked for two frightful days (a really effective sulker; the bath-water and the champagne became exactly the same uninviting temperature). Then he simply left...

'No doubt,' he added, following her back to the kitchen, 'his loss will prove a blessing in disguise. That is how they usually come, I find. You get misfortunes in plain clothes as it were, but not your average blessing.'

Elizabeth, rather dazed by the way in which he seemed to be talking about a lot of things she didn't know about all at once, absently gulped the rest of her champagne.

'I'm interrupting you: I'll go. Let me fill your glass, and leave you to it.'

'It's all right, so long as you don't expect any intelligent response.' She was doing the part of a soufflé that you can do ahead of time. The steak was out and ready; the watercress (the only concession to greenery in the entire meal) was waiting, washed, in the salad basket.

'Do you want your steak *on* pâté *on* toast?'

Before he could answer, the front door rang without stopping for what seemed like ages.

John Cole said, 'I'll go. There's an intercom by the door there. I'll tell you when we want to start on the caviare. Don't, for God's sake, go before I've seen you.' He went.

He's dreading it, Elizabeth thought: perhaps he's still in love with her? Yes. No. If he isn't, she must be very awful for him not to take her *out* to dinner. Surely that would have been the answer?

Voices: a contralto treacle; John Cole's. Door shutting; the woman laughing—a husky, but high-pitched laugh—another door shutting, and silence.

Silence for what seemed ages, but Elizabeth, who timed it, knew that it was no more than twenty minutes. She hummed and hawed about cooking the steak, and something told her not to until both the Coles were safely in his dining-room. But this didn't seem to be going to happen. She fidgeted around the kitchen, fiddling with the soufflé mix, turning the steak in its salt, oil and lemon juice, swinging the basket of watercress. Eventually she sat down, combed her hair and put on a spot more lipstick: her fringe was too long again—it was getting, as Oliver had said, like one of those intensely reliable dogs. Seeing herself for long always made her feel shaky and depressed. She decided to have a proper look at the dining-room.

The paper was like the passages at Covent Garden—broad stripes —only here it was two different fairly dark greens. The walls had several pictures that looked, at first sight, to be French Impressionists, and on closer examination (and bearing the champagne and caviare in mind) stayed being them. The damp patches, the marks on the lime-coloured carpet, the rather low, smoky ceiling, all gave the impression that the room had been decorated years ago—pictures and all—and then simply left. Was this the work of Mrs Cole?

The moment Elizabeth thought this, she heard Mrs Cole's voice; continuous and, even at a distance, seeming too loud. She slipped back into the kitchen: the voice got louder.

They seemed to be taking a very long time to come downstairs.

She put the steaks under the grill; got the caviare out of the fridge and then, her heart beating out of sheer curiosity, made for the dining-room.

Mrs Cole was sitting at the table, but not at the place set for her. She had dragged (at least Elizabeth supposed it must have been she who had dragged) a chair and placed it tremendously near her ex-husband's place.

'Cavvers—goody-goody-goody gum-drops!'

Mrs Cole's voice was naturally rather high, but with a good deal of husky interference which gave her a much wider vocal range than most people. At any rate, her voice certainly made you look at her. Elizabeth looked, and then immediately looked away, because she found Mrs Cole's enormous, pale blue, rather protuberant eyes fixed upon her.

'Is this a little chum of Jennifer's?'

'It is not.' He pushed the caviare over to her while Elizabeth fetched the silver porringers from the sideboard.

'He's a *sodding* awful liar, isn't he?' Mrs Cole laid a thin, white, heavily freckled arm upon Elizabeth's overall. 'You know all about where Jennifer is, don't you, darling?'

'I'm afraid I don't—'

'Miss Seymour has kindly come in to cook dinner. She's never even *met* Jennifer. Come on, Daphne, stop needling, and have some nice caviare.'

Without letting go of what had become her grasp of Elizabeth's overall (the skinny arm culminated in a hand that was shaped like the foot of some bird of prey), Mrs Cole started to dig her spoon into the pot. 'Vere is the *wod*ka?' she asked. Drops of caviare dripped from her shaky, laden spoon and rolled about the table. When some of it was in the bowl, she stabbed at it petulantly. 'No cavvers without wodders,' she said in a sort of voice that a large doll, if it could talk, would talk. She was altogether like a huge, old doll, Elizabeth thought. Even her hair had a very wide parting in it—like doll's hair—and she wore it in a long, permanently-waved bob—like Rita Hayworth in ancient films. Mrs Cole's head and the shoulders of her black crêpe dress were showered with dandruff, and well over and above her Chanel No. 5, Elizabeth could detect the odour of cheap raspberry jam that so often accompanies this condition.

John Cole, without answering, took out a bunch of keys and left the room. The moment that they were alone, Mrs Cole's grip on Elizabeth's arm tightened, and just as Elizabeth was going to pull herself away from this rather surprising and horrible person, she said,

'While he's away—quick! write down her *number*—I only want to *see* her.' She had let go at last, and was fumbling desperately with her bag. '*You* look for me, darling, any old scrap will do—I just want to give her my love.' And for a moment Elizabeth found herself looking down into the huge, heavily made-up doll's face, whose eyes were of such open agony that she felt her hair prickling with shock. She would do *anything* to stop someone looking like that.

The bag, which had seemed quite small, was crammed with dirty, broken, spilt things—loose aspirins coated with brown face-powder, a miniature bottle of Gordon's gin, a grey elastic sanitary belt, a screwed-up packet which could contain no smokable cigarette, a little Disney-type dog made of pipe cleaners, a chiffon handkerchief with a swansdown puff attached, some cloakroom tickets, pencils (broken), Biro (top off), a tube of something that was oozing out at the bottom ...

John Cole was back. He carried a bottle of vodka in one hand, and two very small glasses in the other. Elizabeth, who had been burrowing, as directed, into Mrs Cole's handbag, saw his face, and felt herself beginning to blush. Mrs Cole looked at her with hatred, but there was something helpless about it, and Elizabeth, now feeling treacherous in both directions, put the bag back on the side of Mrs Cole's chair. Her ears were burning, and the steak needed basting.

'What a one you are for locking things up. It would have been awful being married to you when the *Crusades* were on. One would have been *hobbling* about in a chastity belt ...'

When Mrs Cole was trying to be horrible she had a kind of old-fashioned drawl ... Who on *earth* was Jennifer? None of your *business*, you fool. She basted the steak with its juices, finished her glass of (now rather warm) champagne and tried not to hear their voices next door. The trouble was that you could. You couldn't hear absolutely everything they said unless you tried very hard indeed—and possibly you couldn't then—but without trying at all, you could hear enough to make it very difficult not automatically to try. Mostly it was Mrs Cole, who seemed to be talking a good deal, but he was also answering, or arguing with her. Sometimes she shouted, or almost cried out, and once Elizabeth thought she was actually crying, but then she realized that it had been a laugh turning into a paroxysm of coughing.

The steaks were done; the toast fried; the pâté put into position. The watercress was in a silver bowl in which (she had to admit), it looked its best. Now what? Did she wait until rung for, or march in with the next course? Perhaps this was why most cooks in the old days had had such fiendish tempers and took to drink. Hours seemed to have gone by. She decided to march.

The candles on the dining-room table had been lit, which made the rest of the room seem darker. Mrs Cole sounded as though she was in the middle of some rambling accusation. John Cole, who, elbows on the table, almost looked as though he was blocking his ears with his hands, gave a brief affirmative nod as she came in: clearly she had done the right thing. She put the tray on the sideboard, and went to clear the caviare bowls. ' ... but that's what you *always* do, always assume the worst instead of the best, not like me, I always assume the worst instead of the best ...'

They had neither of them eaten much caviare. Mrs Cole's helping seemed to be absolutely everywhere except inside her and the original pot was nearly full. The vodka bottle, on the other hand, was nearly empty. It stood at Mrs Cole's right hand, and as Elizabeth cleared away her bowl, she grabbed the bottle, emptied it into the tumbler which had been meant for water, and sank it.

John Cole said, 'Daphne—'

Mrs Cole said, 'Merry old soul indeed! Christmas; celebrations—fun; coming off your high horse; the trouble with you, Jack, is that you're nouveau riche—that's not like art nouveau getting fashionable with time like bead dresses and bobbed hair: the riche are always with us, and far too many of them are nouveau—they've never been popular for one very good reason—they suffer from moral over-compensation—like cork legs or being a Lesbian—they can't help regarding riches as a kind of drawback they're going to surmount. Nobody goes about saying "he's marvellous, in spite of being nouveau riche." But that's what they want. They all want it. They don't realize that however riche you are, there are some things that money can't buy. Like stopping being nouveau.'

At this point, her head sunk gently forward until it was enjoined with the steak Elizabeth had placed before her. There was a profound and continuing silence. Both John Cole and Elizabeth gazed at Mrs Cole until they looked at each other. Mrs Cole's arms lay on the dark, polished table like pieces of Arctic coastline, each side of her head. It became clear that any move that was to be made was not going to come from her.

Then John Cole said, 'I must take her home: oh dear, oh damn!'

'Shall I—'

'No. You could help me get her upstairs, though. People like this are a dead weight. Hang on a minute here, while I get the car out.' And he left the room in such haste that the candle nearest the door nearly blew out.

He was pretty callous about her, Elizabeth thought, because whatever someone was like, you couldn't help feeling sorry for them if they were being like Mrs Cole was now. Nobody would pass out with their forehead in a lot of hot gravy unless they had got past caring about anything. Except drink and Jennifer whoever-she-was. She went to the kitchen, damped a clean drying-up cloth and tried to lift Mrs Cole's head out of her plate in order to clean it up a bit. This operation, she quickly found, needed three hands: one, at least, for Mrs Cole's head (which was surprisingly heavy), one for wielding the damp cloth, and one for removing the plate of steak. She got the plate out of the way, but dropped the cloth and then lost control of Mrs Cole's head which rolled forward again almost as though it had nothing to do with the rest of her.

She groaned and started to breathe rather noisily, but she must be better off lying on the cloth. 'Poor Mrs Cole!' she thought rather uncertainly. She was very glad when *he* returned.

They carried her upstairs; Elizabeth leading, backwards, with the feet. One of her shoes fell off and apart from her smeared make-up and the gravy she seemed also to have lost an ear-ring, but she looked so absolutely awful by now that Elizabeth rather hoped that neither of them would start worrying about the ear-ring. They'd both begun saying things like, 'Mind the head: can you manage the feet?' so they were hell-bent on trying to pretend she wasn't anyone. The front door was wide open, and so was the car door. Luckily, it was a very large car, but even so, it seemed to Elizabeth that they had, rather heartlessly, to stuff her into it.

Before he got into the car, he said, 'I do beg you not to go before I get back. I'll only be about twenty minutes.'

So she went back and tidied up: cleared the food out of the dining-room (it seemed such an awful waste of steak that she put it all on a dish in case John Cole knew a dog). She licked the caviare pot spoon not to waste that, and it was delicious: she put the pot firmly in the fridge before tackling the washing up—not much of *that*, anyway. Now that it was almost over, she felt very sad: it seemed awful that people should either have lives with nothing happening in them (like hers) or lives where whatever it was that happened was quite so squalid and frightening (like Mrs Cole). *He* might be all right—fall into neither of these categories—but then he was a man, and she had a sinking feeling that most of the *ordinary* bad things happened to women rather than men. Men were probably saved up for heroic death (like her father) or glamorous danger (like Oliver when he'd borrowed someone's quick motor and sneaked into a race at Brands Hatch—all that kind of thing). Perhaps men were largely responsible for the things that happened to women—perhaps *he* was the reason why Mrs Cole had taken to drink! Perhaps Jennifer was her own child, and John Cole wouldn't let her see her own daughter—was, in fact, not only nouveau riche, but wicked, it was simply his glasses that misled one ... And Daddo! she thought, with exactly the same hectic alarm; supposing *he* was wicked and just masquerading as stupid and dull! There was absolutely no reason, she went on, wildly, why on earth stupid people shouldn't be wicked: it was far more likely, when you came to consider it. It was supposed to be far easier to be wicked than to be good, and Oliver had said that one of the hallmarks of stupid people was that they always did what they thought was the easiest thing: the fact that it often turned out not to be that was neither here nor there ...

The front door slammed: why hadn't she *left*? She seized her bag and basket, turned out the kitchen lights, and almost ran up the basement stairs, straight into John Cole at the top.

She ran into him with such force that if he had not caught hold of her shoulder, she would have lost her balance and fallen back down the stairs.

'Steady.'

'I'm going home now.'

'Hang on a minute.'

'I've got to go—honestly.'

But a strand of her hair seemed to have got caught in one of his waistcoat buttons: she jerked, and tore the tangled hairs out by their roots with half a dozen little dwarf mandrake screams of agony. Tears filled her eyes.

'Steady,' he said again, but more seriously.

He took her upper arm and walked her through the nearest door.

'Don't *frog*march me!'

He laughed. 'I couldn't be doing that: you have to be four to one for that. I'm leading you to the nearest comfortable chair which is what one does to girls in your condition.' He pushed her gently into it, and took the basket from her.

'There you are. I say, that's Little Red Riding Hood equipment. Had you suddenly decided that I was a good old-fashioned wolf—look here, what *is* it?'

For the moment she sat down, tears began spurting from her eyes. For a few seconds she glared unseeingly at him, too offended with herself even to search for a handkerchief. He went to the other side of the room and came back with a tumbler so heavy that her hand shook with surprise at its weight.

'The male equivalent of a nice cup of tea,' he said.

'I don't like whisky.'

'As a matter of fact, it's brandy. Brandy and soda. I should have said the male nouveau riche equivalent of a nice cup of tea.'

She drank some, and then said, 'It's simply that things seem awful to me sometimes—nothing, really. Nothing to do with you,' she added, meaning to sound worldly, rather than rude. She gave him the glass to hold while she found her handkerchief, and then blew her nose in what she hoped was a practical and finishing-off manner.

'Have some more brandy. I'm going to have some too.' He handed her back her glass and went away again. It was a very large, dimly lit room, with two fireplaces and windows to the floor each end of it: it smelt of flowers and she was glad that it was dimly lit.

When he came back with his glass, he sat on the arm of a huge sofa near her chair and said, 'We've both had rather an awful evening. It's not surprising that you feel awful.'

'What about Mrs Cole?'

'Don't worry about her. *She's* all right.'

'She's *not* all right! She clearly wasn't at all all right!'

'She was stoned, of course. There's nothing unusual about that.'

Elizabeth was clutching her tumbler so hard that if it hadn't been made of plate-glass windows it would certainly have broken. She took a gulp of brandy for courage and said, 'She was extremely upset about someone called Jennifer.' She was watching him narrowly for a reaction.

'There's nothing unusual about that. She's been upset about Jennifer for years.

'Our daughter,' he added a moment later: and now it seemed to be the other way round—to be he who was watching her. Staring down at it, she was turning the glass round and round in her hands, and even with her fringe it was possible to see from the rest of her face that she was frowning. At last she said, 'Do you mean that she doesn't *know* where her *own* daughter lives?'

'That's right.'

'Who stops her knowing? You?'

'Yep.'

'That's monstrous!'

'Of course, sometimes my security slips up, but not if I can help it.'

'No wonder she is so dreadfully unhappy.'

'Yes, it's not a situation that makes for happiness—'

She got to her feet and looked wildly for somewhere to put her glass.

'I'm going home now.'

'You said that before.' But he rose to his feet and stood towering before her as he took her glass.

She looked defiantly up at him. 'Now I really *am*.'

He stood quite still watching her face. Then, with neat and gentle movements, he took off his glasses, folded them and put them in a pocket: without the glasses, he looked more simple, more serious, and inquiring. He put his arms round her, drew her towards him and put his mouth upon hers. They stayed like that for a long time, motionless and utterly silent.

Then they were both sitting on the sofa: he was holding one of her hands in both of his and speaking quite calmly—as though nothing had happened.

'You see, it's not only Daphne we have to consider: there's Jennifer, too. It got a bit much for her having her mother turn up without warning, dead drunk, falling all over the place at Speech Days and sometimes just any old day—anywhere. You know how conservative children are: well poor old Jennifer kept turning out to have a mother not like anybody else's mother. I had to put a stop to it. Daphne suffers from gusts of sentimental passion for Jennifer and there is nothing children hate more than that. Do you begin to see, at all?'

She nodded: she felt like two people: one inside, and one sitting on a sofa, talking. She said, 'But she can't always have been like this? She must somehow have *got* like it?'

'I don't know when that was. She'd been on the drink long before I met her. When I married her she came off it, because, poor girl, she thought I was going to love her in the way she wanted. But the trouble with alcoholics is that they can't love anyone back, you see: they're too taken up with themselves, and whether people are reassuring and loving them enough, and nobody ever can, so then they feel let down and switch the situation so that most of the letting down will be done by them. That's roughly it, I think. But it's an impossible situation for children: if you have them, you have to try and protect them from bad luck on that scale. I divorced her.'

He had put on his spectacles again, and was observing her, she found, when she looked up.

'Years ago.'

'How old is Jennifer?'

He reflected. 'Twenty in September.'

'I'm twenty.'

An expression she had not seen before crossed his face: then he said, 'That's why I explained this to you. I'm forty-five.'

There was a silence while they looked at each other. Then he took off his glasses again with one hand and put them on a table behind the sofa. 'I want to kiss you,' he said, and there ensued another unknown quantity of time and by the end of it she was lying on the sofa in the crook of one of his arms.

'Now is the moment for me to examine your face,' he said, 'I'm sorry to seem so fidgety, but that means putting on my spectacles.'

'Who cuts your hair?' he asked when they were on.

'My brother.'

'Good Lord!'

'He's not actually a hairdresser.'

'I can see that.' He pushed the hair out of her eyes. 'Anyway, with a forehead like that, it's a crime to have a fringe or bang or whatever it's called. Is it my imagination, or is your hair not perfectly dry?'

'It mightn't be. I'd just washed it when you rang up.'

'*Really*—may I call you Elizabeth? Well, *really*, Elizabeth!'

'It's all very well for *you*—'

'I was waiting for that.'

'How do you mean?'

'Some disparaging allusion to my baldness. Would it help if I told you that what hair I *have* got is incredibly greasy? A little of it goes a hell of a long way; you should be thankful it is so much on the decline.'

'I only meant that you *know* when you are going to work, so you needn't get caught out washing your hair'. She sat up. 'Could I have my brandy?'

'In a minute; you're quite perky enough without it. Let me see your eyes.' He peered very close into her face and she could see two little Elizabeths—like Polyfotos—one in each lens.

'What marvellous, translucent whites you have—like a very young child. Or—let me see—thinly-sliced whites of hard-boiled egg—in case you think the young child stuff is a bit Dornford Yates.'

'Who's he?'

'When we have more time, I'll show you. True to form, I have nearly all of him in first editions upstairs. I'm afraid I've got to take off my glasses again.'

'I'll take them off.'

She leaned towards him as she did this and he kept perfectly still. He was staring at her mouth.

At last he took her head between his hands and began kissing her and this time it was different: it was not enough, and she could not bear it to stop. She clung to him and kissed him—the first time *she* had ever actually kissed in her life; afterwards, she flung her arms round his neck and rubbed her face against his to make the touching go on ...

'I'm going to take you upstairs,' he said. He took her by the shoulders and pushed her a little away. 'Elizabeth: you've never done this before, have you?'

She shook her head. 'It's a kind of love—isn't it?'

'At first sight,' he said.

TWO

·᛭·

CÔTE D'AZUR

OLIVER loved the whole business of flying, and always managed to get a window seat where the view was not obscured by the aeroplane's wings. It was dark, as one would expect at half past midnight, and by the lack of lights below, he guessed that they were flying over the English Channel. He stretched out his legs, threw back his head, shut his eyes and waited for France. He was on his way to Cap Ferrat, to stay with Elizabeth and the fabulous John Cole. Elizabeth had been there a fortnight already: a week ago she had rung him at Lincoln Street—in the *morning*—and said how soon could he come? Not for at least a week, he had replied: he didn't want to sound as though he had nothing better to do as most people who habitually haven't, don't; also Ginny had gone to Eden Roc the day before Elizabeth rang, and the last thing he wanted her to think was that he was chasing her. So he had spent an awful week by himself in London, not getting down to anything more than ever. He'd been to a sale at Simpson's and bought himself some rather stunning bathing shorts. Darling Liz had left him every penny she possessed, but he had thought that if he lived on corned beef it was fair to buy the shorts. The ticket had been sent to him with Mr Cole's compliments: a perfectly charming old-world chauffeur (Scottish) had brought it. He had saluted Oliver and then said, 'Your sister has expressed the wish for a picture of her father which lies on the table by her bed here. If you will entrust me with it, I will have the office send it out.' So Oliver had fetched it for him, and the man had saluted again, and said, 'I hope we shall see you in France, sir. Your sister sent her love and seemed very well when I last saw her this morning.' And then he had popped into a silver Rolls-Royce before Oliver could reply.

Liz really was extraordinary. As far as he could make out (and that surely must be, in her case, the whole way), she had lived a kind of schoolgirl, virginal existence, and then, suddenly, he had got back from seeing May in Surrey to find her not at home which she continued to be all night. When eventually she returned (shortly after he had started seriously to worry), she had been quite different from anything he had ever known her be; excited and dreamy; partly treating him as though he ought to know everything already; partly behaving as though *he* had incurred some minor tragedy; quite incapable of any coherent account of herself, but unable to stop talking about it.

'Do you mean you cooked dinner for him and he seduced you?'

'Well, he couldn't eat much of the dinner. We had caviare for breakfast—not with spoons, though—to revive us because we hardly slept a wink, you can't can you, if you're in bed with people you don't know very well—it's *so* fascinating talking to them in between—'

'Now Liz. Listen to me—'

'Darling Oliver I *do*. Whatever happens. I shan't stop loving you—what*ever* happens everything will be all right. How many hours is it till seven o'clock?' But she went upstairs, without waiting for an answer.

'Isn't it amazing—the first person I meet—' she said, turning on the bath on her way up.

'He's *not* the first person you've met. He's probably about the ten thousandth person you've met—'

'You know perfectly *well* what I mean. I mean the first person I've *met*. Goodness I'm tired! I feel as though I've got roots coming out of my legs that have to be torn up every time I move.' She threw herself on her bed: he stood morosely over her.

'He asked who cut my hair,' she said looking up at him with a wealth of meaning that he couldn't fathom.

'Who *is* he?'

'He lives in Pelham Place. I said you weren't a hairdresser, of course—do you know, he's got a sunken bath *in* his dressing-room?'

'What does he *do*?'

'He's nouveau riche. He told me. He has the most beautiful hands—' she gave a little shiver and fell silent.

He had opened his mouth to tell her to stop being so silly and make sense but she had smiled at him—half triumphant, half appealing (she looked tireder and prettier than he'd ever seen her)—and then, without the slightest warning, fallen asleep. And ever since then ...

And he had not only not set eyes on the famous Mr Cole, he hadn't even spoken to him on the telephone. A few days after meeting him, Liz had announced that they were going to France. She had also said that she was going to ring him to make a plan for his joining them when she knew what the house was like, and sure enough, she had done just that, the day that he'd been giving up hope.

So here he was—in the aeroplane, just in time because he had been getting very tired of corned beef. When the stewardess appeared, he asked whether there was anything to eat. She was afraid she thought there wasn't. What about a drink? He felt in his pockets and there seemed to be enough there so he said yes—a beer. The lights of the French shore appeared below; tiny, twinkling and very yellow, and he began to feel positively excited. The stewardess came back with some beer and a packet of biscuits done up in Cellophane. Most of the other passengers were, or seemed to be asleep.

'It's these tourist flights,' she said, 'they don't issue meals if they can help it: not if it's a short flight like this one, and late-night flight at that.'

It's funny how hungry you have to feel, he thought, to want to eat assorted sweet biscuits. The stewardess was—a bit more than kindly—adjusting the table for his beer. She was the wrong age for him—he liked women of thirty-odd or not over twenty-one; besides, her eyes and her breasts were too close together, and anyway, his hands were far too full with Ginny. So he thanked her lying back with his eyes shut, and she went away. He hadn't told Ginny he was coming. He planned to ring her up—very casually—or better still, encounter her in the pool at Eden Roc ... She was the kind of girl who would wear the scantest bikini and no bathing cap—she'd come up from some dive, with streaming hair and golden waterproof skin, to find him ... Perhaps *that* wouldn't bore her. Ginny's boredom threshold was one of the lowest he'd even read about, let alone met. She combined an attention span about many things that would disgrace a teenage puppy, with a startling, and morbid, capacity to stick to some dreary point—like getting black-heads out of her legs or how many calories she had consumed that day. One of the deadly attractions of people who are easily bored is the challenge of not boring them: it tickled the vanity in a very private place. She often bored him (the other side of the coin): but just when he was deciding that he couldn't stick much more of whatever she was or wasn't being at the time, she did, or said some-thing wholly unexpected, funny and endearing. The fact that she was so frightfully, chronically, hereditarily rich *had* to be treated by anyone of sensibility as a sort of controllable, but unfortunate disease—like diabetes. Regular injections of homespun affection, honesty, and common sense were essential to people in her position if they were not to go into a coma of indulgent self-pity or persecu-tion mania. Blaming your parents provided some sort of domestic release: in Ginny's case she had a good choice; each of her parents had remarried four times, so there were ten people in this relation to her. She lived a kind of upper-class Esperanto: in certain places with certain people; they could come from anywhere, but they had to be able to be in approximately the same position ... It was a very small, jet-propelled and gilt-edged world. Because everybody in it was on the move, they tried to make everything the same wherever they were, and being very rich, of course they succeeded. Naturally, from time to time, they felt the need of variety: Oliver, being only twenty-four, did not at all understand that that was what he was in aid of. He provided a—not very marked—contrast to Scrabble, Martinis, massage, sun tan, water-skiing, in-jokes, and being a socialist in your spare time.

He hoped he was going to get on with—even like—John Cole. Liz—without meaning to—went on not telling him anything really about her lover, so that apart from the obvious fact that he was rich, Oliver simply couldn't imagine him at all. But the fact was that it was a damn good thing he was coming to this villa to have a look

at the situation: after all, he was responsible for Liz; the nearest she
had got, poor darling, to a father: nobody would dream of consult-
ing that overblown cliché that their mother had married, and May—
like Liz—was not noted for her common sense. If necessary, he must
be prepared to take a very firm line with Mr Cole. The mere
thought of this made him feel unutterably sophisticated and responsible—light-hearted with domestic power. He began to wonder
whether he ought not set about becoming an ambassador ...

'Fasten your seat belts.' The stewardess was not leaving this
announcement to chance where Oliver was concerned, and before
he had come out of his doze enough to stop her, she was expertly
fumbling with his belt.

'We haven't arrived?'

'In about five minutes.'

She gave him a smile, more professional than disappointed, and
went her way.

He must have been asleep, then.

Two thirty, French time. He wondered who, besides Liz, would
meet him.

Only Liz. She stood at the barrier, not waving, but looking
intently for, and eventually at him. She wore pale pink jeans and a
dark brown shirt, and her hair shone. She looked marvellous, and
not at all like his sister.

When they could meet, she hugged him without speaking. They
walked out of the airport building, into the warm perfumed air
alive with cicadas.

'It's like somebody endlessly scratching themselves in navy blue
velvet.'

She squeezed his arm and looked up at him. 'I've come alone. John
thought you would prefer that.'

The warm, scented smell continued. She walked them to a white,
open two-seater. 'It's *my* car,' she said, rather defiantly, 'so I'm
going to drive.'

'Do you mean it is *literally* yours?' said Oliver, when they were
sitting side by side with his suitcase in the back.

'Mmm. John said that if you were a kept woman on the Riviera you had to have a few obvious things and it is far too hot for mink so he said a car. And *I* said,' she continued, 'either red with white leather, or white with red leather. So there we are.

'You shall drive it tomorrow,' she ended, as they swept out of the airport on to the Corniche. Warm air and lights streamed by: the sea glittered, palms, oleander, rubbish dumps, dried-up river mouths all lay shrouded in nocturnal glamour.

Elizabeth did not speak, because she wanted Oliver to think she was a good driver, and she wasn't unless she tried. Oliver watched her thin brown hands on the wheel for a bit and then said, 'Come off it, dear. Drive more like a woman, and tell me things.'

She slowed down at once, and said, 'What things?'

'Longing to be asked,' he thought. He knew they were both very happy.

'Where did you get that watch, for a start? What's happened to the good old Gamages Commando-type object you thought you looked so sweet in?'

'It fell in the sea. John gave me this. From a shop called Cartier in Nice.'

'From a shop called Cartier,' he mocked, 'well I never—'

'Well I didn't know you knew about them.' She held out her wrist. 'Isn't it beautiful? It's a man's watch really. John agreed it suited me best. He's very good at choosing things: he says it's because he's had so much practice, but I think he probably started out good at it.'

They were driving through the back streets of Cannes, and a sudden gust of hot fish soup made him remember how famished he was.

'Liz, we couldn't stop for a snack, could we?'

'There's a snack waiting at home: supper, really—a sort of midnight feast. I *knew* you'd be hungry.'

He could tell she was pleased at being right about this.

'Has your John been cutting your hair?'

'Well—actually he did have a go, but he made it so much worse, he got a man to come and do it properly.' Then to avoid being teased, she said, 'How's May, and does she know about me?'

'She's fairly all right, and I honestly don't know. I sort of told her that I thought you might be away for some time, and just as I was trying to work out whether it would be better to say you were here on a cooking job, or come clean about it, she changed the subject. Asked me whether either of us wanted that ignoble pile in Surrey after she was dead.'

'How extraordinary! She must know what we feel about it! Did you tell her?'

'I said we both preferred Lincoln Street. And she said, "That's just what I thought, darling—such a load off what passes for my mind." '

'Has she joined some new society?'

'That's a very clever guess—how *did* you think of it?'

'John says I'm quite intelligent—*very* intelligent.'

'He must be in love with you.'

'*That* wouldn't make him say it. Anyway, has she?'

'Don't know, but now you mention it, there were all the signs. She comes to London much more, and she has that terrible, far-away, secret look when you catch her unawares. She must have,' he said a minute later, 'she's completely stopped giggling: I've noticed that always happens.'

'Do you think Herbert's joined too?'

'No—because they all cost money, don't they? He'd absolutely *hate* that—especially as there's a perfectly good straightforward Church for free. Good enough for a simple, nauseating chap like him.'

Elizabeth swerved unnecessarily to avoid the black streaking shadow of a cat. 'I think he's so awful he's probably mad or actually wicked.'

'Now you're exaggerating. He's just awful. With any luck, the marriage will quietly crumble to bits and May will stop searching for obscure comfort. Can I have one of those?'

He'd been hunting in the front pocket of the car and found the Gauloises. She pushed in the cigarette lighter, and said, 'Light me one too.'

A yellow, floodlit castle appeared on their left.

Oliver said, 'What's that?'

'Antibes. The castle is a sort of Picasso museum: beautifully done; we'll take you.'

'Is your John interested in art, then?'

'Of course he is!' Then she said, 'Sorry: but I can't help feeling a bit edgy about whether you like each other. Men are so *much* worse than women in this way.'

'Are they? Are they really?'

'Of *course* they are!'

He looked at her fierce profile with the short ruffled hair. 'I must say that this adventure seems to have made you very stern and knowing.'

She had turned left and they were driving down an avenue of plane trees, whose jigsaw trunks were exaggerated by the headlights.

'This is St Jean,' she said. It was really, he thought, as though she had lived there all her life.

In the gaudy little square there were still people: the sound of an accordion, cars starting up, an old man morosely smoking a pipe.

'People never all go to bed here,' she said. They had reached the sea again—molten pewter in the moonlight, and dark trees on their right with the warm pine smell. 'The villa is right at the end of the point.'

He knew by the way she wasn't describing it that it must be marvellous in some way or other.

'Will he be waiting up for us?'

'No. He's gone to bed: he thought we'd like a private supper together.'

'Nice of him.'

She opened her mouth, and shut it again.

'But of course he's nice if you like him,' he added.

'I like him,' she said, and at exactly this point they plunged through a gateway and into a drive which, with its continuing archway of dark trees, looked like a tunnel.

The house seemed strung with floodlit arches and beyond that shadowy caverns; the trees overhung it, black or glistening—according to the light. They walked through—past a terrace, into a hall, a room and on to another terrace beyond which stretched dark garden trees, a wall and the sky. There was a heated trolley with soup: another with sandwiches and drink. They ate—Oliver feeling like a foreigner in a dream. He could not tell about his sister. She had sent the servant who met them to bed—with such familiar certainty, that he found it difficult to believe that she had spent only two weeks here. As soon as he had eaten, he felt very tired; Lincoln Street seemed now as far away as it had seemed near when he had got out of the aeroplane at Nice: he longed to be asleep before he started thinking about his life which—Liz and the villa apart—didn't seem to be going too well at the moment: you couldn't keep on expecting gilt-edged stopgaps ...

'You're yawning even faster than your mouth will work,' Liz was saying. She was standing over him and pulling him to his feet. 'Just one quick look outside and then you'll sleep for hours.'

She led him outside the terrace across springy grass to a low wall. Here the garden seemed to come to an end, became a steeply declining cliff, the tops of whose trees were level with their faces. A hundred feet below spread the silver and silent sea with nothing upon it.

'The next place is Africa.'

'I know.'

'He's not conventionally good-looking.'

'No?'

'You don't need experience in loving to love. Necessarily?'

He shook his head. He had not the slightest idea.

'That's all right, then.' Then she took him back to the house.

*   *   *

When he awoke next morning he was in a large, dim room charged with the feeling of suppressed heat, cracked with streaks of sunlight and noisily inhabited by one—apparently gigantic—bluebottle. He sat up to reach for a blind cord and felt the rustle of paper which must have been tucked under his head on the pillow. The blind flew up: sun flooded the room and in his hand was a note from Liz. 'We

125

are swimming and having long breakfast by swimming pool two terraces down. Follow rice stream, starting by french window.' There were three french windows in his room, which he hadn't noticed the previous night as being on the ground floor, but only one window had an O made of rice on the pale blue carpet. Having established that, he delved in his luggage for the stunning bathing shorts and went to the marble inlaid bathroom. The whole suite was like the most successful dentist in the world having you to stay for the night. Marble, gilt, mirrors, faded, painted furniture; hopelessly refined scenes of eighteenth century social life; nylon muslin and rayon satin in flesh tones: ormolu gryphons being door handles and bathroom taps: it was extraordinary, he thought, how things were somehow all right if somebody had once thought that this was thoroughly, entirely, the best they could do. Then he thought that perhaps he ought to become the lover of some outdoor, but mysteriously cultivated duchess, and start an interior-decorating business. Mary London and Oliver Seymour. That kind of thing. He took an extremely thick and luxurious bath towel, and made for the rice window. He knew Liz. She would make it more difficult as the trail went on. But no: she must be very anxious that he should find her before he got cross. A thin but steady stream of rice led across the coarse, green grass (that only foreigners, he thought, would call a lawn) to a corner of the wall where there was a low gate. A grain of rice was impudently perched on the latch. He put it absently into his mouth and turned back to see where he had spent the night. It was, or looked to be a large house; a great apricot coloured nineteen-thirties' sprawl, with a quantity of doors, windows, french windows, columns, patios and at least two large terraces in view—with a good deal of bougainvillaea hanging about (in no other circumstances would purple and apricot be bearable) and a heavily tiled roof descending, in some places, to a height that he could easily reach. Just as he was going to stop looking and get on with the rice, a rat ran smartly along the gutter, paused at the corner, exuding sensibility and sharp practice, and then, having recollected whatever exciting and shady it was that had stopped him in his tracks, made off. Oliver opened the gate and started down the path, or rather steps. Rice was no longer needed, as the way was hedged by aromatic shrubs and the rough biscuit-coloured trunks of umbrella pines: it was both hot and sombre, a charming mixture if you'd been in England for a long time. He heard a man laugh protestingly—a splash and his sister's voice. 'I hope he's not an absolute beast or bore,' he thought feeling suddenly angry and a bit frightened.

They were sitting side by side at the edge of the pool—which seemed floodlit with sun—their legs were in the water and they were holding hands. Their heads were turned to each other: he could see his sister's face but simply the back of *his* head. 'Nearly bald!' he thought, and was fleetingly conscious of half wanting the situation to be perfect, half wanting it to be hopeless. Then Liz saw him; her face changed, and he realized how happy she had been looking.

'It's Oliver!' she said—too loudly, and Oliver wondered whether he was deaf as well as bald.

By the time he reached them, they were both on their feet.

'Oliver: John,' she said, trying to watch both of their faces at once. 'What stunning shorts,' she added before either of them could say anything. Everybody looked at Oliver's shorts; even Oliver, and John Cole said mildly, 'They are, indeed. How very nice of you to come. Do you want to eat straight away, or would you rather swim first?'

'What we're doing,' interrupted Elizabeth rather breathlessly, 'is swim a bit and eat a bit and so on. Come and see.'

And she half dragged him to an open terrace-room built against the wall where a long narrow table was covered with a very delicious looking French and English breakfast. It looked enough for a dozen people. Oliver said he'd like some orange juice and then a swim.

She gave him his juice and said, 'He's nice, isn't he?' a question so patently silly that he squeezed her arm, feeling happy that she minded so much what he thought, and said, 'You bet.' Her hair was wet, sleeked back and held in place by a pair of dark glasses perched on top of her head.

'She looks like some science fiction reptile—or very close-up of an insect, don't you think?' he remarked as they made their way back to the pool and its owner. 'It's partly the freckles—they pop up all over the place the moment you get her out of a night club.'

'I must keep her out of night clubs then,' said John tranquilly. 'I'm devoted to her freckles.'

A telephone rang, and he got up to answer it. He was even taller than Oliver, Oliver realized, and he walked as though he had a low opinion of doorways. On either side of the breakfast table terrace were square little pavilions—changing rooms, he supposed, beginning to get the hang of what to expect—and by one of these was a telephone. He picked up the instrument, listened for a moment and said, 'Well, well well!' in tones of the mildest possible surprise.

Elizabeth said, 'Come on! Swim!' And before she could drag or push him into the water, he jumped. She followed him: she swam very well, and just as he was thinking how seldom—since they were children—they had swum together, she said, 'Do you realize that this is the first time we've been abroad together? At the same time, I mean?'

'You mean together.'

'No I don't. I mean together at the same time.'

'But if we'd been abroad together, it would have to have been at the same time.' Then he saw what she meant and reached out to duck her head under, but she eluded him. The water was so bright and light a blue that it was surprising the drops on her shoulders weren't that colour.

'Lovely water,' he said.

'John says it tastes of American prawns,' she answered, and as she mentioned his name they both looked at him. He had finished telephoning, and was looking under breakfast covers. 'He wants to eat,' she said and swam fast and splashily to the side of the pool.

During breakfast the telephone rang twice more. The first time it was London and the second time New York. With the London call, John said, 'Look here, you know how I love the sound of your voice, but twice before breakfast is overdoing it.' With the New York call he simply said, 'Dear boy, I've known all that for half an hour: London told me,' and put back the receiver.

Oliver ate a huge breakfast, and decided that he liked John:

Elizabeth kept buttering croissants and then dipping them in cherry jam and *then* handing them to her lover and her brother. The coffee was wonderful: there were fresh trout, Charentais melon and raspberries with thick, rich, slightly sour cream. John ate sparingly, Elizabeth hardly at all. She perched on the end of some gaudy chaise-longue, licking cherry jam off her fingers and smiling gently as she looked from one to the other.

'Like a little marmalade cat,' John said. The sky was violet blue and the sun so sharply golden it was like some brilliant daydream, with each pair of them admiring the third so that they took turns at being part of a conspiracy and the object of conspiratorial approval.

'What happens next?' Oliver asked, after another swim.

'We've been asked to the local hotel for lunch—and swimming, of course. Up to you: it's rather like here, really, but with more people. I have to go; but you two stay here, if you like?'

'Coming with you,' Elizabeth said and then looked anxiously at Oliver.

'Fine: anything,' he said. The telephone rang again and when John had answered it, he said, 'The secretary's arrived. So up I go. Why don't you take your brother down to the sea?'

'When will you be through?'

He looked at her again. Whenever either of them did this, the whole place became rich with sexual affection, Oliver noticed.

'By lunch time,' was all John said.

'At the nauseating risk of sounding like Juliet's nurse, I should say you've fallen on your back,' Oliver remarked as they made their way down the blazing little path.

'Juliet's nurse?'

'Romeo's Juliet's nurse. Shakespeare's Romeo's Juliet's nurse.'

'All right, all right.' She was walking ahead of him. She was wearing a lemon-coloured bathing suit that fitted her beautifully, and was excellent with the bronzed hair and freckles and cream of her skin.

'Did John choose that bathing suit?'

'Yes. He likes choosing things, I told you. He's jolly good at it.'

'Do stop boasting about him.'

'I can't. You're the first person I've had to boast *to* about him, so do be fair.' A minute later she said.

'I've got a ring this colour: it looks a bit like tarnished diamonds, but it's something Portuguese called chrysolite.' Then she added, 'I'm so happy that every day seems about like a week, and I can't even imagine leaving *here*. It's extraordinary how when everything is *being* perfect, the future simply doesn't count at all—there's just what happened before, and *now* is everything else.'

Oliver was silent at this, because he had never been as happy as that, and everything she said simply made him start worrying about his future instead of not thinking at all about it, which was what he had been doing before.

Just as he was going to ask her whether John and she were going to marry, she said, 'So you see, in spite of your fears, I haven't had to fall back on a chimpanzee: John says he *prefers* women with furry arms, and he says he'll never let me be anybody's bridesmaid—'

He decided not to ask: it was a woman's question, anyway.

They had their bathe, and lay on rocks in the sun, until Elizabeth said Oliver was too new to lie about without blistering, even though she had rubbed what she described as marvellous stuff all over his back.

'Anyhow, John may be finished with letters.'

She had sprung to her feet.

'So?'

'I don't want to miss any of him,' she said.

They walked slowly back up the terraced cliff path to the villa. It was now very hot: their wet heads steamed; cicadas had reached their seemingly endless zenith; the smells of hot thyme, juniper and resin from the pines thickened the hot and dazzling air. They slipped on sharp, slippery stones as they climbed: geckos froze into gracefully heroic attitudes as they approached, and then, when they got too near, disappeared with jerky speed—like odd pieces of silent film pieced together; butterflies loitered, bees zoomed, there were no birds, no fresh water and no shade. 'A foreign land,' thought Oliver, watching his sister climbing the path ahead of him. All morning, he had been seeing her for the first time as an outsider might regard her; a sturdy body, slender still, because she was so young, but all a matter of neat, solid curves; she could never have passed as a boy.

When they reached the swimming pool, all the breakfast had been cleared away and the pool was blue and absolutely still except for one large moth trapped and drowning. Elizabeth, of course, would rescue it if she noticed it, and he hoped that she wouldn't but she did, so he helped by picking a fig leaf for the creature to rest and dry out on. 'You realize how furry they are when they're wet,' Liz said anxiously. She had gone into the pool and collected the moth on her dark glasses. 'Fig leaves are awfully prickly, do you think it minds?'

'It's about like us lying on coconut matting, but think how pleased you'd be with a piece of that if you'd been drowning.'

She looked at him gratefully. 'Of course you would.'

'Swimming pools always make me think of *The Blue Lagoon*.'

'What's that?'

'Don't you read *any*thing? Or at least hear about things that other people read?'

'Now I do. John reads every day of his life. Novels as well.'

'A civilized man—not a ghastly specialist for a change,' he said, but seriously, because he meant it, and not to hurt her feelings. But she simply picked up the fig leaf, saying, 'I think I'll take this moth up with me.'

When they were on the move again, he asked, 'What novels does he read?'

'People called Henry Green, Ivy Compton-Burnett and Elizabeth Taylor. They're his three favourites. He tries a new one from time to time, but he says they never seem to be so good.'

'Have *you* tried them?'

'He reads them to me in bed sometimes. I really like it,' she added looking nervously at him to see what he thought.

'Fine, so long as it isn't all you do in bed,' he said and she stared at him with a mixture of shyness and bonhomie that was, or would be, if you weren't her brother, entirely irresistible.

'It isn't.'

* * *

The local hotel turned out to be Eden Roc, so Oliver realized that he might well meet Ginny before he was brown, and (worse) soon enough after Ginny's arrival there for her to think that he had followed her. Oh well, he thought while showering. Oh well, to hell with it, he thought half an hour later, when all three of them were having one drink on the terrace before setting off. John wore a pair of dark linen trousers and an unremarkable silk shirt, open at the neck, but decorated with a silk scarf. That was the trouble. He was trying to get Elizabeth to knot it, and she, of course, had not had enough practice at that kind of thing, Oliver thought laughing inside from his kindly hide of adult experience.

'Never mind,' John said, 'I'm probably too old for this kind of thing. Too balding and paunchy.'

'You're nothing of the kind,' cried Elizabeth. 'You just don't hold yourself properly.'

'*You* hold me properly,' he replied in a low voice which was neither teasing nor intense: and over her head, met Oliver's eye seriously, and then smiled: the smile changed his face completely and Oliver realized that he might be old and not particularly good-looking, but that in his case, neither of these things mattered.

On the way to the hotel he told them about Ginny Mole—casually, but he didn't want Liz letting him down by any display of vicarious enthusiasm or too much sisterly curiosity, supposing that Ginny was lunching there and they *did* meet ... supposing that she was lunching there which she easily might not be ...

They went through the splendid, luxuriously cool hotel and on to the western terrace. The walk down its tremendously wide and shallow steps and gravel drive to the sea, Oliver thought and then said, was very like anybody's dream of the kind that they thought interesting but their audience invariably found dull. John agreed, and then went on that if you didn't know enough people who had boring dreams like that *and* told you about them, you could always go to a French film. In fact, a lot of those films were simply made by power-conscious dreamers who had hit upon a method of mass boring people.

'Still you can always leave a film: one couldn't get away from *her*'—jerking his head towards his sister—'and she went through a frightful period of telling you every morning—following you about and telling you.'

'When did I do that?'

'It started when you were about ten. Morning after morning, we had accounts of your flimsy, indecisive, *interminable* sagas—'

She turned protesting to Cole, who took her arm saying, 'I like the morning after morning part anyway.'

Oliver said, 'Why *are* they so indecisive, I wonder? Other people's dreams I mean—'

Elizabeth immediately said, 'Because one's forgotten the vital part: that's why you want to tell it to people—you hope you'll automatically remember. I can even remember feeling that part of it: that something particularly marvellous had happened to me and somehow I couldn't remember what it was.'

John said, 'We must see to it that you don't *always* feel that...'

Oliver said, 'There's Ginny! I mean,' he added a moment later as they looked in vain, 'it was someone who looked jolly like her. She came out of that gate there, and went over there.'

'Then she'll be at the pool. We'll go and have a look at it, to see if our hosts, the Dawsons, are still there.'

The swimming pool, cut out of the natural rock and slung above the sea, intensely blue and sheltered and sunny, was not thickly populated: most people had gone to change and drink and eat, but just as they were leaving, a figure rose from behind a rock whom Oliver immediately identified as Ginny.

Ginny was coming towards them on her way out, but she was doing this so moodily, that she did not see them until the last minute when Oliver accosted her with elaborate coolth, as Elizabeth afterwards pointed out to John. She wore a bikini and sun glasses, both white. She was very small, and delicately made; a sharply indented waist, small, pointed breasts, and arms and legs that gave the impression that their owner hardly ever used them in case they broke. All flesh visible was the colour of heather honey: her hair was black and long.

'Oh Oliver,' she replied, rather as though she had known he would be there, but as an afterthought.

'What an amazing thing,' she added looking up from the minute pebble that she had been scuffing along with small bare feet.

Oliver explained that Elizabeth was his sister, and John Cole was John Cole.

'John *Cole*?' Ginny said, and pushed her huge dark glasses on to the top of her head. 'You've got a villa up the road haven't you? The one Mummy used to have when she was married to Jean-Claude?' Her eyes were like horizontal diamonds from a pack of cards and the colour of dog violets. 'You must be Jennifer's father.' She looked at him, at Elizabeth, and back to him with distinct interest.

'Come and have a drink with us,' said John easily. 'And tell me where you met Jennifer.'

'We were at Lausanne together and we would have gone to Florence only Mummy was having such ghastly trouble over my maintenance. One thing I'll never do and that is get divorced in Mexico—it may seem the simplest thing in the first place, but there's no end to the complications. I say, I can't have a drink with you,' (she had seized Oliver's wrist and twisted his watch towards her) 'I've got to change and have lunch on some filthy yacht with the most boring people in the world. Do you think if one *fined* people like that for being boring they'd get better? A hundred quid an hour and a bonus if they laughed at their own non-jokes? 'Bye then.' She dropped Oliver's wrist as though it was some kind of barrier and prowled lightly away.

'Come to dinner,' called John, who had seen Oliver's face.

She lifted her right hand like someone stopping a bus by way of a reply and disappeared through the changing-room door.

'Does that mean she *is* coming, or she isn't?' asked Elizabeth as they walked up the stairs to the restaurant.

'Time will tell.' Oliver felt obscurely irritated by the whole encounter. He had been afraid that Ginny would express too much surprise at his presence—thereby implying that he had followed her to France when he was pretty sure he would have come anyway, whether she had been there or not—but her total lack of interest in his sudden appearance was far more galling. And John seemed to have run the whole thing ...

'Hope you didn't mind my asking her,' John was saying, 'I just thought it might be fun.'

'Course not. Jolly good idea.'

They went into lunch where Mr and Mrs Dawson awaited them.

In a way, having lunch with two, to him, total strangers was a relief, Oliver thought. It was curiously difficult for him and John to stop being shy with each other: whatever refuge they might take as a team in admiring or teasing Elizabeth, the fact was that their areas of intimacy with her were necessarily entirely different, and apart from her, they had not so far anything else in common. They both knew, he felt, that Elizabeth was worrying over them in that intricately illogical way that girls could, indeed could not *stop* doing, about people they loved. So lunch, diffused by the Dawsons, was a relief. Arnold Dawson had made a fortune out of camping sites and finally holiday camps. He came from Westmorland and had a gentle wedge-shaped face with soft blue eyes to match his accent. Mrs. Dawson also came from the North Country. They were both in their fifties, but whereas middle age had polished and tidied up Arnold, it had softened and blurred Edie, whose clothes fitted her like a badly-made loose-cover, and whose dry, oyster-coloured hair rippled in an uncontrollably old-fashioned manner. She wore Marina blue, a shade of muted turquoise. The Dawsons had married the same year as Princess Marina, and Arnold never liked her to change anything. He called her Mother and constantly told the company what she did, and did not, like — mostly the latter although she looked far too mild to possess so much and such varied disapprobation.

It was the kind of lunch where, having chosen your main course, you went to a vast table covered with beautiful *hors d'œuvres* and took what you liked or wanted. 'Now Mother, there's not much here for you, that's plain, but we'll do our best.' And Oliver and Elizabeth watched him allowing her one sardine, 'You're not too keen on them, but you don't *mind* them in moderation,' two bits of beetroot, 'That's safe enough,' and half a hard-boiled egg off which he carefully scraped the sauce, 'She can't *abide* her food mucked about.'

'No, I can't see anything more,' he said after careful scrutiny. 'You'll have to make it up with the steak.' He spoke, not loudly, but with unselfconscious deliberation, and her embarrassment at his behaviour was clearly routine; he was drawing attention to her, but he had been doing that for a good thirty years: she merely plucked his arm, said, 'That's fine, dear' and smiled at the general company for support. He took her back to the table where she sat by herself while the rest of the party made their choice.

'The thing is,' Arnold said in generally audible confidence to John and Elizabeth, 'she doesn't really like travelling abroad—does it to please me, she knows I like the sun and a bit of a change. A lot of it's the food you know, but if I take enough trouble over that, and she gets her paper every day, it's not so bad. I had a yacht once but she couldn't stand it, she's so prone to sea-sickness—put her on a mill-pond and she wouldn't be able to keep anything down: I said once, Mother I don't know how you manage a bath without trouble. I fly her everywhere nowadays: she doesn't mind that so much. You can't change your ways at her age, you know, and you can't *make* ways you never had.'

Elizabeth said something faintly about the sun being nice for her anyway.

'Oh not the *sun*!' he said. 'Put her in the sun for five minutes and she's out in a rash—and that's followed by blisters which I wouldn't like to describe … I think I'll go back if you don't mind, she's all by herself.'

'As though he was one of the best, frightfully kind, owners of a dog,' Elizabeth remarked afterwards. John Cole laughed.

'He's a born owner, anyway,' he said.

After he had asked and been told about Mr Dawson's empire of holiday camps, Oliver said, 'Perhaps he'd give me a job.'

John said casually, 'Are you looking for one?'

'In a sort of a way. The trouble is, you see, that as I know what I like, I *do* mind what I do.'

He looked up to see how this was taken and found Cole regarding him with impassive intentness. He did not reply.

* * *

They found out that Ginny *was* coming to dinner. On John's suggestion, Oliver rang the hotel and asked her if she would like him to fetch her.

So off he went in Elizabeth's white car in a silk shirt borrowed from John.

'It would be a frightfully good thing if he *did* find out what he wanted to do.'

Elizabeth was having a shower while John shaved, so she did not hear his reply. When she emerged, sleek and streaming, a few seconds later and said 'What?' he simply laughed. 'I must say that catching you in your odd, dry moments is almost impossible. It's like living with a seal or an otter.' Before she could say 'what' again, he wrapped her in a gigantic white towel, wiped her mouth with a corner of it and kissed her.

'Seriously, about Oliver—' she began.

'I was kissing you with the utmost seriousness. What about Oliver?'

'Well—what about him? Honestly, John,' she sat on the bath stool hugging her knees, which she always did, he had noticed, when she was settling down to some insoluble confidence, 'I don't want him turning into a lay-by—oh, you *know* what I mean: I do think it's absolutely extraordinary how men don't stick to the point—'

'Come next door—'

'Why?'

'Don't ask silly questions.'

'You're not going to carry me!' She slipped on to the floor still wrapped in her towel. He stood looking down on her for a moment, then collected the four corners of the towel and started dragging her at a surprising speed across the marble floor to the bedroom.

'Sometimes in my loathsome way I even have to *drag* them into bed.'

Very much less later than it seemed to either of them, he said,
'You *are* like a little cat: just as firm and graceful — just as neat and
sweet and only slightly less furry — '
'You would prefer me even to Ginny?'
'Ginny?'
'Her body, I mean.'
'I thought that was what you meant. I do. I don't like girls who
are all chicken bones and a mass of dangerous corners. I like firm,
rounded people.' He propped himself up on one elbow. 'Are you
happy, Eliza?
'You don't mind my being so much older?'
'Or having been married and having a grown-up child?'
'Or blind as a bat and nearly bald?'
'Then you shall have a drink: anyone as broad-minded as that is
bound to be thirsty.'
He picked up the house telephone and said, 'Two large Paradis,
please, Gustave. What a ridiculous name that is. Like a villain's
chauffeur in Sapper.'
She pulled the sheet over her and watched him collecting clothes
for the evening. Then she said, 'Are you? Happy, I mean, as well?'
He looked silently at her for a moment, and then said, 'Oh darling!' a word he had never used to her before.
Afterwards, Elizabeth remembered everything about that time:
the comfortable, untidy room with damp towels, ticking clock and
smell of gardenias; the small sunset breeze ruffling muslin by the
balcony windows, and outside, a fiery sky against which small bats
occurred and dropped to nowhere like huge pieces of ash. She lay on
the bed until the drinks were brought, and afterwards she also
remembered thinking lazily that when you were entirely happy
fresh raspberry juice and champagne seem a natural drink. John
padded about in a very marvellous dressing-gown, 'It's meant to
blind people to my true appearance,' trying to decide what Elizabeth
should wear. 'You've jolly well got to wipe Ginny's eye, that's for
sure.' The coat-hangers clicked against one another. 'My bet is that
she will wear white, so you'd better be in colour.'
'Why couldn't I be in white, too?'

'Because with her black hair it will look as though her mother uses Persil.'

While he was choosing, they heard Oliver returning in the car.

'Oh lord! I'm not dressed at *all*, and we never talked about Oliver!'

He threw a pleated lime chiffon dress at her. 'It won't take you long to get into this, and we've got plenty of time to talk about Oliver.'

'Have we? Really?'

'All our lives.'

He told Gustave to give Oliver and his guest anything they wanted to drink, and sat on the end of the bed. 'You have lovely hair. The colour of highbrow marmalade. Wait!' He seized a spray full of Bellodgia. 'Shut your eyes; keep still—no turn round—fine.' The room smelled of a million gardenias now, and the sun had sunk out of sight.

* * *

There was a little more time when they went downstairs to find that Oliver had taken Ginny to see the pool. They sat on a sofa with another drink talking about him quietly; Elizabeth explained—not again, but in the context of Oliver—how awful their stepfather was, 'The kind of man who'd almost *force* you not to settle down in case he started approving of you. Oliver simply loathes him: breaking up his marriage with May is Oliver's dearest wish,' and John sat regarding her benignly with his glasses on and not saying anything. A relative of Gustave's came and lit the candles on the dining table: instantly, moths collected for their doom: and just as Elizabeth was starting to worry about their fate they heard the others returning; Oliver's voice and Ginny's little exclamations of bare incredulity. John picked up Elizabeth's hand and kissed it.

Ginny wore the smallest white dress Elizabeth had ever seen in her life. It fastened on one shoulder with a huge gilt buckle: 'She looks like someone in a Roman epic,' Oliver explained. All her nails were painted gold and her hair was carelessly piled on top of her head. When Elizabeth said what a terrific dress it was, Ginny replied that it was absolutely all she'd got.

'I think the pool's just top *dog*,' she said to John Cole during the *langouste*. 'Mummy always meant to put one in, but Jean-Claude was so *fright*fully mean and kept saying what was the sea for. He should have been stung to death by jellyfish and Portuguese men-of-war but it didn't happen to be a good year for them. I collected a whole lot in a suitcase and put them in just as he was diving off that board but he didn't even notice. I think success spoils men far more than women, don't you?'

'I'm glad you like the pool,' John said, 'I thought we'd come back and swim in it after the night club.'

'Take my father, for instance,' Ginny continued, 'oh good about the swim; Mummy said he was absolutely charming until he made that movie with her, but with just the tiniest speck of fame he became ghastly. I'm sure it's all right what *you* do,' turning to John. 'After all, you're not in the least famous are you? Just rich.'

'That's it.'

Then, just as Oliver was saying, 'Anyway, Ginny, you'd be a rotten judge of character—' the telephone rang, and after an interval Gustave came for John, who got up saying, 'Do go on with the duck—don't wait.'

He did not come back until halfway through the duck, and the moment Elizabeth saw his face she knew that something was wrong.

'That was Jennifer,' he said looking at Ginny. 'Apparently you've invited her to stay.'

'I just called her up this afternoon and told her to come on out. I didn't invite her to the Roc. I assumed she'd be staying here.'

Elizabeth realized that it was worse than she had thought when he came back on to the terrace. 'What time is she arriving?' she asked, she hoped, casually.

'Tonight. On the same plane that Oliver came on.' He met her eye with no expression at all.

That was that. They finished dinner and went to the night club. When he was dancing with her, John said, 'You know this changes things?'

She looked at him dumbly—suddenly so frightened about them she couldn't even ask what things.

'I've told the servants to move me into another room. I didn't want it to be like this. Jennifer's not—I've given her too rough a time. Damn that interfering little girl.'

There was an act at the night club whereby they collected somebody off the floor and asked them a string of questions: the trick was that you must not say 'no'. If you succeeded for long enough you got a bottle of very nearly undrinkable champagne. Ginny achieved this, and behaved as though it was really an achievement. She was unaware of tensions. Oliver knew that Elizabeth was anxious, and Elizabeth became increasingly frantic about John, who seemed to have retired from the scene—seemed hardly to know her. Oliver danced with her and said, 'Don't get so worked up. Of course she'll like you.'

'It doesn't just seem to be that.'

'What is it, then?'

'Don't know.'

He hugged her. 'Anyway—I'm here.'

'*Why* did Ginny do it?'

She felt him stiffen. '*I* don't know. They're friends: I expect she just thought it would be fun to see Jennifer.'

She didn't answer that: Oliver was too mad about Ginny to *want* to understand.

Later, she danced with John and they didn't talk. Night clubs were bad for seeing anyone's face but her neck ached with staring up at him. When the music stopped, he wrapped his arms round her. Then, she said, 'Do you want me to go away?' But he didn't hear her because of people clapping the band, and she hadn't the courage to say that again.

Back at their table he said, 'I'm going to take you home now and Oliver and Ginny can make their way later.'

When they were well out of Cannes, he drove very fast to a small café they'd never been to before. 'We're going to have a spot of coffee and cognac.'

They sat at a small table in a dark corner, and he said, 'Of course

I must explain a bit: of course I must do that. I was going to, anyway, but I thought I had much more time.

'Jennifer is—she's had a rotten childhood, of course. You know she's the same age as you?'

'You told me.'

'Twenty. Well—she doesn't seem like twenty at all. She's fearfully young for her age.'

'Where does she live?'

'She wanted her own flat in London: she shares with two other girls. She's just started at an acting school—last term, I mean. Of course it's holidays now. She's got a sort of flat in the house in Buckinghamshire. To use when she feels like it. She sometimes spends a week-end there with me, but she's always hated making plans. She wants to be free. You know.'

He met her eye at the end of this with a smile that was apologetic and also curiously urgent—as though beneath or inside his random remarks about Jennifer there was some anxious and secret message to be conveyed. She wanted to ask quite simple—probably stupid—questions like, 'Will she resent us?' or even, 'Has she any idea about us?' but she didn't ask because she felt that she knew the answers and they would be all wrong.

There was a short silence and then he said hopelessly, 'I'm sure you'll get on.'

He paid for the brandy and drove her home. Ginny and Oliver were not back. He stayed in the car and she felt another wave of fright.

'Are you going to bathe with the others?'

'Are you going to the airport now?' She knew it was far too early for Jennifer's plane.

'I might as well.'

'I shall go to bed.'

He nodded agreement to this dreary plan, and so she got out of the car and made for the house. As she reached the steps, he called, 'See you in the morning!' in a hard, cheery voice. She was nearly crying, and found that Ginny's stopping-a-bus gesture was the best answer to that.

In the bedroom—now most obviously and merely hers—she lay

on the bed resenting Jennifer, needing Oliver, despising Ginny, worrying (illogically, surely?) about May, her mother, whom she had so heartlessly and gladly abandoned to what Oliver had described as a living death worse than fate, *loathing* Horrible Herbert, hating Jennifer (why on earth should *she* mind her father being happy?) wanting Oliver just to be there teasing her and making light of her feelings, wishing she didn't think Ginny was so heartless and *decadent*, feeling guilty that she had so often and so adroitly avoided going back to Surrey for week-ends; perhaps May felt as abandoned by her as *she* now felt abandoned ... Perhaps it all served her right ... Then she could no longer stop thinking about John; could think of no one else and got rid of all her tears.

* * *

'What's up?' John Cole asked his daughter.

'How do you mean, Daddy?'

They were lying on the sea raft a hundred yards out from shore and there was no one else within range.

'Why are you making everyone feel uncomfortable?'

'I don't think I'm making *every*one feel uncomfortable.' She started putting on more lotion from a bottle that she wore tied to her waist. Her skin was very white, and had constantly to be protected from the sun.

'Well, you're making *me* feel awful. I don't like my daughter being unfriendly to my guests.'

'Guests! Honestly, Daddy! Come off it! She's not a guest.' She wore a red linen hat with a flopping brim that suffused her face with a pink glow: it wasn't all her natural indignation.

Before he could reply, she put down the bottle of lotion, gripped her knees with hands that were so like Daphne's, and said:

'Listen, Daddy! How would you feel if I was sleeping with a man twenty-five years older than myself?'

'It would depend upon what *you* felt about him. And what he felt about you.'

'I'm not talking about feelings. I'm talking about the plain facts of the matter as any outsider might see them.'

'Why?'

For a moment that silenced her: she gave a deep (patient?) sigh.

'How long have you known this girl?'

'Jennifer do stop cross-examining me—not very long—a few weeks, why?'

'All I can say is that it seems very odd to me that someone of *twenty*—someone exactly my age—who hasn't got any money would want to risk setting up with somebody old enough to be her father. I suppose you gave her that car!'

'Why not? She hadn't got one.' But flippancy was useless with her.

'I may say that she tried to conceal the fact that you gave it to her.'

'I think,' he said with both patience and revulsion, 'that she was trying to be tactful.'

'Tactful! Why should there be any need for tact?'

'Jennifer I've had enough of this—I warn you—'

'So have I! I don't see why you should abandon Mummy simply in order to indulge some kind of Lolita complex—you're just infatuated and at your age it's disgusting!'

When she was like this, pale grey eyes protruded, chins became one, bosoms heaved, thighs quivered. To be responsible in any way for her existence filled him—as it always did—with a disgust so murderous that immediately afterwards he felt as he imagined some-body might who had actually committed a murder in a sudden fit of hatred and loathing. This was his daughter: his *only* daughter: if he was responsible in one way for her unfortunate appearance, it could be said that he had only himself to blame if he was unable to fall back, as it were, upon her character. She was, she must be, literally what he had made her. Poor girl, then. In the same way that he could not bring himself to speak of Eliza to Jennifer, he surely owed Jennifer the same loyalty. They must simply be kept apart. She had begun to cry now: he was afraid that her acting school had simply oiled the works where histrionics were concerned.

'There, there,' he said, 'I really can't remember when I last took a nymphet to a motel. And it's a bit unkind of you to keep rubbing in my age: an astonishing number of people regard forty-five simply as the gateway to maturity.'

But she simply looked at him with wet, resentful eyes and said, 'I do wish you wouldn't be so hard and cynical.'

Over her head, on the top terrace by the villa, he saw the tiny figure of his love. She was walking very slowly, and then, because she stood still for a moment, he imagined that she was looking out to sea, to the raft, to him. He wanted to wave to her, but knew that the gesture would be misinterpreted by both girls. Must keep them apart, he thought again.

He suggested a swimming race back. Jennifer was a very good swimmer and would easily beat him.

∗   ∗   ∗

'I'd rather go if you don't mind.'

'I *do* mind.'

'I feel as though you are a bit ashamed of me.'

'It's not *you* I am ashamed of—it's myself.'

'But that's just the same for me, don't you see?'

'Yes I do. Darling: I'm so sorry about it all. But I'm sure she'll get used to the idea: it was just rather a shock.'

Silence. Then he said, 'Please—Eliza—you won't abandon me entirely, will you? Will you?' But she looked at him with that bright, trapped look of someone who was prevented only by pride from crying.

Jennifer's footsteps—voice. 'Daddy!'

'Coming!'

'Don't bother. It's only, do you think Elizabeth would mind *awfully* if I borrowed that car you gave her to drive Ginny back to the Roc?'

She shook her head then, saying, 'Of course I don't mind,' pulled the key on its ribbon over her head and handed it to him. Their hands touched and all the other starvations shouted out. Jennifer came in and said, 'I'm sorry!'

∗   ∗   ∗

Two days later she and Oliver left. It was all quite civilized: everybody told somebody else quite acceptable lies: Oliver said that their mother was not well and wanted Elizabeth to come home; John said how sorry he was that they had to go; and Jennifer said what a pity it was that she was losing her chance to get to know Elizabeth as they must have so much in common. Other things were said, of course.

'Can't you stop her?' Oliver asked Ginny.

'Stop who?'

'Don't be an idiot.'

'Jennifer thinks her father should go back to her mother,' said Ginny primly. 'It's mad, of course. People never go back to people— except in books. Look at Mummy: she's always going back to people in movies but she never does in life.'

'Can't you tell her that?'

'Oliver don't be so *dim*! It's not *really* what she thinks. She just wants her father to herself.'

'Well, if you knew all that, it was bloody of you—' And they had a frightful row which ended with Ginny saying she was going to Martha's Vineyard, she was sick of France, and Jennifer was right about one thing—young men were a pain.

* * *

They left on a three o'clock plane after an extremely uncomfortable lunch at the villa. Ginny came to it, but she was not speaking to Oliver. John and Elizabeth did not speak to each other. Oliver, who loathed her, ignored Jennifer, who was chattering at Elizabeth with a placating eye on her father. Nobody ate much, and in the end Oliver and John had a desultory conversation about the early winter days of the Riviera, Katherine Mansfield, and Gjieff. As soon as coffee had been served, Elizabeth, who had refused it, said that she must go and finish her packing.

'I'll help you, if you like.'

Elizabeth stopped at the end of the terrace. 'No thanks, Jennifer. I prefer to do it alone.'

Oliver said quietly to John, 'I think it would be better if we had a taxi, you know.'

'I'd arranged for Gustave to drive you. I'm not coming to the airport—don't worry.'

Somehow or other, the cases were put in the car, various farewells got through and they were off. Oliver looked at his sister. She sat rigidly, staring out of the window away from him. She was wearing the dark blue linen suit in which she had left Lincoln Street, and there was a white stripe on her fingers where the ring had been. Oliver took one of her hands and held on to it. Neither of them knew how much English Gustave understood, so they said nothing.

In the aeroplane, once they were up, Oliver said, 'Have a huge brandy.'

She looked at him for the first time, and he could tell by her thick upper lids that she must have been crying after lunch. 'That's another thing. I've only got ten bob.'

'Ha ha! I thought of that. Look what I've got.' And he pulled out of his breast pocket a bundle of notes. 'I haven't even counted them yet.'

'Oh Oliver! Where did you get that.'

'Don't sound as though you've never seen a five pound note in your life before. They haven't come from outer space.' He lowered his voice. 'Loot: from that damned awful little bitch.'

'Not Ginny!'

'Of course not. I never take money from women I *have* loved. No—the real, prize, first-class, hysterical, neurotic, hideous, boring, megalomanic little bitch: Jennifer Cole. I popped up to her room after lunch and took what I fancied.'

'Oh Oliver!'

'Oh Elizabeth! I call it meagre revenge. It doesn't matter to her: I bet she just asks for and gets whatever she wants. She probably didn't know what was in her Hermès wallet. Let's see. Five, ten, fifteen, twenty, twenty-one, two, three—ten. That's going to keep the wolf from the door: and anybody who saw Jennifer would only have to show her to the wolf—she wouldn't need money.'

'It's stealing.'

'That's what it is. And if you asked me whether stealing twenty-three pounds ten is as bad as what that little bitch has just done, I'd say you want your head examined. Anyway.' He ordered the brandies and ginger ale. 'That's to satisfy your puritanical urge. All women feel reassured by long drinks—even if there's twice as much alcohol in them. Darling Liz. It's not as bad as you think. You've kept your watch, I see. So you must regard the situation as not entirely lost?'

'Do you think it was wrong? I didn't want to seem pettish. I left everything else, but he knows I lost my other one. I don't understand anything about it.'

'Of course you don't.' The brandies had arrived and he poured the ginger ale, mixed it up with his finger. 'There. A nice, brotherly drink. Swig it back. The situation is perfectly simple, really. Jennifer doesn't want anyone competing with her for her father's affection. How about that?'

'That part is not in the least difficult. But what does *he* feel about it?'

'Oh—there you have me. Haven't the slightest idea. Can you imagine what on earth made May marry Herbert? People are so keen on explaining every nuance of human behaviour that they fall back on the kind of invention that tells you more about *them* than it tells you about what they're explaining.

'Although I'd hardly call either Daddo or Jennifer a nuance,' he added a bit later. 'Go on: drink up, and we'll have another. We've got to face Lincoln Street after I've been alone in it for a fortnight. We need a spot of blurring and bracing.'

Just before they were landing, she said, 'I do need to know what he feels, though.' She had had the two brandies, and was now simply relaxed and unhappy.

It was raining in London and looking its August worst. In the bus she cried a bit, but silently, and then, holding a bit of his coat sleeve, said, 'It would be so awful without you—you can't imagine.'

'Don't cry too much; there's nothing to blow your nose on but five pound notes. Think of me. Think of wicked horrible Ginny buggering off to Martha's Vineyard in order to get away from me. Think of my broken heart.'

'Oh yes! Poor Oliver! Do you mind awfully about her? I mean—*is* your heart broken?'

'A bit,' he said, 'but don't worry—it's smaller than yours.'

THREE

SURREY BLUES

IT wasn't until after Elizabeth had rung up that May realized how down she had been. Three or four times a day she had been telling herself that this was absurd. The weather had been good: Herbert had alternated trips to Lord's with a much keener and more practical interest in the garden than he had shown before. He treated the lawn with various chemicals, hosed it, rolled it, mowed it, and walked about it discussing its future perfection and the possibility of croquet. It kept *him* happy. He was just the kind of man to get obsessive about lawns, she thought. Mrs Green had been angelic: especially when May's indigestion had been so stupidly bad that she hadn't felt like cooking—let alone eating—anything. Mrs Green had even got her nephew to repair May's electric pad because she simply couldn't get her feet warm at night. Of course she worried about Oliver—not having a proper job, not seeming to care to get on with his life—but what she had already learned from the League had taught her to despise that kind of practically dishonest concern. Dr Sedum would simply ask *who* she was really worrying about— Oliver or herself? And as it was clearly worse to worry about herself, she knew that that was what she must really be doing. Elizabeth she suspected of being in love; a perfectly natural and reassuring condition. Lavinia had said that the impression she was creating upon other members of the League was largely favourable. The few people with whom she had obliquely discussed the difficulties of living with Herbert had treated him as a chronic natural hazard—like a degree of fall-out or the build-up of pesticides. It had—reasonably enough—been a reflection upon *her* that she was allied to such a man. Quite right (she was sure that anybody who could point to any of her behaviour and pronounce it shoddy, dishonest, underhand in some sickeningly unconscious manner must be right): but the facts were that she had to go on living and dealing with what she had done. The house, for instance. The curious thing about that was that she (not forgetting darling Oliver and Elizabeth) seemed to be the only person who really hated this awful house. Herbert, naturally (it was he who made her buy it), adored the place; but, far more mysterious, Dr Sedum and co. seemed *also* to think well of it. Lavinia had pointed out that many of the rooms were ideally suited to communal activities, although she was maddeningly unprepared to say what they might be. May was in a curious position *vis-à-vis* the League. At steady intervals she was invited to a Time—in a garden flat in St John's Wood—but she could not go unless it happened to coincide with one of Herbert's cricket days. When she *did* go, she came away feeling curiously depressed. This was partly because everybody except her seemed to understand everything that was going on, and partly because, this being so, she *pretended* to understand when she did not. There were usually about nine people, one of whom was allegedly in charge and who read something and then asked other people what they thought about it. Everybody spoke in very calm, deliberate voices—as though everything was unspeakably bad but they had faced up to it. Nearly all of what people said was in the form of a question—so all the talk was like some wavering chain with an occasional bead. The reading matter was so wide, as well as high-minded, as to be (to May anyhow) totally obscure. There had been one paper where it had started with primary colours and May had thought, oh good she knew what they were, but in no time the Trinity, the Milky Way, the Three Bears, fairy stories, triumvirates, geometry, Shakespeare's plays, being-more-civilized-than-allowing-oneself-to-be-presented-merely-with-the-alternative had all been thrown into the breach until the air was heavy with cigarette smoke and the whole of philosophy, and people were even pretending to want to interrupt one another. Einstein would be dismissed as clever (?) and Krishnamurti as not a realized man (?) The question marks saved everyone from noticing how far someone had stuck his neck out.

No wonder May left with indigestion—of a different kind from her run-of-the-mill prosaic kind—and wondering as she took the tube to Waterloo whether these symptoms, both physical and mental, were just the result of being fifty—i.e. too old for serious mental or spiritual effort. Herbert simply made her feel older by wanting her to make a will, because, he said, things could be so difficult with stepchildren if it wasn't all cut and dried. When she'd rung up the only lawyer she'd ever known because Clifford had used him, he said the same thing. But when she'd told Herbert this, thinking he'd be pleased, he'd got quite shirty, as darling Clifford used to say, and said he'd got a perfectly good lawyer already, there was no need for her to go ringing people up behind his back. Sometimes it seemed impossible to do anything right, and she really felt so wretched a good deal of the time that she seemed to have no energy. Herbert, who talked a good deal about her state of health, said he was going to take her into Woking to see a tremendously good doctor, but when she suggested getting on with this scheme he said give it a few more days with the pills he'd always used in India for *his* indigestion, and the hot drinks he brought her every evening. Twice Herbert made appointments about ten days in advance, and on both occasions she felt so much better that the first time she refused to go at all, and the second time she only went to please Herbert.

All in all, she was very glad when Elizabeth rang up and said she was coming down for the week-end.

They were mutually surprised by each other's appearance. May thought that Elizabeth looked dreadfully unhappy, and Elizabeth thought her mother looked worryingly ill. Neither of them mentioned these facts. They talked instead about Oliver, who *might*, apparently, be going to get some sort of job on a London newspaper; about Alice, who was apparently pregnant; and finally about Claude, who had taken to hunting all night in muddy and dank places and drying off luxuriously in the linen cupboard to which he seemed mysteriously always to have access. He had also kept such a sharp eye on any food imported into the house not specifically for him that he no longer bothered to kill and crunch up bluebottles. 'His one asset, from our point of view, simply thrown away. He's tripped Herbert up twice in passages when we haven't had spare bulbs and Mrs Green thinks his moulting gives her asthma. Somehow the awfulness of Claude is very consoling.'

Elizabeth looked at her mother's profile (she had met her daughter at the station in the Wolseley, which she drove with great care extremely badly). It was easy enough to imagine what her mother needed to be consoled about: Daddo and the horrible house. Apart from May's beautiful English complexion (that Elizabeth supposed she must be noticing so particularly because everyone in the South of France had been too brown to have one), her face looked as though she had lost too much weight too fast. Elizabeth felt that as well as looking ill, her mother did not seem to be happy. Nobody who thought of Claude as a consolation could be *very* happy.

'How is Alice getting on?'

'It sounds as though she is having a baby: at least she has absolutely every Victorian symptom. She writes me extremely long letters, and the moment I have screwed up the energy to reply she sends another one. Imm*e*diately. She wants to come and fetch Claude, but she says she's so sick in *any* vehicle that she dare not risk the train.'

'Perhaps I could take him to her!'

'Oh darling, that would be kind. Alice simply adores that cat, and on top of everything else she sounds a bit homesick, although how *anybody* could be homesick for this, I cannot imagine.'

They had swept precariously round the drive (May treated all corners—even gentle curves—as dangerous) until the monstrous builders' folly was in view. Oliver, who never tired of insulting it, had once said that it would be ideal for an American film producer to do a B feature on the haunted-house theme. Beams, battlements, leaded windows, nail-encrusted doors, awful, useless chimneys that looked as though they had been knitted in moss stitch, liver-coloured bricks, ill judged pieces of roughcast (dinosaurs' vomit Oliver had also said) made the place a landmark: it was called Monks' Close, and Oliver had also said how lovely it would be if you opened the hideous front door one day and found it chock-a-block with monkeys.

Herbert was standing in front of the front door to greet them. He wore cricket flannels, a white shirt and a panama hat and carried a syringe. He waved this last in greeting and then stood elaborately at attention as the car drew to a halt.

'Well well well *well*! Here you are. Welcome home, m'dear. Don't bother with the car now. I must say, Elizabeth, you're looking remarkably well. Flying the nest seems to agree with you, eh?'

Elizabeth had never known him so affable. He even made her a fearfully weak gin and tonic without being asked: but she took her small suitcase up to her room by herself. It was exactly as awful and the same. It seemed to her as though she had been away for—not a hundred, but about ten years. The thought that forty-eight hours ago she had been with John in the villa drinking Paradis and feeling so happy that she could notice *everything else* seemed extraordinary now. In the cupboard were a few outgrown, or at least outloved, clothes: they seemed both girlish and faded. The horrible bridesmaid's dress was there, too. How John would have laughed at her in that! The trouble was that she could not bear to think about John—in case it was no good thinking about him. The great thing was to think about other people: May, for instance, and even Alice. She washed her hands and combed her hair, collected some cigarettes out of her case and went down in search of her mother.

May had made dinner and to her amazement, the colonel had more or less laid the table, so there was nothing to be done.

'It's not very exciting, I'm afraid darling,' May said. 'Just steamed plaice and some baked apples. We've taken to eating very little in the evenings.'

'That's fine. I'm not especially hungry, anyway.'

'Well, Herbert is trying to keep his weight down, and eating at night doesn't seem to agree with me at all these days.'

Elizabeth watched Claude, who was crouched on the back door mat cracking drumsticks with his head on one side, almost as though he was testing them for sound.

'He seems larger than ever.'

'He is. He must be: I can really hardly lift him now. That is
another problem: he'd never fit into his cat basket. Darling, would
you like another drink?'

'I'd love one: what about you?'

May shook her head. 'I've had my little cocktail. The drink's in
Herbert's den.'

In summer, the den looked merely dingy rather than dank. It
had an unreasonably high ceiling with unfunctional beams. The
furniture, a nasty mixture of pitch pine and mahogany, was bilious
from the evening sunlight which filtered in through the narrow,
heavily leaded windows. The flat surfaces of the room were ranked
with photographs of the colonel, in uniform and out of it, in various
hot and cold countries, and accompanied by an assortment of
animals—alive or dead—as his sense of occasion had seen fit. There
were also a number of metal filing cabinets—unlabelled and locked.
Elizabeth found that she was looking at each awful room quite
freshly, as though it had absolutely nothing to do with her.

Herbert was sitting in his large chair with his head thrown back
listening to the cricket news from a small and badly serviced radio
resting on the arm of his chair. A whisky and soda lay within his
grasp. When he became aware of Elizabeth, he went through the
bizarre and contradictory motions of not getting up out of his chair
although he knew he should: or, possibly, seeming to get up out
of his chair and then not managing it because he was listening too
hard to the radio. Elizabeth took advantage of this pantomime to
make signs at the drink and herself, and with the barest flicker of
hesitation, he seemed to agree. Luckily for her, the drink was still
unlocked, but pouring a slug of gin under Daddo's eyes, as Oliver
had been wont to remark, required the most artistically unsteady
hand if one was to get a decent drink. There was about a third of
the bottle of tonic left from her first drink. No ice: no lemon.
Just as she was deciding it was worth the journey to the kitchen
for, at any rate, ice, the news came to an end.

'Ha! M'dear—you should have let me do that for you.' He had
switched off the radio. 'Lost without m'cricket. Haven't been up
so much this season with May being a bit off colour.'

'She doesn't look well: has she seen a doctor?'

'First thing I thought of. Got her to one in the end. Bright young chap in Woking. Mark you, had to make at least two appointments for her before I could get her there. She won't take enough care of herself, you know.'

Elizabeth asked what the doctor had said, but he was hunting for the drink cabinet key on his vast and crowded key ring: he didn't seem to have heard her.

'What did the doctor say?' she asked again.

'What? The doctor? Oh—he thought she'd been overdoing it. Alice's wedding and all that. I told him the moment she knew she was coming to see him she seemed much better—much more like her old self—and he produced some fashionable twaddle about psychology—they all do it now, you know, can't stop 'em, even got it with M.O.s towards the end of my time. Personally and between you and me, I don't think *any* woman of her age likes to admit to herself she can't do as much as she used to when she was younger. I don't say it, of course, but my view is that she should rest more, settle down a bit, all this dashing up and down to London takes it out of her. Wish you'd have a word with her about that, m'dear.'

His pale blue eyes were fixed upon her face: he looked anxious, tactless—or rather as though tact was an almost unbearable price to pay for him getting things right with people—and above all, as though he needed help of some kind if only he could explain the kind ... She began her customary retreat from dislike and ridicule: it was unfair, worse than bad taste, wrong for her to laugh at her mother's husband with her brother. He was like she was; simple, not specially clever or good at understanding things, but here he was, clearly doing his best. She smiled at him (she had no idea how anxious her smile was) and said that of course she'd do anything she could. The colonel seemed tremendously relieved by what she said. They finished their drinks in an unusually companionable silence.

After supper, the remains of which were clearly going to provide an ample snack for Claude, the colonel insisted on putting the car

away without help. May and Elizabeth piled the dishes on to the
rickety trolley and wheeled it down the stone passage, through the
baize doors that stuck and squeaked, to the kitchen. Claude emerged
unhurriedly from the larder where he had had a rather unsatisfactory
check-up.

'Do you mean you *still* haven't had the larder door fixed?'

'No: like so many things, I still haven't done it.'

Her mother's voice sounded despairing, and Elizabeth, going to
hug her, realized that she was very near tears. 'Darling—what *is* it?'

'Don't know—feel so awful—don't tell Herbert—headache—
lovely to have you here—'

A bit later, she said, 'I've had my little moan. Feel *much* better.'

Elizabeth offered her a cigarette, and she took it doubtfully.

'It might be nice; but often they make me feel sick, these days.'

Elizabeth said, 'Do you think you might possibly be having an
ulcer?'

'The doctor didn't seem to think so. Herbert took me to one in
Woking. And I saw someone else in London and they thought
definitely not.'

'Who did you see in London?'

May had lit her cigarette and now turned to throw away the
match. 'Oh nobody you would know, darling: but he was most
reassuring.'

Here, the conversation was interrupted by Claude, who was sick
and tired of waiting for his plaice. He stood on his hind legs and
reached an arm across the top of the trolley until he'd hooked a
backbone off what, unfortunately for him, turned out to be the
colonel's plate—the only one of them who'd eaten all his dinner.
He shook it free and tried again, knocking over and breaking a
glass half full of water. This gave him a horrible fright, but this time
he held on to a hardly-eaten fish and retired with it under the table.

'Isn't he ghastly?' said May fondly. 'The dustpan's over there.
It isn't as though he's intermittently awful—he never stops being it.'
And what with getting the fragments of glass and the sticky glue
of fish bones and skin off the floor, nothing more was said about the
London doctor. Later, Elizabeth made her mother some hot milk

and took it up to her in bed. There she learned that Herbert, who was shutting the dogs in, had taken to doing this every night.

'He's very sweet about it. He's bought Horlicks, and Bournvita and cocoa, and I never know which it's going to be.'

'That's good.' Elizabeth tried not to sound surprised. 'I'm afraid I've just put a little nutmeg in this.'

'Delicious, darling. Now off you go to bed—you look tired and we've got the whole of tomorrow to talk.'

But somehow or other, they never did talk. This was because May was afraid of Elizabeth telling Oliver about Dr Sedum and his laughing at her, and also because Elizabeth was afraid of breaking down completely if she began to tell May about John. So long as she never said even his name to May, she could pretend that the whole situation—including having to go away because of awful Jennifer—was unreal, or at least that the going away part of it was unreal. For minutes at a time she did not think at all about it, and then, just as she was beginning to notice in perhaps a rather sickening, congratulatory way that she had not thought about it, it filled her mind; John, unhappy, apologetic, at a loss, giving in to blatantly horrible Jennifer, so that there was a kind of double pain of seeing him give in and send her away and of actually going away. Thinking about it after not thinking about it was always worse. Going to bed was, of course, the saddest time: better at Lincoln Street because Oliver was always about, but here, at Monks' Close, it was really awful. She was even glad of Claude, who turned up reeking of fish to lie on her bed. He waited until the lights were out before he began a vigorous all-over wash that shook the bed for about forty minutes. At least the maddening absurdity of him stopped her crying.

Next day she knew she couldn't bear to stay much longer. It was having nothing to do—except things that she didn't really have to do—that made it impossible to stay. By lunch time, after she had fed the dogs, gone to the village shop for some rennet to make her mother a junket, made it, talked to Mrs Green, been shown the possible croquet lawn by Herbert (she was trying not to call him Daddo any more as he was obviously being so nice to May), been offered, and accepted, a South African sherry, it seemed as though she had been back for months; and just after she had tried the sherry, forgetting and remembering how much she had always disliked it, she also had a moment of actual panic because it seemed to her that far from time making things better about John, it was making things worse. Already they seemed to her about as much as she could bear. May had tried asking her about her job in the South of France, but she had been waiting for that, and her dull answers came out so pat that they quenched the kind of mild curiosity known as 'showing an interest' that was all May thought proper with her grown-up children. The colonel asked her whether she'd been to Monte, and when she said no, told her how much nicer and cheaper it had been in the 'thirties.

After lunch, she offered to take the dogs out, and when she got to the village, she rang Oliver who was in.

'Goodness me, you haven't got much stamina, have you?' he said in a rather jeering voice (she had got him out of the bath).

'Well you only stuck it for the inside of one day.'

'Quite a contrast to Antibes, I bet.'

'Oh—don't!'

'Do you want me to ring up or send an urgent telegram?'

'Ring up, I think.'

'Have you got any money?'

'Only what I left you with: minus train ticket, of course. Surely you haven't spent all that dough you got?'

'Don't say "got" in that suburban voice. Stole you mean. No, I haven't. I'll buy us a lobster if you come back in time to make mayonnaise.'

'Ring up in half an hour then. Is there—are there any letters for me?'

'Afraid not.'

So Elizabeth was half dragged back to the house by the large, dull dogs, but with a lighter, if more guilty, heart.

May accepted her going with the usual good grace: there was an awkward moment when she reminded Elizabeth of her promise about transporting Claude, but it was agreed that May should come to lunch at Lincoln Street next time she was in town, and bring

Claude with her. The colonel said it was a pity she was going when she'd only just come, and Claude yawned for such a long time that she thought perhaps he had forgotten what he was doing, but eventually he shut his mouth and then his eyes very slowly like sliding doors. May drove her to the station while they reassured each other about what they had not really discussed. Elizabeth said, 'You *will* see another doctor, won't you, if you go on having this stomach bug or whatever it is?' And May said, 'Of course, darling, but it's bound to go: everybody's been having it; even Herbert hasn't been feeling quite the thing.'

As they drew up at the station, May said, 'Darling, don't work *too* hard. You don't look as though you're having enough fun. Make Oliver pull his weight.' And Elizabeth said, 'Oh—I don't do too badly. Yes, I'll tell Oliver: perhaps he's got this job.'

They kissed and Elizabeth told her mother not to wait, and May said that she'd just walk on to the platform, but she *did* wait for the train, and kissed Elizabeth again and then immediately started walking back down the small platform: it was then that Elizabeth noticed how much weight her mother must have lost.

Waterloo: the bit of time walking down the platform when you knew you weren't going to be met, and you could imagine that you might have come from anywhere; you had to jazz up the departure because there wasn't enough to be said about arrival. You could only like London at the beginning of August if you knew it very well the rest of the time. She took trains to Sloane Square and then walked—with one or two rests from the suitcase.

When she rang the bell, the door of Lincoln Street opened rather slowly and she couldn't see anyone. Then Oliver said:

'It's me. Behind the door. I'm naked. I knew you'd come if I took off all my clothes.'

'Is that why you did?'

'No—you *fool*! I was just going to try out a new stuff that's supposed to turn you brown while you wait. Give it to me.'

He took her case and they padded upstairs. Oliver collected a bath towel and Elizabeth flung herself on the sofa saying, 'Anything to drink?'

'I must say high life has made you very demanding.' But when he got nearer to her, he saw that tears were sliding down her face. 'Liz!' He rubbed his face against hers. 'It's nothing like as bad as you think.'

'How isn't it?'

'I've made a marvellous drink for you. And there is a huge lobster in the fridge, and I went to Buck and Ryan and bought some immensely useful-looking tools that will do for picking the best bits out as *well* as screwdriving. I bought a bottle of Pouilly Fumé —costs the earth, I must say—to drink with the lobster and a packet of Gauloises for nostalgia—'

'Oh don't, Oliver! It's only—seventy-two hours since we were there!'

'*That's* why you haven't heard from him. Oh yes, and I was out last night so he might easily have rung up if he can ever sneak away from loathsome Jennifer. Now—first you're going to get a bit drunk, and then you're going to get indigestion, but the whole thing will turn out to have been worth it when you look back on the evening—you'll see.'

'What about the mayonnaise?' she said about half an hour later.

'Do you think if I brought the ingredients here to you you could manage it?'

They'd each had three tremendously strong Negronis and Liz had just remarked that he had a lovely easy name to say when drunk.

'Standing on my head.'

'That won't be necessary. You're not at the Palladium now.'

When he had assembled everything, and she was sitting with her feet tucked up under her on the sofa stirring away, she asked, 'What about the job?'

'Which job?'

'The newspaper one.'

'Oh that. Well I've got that in a way. Freelance. As a matter of fact I've got three jobs. Haven't let the grass grow under my feet. Can you imagine *anyone* doing that in England? Rheumatism and awful metal notices telling you to keep off it, and dogs peeing and worms casting and even policemen asking you to move along.'

'What are your other jobs?'

'Well—one of them's rather silly, really. The idea is that I should do a TV ad for the people who make this instant brown stuff. And I wanted to see if you could watch it working.'

'You're brown already.'

'Not really. I'm simply not that British un*earthly* white. This is supposed to turn you Nescafé olé, as the international slogan might well go.'

'What's the third job?'

'Well that's a bit queer, and I'm not supposed to talk about it. I answered an ad in the paper. All they seem to want you to do is to watch things.'

'What on earth do you mean?'

'Not absolutely *anything*, of course. They ring you and tell you to watch, say, 29 Pelham Place.'

'How do you mean—watch it?'

'Who goes there, etcetera.'

'Oliver! That's simply spying!'

'That's right. An immensely fashionable occupation. Not very well paid at my level, but still not negligible.'

She put down the fork in the mayonnaise bowl.

'Look here, Oliver, honestly!'

'Before you start all that, I'm going to get the lobster. You may think you're a stanchion of society, but I know bloody well you couldn't walk down a flight of stairs without help. So off I go.'

While he was assembling dinner, she sat in a state of semi-alcoholic despair about life: about Oliver: brilliant at Oxford; no fool, really by any standards, fiddling about with sleazy old part-time employment kicks. And what was she doing? Cooking for unknown, boring, quantities of people. Their father had died fighting the Second World War. May was hanging out with that silly boor in the home counties. Who was enjoying what? And what about John? What about John? What about him? *What?* Was the world ruled by Jennifers? Once it was certain that you could get no pleasure from anything, were you automatically in a position of power? Where the least you could do was to see that other people did not enjoy themselves? What was the *point* of being as clever as Oliver if people only asked you to do silly things like watching houses and putting idiotic stuff on your back? Why should children — like Jennifer — exercise this fearful blackmailing jurisdiction over parents? Jennifer was the same age as *she* was — grown up, in fact: no longer in need of — supposing *she* had made that sort of fuss, she supposed that she (and Oliver, of course) could have prevented May from marrying Herbert. They could have made May feel so awful about it that she would have given up the idea. Perhaps that was exactly what she ought to have done. This thought quickly took hold to the exclusion of any other.

'Crying again, I see.' He dumped the tray on the coffee table. 'Everything is your fault, I have no doubt, and by the time I've reassured and comforted you about that, everything will be *my* fault. Better if we both got down to a nice dose of strontium 90.'

'What?'

'Liz, dear, do stop snuffling and blow your nose. Lobsters, as you clearly didn't know, are chock-a-block with strontium 90: not as much as crabs, but still enough to worry some people. There.' He handed her a plate on which was half of an enormous lobster, some chopped pieces of tomato and a length of cucumber. 'You've *cried* into the mayonnaise!'

'It won't hurt it.' She stirred up the bowl a bit. The lobster looked far too big. He was pouring out the pale, delicious wine.

'You'd better eat some bread: this'll taste awful after Negroni.'

On the tray were a collection of what looked like burglars' tools. While she was fingering them, Oliver tied a large tea towel round her neck.

'Now: we are going to enjoy this: you may think I'm wasting my life, but I'm not going to have you wasting my lobster.'

'What about *you* having something round your neck?'

'No point when it's just skin.' He was still bare to the waist, but had put on a pair of jeans and some vicious-looking sandals that a friend had brought back from Marrakesh.

The lobster wasn't too big, and the burglars' tools turned out to be extremely useful. Oliver was the ideal person to eat a lobster properly with, she thought: you could crunch and probe and lick and he only thought the more of you.

After the lobster there was half an extremely ripe Camembert and some crusty bread and finally half a bottle of brandy.

'It is so awful changing one's standard of living with too much of a jolt,' he said. By then she had told him about May and how Herbert had seemed to be nicer, and he had said that May would be bound to feel ill if she lived with such a bore and he, for one, did not believe that Herbert was ever *really* nicer, he must be pretending. Elizabeth argued a bit—that people surely didn't throw *up* for psycho-whatever reasons, and Oliver said oh yes they did. She had hiccoughs by then and you never win an argument with them. Oliver gave her a mediocre fright and some more brandy. Then, she said,

'Now, Oliver—we've got to talk about you.'

'What are we going to say?

'Oh, *I* know,' he added, when he'd had a good look at her face. 'The trouble with me is that all my life I *haven't* wanted to be a doctor. I've got no sense of purpose. You get that with rather charming, spineless people sometimes, and with me you've got it. I simply want a tremendous lot of money for nothing. Nearly all work that people do seems to me so absolutely awful that I'd rather live from hand to mouth. I haven't quite got that sense of showmanship required for the Church, or the Bar or the stage. I haven't the senses of responsibility and greed that would make me any good at business. I only like nature in amateur quantities, so farming is out. (Also—I could never fill in the forms.) I've thought seriously of crime, but prisons are full of such *frightfully* boring people all wanting to tell you every single unfair thing that has ever happened to them. What else is there? Oh yes, the Services. Now them I wouldn't mind so much if you could choose at all where you went, and didn't get chucked out the moment you'd got any good at it and had a chance to tell other people to do the dirty work. Also they are tremendously keen on people having spines. The arts sound more fun and I might end up on that kick somehow or other, but deep down they're horribly hard work and you get your sense of dedication creeping in: I'd have to be a charlatan. I thought of running a brothel—rushing to Victoria station and saying, "You like my sister? Very clean"—what else is it they say?—but somehow that is a mixture of business and vicarious pleasure. No: I'm afraid I've simply got to marry a very rich girl and let people say what a marvellous chap I would have been if I hadn't done that. So I'm quite prepared to talk about Ginny. The trouble is, I don't think she has the stamina for marriage, and the other thing is I'm really very fond of her in between when she's not being spoilt and boring. What do you think of her?'

Elizabeth, who felt as though she'd been holding her breath without warning for far too long, hiccoughed in spite of this and said that she didn't think marriage was a way out. For a man, she added.

'What about a woman? I mean one could look at it from Ginny's point of view. It might be a way out for her. You don't like her, do you?'

'I don't have any feelings about her.'

'With you, that amounts to dislike. Well, of course she's not the *only* rich girl in the world. I don't think we ought to marry people each other don't like, do you?'

She shook her head, hiccoughed again, and held her glass out for more brandy.

'Like a Gauloise with it?'

She nodded.

'It's a pity we've got to marry anyone, really: we get on so well. The only trouble about incest must be getting yourself to feel like it. Otherwise it strikes me as a very harmless and economical arrangement. It's funny how brandy seems to make me talk and shuts you up. Can't you think of *anything* to say?'

'It's my hiccoughs. But what would we do about children?'

'Have them, of course. With your looks and my brains (I must say, Liz, that you really have quite *suddenly* got much prettier) they'd probably be marvellous. And think how nice for May not having any sons- or daughters-in-law: cutting down family friction to the minimum. I suppose I could be an amateur detective, but there's nothing I really want to find out—in that sort of way, I mean. I would love to know what we're all here for. The only people who've taken any trouble about that got so bogged down with knowing what *they* were for.'

'What?'

'Taking trouble about what we're here for, silly.'

'Anyway, I can't marry you. I don't think I'll be able to marry anyone.'

'Watch it! You're going to cry in a minute. You mean because the only person you want to marry is John and you won't be able to because foul Jennifer will bitch it up?'

She nodded, put down her glass and started looking for her handkerchief.

'He is the first person you've ever fallen in love with.'

Miserable tears had started streaming down, and no handkerchief.

'Look, darling Liz: most people have to try dozens of people before they find the right one. He isn't the only man in the world.'

'He *is!*'

'Oh dear. O.K. I was afraid of that. Because you see the course that *yawns* before me, don't you?'

She rubbed her face with the tea towel.

'No.'

'It's up to me to seduce and elope with Jennifer. Thereby getting her out of your way and remaining true to what I know would be generally accepted as a sordid ambition; but I do feel that that simply means one must exercise even more loyalty. She is awful, though. I suppose if I was drunk and always wore dark glasses I could just about bring it off. But then, you see, *you* wouldn't like me marrying someone you didn't like, would you? How will it all end I wonder.'

'You don't know how awful I feel.'

'Now then. Your situation is by no means hopeless, and the best thing you can do is think of others. That usually makes one feel so frightful that one can stand any parochial anguish. Think of Alice.'

'Oh dear.'

'You see? You can hardly bear it at once. You just think of how you can brighten her perfectly dreadful life.'

'Claude!'

'What about him?'

'I promised May I'd take him to Bristol for her.'

'What on earth made you do that?'

'You know how when you're bored you'll pledge yourself in the most tiring ways. Alice is pregnant; she can't travel to fetch him, and nobody seems to think he could go anywhere unaccompanied. So I said I'd do it.'

'You do it and then you can tell me all about their horrid little happy home.'

'You are absolutely beastly.'

'No. Just accurate. But if Alice wants Claude and you are at all sorry for her, it is the least you can do.'

FOUR

·ᚙ·

BLUE FOR A BOY

ALICE was so excited at the double prospect of Elizabeth and Claude that on the morning of the day that they were due, she hardly minded being sick. She was usually sick about three times before eleven a.m.: once after she had fried Leslie's bacon and eggs, once after she had mopped and cleaned up after the hysterically dirty puppy that was Mrs Mount's newest token of kindness to her daughter-in-law, and once after she had obeyed Leslie's command that she have a nice cup of hot tea, or coffee. Leslie had usually gone to his office before she got to the puppy-cleaning time. Then she would go and have a bath. The cold sweat, the dizziness, the soiled disorder of her body usually revolted her so much that she had to try not to be sick a fourth time. So far as she knew, she was six and a half weeks pregnant, and the doctor had said that many people suffered from morning sickness for the first three months. She explained that she often felt sick in the evenings as well and he said that often happened, but with most people it was one or the other. The idea of another six weeks of feeling like this was so terrible, that she simply retched and crawled through each separate interminable day. After her bath, she did the housework very slowly while the puppy yapped round her. If she shut him into any room he made a mess in it and then yapped and howled to be let out. Sometimes she put him out into what would one day be their garden but was still just a rectangle marked off by a paling fence. As soon as he found he could not get out of the garden, he yapped to be let into the house. He was (more or less) a miniature poodle and his nature was both disagreeable and demanding: he smelled faintly all the time of shit; she no sooner got rid of one set of worms than he contracted another; his breath offended her, particularly in her present condition; he had a capacity for yapping that seemed almost electronic; he was hardly ever obedient, and totally undiscriminating in his affections; he ate so fast that he nearly always threw his food up; he seemed quite unable to keep any parts of himself clean and his grasping claws ruined any pair of stockings she wore. His expression was unreliable and silly and she could not get fond of him. Leslie thought it was wonderful of his mother to give her a dog—it was company, as he kept on saying: he did not seem to think that it mattered what kind. She took him shopping with her on the days when she felt strong enough and he strained on the lead, strangling himself, winding the lead round and round her until she was immobile, peeing every two or three yards, yapping at any other dog. When she felt really weak, she would leave him in the bathroom and go guiltily off without him. She would buy food for supper; things at the chemist and the ironmonger for the house; she would get herself some books from the library and occasionally she would eat lunch of some kind in a tea shop or women's café. Then she would walk slowly home, clean up and let out the dog and lie down with one of the library books. In the afternoons she did not feel sick, simply overwhelmingly tired. She would read two pages and fall into a heavy sleep. The house was still far from finished, and she did nothing at all about preparing for the baby in whom, when alone, she just did not believe. She would wake at about five, force herself to get up, and start sewing Rufflette tape on to half-made pairs of curtains, slicing french beans for supper, or marking some of the wedding present linen with indian ink and a tiny, spluttery pen. By the time Leslie returned she was just beginning to feel sick again, but gave the appearance of having been at wifely occupations all day. He would make himself a drink, switch on the television and tell her about his day in a raised voice over it, while she struggled with nausea and supper. After they—or sometimes he—had eaten, he would watch more television with another drink. He always asked her how she was feeling; he was very bucked about the baby and said several times a day that he was sure it would be a boy. Once or twice a week his family either turned up or summoned them. These were the worst evenings. Otherwise, she could get into her housecoat after dinner and read or watch television with him. At about ten she got hungry, and what she liked best was anchovies on water biscuits. When, eventually, they went to bed, Leslie left her alone which was the single best thing about being pregnant, she decided. He would kiss her forehead, pat her hand, sometimes—maddeningly—stroke her belly, but he seemed to regard sex as unnecessary.

There were terrible days when Rosemary turned up in her little second-hand M.G. and talked and talked: it was extraordinary how people telling you things could wear you out: the only hope was that one day Rosemary would have told her everything and would then stop coming. And this was odd, because nearly all the time she felt more lonely than she had ever felt before in her life. Always, before, there had been so many things to do for her father that she had not needed to bother about how she felt. She had always wanted a friend, but somehow Rosemary would not do: she seemed to treat Alice like an inversion of the radio—she simply turned Alice on as a listener.

So when Elizabeth wrote to say that she would bring Claude down and could she stay the night, Alice felt as though it was a turning-point. Things were bound to get better once Claude was there, and Elizabeth must care about her or she wouldn't go to all the trouble: Claude would not be an easy person to travel with. After she had told Leslie and he had remarked kindly that that was very nice, she started feverishly to get the spare room into some sort of order. The bungalow was tremendously full of wedding presents, and as they were mostly either ugly or useless, and often both, Alice had been dumping them in the spare room. Elizabeth had only given her twenty-four hours' notice (never *mind*) so after Leslie had gone and she was more or less over being sick, she set to work. It was lunch time before it occurred to her that Claude would be unlikely to take kindly to the puppy. He disliked all dogs intensely, and a puppy in his own house was a kind of double insult. If *only* Mrs Mount would take it back! She had a sandwich lunch (anchovy and cucumber) and finished the curtains for what she by now called Elizabeth's room. She had telephoned Lincoln Street and made all the arrangements: they were travelling by the morning train, and she would meet them in a taxi if Leslie could not let her have the car. She spent an hour or two with her cookery books trying to think of the best things for dinner: Elizabeth was such a good cook and Leslie preferred very plain food. She decided on lamb and summer pudding which she made well because her father had particularly liked it. In the afternoon she went to buy the meat and fruit and she took the puppy with her to make up for probably being horrible to him tomorrow.

That evening, because Elizabeth was coming, she realized how very little she and Leslie said to each other; up until now it had not seemed especially strange that she and Leslie talked to each other much less than she had talked with May, for instance. But now she was afraid that Elizabeth would think it very odd, and in a desperate, last-minute effort to alter this situation, she tried to chatter to Leslie. But Alice trying to chatter was so unusual, unlikely and unsuccessful, that after a short time Leslie asked her whether she was feverish, and after she'd said 'no', she couldn't think of anything at all.

The next morning, she bought half a rabbit and some whiting for Claude. Leslie needed the car, so she took a bus to the station — a queasy, but not disastrous progress. She was far too early, but it did not matter. It was a baking hot day and when she reached the platform, the station smelled of cool dirt. She sat on a hard bench and wondered whether anybody could tell, by looking at her, that she was pregnant. Perhaps Elizabeth would stay for several days — for quite a long time. Her hopes rose as the train did not come. Very few people were waiting for it, those that were had a holiday air: red-faced women in sleeveless dresses with shopping bags and either silent little babies in blue and pink nylon, like elves, or something out of an egg, or hot toddlers in dungarees, burdened with awkward and favourite possessions, who tugged at any free hand to try and make something happen.

The signals changed; a feeling of routine or professional expectancy charged the station. Two porters appeared. An old man who had been walking down the track, climbed up on to the platform.

A case of carrier pigeons was moved nearer the line, and somebody cleared their throat into the loud-speaker.

She hardly recognized Elizabeth: new clothes, her hair cut differently and her tan made her look a different person—almost unbearably glamorous to Alice, who had found her marvellous enough before. She wore a dark blue linen coat and skirt and carried a small red case. Claude was surely not in that?

They kissed, rather shyly, and Elizabeth said:

'They wouldn't let him travel with me: he's in the guard's van. I did go and see him several times, but I don't think it made much difference to him.'

The guard was putting what looked like a small picnic basket on to the platform. When they reached it, Alice saw that it had a label saying, SEYMOUR, BRISTOL on it. No sound came from the basket. She bent over it.

'I don't think you'd better open it here. He might rush out.'

So she waited until they were in the taxi.

Claude, looking even larger than she remembered, crouched on his old blanket inside. He looked up at her and opened his mouth, but no sound came out.

'Oh dear. I'm afraid he's lost his voice. I'm not surprised, I must say. He went on and on about how much he hated everything all the way to Paddington and whenever I went to see him in the van.'

She stroked him, and he winced as though he was past any such attention. He went on opening and shutting his mouth and staring resentfully at her: he smelled faintly of circuses. It was lovely to see him again.

'It is kind of you to bring him.'

'That's all right. It's jolly nice to see you again.'

'You look very sunburned.'

'I've been in France.'

There was a silence. After a bit, and after thinking what to say, Alice said, 'Our house—it's a bungalow, really—is on a new building estate, so everything looks a bit unfinished.'

'I'm longing to see it.'

During the rest of the taxi ride, she asked about Oliver and May, and, finally, her father. Elizabeth was funny and animated about Oliver, said that May did not seem to be very well, and said that Alice's father seemed to be looking after her as much as he could.

After that, she suddenly started feeling very sick—so much so that she had to tell Elizabeth.

'Do you want to stop and get out for a bit?'

'It's all right.'

After a bit, she said, 'I'll tell you if it isn't.'

The road to 24 Ganymede Drive was only half made up. They lurched and jolted and dust came in through the windows, so Elizabeth shut them. As she leaned across to do Alice's window, she said, 'Are you excited about the baby?'

And Alice answered in a colourless voice, 'Oh yes.'

They opened the tricky little gate and walked up the path. Elizabeth insisted on carrying Claude's basket. The moment Alice put the key in the lock, there was a frantic yapping. The puppy, who had hurled himself against the shut door and fallen over, had picked himself up in time to hurl himself at them when the door was open. There was a heavy lurch in the picnic basket, and Elizabeth tried to hold it higher from the ground.

'Wait a minute; I'll shut him in the bathroom. Please go in the sitting-room, Elizabeth.'

Elizabeth had plenty of time to look around the sitting-room. It had streaky black and grey Marley tiles on the floor, a fireplace of the kind that Oliver had once described as Builders' Revenge, with cute little shelves made of tiles. There was a coffee table also made of tiles—rather improbable tropical fish—a sofa and two arm-chairs upholstered in black imitation leather, a corner cupboard of limed oak and a rather large cocktail cabinet of walnut veneer. On this stood a wedding photograph of Alice and Leslie. Alice looked as though she had just sneezed and Leslie seemed to have too many teeth. The curtains were blue linen, and Elizabeth suspected that Alice had chosen and made them. There was a fluffy rug the colour of beetroot juice in front of the fireplace. There was a reproduction of Degas's 'Dancer' in colour, and a mirror with the most serpentine wrought-iron frame. In the corner cabinet were some silver cups that she guessed Leslie had won playing golf. She had put Claude's basket down in the middle of the room, but she knew that Alice would want to open it herself. Just as she was beginning to wonder what could have happened to her, Alice came in.

'The puppy had made another mess: I'm so sorry.' She looked rather green.

The basket was opened and Alice lifted him out, Claude turned his head from her and jumped clumsily to the ground. He then prowled slowly around the door and the windows with exaggerated caution, his belly touching the ground. When he could find no way out, he went and crouched under the coffee table. He looked dusty and disgruntled. When Alice went to stroke him, he got up wearily and crouched somewhere else.

'He doesn't remember me!'

'He's just upset. Perhaps he's hungry.'

She fetched him a plate of rabbit: he sniffed at it and sneezed.

'Perhaps he's thirsty.'

Milk was brought. He grudgingly drank some of that, and then, with a gesture that seemed to Elizabeth deliberately involuntary he knocked over the saucer with one paw. Alice had made him a tray with sand in it. He sauntered to that ('He's feeling more at home!' Alice said) and spent about five minutes walking round and over it, scuffing sand out, settling himself with his face turned towards the ceiling and a fixed expression and then changing his mind. When most of the sand was on the floor he got into the right position, his eyes became glassy and one natural function, at least, was achieved.

'Do you think he will get on with the puppy?'

'No. I know he won't. My mother-in-law gave it to me: I asked her not to but she did. I don't know what to do. Perhaps they will keep out of each other's way.'

But this, of course, was not possible in a small bungalow. After they had had lunch, Alice and Elizabeth made the experiment of bringing the puppy into the sitting-room. Claude uttered a single cry of rage and despair and tried to get under the sofa while the puppy gambolled around and fell over him. He swiped at the puppy who retreated yelping. As it was clear that he could not possibly get under the sofa, he jumped on to it and crouched there swearing continuously under his breath. The rest of the afternoon was in the same key and Elizabeth realized that the situation was a crisis for poor Alice. 'You see, Leslie *likes* the puppy because his mother gave it to us. He doesn't do anything about it, but he would never agree to getting rid of it. What shall I do?'

Elizabeth did all she could. She helped with dinner: she cleared up after both the puppy and Claude. She even took the puppy for a short walk and he laddered her stockings. Taking these off in the spare room that had been shown her with such humble anxiety for her comfort, she saw how brown her legs still were and felt so miserable, so homesick for John, so bewildered by the sudden, horrible, inexplicable change in her life, that all Oliver's cheering-up went for nothing and she wept. As she was washing her face she remembered what Oliver had said about having to spend a fortnight in Cornwall with Leslie. Being in this house made that seem about like having measles compared to a life sentence. It was all too clear that poor old Alice was not happy. Why on *earth* had she done it? A mystery: and as Oliver had once pointed out, many of them were horrid if you got at all close.

Leslie came back at a quarter to six, and by then Elizabeth felt as though she'd been in the bungalow a week. He embraced her facetiously, kissed Alice with more social practice, and said he'd make them all a drink. This was a good idea, but when he went into the sitting-room to do this, he encountered Claude, who, having demolished the plate of rabbit and a raw whiting, was grandiosely engaged upon the only other natural function left to him. The smell was awe-inspiring and Elizabeth had to admit that it was reasonable of Leslie to object. So Claude and his tray were moved to Elizabeth's room: she said she didn't mind a bit. (This was true: she felt she would never mind anything again.) But Leslie was somebody who continued to discuss something after it was over. The windows had all been opened; the puppy had been let in, the drinks were made, and Leslie had only just got into his stride about what coming into his home and finding Claude doing that

had been like. After two gins and tonics he was still on the subject
of how much worse (worse?) cats were than dogs. 'You've got a
nice little pup for company,' he said over and over again. 'You
don't want a dirty creature like that.'

They had dinner in the dining alcove. Roast lamb, mint sauce,
rather old new potatoes and ageless, frozen peas. The summer
pudding was excellent, and Elizabeth told Alice this but the poor
thing was by then too distressed to eat any of it. While she was
making coffee, Leslie told Elizabeth that women who were expecting were always touchy; his mother had warned him of it; he was
glad of course that Alice had a stranger on the way and that he was
sure it would be a boy. Elizabeth looked at her beautiful watch
while he was getting his pipe: it was twenty to nine. She went to
the kitchen to see if she could help with the washing up and found
Alice in floods of tears. There is a curious sensation of genuinely
trying to comfort somebody who is sincerely unhappy when they
are utterly unused to being comforted. Elizabeth found that you
quickly reach a point where anything you do feels dishonest; you
are embracing or stroking a tree, not a person; any words you say
sound as though you have not understood or do not care: added to
this, she felt that if Leslie came into the kitchen and found them,
a kind of spurious treachery would be added to the scene.

They went to wash Alice's face and to see Claude in the spare
room. At first they could not find him but this was because he had
gone to sleep on Elizabeth's bed *in* her open suitcase and mysteriously covered himself with her white cashmere cardigan. It was
Alice who found him and who sank to her knees beside the suitcase
to tell him he'd been hiding. He stared at her coldly: his whole
routine had been upset and grudges were very much his line, but
Alice seemed neither to know this or to mind. 'The thing is, Elizabeth, that he *is* my cat and I can't—I don't see why I should—'
and Elizabeth realized that she would start crying again if something were not done about it.

'Of course he is,' she said briskly. 'I'm sure they'll settle down
together in a day or two. Don't you think we had better take the
coffee in to Leslie before it gets cold?'

Alice nodded dumbly, sat at the dressing-table to powder her nose and met Elizabeth's eye in the glass. It was funny, Elizabeth suddenly thought: if you didn't say *anything* to Alice you felt she understood everything you hadn't said, but if you *said* anything at all, somehow you felt that whatever you'd said had been wrong and all communication with her got blocked. She was trying to smile now: but as Elizabeth touched her shoulder—rigid with the inexperience of being comforted—the smile somehow turned into a face that Alice was making—absurd and repelling: you had to think hard to be sorry for her.

But as soon as they were back in the sitting-room with the coffee, she felt sorry for Alice all right. Leslie put down his evening paper and started.

He didn't want them to think him an unreasonable man, as a matter of fact that was the last thing that he was, so he defied anyone to think it, but he *did* believe in plain speaking, he'd never been someone who minced their words and he had no intention of starting this evening. Everybody had got their coffee by now, and the two women were seated looking—he thought expectantly—at him. In fact Alice was trying not to hate him, and Elizabeth was trying not to yawn. What it amounted to—after what seemed like hours but was, in fact, about forty minutes—was that Leslie would not have that cat in the house. At any price, he had reiterated many times as though there could possibly be one. The third time that he said that Alice had got the puppy after all, Alice said that she had had Claude first and that she didn't really *like* the puppy. It was a present from his mother, Leslie said, thus putting it beyond the realm of liking. The argument about whether Claude was clean in the house began. Leslie said look at what he had had to come home to, and Alice said that as soon as he was settled down, Claude would use the garden, but this simply drove Leslie back to square one: he would not have that cat in his house. Just as he was saying that Alice had got the puppy, after all, the telephone rang, and this was so loud and surprising that Elizabeth, at least, jumped, thinking 'Thank God' without knowing why. Leslie went to answer it (the telephone was in his study) and came back a moment later saying that the call was for Elizabeth. This seemed both to amaze and annoy him. Wondering what on earth Oliver was up to now, Elizabeth escaped to the study.

'What *are* you doing in Bristol?' said John Cole's voice.

It was John. It wasn't Oliver—it was John.

'Are you there?'

'Yes. I'm in Bristol.'

'Yes, I thought you must be. Do you want to stop being there? Because if you do, I'll fetch you.'

'Now—would you?'

'Yes. I'm at London airport. That should just give you time to pack.'

'Oh! I don't think I *can*, though. I'm supposed to stay the night here: at least. I mean I haven't even *been* here for a night yet.'

'Couldn't you explain to them?'

'Well—no, I couldn't really. Not enough to stop people feeling hurt.'

There was a pause, and then he said, 'All right: what about tomorrow morning?'

'That would be O.K.'

'Would it be lovely as well as O.K.?'

But as soon as she didn't answer, he added quickly, 'Jennifer has gone to Capri with some of Ginny's set.' Then he said, 'Oliver said he didn't think you'd mind my ringing you, but I quite see about staying the night. Would ten o'clock tomorrow morning suit you?'

'Yes. I'm sorry, I'm no good at talking on the telephone.'

'The trouble is that there's nothing else you can do on it really. Never mind. Tomorrow; ten o'clock.'

'Have you got the address?'

'I have.' She waited; there was a faint click and then the dialling tone. He never said goodbye.

She put the receiver down and walked unsteadily back into the sitting-room trying to compose her face to suit the now so distant as to be meaningless situation of Leslie versus Claude.

Leslie was definitely intrigued, as he put it, by Elizabeth's telephone call. This was partly, Elizabeth felt, because he was rather rudely amazed that *anyone* should want to call her long distance, and partly because she sensed that he had wrung from Alice some form of capitulation about Claude, and, having got his own way, was breezily determined to change the subject.

The young man sounded definitely intriguing, Leslie repeated; was he someone they might have met at the wedding? Which was absolutely ridiculous, Elizabeth thought, since he must know perfectly well that apart from the caterers everybody at the wedding had been some sort of actual or potential relation.

No, she said.

Well people didn't phone people for nothing; that was a fact and certainly not at this hour of night, so perhaps there might be another wedding that they'd meet him at?

He was like Rosemary in plus-fours, Elizabeth thought, but even *he* could make her blush.

He was a friend of hers and Oliver's, she said: he happened to be in the neighbourhood and Oliver had suggested to him that he pick her up. Which he was doing tomorrow morning at ten o'clock. And from coldly and casually not looking anywhere, she turned to Alice with something like entreaty. Alice made an effort to smile and said that she thought perhaps she would go to bed. Would Leslie take the puppy out? Of *course* he would. Where was the poor little chap? In the kitchen in his basket. When he had gone, Alice said:

'Would you mind very much having him in your room tonight? Claude, I mean,' she added.

'Of course not. I'd love to have him.'

Alice followed her to the door of her room. 'He's very good at night: as long as he's got someone warm to lean against and you don't turn over too much.'

'I'm sure he is: I'm awfully sorry, Alice.'

They kissed clumsily; Alice's eyes filled with tears and she said, 'Just bad luck.' Then she had to go without saying good night to Claude, because Leslie and the puppy had returned.

But with Alice gone, all pity, all dismay vanished. It was almost impossible to feel really happy *and* really sorry for someone at the same time—or at least *she* didn't seem to be managing it: of course she wasn't simply happy about John—they were going to have to have a serious talk, about Jennifer and everything. It was more a mixture of tremendous relief that she'd heard from him, and excitement at the thought of seeing him, and apprehension about what seeing him would be like. 'This time tomorrow,' she thought, unable to think any more than that about it.

Claude still lay in her suitcase, but now his tail hung out and down the side of the bed like a bell pull in a Beatrix Potter story. She lifted him out of the suitcase on to the bed, and without the slightest pause he started to climb into it again. So then she lifted the suitcase on to the floor and he got out at once. He had no intention of spending his night on the floor. When she was in bed and had turned out the lights, he subjected her to nerve-racking minutes while he walked over her dressing-table hitting things and knocking them over. She called him, and after a suitable delay, he landed with exaggerated caution on her neck. He then tramped wearily over her, testing various places to see whether or not they could be expected to take his weight, until he finally settled in the crook at the back of her knees. Here he sneezed eighteen times and then got down to a thorough all-over wash. His muscular and rhythmic tongue shook the whole bed for what seemed like hours. But he did one good thing. From thinking that she would not be able even to shut her eyes, he made her long for him to shut up and let her fall asleep. Eventually, he did.

John arrived punctually at ten. Leslie had left for work, it having been made interminably clear that Claude was not to be in the house when he returned that evening. Elizabeth left them alone together and heard Alice saying goodbye to him and then the outbreak of his fury when he found himself back in his travelling basket. She had tried to do the breakfast washing up but Alice had stopped her; 'You'll leave me nothing to do.' So now she stood in the sitting-room by the front windows that looked on to the small blazing desert that was to be a garden when, as she had heard it variously put, Leslie got round and Alice faced up to it. The thought of being Alice was, at the moment, so awful, and the

kind of chance whereby *she* had escaped this fate so utterly mysterious that she felt a kind of moral sadness for the world ... She
could see the car.

The bungalow gate made him look even taller than usual—
turned him into a kind of Gulliver; he stooped to undo the fussy
little catch, but really, he could just as well have stepped over the
whole thing; she rushed to the front door and opened it before he
had finished striding up the concrete-scored-to-look-like-crazy-
paving path. He beamed discreetly at her, looking much browner
than he had looked in France. Alice appeared in the doorway of
the guest room and Elizabeth, introducing John, suddenly saw her
as a complete stranger might do: a large, ungainly girl, but striking
in a gentle, picturesque manner, as much out of proportion and
place here as, say, a Labrador in a hen coop. She was very pale,
but blushed when John shook hands with her and immediately
started to apologize for Claude about whom John, as yet, knew
nothing. Elizabeth, who had thought that perhaps they would have
to endure coffee and each person trying to think of things to say
that would be all right for the other two, realized from her glazed
expression and oddly trembling mouth that she was very near
breaking down again: it would be better if they left as quickly as
possible.

So this they did. Claude, whose protests had settled in volume
much as a long distance runner adjusts his speed to the course,
was put on the back seat with Elizabeth's small red case beside
him. Elizabeth thanked Alice again for having her: they kissed,
and their noses bumped together painfully.

'I promise I'll take him home to May.'

'I know: thank you so much for coming, Elizabeth.'

She stood at the gate—it looked absurdly small beside her, too—
and waved to them like someone who had never done it before.
When Elizabeth turned back for the last time, she was still waving.

As soon as they were out of sight, John stopped the car and put
Claude's basket in the boot which he propped open. 'I've nothing
against him, you understand, but I want to keep it that way.'

'As long as he can breathe.'

'Lots of fresh air in that boot.'

'He loses his voice in about forty miles.' She couldn't help feeling a bit guilty about him.

'Where are we going?' she asked some time later.

'Somewhere nice: *I* don't know. Let's just—see.'

They were out of Bristol by now, into the rich green and multi-coloured country: fields of ripe corn; hedgerows overgrown with flowering brambles; cottage gardens choked and blazing, the thick, grassy verge crammed with poppies and buttercups and cow parsley ... She thought of Alice jammed in the house Leslie had built, pregnant, and still, in spite of marriage, lonelier than she had seemed before: of her mother, doggedly frittering her time away with menial and unnecessary tasks for a bore; and of Oliver, wasting his brilliance and youth for lack of opportunity or purpose or something like that ... She did not want to think about Oliver; in fact, in her selfish way, she did not want to think about any of them: they all added up to life being some kind of tightrope; if you were on it and didn't look down, everything seemed easy, but if you even began to look down ...

FIVE

ONE FINE DAY

W HEN she could no longer even hear their car, Alice turned back to
the bungalow. It was going to be another baking day. She had
planted three white geraniums in the piece of earth that she had
marked out for a flower-bed, and already their lower leaves were
wilting. In any case, only three plants in a whole garden looked odd
and wrong, but it had been too late to sow the lawn and the man who
was to turf it had not turned up. There was no shade in the garden,
it was really just a rectangle of ploughed-up earth with a garden
path laid at one side of it. Then there was the house with the puppy.
The black dots that lay in wait one inch from her eyeballs took yet
another curtain call—diminishing as though sinking to the bottom
of a curtsy and then bobbing up again. She started walking up the
path, trying to find things to notice that would stop the sick, empty
feeling that seemed to come and go but always to come back. The
puppy was alternately hurling himself against the study door and
howling. The thought occurred to her that it would be possible
just not to go into the house at all; she was perfectly in control of
herself—all she had to do was *not* go on walking towards the front
door: she could stop everything as simply as that ... But still she
would have to be somewhere. She shut the door very slowly and
leaned against it: breathing had become something she was having
to notice to make sure it went on happening. She went into the
sitting-room meaning to sit down somewhere and wait for things
to get better, but the room, when she reached it and looked round
her, seemed so horrible, so arranged to expose her as an alien,
neither at home nor even at ease, that she couldn't sit alone there.
In her underclothes drawer in the bedroom—hidden beneath the

pastel Celanese and nylon lace—was the red-leather book that she had bought in Barcelona. It had thick, white paper with gilded edges. Into this she copied her poems when they were as finished as she could make them. She took the book back to the sitting-room and sat for a long time with it on her lap. Sometimes she looked at the poems: she knew them by heart, and also exactly what they looked like in her writing on the page, but it was comforting to look. They were never really what she had meant, but they reminded her of whatever that had been; it was the nearest she got to being able to tell anyone anything, and in reading or recalling them, she was able to become somebody else whom she was telling. This made it the opposite of lonely. The last poem was about the bird in Cornwall.

* * *

'But it said: PRIVATE ROAD!'

And John, maddeningly like Oliver, replied, 'So it did.'

They were driving through a beech wood, a chequered, green cavern—ahead was the sunlit, tunnel-shaped exit: it looked dazzling and mysterious, but then they were out and it was just ordinary summer afternoon light. On either side of the narrow road were hedge and meadow, the road curved, declined, and then straightened, and on their left, the other side of a field, and set a little above it, was a very square and pretty house. John stopped the car. It was built of stone so bleached by the sun that it was neither grey, nor white, nor cream. The shallow roof was almost concealed by elaborate stone coping, and the middle of the front was entirely covered by wisteria. John got out of the car.

'Where are you going?'

'To explore. Come on.'

'I'm sure it's private property.'

'Awful for them if it wasn't,' he said cheerfully, and opened a wicket gate. There was a wide path of cropped or scythed grass which led straight across the meadow towards the house. This, she now saw, was in fact set on a terrace some ten or twelve feet above them, that was faced with the same stone and contained a black painted door in the centre and at their level. John was striding towards this. She followed him because if he was going to get into trouble it would be disloyal not to get into it with him, and also perhaps she might prevent him from doing anything too idiotic. The door would be locked anyway, she betted. But to her dismay, he opened it easily and walked through.

'John!'

'Don't you want to see the house? I thought it was rather pretty.'

She caught him up. 'John honestly!'

He had begun on the flight of shallow stone steps that clearly led up to the terrace above them.

'It's August,' he said. 'People who live in this sort of house are always away then. Don't be such a little stickler: you know we don't mean to do any harm.'

'Gardeners,' she said: it was awful being shown up as craven and law-abiding.

'We can always deal with them.'

They had reached a lawn path hedged with sweetbriar. He picked a piece of this and held it out to her. 'Pinch it.'

'There you go—*taking* things now!'

'Where's your sense of adventure?'

'Oh—don't *shout*!' They were now only about twenty yards from the house from which there was no sign of life. Blinds, she saw, were down on the upper windows: perhaps everybody *was* away. 'What do you want to do?' She felt it would be better if she knew.

'Just have a look round.' He seized her hand and walked her rapidly up to the long, narrow windows of what turned out to be a dining-room. 'Dinner is laid for two,' he said after peering in.

'They must be somewhere about, then,' she said, trying to sound reasonable rather than terrified. But already he had gone ahead and was disappearing round the corner of the house. 'It would be worse to be caught without him,' she thought. Bees in the wisteria were making the outdoor equivalent of ticking clocks in empty houses—too loud and the only noise she could hear. She followed him, and away from the bees became aware of her heart beating.

Round the corner was a conservatory tacked on to the house. It was quite large, and hexagonal in shape. The garden door stood propped open by a watering can, and she could see that it had a black and white marble floor. There were pots of geraniums and fuchsias, a table and various garden chairs, a french window leading into the house, but what really struck her was a tea trolley laid with an elaborate country tea and a kettle actually over a spirit lamp.

'John! Honestly! They'll be coming to have tea any minute.'

But he simply went in and took a cucumber sandwich and then flung himself into a basket chaise-longue. 'If anyone else *does* turn up we can always ask for more cups. Come and have a sandwich, dearest Eliza. They're awfully good, they've got that touch of curry powder in them.'

She stared at him: he was smiling—nearly laughing.

'I own all these sandwiches,' he said.

'Is this your house then?'

'It is, actually.'

She stared at him a second longer and then burst into tears. 'Absolutely *beastly*—you are!'

'Darling Liz—I couldn't resist it; it was only a joke—'

'Not at all of a joke!'

'You were so funny: I never knew you had such a law-abiding nature—' He got out of the chair; she was crying more; he would have to apologize to make her feel better. 'I'm terribly sorry, and I'll never do it again—'

But she interrupted, 'You couldn't! I know all your other houses.'

'Oh no, you don't. There is yet another, in Jamaica, so I could do it again, but I won't. Cheer up. Think how much better it will be to have a nice tea than be chased off the premises by an angry and righteous owner. I'm not angry or righteous.'

'You're just smug and horrible.' But she mopped up her face and sat down and made the tea for them both.

* * *

Leslie had felt quite upset by all the fuss about the cat. The point wasn't that Alice was unreasonable—there was no question but that she was *that*—it was whether in her condition he shouldn't perhaps have tried to humour her more?

Naturally he didn't want her to be upset. The worst thing about marriage—in its early years at least—seemed to be the terrible way you couldn't take anything for granted—had to keep on noticing the other person, making allowances or putting your foot down, not to mention changing all your social habits, it *was* taken for granted you'd do that. And what did you get for it? The cooking wasn't up to Mother's, although it wasn't bad. Company, but really when he came to think of it, he wasn't at all sure that women were much good at that side of life. He wouldn't have married a vulgar bit like Phyllis Bryson for instance, joining in the laughs at men's stories in the pub: no thanks, not for him. There was the sexual intercourse side of things, but here again, you ran into trouble. It had become clear to him by degrees that Alice didn't seem to be all that keen on it—intercourse, he meant—not that he would necessarily have thought the more of her if she had been; when you came to think of it there wasn't any way that a woman could be enthusiastic about intercourse and still be what for want of a better word he could only call decent. So it wasn't exactly that he wanted Alice any different in the dark to what she was, so much as, being a normal man, he sometimes felt he could do with a change. He supposed that when she'd had a couple of kids everything might settle down and become more normal. After all, everyone went through it. This last reflection cheered him up and he decided to phone Rosemary to see if she could pop over to Alice and cheer her up a bit.

'Down in the dumps, is she?' Rosemary's voice had the kind of cheery, professional concern that implied that this was nonsense of Alice, but that it could be dealt with by someone who knew how. Leslie explained about Claude and Elizabeth coming for the night.

'Deary me: what a storm in a tea-cup! Not to worry: I'll drop over and see if I can't take her out of herself.'

Leslie put down the phone much relieved. Rosemary was a good sort; she could be a real tonic if she tried. Alice always seemed especially pleased to see him on the days when Rosemary had been over.

✳   ✳   ✳

After tea, he said, 'Elizabeth! We've got to talk. Shall we do it now, or would you rather wait until after dinner?'

'I'd rather start now.' The thought of waiting for a serious talk once you knew that it was going to happen was awful.

'I don't even know whether talking about it is going to make you understand, but at least I've got to try.'

'Yes.'

There was a very long silence. A Spanish servant had cleared away the tea and been given instructions about the car and Claude. He had asked what time they wished to dine and then padded quietly away. The silence went on much longer than just waiting for the Spaniard to go.

'Goodness! This is much worse than I thought,' he said at last.

'The thing is, I must have seemed an awful coward in France: when Jennifer came and everything went to pieces. Well, you see, I *am*: that's what she does to me. I don't mean it's just about you, any more than I mean that there have been a lot of other girls. It's really anything I try to do except make money. It's partly why I've got so much money and hardly do anything.'

'*Why* does she?'

'There are two aspects of that question. Why does she *want* to stop me having any kind of life, and how does she manage to succeed?'

'Well, start with why she wants to.'

'That's not very difficult. Jennifer, at a very early age, was deprived of her mother. Even before that, she was deprived of a motherly mother, if you see what I mean. Howling egocentrics like Daphne take up having children like archery or the harpsichord; they soon find you have to work at it far harder than the effect seems worth. Jennifer was never an easy child. When I finally divorced Daphne, she was old enough to know what was going on in a way, but she certainly wasn't old enough not to look at the whole thing entirely in terms of her own loss or gain. She'd lost a mother: she'd won me as it were. I've been a kind of hostage for her security ever since. Children seem to be rather good at that.'

'But—she isn't a child now, any more, is she?'

He looked slightly taken aback: then he said, 'I told you, she's very young for her age.'

'But she still doesn't have to be treated as a child, does she?'

'I'm not at all sure that I know how *else* to treat her.'

This seemed to stop either of them having anything to say.

'We've got plenty of time to talk about this,' he said in the end. 'Do be sure of one thing. Somehow I've got to make you understand, in fact we may have to stay here until you do. Come on: I'm going to show you the house.'

* * *

'So having thought about it a great deal—' she corrected herself, 'as much as I possibly could—it did seem that this was the only useful contribution I could make. Even though it is only pot*en*tially useful.' And she smiled apologetically: in spite of feeling like death, she might easily live to be eighty …

Dr Sedum seemed to clear his throat and say something at the same time.

'I'm sorry: what did you say?' It had sounded like 'furry concerns' which it couldn't have been.

But it was family considerations that Dr Sedum had mentioned.

'Oh no: that's—they're quite all right. I asked my children, Oliver and Elizabeth, you know, and they would both *far* prefer to have the little house in Chelsea. So *that* is all right.' She paused, because, actually, the rest of it—meaning Herbert, wasn't: yet.

'I shall have to discuss it with my husband of course.'

Dr Sedum nearly shut his eyes and rocked slowly backwards in his huge chair.

'It's just a matter of telling him, really. I mean—much though he seems to love the place, he couldn't possibly manage there without me. He'd be fearfully lonely and uncomfortable and he hates being either of those things. It's just a matter of telling him,' she repeated, beginning to dread the thought.

They were sitting in the sitting-room in Dr Sedum's mews in Belgravia. In spite of it being a hot and sunny afternoon, the room was so dark that May would not have been able to see to read in it. This also meant that it was difficult to see Dr Sedum's face clearly, which in turn meant that it was harder than usual to understand what he said. In the spring—the only other time she had been there—there had been lamps lit and it had been much easier. But now, although the curtains were not drawn and there were windows at each end of the room, she could see that one of them faced a quite alarmingly close, black, brick wall and the other was entirely covered by the leaves and branches of some dusty evergreen. The room smelled of coffee and stale clothes. Dr Sedum always offered people coffee and they always accepted, and a girl called Muriel who typed all day in a tiny little room by the entrance door always heated it up a bit and brought it in. There was a sugar substitute and some powdered milk in a pottery jar that you could have as well. May had had some powdered milk, as she was afraid that black coffee (which had at one time been instant and then constantly reheated) would make her indigestion worse.

Dr Sedum said something that sounded like 'evil suspense'. It couldn't be that.

'What?' she said.

It turned out to be 'legal aspects': he wanted to know if she had a good lawyer.

'Oh, I think so,' she responded vaguely. She had thought that lawyers, by the nature of their profession, being fair and everything, must really all be the same. 'He was my first husband's lawyer,' she added. Lawyers, she felt, were not a thing in her life that Dr Sedum could expect to change. But he just smiled in a conclusive manner, and said let him know how things went, so she knew that the interview was over before they had had time to talk about anything in the least interesting. He shook hands with her at the head of the steep and narrow stairs, and Muriel met her at the bottom. Through the half-open door to Muriel's office she could see that someone

189

else was waiting to see Dr Sedum and she wondered if they, too, had had to think up some great practical reason for the privilege of spending half an hour alone with him.

*   *   *

'*You* say something about it.'

'What shall I say?'

'Well you could at least ask questions,' he said—not only irritably for him, but pretty crossly for anyone, Elizabeth thought. Still, questions seemed a sensible idea: the only difficulty was that they were all very hard questions for *her* to ask.

'Do you mean that she—Jennifer—will make things awful whenever she turns up?'

'I suppose I mean that she might.'

'When mightn't she?'

'I suppose if she got used to the situation—felt it didn't threaten her: or, I suppose, she might fall in love with someone herself.'

There was a silence while these distant possibilities receded still further.

Then, using a certain amount of courage, she asked, 'Is it our having an affair that she finds so objectionable?'

'Don't know: don't think so. You mean, if we were respectably married, she'd be all right?'

'I did mean that; yes.'

'I don't know,' he said again. 'The trouble is that one can't do that sort of thing as an experiment. It would be so frightful if we were wrong about it.'

'But it *couldn't* be an experiment—from the point of view of Jennifer! I mean it simply isn't enough her business to be that!'

'Perhaps it oughtn't to be—but it is.'

'It certainly oughtn't to be,' she said feeling angry and wanting to cry. 'She's not a child; she's twenty. Like me!'

'She's not like you—at all.' He said this very sadly, and she began at once to feel less angry and more sad.

They were sitting in the window seat of his dressing-room.

Outside, the orange and violet of the sky was slowly darkening out: milky mist was rising from the meadow and a young owl was trying out his cry that sounded with sudden, juicy, jack-in-a-box ease— probably frightening even him Elizabeth thought.

'You have to give her a chance to grow up?' she said with a slight question at the end so that it didn't sound too obvious or patronizing.

'But we can't get married to do it,' he said. 'Come on—we'd better go and have dinner.'

* * *

'... in witness thereof I have hereunto set my hand this blank day of blank nineteen hundred and blankety blank.' He cleared his throat, took a final swig of the cold tea and looked expectantly at his audience. 'I sign it of course; George Frederick Herbert etc. etc.' He made a point of never telling people like Hilda his real surname: you never knew what that kind of woman might get up to if she was given the chance.

He had been reading for nearly twenty minutes. Mr Pinkney, that solicitor chap, had drawn up a draft according to his specifications which, broadly speaking, were that he was leaving everything to his dearly beloved wife Viola May: he had fetched it that morning, lunched at the club where he had tried unsuccessfully to interest the member who had introduced him to Mr Pinkney with the results of this introduction—the member had simply said all wills made him feel morbid, old man: so now, after a little spot of dash with her, here he was reading the thing to Hilda. He had read over the whole caboodle in Mr Pinkney's office and again over his lunch at the club, but somehow, to get the full flavour of it, it needed to be read aloud, and by God it brought out the best in him when he did. He read well—hadn't fully recognized this talent in himself—and felt staggered, confounded, positively intoxicated by his own generosity. He was leaving everything, every single blasted little thing to Viola May. Not simply his shares, but clothes, weapons, mementoes, books, the car, the dogs, a hell of a lot of snapshots of damned interesting and unusual places, some jolly good books—well he'd mentioned them, but not what they were: classics, mostly, but some pretty rare books on India as well—eye-witness accounts of the Mutiny, for instance, which some feller had had privately printed—all long before his time, of course, but after all, he'd served there, knew the country better than most, and that book was a piece of exclusive history as it were; probably highly valuable if truth were known and by no means the only rare book of the lot; then his stamp collection—heaven only knew what that would fetch ... then there was all the furniture he had bought for Monks' Close; hundreds of chairs, whacking great pictures, filing cabinets, fire-irons, his transistor radio set. All his clothes were made of far better cloth than you could buy nowadays, so even they would fetch a good bit ... his mind was crammed with these and other generous assessments (he'd insisted on Mr Pinkney itemizing his possessions in groups or catagories—otherwise the whole document would have been barely two pages) and he had to admit that the whole thing sounded very well ... He looked across the small room to Hilda again. She was sitting in the other chair—the upright one—with her feet on a small footstool, her hands tucked into her kimono sleeves, her plumpish chin resting in the vee of its low neckline, her eyes indubitably closed. How like a woman! A feeling of hatred for her surged up, made his gorge rise as the saying went, only it didn't stop but went on up to his head so that he felt that something up there was going to explode. Steady on! The doctor had said months ago that his blood pressure was up and that he shouldn't indulge in undue agitation: a nice thing if having just read his will he was to drop dead! He could see the funny side of that: nobody could say he hadn't got a sense of humour. He started to take deep, quietening breaths and just then, Hilda opened her eyes and said, 'Very nice, Bogey.'

'That seems a peculiar word to use.'

'Well, striking as well. You've got such a lovely reading voice, it wouldn't matter what you read. A really lovely voice,' she repeated. Her mouth opened in the perfect O of a yawn and she laid the palm of her hand over it before any sound could come out.

Of course she'd been asleep; he wasn't easily fooled. It had been foolish of him ever to think that she had the intelligence to be interested. He decided to be getting along. Where? The thought of tooling back to Surrey and a quiet supper with poor old May was suddenly depressing. He didn't *enjoy* her feeling so under the weather, dammit, it was just that some things could not be helped. It wasn't much fun for *him* sitting it out week after week, but you couldn't always do things just as you wanted to—had to take a long view and all that.

He got to the door before Hilda reminded him about the money. Then she reminded him that it was an extra thirty bob—she wasn't one to forget the money, was our Hilda! He said this as he chucked her rather painfully under the chin before she shut the door. What he would do was have a spot of dinner at the club and see if anyone felt like a game of billiards. He could telephone May from the club: women always appreciated little thoughtful gestures of that kind ...

*   *   *

'The worst thing is, you see, that I don't—I can't—I simply feel terribly guilty about her. All the time. As though the whole of her was my fault.'

They were lying in bed, both of them still and Elizabeth silent as well.

'Most fathers love their daughters:' he gave a short, unlifelike laugh, 'sometimes they're supposed to love them too much. The trouble is that I never have.

'I never meant to say any of this to you, in fact, I meant very much *not* to say it. The fact is that you only really feel guilty about people you don't love. The other thing is that if you feel guilty about somebody, something sad and knowing in them finds out *and* knows the reason why. Then there is the shady little game of trying to compensate them.'

'How do you mean?'

'Oh giving them things, and putting up with being bored or inconvenienced by them, and hating anyone else to criticize them —all that. And of course they play that game: why not? Nearly everyone settles for what they can get in the end.'

'Do they?' The thought appalled her, but she felt that she must remain non-committal.

'If she'd had a normal sort of mother I suppose the whole thing would have been less emphasized—'

'Do you feel guilty about *her?*'

'Daphne? Oh, years ago, I did; before we parted company. But I got so cross with her for always letting Jennifer down that there stopped being any *ought* about loving her—Daphne, I mean—'

'Well I don't think there should be any ought about loving Jennifer now. I can't see why she shouldn't see her mother if that is what either of them wants, and if they don't, let them sort it out on their own.'

'You think the whole thing is a storm in a tea-cup,' he said coldly, a minute later.

'I think you'll simply turn Jennifer into some sort of monster if you go on protecting her *and* letting her bully you.'

'Perhaps that is what I want. To prove that she's a monster, so that I am excused for never having loved her. That's a convincing little by-way psychologically speaking, wouldn't you say?'

'I don't know.' She sat up and swung her legs over the side of the bed. 'I don't see why you have to be so determined that she'll bring out the worst in you. I'm sick of psychology anyway and the way people keep falling back on it. I thought we were going to talk about what we were going to *do*—about—everything, not just go on and on about what you and Jennifer feel or don't feel about each other.' She realized rather belatedly that she was naked, which somehow didn't go with feeling angry, so she seized his dressing-gown and started cramming her hands into the armholes.

'Where are you going?'

'Have a bath.'

He sat up and began getting out of bed. 'It's no good, Elizabeth: girls *do* feel strongly about their fathers—nobody can get round that.'

'I wouldn't know: I never even saw mine.' She tried to slam the bathroom door, but it shut and then swung open and he was standing there. They stared at each other: it had never been like this before and the horrible novelty made both of them speechless. But only a few seconds later, he said,

'I think we'll postpone the ugly rush to grovel.' It was going to be all right: not the same—but all right.

* * *

Oliver had been relieved when John Cole had rung up inquiring for Elizabeth. He had been extremely resourceful about getting the Bristol telephone number, which Elizabeth had written with her finger on the greasiest bit of kitchen ceiling just above the gas cooker without telling him that that was where she had put it (he'd worked out at lightning speed where she had been when she'd taken the number) and he'd finished the conversation with what he hoped was just the right degree of nonchalant friend-liness: 'Goodbye, then: hope you find her,' was what he had said. But then, noticing that he felt relieved that *that* was all right, he began to feel slightly irritated; either he had to keep on feeling sorry for Liz, or else she was having a bloody marvellous time. On the whole, he preferred being sorry for her, partly because he saw more of her then. But what about *his* life? When anyone else asked this question, he would airily shut them up (that was one thing he liked about Ginny; she only ever asked him what he was going to do that evening) but sometimes, like *this* evening, he started to wonder about the whole business and found it difficult to stop. Bitter little tags after Housman (after all, *he* was twenty-*four*); famous men with melancholia; philosophy seeming to go *on* finding out that man was vile; the revolting expense of the slightest luxury; the rank bad luck of not knowing exactly what he was for; the frightful lack of saints or anyone seriously different from and better than anyone else (he could keep his discontent on quite a high plane if he tried); the feeling that though he was not particularly happy or well off things could quickly get infinitely, alarmingly, much worse; the sensation he sometimes had of peddling his own life endlessly uphill—having to keep at it all the time or at the best nothing happened; at the worst one could slide with unearthly ease into some abyss—the alternative to which certainly didn't seem to be a bloody marvellous time. Sometimes he thought it was because she wasn't very clever that Liz nearly always seemed to feel all right; sometimes he thought that perhaps he was simply living in the wrong time. In what other century would he be sitting on a cramped and crumbling balcony looking on to a dull, dusty street whose air was thick with diesel fumes, eating a Mars Bar that had clearly been kept too long, while from some open window or other a gobbled Oxford voice roved suavely round the world remarking on its chaos, and *he* wondered what the hell to do that wouldn't cost too much or be too boring? He began thinking how else it might have been at various times and ages ... Hock and seltzer with Oscar and Robbie—a delightful dinner for about seven and six (he decided not to bother about inflation: calculations about which would ruin imaginative nostalgia) ... or he might be lying in a hip bath in front of a coal fire in a huge bedroom, frequently waited on by pretty young maids with rosy cheeks and tiny waists, then dressing for the house-party dinner before the ball where he would dance with a delightful young creature called Maud or Gwendolen—in white, of course, with ivy leaves in her hair. There was a bit of a gap here, but there he was again, or could be, downing his second bottle of port (unfortified, naturally, in those days) with a group of chaps who knew a thing or two about the army, the navy or the Church, with whom he would have dined by now, before riding to drink tea with some delightful sisters called Mary and Ann and Elizabeth and Jane, whose simple life in the wilds of Hampstead had all the charm that reflects upon true elegance of mind and refinement of nature ... they would run to greet him on little slippered feet, muslin skirts flying—the youngest barely fifteen but already proficient at all the sweet and useless accomplishments that were thought proper and desirable: netting, fan- and table-painting, making pens and embroidering anything they could lay their hands on. Earlier—he was getting hazy about how much—he would be riding back from a jolly good day's hawking—a castle this time, but nice and clean—they'd only have been there about a week: the smells would be merely festive, roasting wild boar and hare, perhaps a swan or two; a serf would run to his stirrup with a beaker of spiced—ale would it be, or mead?—and up some tortuously twisting stair would be someone with immensely long hair called Margaret or Philippa, who'd had nothing to do all day except wait for him …

When the telephone rang, he was so physically wedged in the balcony that quite a lot of plaster fell on to the dustbins in the area by the time he got out, and he had time to get excited about who might be ringing him up.

It was May: not even a girl he wasn't particularly attracted to or had got tired of, but his mother. He snorted and she immediately asked him if he'd got a cold.

'Good God, no!'

'All right, darling; I only asked.'

'I should have thought you'd had enough practice at being a mother not to ask that sort of thing.'

'Clearly not.'

That was better. He smiled, and said, 'Where are you and what do you want?'

'Well, I thought we might have a drink together.'

'Where *are* you?'

'In a call box. Is Elizabeth there, because do bring her if she is.'

'She's in Bristol.'

'Well get into a taxi and come straight away darling, because I'll have to catch a train—hurry up—'

'We'll never meet if you don't tell me where you are—'

'Knightsbridge tube station: don't be long because there may not be anywhere here to sit down …'

She was standing anxiously at the Sloane Street entrance: she looked as though she could do with a drink. He paid off the taxi and took her to a pub in Kinnerton Street. When they were both established with glasses, he said, 'What have you been doing all by yourself in London? Isn't it a bit risky to be seen after shopping hours in Sloane Street?'

She blushed faintly, but retorted, 'It has always amazed me the way the moment you have a life of your own you assume that I

can't possibly have one. You behave as though I should only come
to London for the dentist and Peter Jones. I might easily have friends
and interests of my own, you know.'

'Oh, I doubt it. At your age I should have thought—'

'And what are *your* interests may I ask?'

'You really mustn't try to change the whole *tone* of a conversation with no warning like that. I've got no news. No news is bad
news with me as you've probably noticed, and as I find it very
depressing, I've nothing to say about it. It really is awful,' he went
on a moment later after he had refused to meet her eye, 'the way
you keep on wanting me to start something and I keep on wanting you to stop.'

They looked at each other; both knew which way the conversation was going; but the familiar challenge—the routine reluctance—
was too much for either effectively to resist.

'You want me to set about almost *anything* from nine to five—and
I hope you jolly well realize that at no other time in history would
your maternal instinct take such a poky and squalid form—while
I simply want you to stop living with such a preposterous bore. I
want your life to be nicer while you seem to want *my* life to be
harder—harder and even more boring.'

'You're bored because you *don't* do anything.'

'Am I?'

'Everybody has to have some sense of direction.'

'Do they?'

'After all, we all know that externals don't matter in the least.'

'Is that so? And if it is—so, I mean—why do you care whether I'm
doing anything or not?' Then, lowering his voice, he added, 'I suppose
you realize that everyone is so fascinated by the thrust and parry of
this conversation that they're not only not talking to one another—
they're not even *drinking*. I won that round. While I get us a refill,
you think of three reasons why you should go on living with Daddo.'

He was quite right; it was a small bar and the few customers all
had that glassy air of covert attention to someone else's business.
Even the landlord put down his paper with a hearty start when
Oliver reached him with the glasses. Three reasons ... But the

moment there *had* to be reasons for being married to somebody there weren't any. When Oliver came back with their drinks she smiled firmly and said, 'It's ridiculous of you to blacken poor Herbert in this silly way. Anyone would think he was some kind of *criminal*. I admit he's a weeny bit—old-fashioned in his ways; staid— what you doubtless call dull, but he means well—in fact he's really very kind and protective—he *minds* what happens to me ...' To her discomforted amazement, she seemed to be crying: tears that could not have come from anywhere but her own eyes were slopping on to the drink-rimmed table and Oliver seemed enormous and blurred.

'... a dry eye in this family's a full-time job. Sorry, darling. Darling May, I swear I'll never criticize him again: if you don't stop crying you'll qualify for a short which I don't have enough cash for. So do try to stop because you know how mean I am.'

'Buy us both brandies,' she said when she was over it.

'Let's have dinner,' he said when the brandies were gone.

'Oh darling—I would love to, but I can't. Poor Herbert would feel so abandoned if he gets back and I'm not there.'

So he took her to the station and she caught the seven fifty-five. The cab passed Herbert's club where he was drinking a gin and peach bitters and reading the *Evening Standard*.

*   *   *

When Oliver had seen his mother off (standing on the platform watching in case she waved, with 'Colonel Bogey' on the amplifying system) he had so little money and so little to do that he walked. On Westminster Bridge he wondered about becoming a politician, but then somehow he felt that it might seem to imply a basic sympathy with the status quo and he wasn't at all sure that he had enough of that ... When he got to Victoria Street and passed the Army and Navy Stores, the idea of being an explorer came and went. There was hardly anywhere left to explore that wasn't so nasty and difficult to be in that one wouldn't really enjoy it ... He plodded on. It wasn't that he liked not being able to think of anything to do: it wasn't even that he didn't try to think of something,

it was simply that the only things that seemed to him at all nice—
like living with darling Elizabeth or meeting a new, wildly attractive
girl and going to bed with her long before he knew her too well—
were neither of them money-spinners, and delicious meals and
foreign holidays clearly used money up. He knew he was meant
for better things: it was just a question of knowing which ones.

* * *

'What you mean is that if you married me I might *get* to want children, and then, whatever we said or did about it—everything would
go wrong?'

'Something like that;' he was watching her face very closely.

'Oh.' She knew he was watching her and kept her face deliberately still, not realizing that he would notice that as much as he
would notice anything else.

They were sitting at the end of a small lawn edged with yew.
Behind them, on a stone pedestal, was a stone lady whose naked
back was turned but whose downcast profile was visible as she
looked for ever over her shoulder and down upon the lawn.

'Why are you so sure I'd want them?'

'I'm not. It simply isn't a risk I feel able to take. At the moment,
I mean.'

After another long pause, she said, 'So what do we do?'

'It isn't lack of love. I can't imagine loving anybody more than I
love you, but I still seem to have some of the perfect fear left over.
Darling.'

A little of the strained unconcern left her face as she repeated,
'What shall we do?'

'Not part, and stay as we are together at the moment, that means
nothing. We'll do nothing: just live.' He took her hand and stroked
the back of it gently. 'Do you like this house?'

'Best?'

'Good. We'll spend all my spare time in it.'

'We'll not get married and not have children but stay together,'
she said, but asking for confirmation.

'What do you think?'

'I don't mind about the marrying or children part: I just want to stay with you.'

PART THREE

December

ONE

·⚬·

JAMAICA

THE trouble was that if she relaxed she fell out of the bunk and if she braced herself against the next quivering, uneven plunge, she could not get to sleep. John was all right: he was so tall that even lying as diagonally as his bunk permitted he was naturally wedged, and provided he didn't try to move he seemed to be safe and able to have long refreshing sleeps that Elizabeth quite envied. Sometimes she would give up trying to sleep and kneel upright to look out of the port-hole. The sea and the sky—an angry grey and skim milk that heaved and pounded and lurched—were so tilted and confused together that she felt quite glad to have this scene bounded by the round, brass rim. Sometimes she struggled with the giant screw that made livid rust marks on the glossy white paint until she could free it and swing the window open. Then a strong soft wind beat against her face like the damp wings of some powerful bird; she could put her head out and feel it more, withdraw, and hear the domestic creaks of wood straining against the sea and feel more sharply the vibration made by the engines—a kind of solid and busy reassurance. It was not a bad storm, just ordinary Atlantic December weather, they said; the forecast—after a day or two more—was good, they would all be sitting out on deck sunning themselves, they'd see. Elizabeth did not care. She did not feel in the least sick, and was perfectly happy. This was the third day out, the time was so packed with traditional activity that they seemed to be living in crowded slow motion, and already she felt as though they had been in the ship for weeks. The first thing was China tea at seven in the morning with the breakfast menu, as John liked to have that meal—a large one—in privacy. 'I like tea, and then you, and then breakfast.'

Getting up took ages because of having to hold on to something nearly all the time, but there were nice things about it: the shower was like a scorching cloud-burst and could be salty or fresh; shoes got cleaned every day and towels seemed always to be new. On the first morning they had got themselves wrapped in rugs on deck and were given cups of steaming Bovril—called beef tea—as though, Elizabeth thought, they were really precious and had been frightfully ill. That morning they had also walked—round and round—holding hands and not talking at all. Even then she had still been worrying—had not been absolutely certain: and so the newly-minted feeling of beginning, of being festive and shining and unused, had been rubbed with anxiety. She couldn't, or wouldn't, ask: it was then that she discovered how often someone may inquire about the welfare of another simply in order that—having got the right answer—they may dismiss them from their mind. Of course, *she* didn't want to do that, but if she asked, he might have to lie and that was something that he shouldn't have to do—with her at least. So they walked until he said, 'That's enough to earn us a drink,' and they went in to the large saloon where the tables and chairs were screwed to the deck and she found that he had ordered a bottle of champagne and wondered if that, too, didn't smack a bit of going through the motions until he had said, 'I asked for this because it was our first drink—do you remember?' and when he smiled at her she remembered the first time he had ever done that and the extraordinary difference it made to his face.

'You're smiling a great deal,' he said.

'Am I?'

'Every time anyone looks at you.'

'Oh. Oh dear.'

'They're all loving it. It's an excellent thing, really, because a good many people with fringes look rather stern in repose. Dear Mrs Cole.'

The first lunch time the saloon was fairly crowded; the wind was freshening, but only enough for people to make jokes about it. The menu was enormous, the tables elaborately set with linen and silver and flowers: stewards charged skilfully through swing doors and rushed about with a high degree of bustling order. The captain sat at a round table with seven such hideously boring-looking, although otherwise assorted, people that John and Elizabeth (alone at a table for two) spent most of the meal trying to think what they could all be. In the end they settled for a sociologist, his wife, who wrote children's books, an ex-mountaineer who'd made a belated fortune out of windproof garments, and *his* wife who bred Afghan hounds, and a bucolic man who'd always been a baronet with a woman who'd always been just a wife. That left one lady whose appearance was so ambiguous that it was far from clear what she could ever have accomplished. A widow of one of the directors of the line, they decided weakly.

'Poor captain.' On this particular day, Elizabeth had been disposed to think everyone more unfortunate than herself.

After that first lunch, she had slept for three hours and woken to find John sitting by her bunk with tea.

'In case you are harbouring the slightest doubts I'm really finding being married to you much nicer than I thought.'

Later they played backgammon and drank Planter's Punches in the bar. That night it began to get rough and now here it was, just about as rough as she felt she could manage. Already, quite a lot of people couldn't manage it. The captain's table had shrunk to the ex-mountaineer, minus wife, and the captain. Table-cloths were damped, the ledges round the tables were up, but still whole table-fuls of glass and china crashed to the ground. The stewards charging through the swing doors often lost the contents of their trays before they reached the few stalwart passengers who continued to appear for meals, but morale seemed high, the ship was excellently run and the large jovial captain exuded efficiency and good will. Walking round the deck was out of the question now: they ate and read (backgammon was no good as everything slid about too much) and had drinks, made love a good deal, and John slept while Elizabeth dozed and dreamed.

The wedding had only escaped being awful by its shortness. She had spent the night before it at Lincoln Street with Oliver. 'At least you're not having to put up with me in pink net. Or Daddo making speeches,' he added after a time. They were both sitting on her bed;

Oliver was polishing her shoes and drinking Guinness which he said made his spit more nourishing to shoe leather. John had particularly not wanted family about (the Jennifer situation) and Elizabeth, with reasons none the less violent for being indefinable, seemed absolutely determined on keeping the colonel and John apart. They had met very briefly when Elizabeth and John had returned Claude to Monks' Close: they had arrived without warning at the innocuous hour of tea time, but this had so enraged the colonel that May had thought he was going to have a stroke. They had 'broken in' on him when he was in the greenhouse mixing something up for the lawn; no common courtesy left—he'd looked up from measuring something because he thought he'd heard a sound behind him, and there was this giant stranger without so much as a by-your-leave standing over him—enough to give any honest feller a heart attack. He'd lost his temper: not for long, but enough to make everyone feel intensely embarrassed; then he'd stalked off to find Elizabeth's mother. Poor May had made the mistake of offering them tea, which was accepted, and this had made the colonel stalk even farther—down the drive in fact, with a clashing of gears in the old Wolseley. May had had such an awful time with him afterwards that she had collapsed—in tears—and the next day had gone so far as to suggest that perhaps she and Herbert were not really suited ... but he wouldn't hear of that ...

So in the end only Oliver and McNaughton, the charming Scottish chauffeur who had brought a bunch of dahlias grown by himself, had come to the registry office. They had all waited in a small, ugly room until called into a larger ugly room where the ceremony was performed. After Oliver and McNaughton had witnessed the certificate they went back to the first room, already full of the next wedding party; people staring at their own white shoes and the gap between their hands on their dark blue serge knees; people speaking so quietly out of shyness and discomfort that in the end they said everything again much too loudly. It all looked a bit like having a collective tooth out, Oliver had said. They had packed into the Rolls and McNaughton had driven them to Claridge's where John had taken a room. McNaughton parked the car and joined them for a drink or two and then left them. Elizabeth had wanted him to stay to lunch, but John had said that McNaughton had been quite firm about that. You could drink with anyone, he had said, but you couldn't enjoy a meal outside your own class. He'd fetch them at three. They were driving to Southampton, to catch the boat for Jamaica. As soon as McNaughton had gone, Oliver had said that if they didn't mind, and even possibly if they did, he didn't think he would come to Southampton: he'd feel too awful for too long coming back. The other two immediately said of course not and how much they understood, but everybody was a little dashed by this: Elizabeth had begun imagining him going back to Lincoln Street by himself until he said don't worry, he was going to a smashing party that evening. They had a very delicious lunch beginning with oysters and ending with crêpes Suzette. Outside it was raining and there was an east wind, and when she hugged him, Oliver said, 'You can always tell if she's healthy by the state of her nose: ice-cold at the tip—even in August. Just like a dog, really.' Then he and John had shaken hands and John had shivered and said, 'How I hate saying goodbye to people.' He looked as though he was surprised that he'd said that.

Elizabeth had watched Oliver waving and then turning away before (of course) they were out of sight. 'People shouldn't do that,' she said aloud but really to herself.

'What shouldn't they do?'

'Turn away while you can still see them doing it. It doesn't sound as though they don't care enough; it sounds as though they don't care at *all*.'

'Look, or looks. I see what you mean. But it's supposed to be bad luck to wave someone out of sight.'

'I bet it isn't. I bet that was just invented by someone very lazy at seeing people off.' A tear bounced on to the car rug and then sank greedily as though into moss.

John took her hand. 'I know what it is.'

'What?'

'You're so happy, you need the luxury of a small grief. We'll ask him to stay if you like,' he added.

She shook her head. 'Much better for him to try to get a job. You're quite right about luxury and small griefs. It wouldn't work the other way round, though, would it? I mean if you are really sad *or* miserable something nice but small isn't the slightest good.'

'I know,' he said, but when she looked anxiously at him he said, 'If you start worrying about me I'll get your passport out and show it to people in the ship.'

The Customs and Immigration men seemed quite unmoved by her picture and handed back both passports as though John was not married to and taking abroad a dangerous criminal lunatic. When Elizabeth pointed this out, he said, 'Oh yes, they did. They notice everything. But they're very patriotic, you see. They realize it must be good for England.'

In their cabin had been a bowl of shop roses with a card from Alice. 'Wishing you every happiness,' she had written in her upright childish hand. She must have gone to some trouble to get the card sent to the Southampton flower shop. There were also some orchids from Lady Dione Havergal-Smythe and Mrs Potts, whose name was spelled Fopps (Lady Dione's had come out perfectly). By the second day out the flowers had to be put in a bucket and wedged in the bathroom, and they died very soon after that.

The fourth day it was fine; not smooth or hot enough to fill the swimming pool but good enough to go out: the sea was the steely blue of some roads—the great diagonal shoulders of water were still capped with creamy feathers, and above, the sky was boisterously blue and white. They walked, round and round the deck past rows of people swaddled in rugs on long bony chairs looking like Channel-crossing jokes in *Punch*, past the sardonic looking sailor who was greasing staples very slowly on steel hawsers, past the officers' quarters (a little above them) from which came snatches of curiously sedate jazz accompanied by whiffs of coffee and bacon, to where they could look down upon the bows of the ship ploughing vigorously towards the horizon: round to the starboard side (no sun and so no passengers except for a pair of earnest table-tennis players), past a cabin—one of the two really grand ones—from whose open window they could hear an angry lady explaining why she preferred flying everywhere: for six rounds they found her in full spate. Eight rounds were supposed to be a mile, but any kind of repetition makes things seem longer, and they stopped, by mutual consent, at a mile and a half. It was extraordinary how much they seemed to agree with each other, Elizabeth thought.

The next day it was perfectly fine and there were flying fish— like small silver darts—that shot suddenly from the sea to stream their arcs through the air before they vanished from sight. The pool was filled—with sea water; Elizabeth, who had said that she wanted to bathe, got into her bathing dress before she had changed her mind.

'Why have you?'

She was standing in the middle of the cabin before her dressing-table. She looked at him crossly and he knew she was anxious.

'I just don't want to.'

'But why not, darling?'

'*You* know perfectly well.' And when he was silent at this, she said, 'You can *see* why not. I'm portly.' She looked down at herself with distaste.

'Oh. Well *I* can't see anything portly about you at all.'

'You can. You're just pretending. Of *course* you can.'

'I really can't you know.'

But she interrupted almost triumphantly, 'That shows you'll mind when you can. You wouldn't sound so consoling if you didn't secretly mind. You know perfectly well I'm portly now and it's going to get much worse.'

He put down his book, took off his reading glasses and put on his ordinary ones. 'Ah; you're not crying. You have a fearful capacity for sounding as though you were, and then, on the other hand suddenly doing it when you haven't sounded like it.'

'Stick to the *point*. I thought it was women who were supposed to be so bad at that.'

'It is, but I am as well. Women and me.'

'You're nearly laughing! It's no joke, I can tell you, having to face the prospect of my whole relationship with you being ruined just because of any old Tom, Dick or Harry or whoever's inside me'.

He did laugh then. 'Oh I do think you ought to know that. I

mean, if that's what you're facing, I do think you ought to know who's making you face it.' Without the slightest warning, he picked her up and carried her to his bed. 'Now Elizabeth. Now then,' he said, raising his voice to prevent her interruption, 'why on earth you should feel that having our child will ruin our "whole relationship" I can't think—'

'Of *course* you can!' she said, or this time cried, again. 'It's obvious. I'll look more and more awful until even you can't love me. A lot of people's teeth and hair fall out.'

'Nonsense.'

'Well they have millions of stoppings,' she amended sulkily, 'and some people's hair goes all dull and greasy.'

'Heavens, how horrible!'

'And supposing it's a hideous criminal or simply a terrifically dull child. People do have them.'

'I know. Look at Jennifer.' He met her eye easily, and she flung her arms round his neck. 'It's all right, darling. Jennifer *is* dull: and seeing that—being nasty *about* her as you would say—makes it much easier to be nicer *to* her.'

'You really don't feel guilty any more?'

'Yes, I do, but I can manipulate it: the acme of success in middle age. Arrange your guilt to suit your means. Thanks to you, I've done that. Don't worry. This new Cole won't be dull: at least, not to us and that's what counts.'

A bit later, she said, 'Well—even if it starts all right, I may be such a rotten mother that it immediately grows up awful. Nearly everyone says that they had something frightfully wrong with their childhood which proves that it must be a jolly difficult thing to get right so I bet I won't.'

'Won't what?'

He had been stroking her neck absently: she was curled up against him but he was so much larger that he could look down on nearly all of her.

'Get the childhood right and stop it turning out to be a wicked monster.'

'If you really hate looking after it we'll get a nurse: then it will

grow up with all the old-fashioned neuroses instead of the fashionable ones.'

'Oh no! I'll do it. Other people might get it even wronger.'
He smiled then, perceiving that she was now enough reassured.
'It's marvellous the way you aren't sick. How do you feel?'

'Perfectly all right. Goodness knows, I've *had* the being sick part.
Nearly three months of it. It's extraordinary: I don't feel anything
at all. Except a bit important,' she added after thinking about it.

* * *

Alice lay perfectly still: after a second or two, the puppy whim-
pered, came up to her and licked her ear and a piece of her forehead.
The thin dark ice that she had not seen at all on the crazy-concrete
paving was now splinter-cracked into a huge clumsy star. The air
was so cold that it still made her gasp if she even started to take a
deep breath, so she decided she'd better not try again. It was so
cold, that not only were her face and hands icy, but when she
touched her smock it was just as bad—like clothes on a dead person.
But she wasn't entirely cold because there seemed to be a kind of hot
spring inside her that was gently welling up and keeping her legs—
or at any rate her thighs—beautifully warm: she had at one and the
same time a feeling of disaster and a sense of comfort, and it seemed
a pity to change this by moving or having a thought—or anything
at all. The puppy was irritating: kept coming up to her with its
little frowsty breaths and complaints—disturbing the peace, which
indeed it had always done. Her ankle hurt: this discovery was of
course a nuisance and should also have been a relief; it wasn't
though. By turning her head rather uncomfortably she could see
that the jigsaw gate was hung with icicles: it was cosier to turn back
to her own open front door. The house must be getting cold, and
just as she found that she couldn't help wondering how long she had
lain on the path (after, it was obvious of course, tripping somehow
and falling on the ice) she had suddenly—but thank God gently
to start with—a pain that was like a skewer, or an enormous long
butcher's knife stabbing the bottom of her spine and then probing,

feeling the best place and way to split it. The pain—so intense for the apparent gentleness that at first it seemed as though it ought to be a laughing matter—accelerated without warning into something past the beginning of a scream. It was like missing a bus; hopeless too quickly for screaming to help. Then, just as she was wondering who *was* screaming, it all stopped—or seemed to—turned into a bit of pain, discomfort, and then nothing again. The funny thing was that as soon as it was over the whole thing seemed like something she had read in a book: 'a dreadful pain like a sword pierced her back with mounting waves of agony,' that kind of stuff: rather dull and nothing to do with her at all.

It wasn't just her ankle—it was a long way up her leg. She shifted to see if she could see any damage; she was of a size that made look-ing at any part of her legs difficult and it seemed to her ages since she'd seen her feet when she was standing up. But after twisting a bit she could see that she had a horrid graze from her ankle bone nearly up to her knee. Her stocking was rent, but bits of it were sticking to the rather dirty and clotted-looking wound. When she tried to reach the stocking to pull it away from her leg—perhaps take it off if she had the energy—a piece of paper slipped out of her hand. 'Half a pint of double cream today please,' it said. *That* was what it was. She had been going to put a note on the gate for the milkman, and the puppy, or dog it was really by now, had suddenly shot past her in the doorway and she'd lost her balance. It always behaved like that—rushing out the moment you opened a door as though it had been imprisoned all its life, but once out, it had no sense of adventure. It had come back to her again, sniffing the graze on her leg, and now, with its head turned away from her it was intently licking the path: licking up the bits of ice? she won-dered, and then it moved a bit and she saw that what it was licking—almost lapping up—was blood; very dark red, and surely far too much to have come from her leg? Nausea, terror, had hardly a chance before the skewer interrupted with total efficiency: this time she could not imagine how she had stopped feeling what it had been like last time. After it, she was possessed by a sense of irritable urgency: she had to do a lot of difficult things before it happened again (which she now knew it would) but she didn't know what they were. Well, she'd have to move; she couldn't do anything lying on her own front path like that. When she finally got to her feet, and started to lumber back into the house, she realized that it certainly wasn't blood just from her leg and it wasn't even only blood. As she almost fell into the chair by the telephone in Leslie's study she thought—quite easily—'I'm losing the baby, then,' and like her first feelings about the pain, she could have been reading about it in some magazine story, without much interest.

∗   ∗   ∗

Lavinia could be awfully tiresome: even when she was a child, she had displayed what May—having just been wretchedly subject to it—now called arrant curiosity. It was really not, or, at any rate hardly, her business what May so urgently wanted to see Dr Sedum *for*; if she was any kind of sport, she would simply have accepted May's word for it and just driven him down when May told her to —or perhaps suggested, was a better word. Heaven knew she didn't want to dictate to Dr Sedum, but the circumstances did seem to add up to a kind of emergency and May always felt at her worst in those. In any case, one false step, spiritually or practically, and she might be cast aside like old gloves or a petty sin. No—she had to see Dr Sedum, and due to her rotten health Mahomet was going to have to come to the mountain (whenever she faced that phrase there was the fear of getting it the rude way round for the other person). And the only member of the League (that she knew) who could drive Dr Sedum down to Monks' Close was Lavinia. So why couldn't she just *do* it, and stop asking niggling, maddening, *pertinent* questions? She didn't at all seem to understand that (a) it was always alarming using the telephone when you weren't quite sure where Herbert was, and (b) that he went through all the toll calls with a tooth comb and would be sure to ask what this one had been. Why on earth not ring people up in the cheap time, he would demand, not realizing, of course, that he and the cheap time most unfortunately coincided. He was *always* at home in the evenings unless he was actually in London, but since she'd been feeling so awful, he had stayed at Monks' Close. This was both kind and tiresome of him: fearfully kind if you didn't want a life of your own, and a tiny bit tiresome if you did. Anyway—after it taking far too long (from the toll-call-in-the-morning point of view), Lavinia had agreed to drive Dr Sedum down for the afternoon. (Herbert, with even less reason than Frank Churchill—he had far less hair—had gone to London to get it cut. He was going by a late morning train and would try to get something to eat at his club, he had said.) The moment that he was gone (the old Wolseley was audible for miles), she began to get up. One of the most frightening things about her these days was the way she often couldn't properly feel her feet—swinging them over the side of the bed, she sometimes didn't realize when they hit the floor. This morning she watched carefully and—perhaps because she was watching—she thought she could feel them a bit better than usual. This morning the fears that she pretended to herself were nameless seemed not so much to be that as without other substance; everybody thought they were dying of some fatal disease at one time or other in their lives. She had a slow, hot bath and put on her warmest jersey with her blue suit. The day had begun with frost and fog; the latter had cleared but the sky was leaden, without either cloud or sun: it was a typical English December day and Herbert had remarked (as he always did when it was either cold or wet) how homesick he had been for weather like this when he had lived in India. This seemed to May extraordinary and Oliver had agreed—had remarked that the Indian equivalent of *that* kind of homesickness would be missing cobras very badly and must therefore, except for a very small minority largely made up of other, immigrant cobras, be nonsense. Oh dear, she did miss her children: she didn't want them to be younger or smaller again, she simply missed their frivolous company. She lunched off a large glass of milk and tried to think about the Absolute so that she would be in the right frame of mind for Dr Sedum. Even with months of practice and Help in the form of Times galore she did not feel that she had got any better about this—in fact she often felt that she had actually got worse: it was extraordinary how trying to hold on to one thought was like trying to hold your arms over your head, or even stretched out like poor Jesus: she hoped He hadn't been expected to do both things at once ... There she went, thinking about the difficulties of doing something rather than the thing itself. The trouble was that she was really dreading the interview with Dr Sedum (although it was always, of course, wonderful to see him). It would be less wonderful to have to see him with Lavinia, but, on the other hand, Lavinia would probably understand the horns of her dilemma and possibly help.

She felt too weak to do all the scene-shifting required to use the morning room; the den, or study, would have to do. She dragged in a second comfortable chair—for Lavinia—and collected a second electric fire: even so there were simply two small areas of scorching heat in an otherwise freezing room. Mrs Green—whose days at Monks' Close were yet further reduced by the quiet but inexorable decline of her bicycle, was not about: it *was* one of her days but she couldn't come. She arranged a tea tray in the kitchen and put the huge kettle on the kitchen range: in spite of it, the kitchen seemed very cold and the passages were so icy that she had taken to travelling about them in her oldest overcoat. She filled a hot-water bottle with water from the tap for a foot warmer and sat in Herbert's chair to wait. As there were two electric fires, Claude sat with her.

They were late; it was nearly half past two when the dogs' barking warned her of the car. Those poor dogs! Nobody took them out now that Alice had gone.

Dr Sedum wore his muffler and Lavinia had a fur coat: they were both smiling, which they went on doing without saying anything while May helped them off with their coats and led them to the study (as she always called Herbert's den when he wasn't there). Dr Sedum sat in Herbert's chair and she put Lavinia in the other nice one. Claude took one look at them and then slunk out of the room as though they were infectious and it would be very danger-ous for him to stay even a moment.

Dr Sedum stopped smiling, leaned slightly forward and exclaimed 'Now!' rather as though he was starting a race.

'It's about the house; this house.' If she had thought Dr Sedum had stopped smiling before, she must have been wrong. He really stopped now. 'Herbert—my husband—seems to regard it as half belonging to him anyway. And when I pointed out—I had to try and make him see that I had bought it, he said it was the only thing he really cared about. So I don't see what—I simply can't think how to—'

'Are you trying to say that you want to go back on your word?'

'No—of course I'm not!' It was much easier to talk to Lavinia even if all you were doing was trying to shut her up. 'But can't you see how awkward it is? I mean it means practically leaving it to the League behind Herbert's back!'

Nobody answered this. After a moment she said, 'It seems rather shabby to me.'

There was a pause during which she noticed that Lavinia looked knowingly at Dr Sedum, who, while he did not return the look exactly, did not snub it either. Then he cleared his throat softly and spoke about one's image of oneself for a long time, at the end of which she felt both confused and ashamed. She could see that it was awful either to do or not to do things simply because you minded what other people thought of you: it was, or could be, a sickening kind of vanity and she had little doubt that this was probably what had caused her dilemma. She *wanted* to leave Monks' Close to the League, but Herbert would mind this and she minded Herbert minding. Yes—but *oughtn't* she to mind? (Him minding?) Or was it (she knew that often one's feelings were exactly the opposite of what one supposed them to be—it was so lucky and calculable that they should be *exactly* the opposite) that perhaps she *didn't* want to leave the house to the League but was afraid of what they would think of her if she didn't and was therefore sheltering under Herbert's alleged feelings? Or was she cold-bloodedly using the house to see who would give her the most attention and interest—Herbert or Dr Sedum? She wondered which of these possibilities was the worst: if she knew *that*, she probably—almost certainly—would know which she was culpable of. It was amazing, she thought, how Dr Sedum could show you in a moment how worthless you really were...

Lavinia suddenly, surprisingly, offered to make some tea for everyone. May, very gratefully, explained that she'd got a tray ready, showed Lavinia the beginning of the way to the kitchen and returned to her uncomfortable chair opposite Dr Sedum. Lavinia wasn't such a bad sort after all.

'I'm sure you're right,' she began; 'one's motives are nearly always suspect, aren't they? At least, I don't mean *your* motives, of course,' she felt herself blushing at the idea; 'I mean mine, of course. It's partly because I'm rather stupid—have never been able to think clearly about anything at all—that I couldn't think what to *do now*, you see. And I haven't been feeling too good lately, either, which hasn't helped.'

Dr Sedum lit his second cigarette, and then, as a gigantic after-thought, offered her one. It was likely, he said, that her poor health was due to her sense of conflict; nothing was more exhausting than Wrong Imagination and Wrong Imagination was something so many of us suffered from. It often prevented events from taking their natural course, speaking of which, at what stage had things got blocked, as it were? He seemed to remember that she had men-tioned some lawyer in July...

'Oh yes! I've done all that, I went to him very soon after I saw you. But you know how long everything takes. It wasn't my *lawyer's* fault,' she quickly added, 'it's just that I don't get up to town as often as I should like, and when I do only half the things on my lists seem to get done. He did a draft and sent it to me but the envelope made Herbert so curious that I didn't like—I felt I couldn't—so anyway in the end I told him to keep the actual will until I could get to London, and even then, you see, I have to think of a reason for going to London—it really isn't at all *easy*!'

Dr Sedum said something stern about easiness and she hastily agreed because she wanted to ask him something else.

'Dr Sedum! Do you think that perhaps there is a possibility that I *am* ill—that I am *not* imagining it?' She looked earnestly at him, in case—only out of his extreme compassion—he might soften the blow. He smiled, and she realized immediately that it *had* been a silly question, but he answered at once with what she recognized was his most indulgent kindness.

There was *always* the *possibility*, he said, that she was not imagining what she thought to be her state of health: anything was possible, and everything was conversely improbable; it was essential that one consider one's own nature in the light of events, but for most people this kind of consideration was a life's work with no knowledge of how to go about it. This was what the League was partly for or about. He was sure that as she understood better how to use her life for the glory of the Absolute she would find that minor anxieties dropped away like so many .dead leaves ... Before she had finished thanking him, Lavinia arrived with the tea trolley. Tea was quite gay: Lavinia poured out and generally was so much at home that May felt as though she was a guest at a delightful small party. Of course Lavinia knew Dr Sedum—really *knew* him—and was also a senior member of the League, often standing in the centre of the Circle at Times.

After they had gone, she reflected that Herbert had taken her to that doctor in Woking whom he said was so good and that when she'd taken the powder stuff prescribed she had seemed to be getting slowly better. The prescription was repeatable, and she decided to get some more.

Lavinia and Dr Sedum encountered the colonel three-quarters of the way down the drive, which was generally too narrow for two cars to pass one another. Lavinia made one of those coquettish gestures of despair that most middle-aged women would do well to outgrow, but the colonel lifted a majestic hand and then backed noisily and damagingly to the entrance gate which he nearly rammed. As it was, he parked so that it was very difficult for Lavinia to edge the Bentley past him: she wound down her window and leaned out in an attempt not to graze his wing, calling cheerfully, 'How do you do! I am a cousin of May's and we have just been paying her a visit!' In League language this was being adroit; to the colonel it was plain worrying. He drove slowly up the drive in first with bits of broken rhododendron dropping from the luggage rack, wondering what on earth May had been up to.

'What on earth have you been up to?' he asked as soon as he could.

'How do you mean? Oh! Lavinia! She dropped in to see me. My cousin: she married a man in Texas who's dead—I mean he died last year.'

'Who was the feller she was with?'

While May was wincing at the idea of Dr Sedum being described as a feller, he went on, 'Looked like a doctor, to me.'

'Herbert, you really are extraordinary!'

'What on earth do you mean?' While she might be delighted by his perspicacity, he was too alarmed for complacence.

'Well—he *is* a kind of doctor—in a way.'

'What do you mean—in a way?'

'I don't know actually.' She did not want to discuss Dr Sedum too much. 'He's not a *medical* doctor at all. But there are hundreds of other kinds, aren't there? I just know that he is one. He's called Dr Sedum: a friend of Lavinia's.

'I know what,' she said as she trotted after him into the hall. 'He's a doctor of philosophy. I bet you that's it.'

'*I* don't mind what he is,' he rejoined, now that he no longer did.

Neither of them wanted to explore Dr Sedum in depth.

TWO

⸻ ⚬ ⸻

GINNY

OLIVER woke up remembering quite clearly how awful he'd felt when he went to bed and looking forward now to having slept some of it off. He opened his eyes very carefully; it was still dark, but then it nearly always was these days. He rolled his eyeballs gently and swallowed. It was no good pretending that it was just a hangover any more: both movements made him wonder if he was at a not too distant point from death. He tried to shift his legs to sit up, but they seemed immovable. Just as he thought, 'God! paralysed!' he remembered the vast and weighty Labrador who was a temporary P.G. at Lincoln Street. She was a noble and resigned creature, hell-bent on loyalty, and given the absence of her owner she turned all her attention on to Oliver. Now her tail thudded against his ribs that he realized were actually aching—as though bruised. She got to her feet and stood on and over him (her nose was refreshing, but her tongue felt like his—hot and abrasive): then, with a heavy, faintly artificial, sigh, she cast herself anew upon some more of his aching and bruised bones. With his free arm he knocked over the glass by his bed and turned on the lamp: he'd drunk all the water anyway. It was ten to six; as he registered this, the Labrador heaved herself up again, jumped or fell to the ground and firmly scratched some more paint off the door. She wanted to go out, and that meant both of them, whether it killed him or not. When the father of a friend of his had offered him ten shillings a day for keeping and looking after Millie, he had, on accepting, jolly nearly said it was too much, but he hadn't and it wasn't. He wrapped himself in his eiderdown, crammed his feet bare into outdoor shoes and padded down the steep stairs. His head throbbed in a way that made him feel as though it was one stair behind the rest of him. Millie had not yet worked out which way the front door opened and there was some bulky confusion before she finally made her way to the street, casually bringing Oliver to the ground in her progress. It was freezing cold and Oliver's teeth immediately began to chatter: Millie, on the other hand, no sooner reached the fresh air than she began to amble. He gave her one chance which luckily she took before calling her back into the house. Upstairs he put on another jersey, took the last three aspirins and got back into bed. Millie had managed to get her fur icy in those few minutes but her stomach was warm and on the whole he was glad of her company. Together they fell into stupor.

Oliver was working at Harrods, for December anyway. He was doing this because he found that life at Lincoln Street without Elizabeth was more expensive as well as being far more uncomfortable, and he had chosen Harrods because he hoped to see some of his friends there buying their Christmas presents. So far the friends part of it had been a dead loss; a woman who'd taught him not much French when he was about ten who looked just the same and just as nasty, and who immediately remembered him with shrieks of Gallic hypocritical surprise, and someone he'd never liked whom he'd known at Oxford and to whom he owed five pounds. Still, he'd only been at it a week—selling ties and handkerchiefs to desperate women—it was certainly the only time of the year to sell in the men's department, but on the whole the crush and rush was such that you never got to know anybody ... By Thursday, he was feeling pretty fagged, but he put that down to the ghastly hours he was having to keep. He got up at seven in order to give Millie a decent run before going to Harrods. He walked there, but took a bus back in the lunch hour in order to take Millie out. Back in the evening and she would greet him with overwhelming vigour but clearly expected more exercise. Her horse-meat meal nauseated him so much that he hardly needed dinner, but he would take her to the pub where she behaved beautifully and everyone would tell him what kind of dog they had or had had. On Friday he woke with a sore throat and a headache, but it was pay day so he struggled through and had a rather longer session at the pub than usual, partly because it was so cold outside and partly because after a couple of whiskies he felt so much better. But the feeling-better wore off sharply on the short, but agonizingly cold, walk home and by the time he went to bed he felt very ill indeed but pretended and hoped that it was because he'd drunk too much. By ten to six, however, he was trying to tell himself that he'd only got 'flu.

At eight o'clock the telephone rang. It was Ginny.

'I thought I'd call you,' she began, 'because I've run out of money and I thought you'd be the least bad-tempered about it.'

He took a deep breath and said, 'That doesn't sound as though you have a genius for friendship, I must say.'

'For God's sake, Oliver, don't try to be clever: I've been on an aeroplane all night and I'm bushed.'

'I've been under a Labrador all night and I've got 'flu. At least,' he added, 'that's the least that I've got.'

'What's your cash situation?'

'Approximately twelve quid.' He was just starting to say but he needed it, when she said (far too loudly: it hurt his ear) 'Oh goody! London here I come!' and rang off.

'She's got a nerve!' he said—several times—to himself: trying to work up a sense of pure indignation (that worthless little chit turning up just when it happened to suit her) to counteract the spurts of excitement and fury that were already stopping him thinking clearly. He hadn't seen Ginny since that—very necessary—quarrel about her getting Jennifer to Cap Ferrat, although they'd had one or two horrible conversations that had begun with her apologizing nothing like enough, showing that she didn't really care about having ruined Liz's holiday, and him telling her this, whereupon she instantly stopped apologizing at all and simply said in the same breath that she hadn't done anything and he was an idiot to mind the tiny thing she *had* done. There had been two conversations exactly like that. 'She's got a nerve!' he said again as he realized that his fury was not because she was coming, but because he was feeling so awful when she was. There were two things he could do, he told himself. One, get up as quickly as possible and just not be here by the time she came, and two … but in the middle of not being able to think what two was he absent-mindedly swung his legs over the side of the bed and sat up. Instantly he felt so frightful that he lay down again. There were two things he could do: one, was to keep absolutely still until he either died or recovered however long either condition might take to achieve …

The door bell was ringing and Millie's broadsword tail was lashing his Adam's apple: she was out of bed facing the door with her back to him; she knew perfectly well that bells meant that people had to answer them and this meant that she, Millie, had the chance of getting the hell *out* of wherever she might be—her chronic wish.

Ginny stood drooping on the doorstep looking even smaller and more fragile than usual in a stiff, felty coat the colour of mustard (English, not French or German).

'It's four pounds ten,' she said. Then she jerked her head backwards in the direction of her driver who looked quite frighteningly like Prince Philip and added, '*he* says.'

A typical Ginny way of getting out of it; announcing the price and then putting it all on to someone else. He'd left the money upstairs oh *damn* because if he sent Ginny for it, she might give away all he'd got.

'Well, that seems rather a lot to me.' His no-nonsense smile was being ruined by chattering teeth.

The driver straightened up from a fulsome exchange with Millie.

'It seems a lot to *me* sir,' he said cheerfully, 'but there it is.' Then he added, 'It's the time of day, you see, sir.'

'Oliver do hurry up: I'm simply freezing!'

Then, while words were failing him, she cried, 'Oh darling— it's so marvellous to see you again, you've left your wallet upstairs I bet, I'll get it for you.'

Millie bounded after her into the house. It was easier to let her get the wallet—he couldn't, he thought, *manage* another trip to the top of the house and down again. 'It's in my jacket,' he called. It was going to be tough bargaining with Prince Philip when he was wrapped in an eiderdown. Still he'd *earned* those twelve pounds; they were damn well going to slip through his fingers the way he wanted them to. The driver was unloading Ginny's luggage— black-and-white striped canvas—and carrying it piece by piece to the bottom of the flight of steps up to the front door. No tip, thought Oliver viciously. Just as he was thinking that, Millie bounded out of the house again with the wallet in her mouth which she tenderly laid at the driver's feet. Her tail was wagging gently and she had an expression on her broad face that was both creative and benign. By the time Ginny had appeared, Oliver had given the driver five separate pounds and was thanking him profusely for the filthy ten shilling note produced as change.

'There we are, then,' said Ginny after he had staggered up the steps for the last time with her luggage. She hadn't offered to carry any of it, but when he tried to look at her morosely, so that she would ask him what was the matter and he would tell her, everything went dark and a stair or a banister or something struck him across the face. When he came to, he was flat on his back.

'... oh *Oliver!*' She sounded distraught, and without much effort he kept his eyes shut to hear some more. Just then, she dropped an ice cube into a sort of niche above his collar bone. He sat up and it rolled down to an even more private place. He glared at her. 'Oh God! Honestly.'

'Don't worry: it'll melt in two ticks: you've got the most ghastly fever. A tear went on your face just now and it sizzled like a drop scone.'

'Have you been crying? Have I been out for ages? Can it be that deep down you care for me?'

But she answered with disarming truth, 'Don't be silly: you know perfectly well I haven't *got* a deep down. But yes, you have been just lying there. Long enough for me to look up Dr Garth-Elwyn-Garth's number, anyway.'

'Who's he?'

'He's the most eminent gynaecologist in England. Mummy swears by him.' And when he burst out laughing, she said crossly:

'Oh shut up! I don't *know* any other doctors in this country. It would be easy if we were in an hotel—you just ring up and say you want one and he comes. Why don't we just slip off to Claridge's? They've got everything there.'

'I thought you'd run out of money.'

'I have. You have a bill, stupid.'

'But you have to pay it in the end, idiot. Thanks to you, I've now got seven pounds ten. And thanks to you,' he added most unfairly, 'I've probably lost my job.'

'It'll probably bring out the best in you.'

'What on earth do you mean?'

'Nearly every great man has been poverty-stricken and diseased at some time or other.'

'Nearly every kind of man's been that. There's absolutely no guarantee of what it brings out.' She was sitting cross-legged on the floor in front of him. The black fox beret she was wearing made her face look unbearably fragile.

'I must go to bed,' he said.

'I must have a bath first, darling—I've been travelling such ages.'

'I didn't mean bed with you: I'm much too ill,' he said and immediately wondered whether this was in the least true.

But in fact Oliver really was quite ill and Ginny surprisingly stayed and looked after him, proving fairly efficient in some— exotic—ways. She ordered food, for instance, not just from Fortnum's, where her mother had an account, but from the Star of India and Fu Tong as well. She used what she called her hocking diamond which travelled everywhere with her in a dented Elastoplast tin and got what seemed to Oliver a fantastic sum from the pawnbroker. With this she bought some clean sheets and sent all the others to a laundry. She bought Aristodog for Millie so there was no horrible horse-meat to cook, and bought muscat hot-house grapes for Oliver that he worked out cost about one and ninepence a grape. She bought mimosa that lasted only a day but was worth it, and Campari and champagne that she mixed with a shot of Pellegrino. She bought him paperbacks and L.P. records and a transistor radio and a pair of pyjamas from Harrods. For herself she bought sixteen different lipsticks for her collection and an auburn wig. When Oliver got better, she wrapped him up and took him in taxis to the Curzon Cinema and the Starlight Club and the Reptile House at the Zoo: Just 'nice, warm, cosy places,' she said. Once she cooked him the most terrific dinner. It took her all day, and even the day before she was abstracted and snappy thinking what to cook. But it *was* a stupendous meal: Oliver ate until he was bursting but there was a lot left. 'Marvellous!' he said. 'Better than Elizabeth?' 'Different,' he'd answered shortly. Liz was not a good subject for them because of the Jennifer incident. 'What will you do with all the remains?' She was setting aside a good deal of a cold goose stuffed with cherries in a rather dismissive manner. 'Oh we shan't eat any *more* of it. I'll find someone: a tramp or some of a movie queue—they're usually so bored they'll eat anything—what shall we do? I feel boredom coming on.' She was wearing a lilac-coloured Pierrot suit with large, watery black spots and a huge white frilly ruff round her neck. 'Couldn't we have a party, or something? It'd be a good idea, really, because I've got to go to Dublin in a minute.'

'*What?*' She'd never said a word about Dublin.

'You know. For Christmas. I only stopped off here for Christmas shopping. I'm meeting Mummy and Roderigo there—' she looked at her watch, 'the day after tomorrow, actually.'

She looked so very pretty and unreliable that he felt he must have a serious conversation with her.

'Ginny! We've got to talk.'

'No, we haven't. No need at all.' She looked nervous and lit a small cigar.

He thought of how she had been the last five days: domestic— in a way—efficient: she had not minded ringing up the right person at Harrods and explaining the situation (which meant, of course, that he had lost his job) any more than she seemed to mind his feverish sweats, the dirt in the house, the persistent quiet problem of Millie but above all, the fact that he was—or had been—literally in no state to entertain her in any sense whatever. Except for going to bed, of course.

'*I* need to.'

'Talk, then.' She looked away from him then, as though it would be rude to watch anyone doing *that*.

He was lying on the battered old sofa in the sitting-room and she was curled up in the only serious chair.

'Well, I thought it would be an awfully good thing if we got married. There you are: as beautiful as the day, and rich and young and tremendously needing a stable background—' but she interrupted, 'What ghastly cheek of you to say that! I must say!'

'Ginny, it wasn't meant to be. But you can't want to spend all your life flitting from one hotel or villa or rented house to another doing nothing but try to amuse yourself.' As he said this, it sounded like something anyone could easily go on doing, but it was also something that almost everyone who had never done it decried, so he went on, 'I mean, it was all very well when you were a child and dependent upon your mother and all that—'

'Never been that! You don't know Mummy! You can't be dependent on her! Anyway, the sort of people who talk like you, dreary old Oliver, wouldn't at all approve of me marrying like that—as a kind of escape. *So?*'

He sat up. 'I should have thought you would have wanted your own life, at least—'

'How would marrying you make any difference to that?' She lay back sideways in the chair with her legs swinging out over one arm.

'Don't be dim on purpose. I mean having your own house—'

'Don't *you* be so silly. You don't have to be married to have a house and lots of people who *are* married don't have them. I don't see the connection. If you are going to go on being so boring I must have a drink.' She got up—almost leapt up—and prowled over to a Fortnum's carrier bag from which she drew a bottle.

'Are you always so rude to people who propose to you?'

'Yes. Now you'll have to wait while I get some salt and glasses.'

While she was gone, he shut his eyes frowning and trying to think why things were going so badly. Something to do with her neurosis, he decided, and he'd touched some raw and painful bit in her.

She brought very small glasses, an eggcupful of salt and a saucer of cut-up, very small, green lemons.

'Tequila,' she said. 'Help yourself.'

He watched while she filled a glass to the brim, put a pinch of salt on the edge of her hand, ate the salt, knelt to drink, and then squeezed the lemon juice down her throat. This was the kind of thing she did in a manner both practised and dashing. When she was licking her fingers, he said:

'I can't take neat lemon juice.'

'It's lime; much nicer than lemon.' She had another shot as quick as lightning and then said, 'Now—you can go on.'

'Being boring?'

She shrugged her shoulders so that the frill hid her ears.

'It's not difficult to bore you: there's no challenge there.' But even that didn't seem to move her, and she remained frozen in the shrug.

He tried the tequila minus all the salt lime nonsense and it was like a small, disgusting explosion at the bottom of his throat.

'People who are most easily bored are usually the most boring.'

'If you think that, why on earth do you think you want to marry me then? You're silly not to have salt and lime.'

'Because it's not the only thing about you.'

'I'll tell you something.'

'What?'

'Let's both have another swig first. You may find you needed it.'

In silence, he waited while she poured the drinks, put salt on what she described as the lockjaw bit of his hand and got the limes handy. Then she said, 'Right,' and they went through the ritual. He began to see the point of tequila, and was just about to say so, when she remarked,

'It's time you knew, I think, that I don't have any money.'

'What do you mean?'

'I mean I'm not in the least rich—any more. I used to be, but now I'm not. Not a peseta, not a cent, not a threepenny bit. That's why I called from the airport. I'd run out.'

There was a silence while she watched him and he tried to think what he thought. Ginny bored but with money was not an easy proposition, but Ginny bored and without a sou made him feel really nervous. And the economics of the thing: living with Ginny was more a case of two could live as cheaply as about seventy-four … even if they both worked like mad at Harrods from morning till night …

'Why did your mother do it?' he asked.

She shrugged again. 'Mightn't even have *been* her. The only time my parents actually liaise is when they think up something nasty for me. They always seem in complete agreement over that.'

Oliver drank some more tequila a bit too fast. This made him choke and Ginny laugh.

'Is it fury you're choking from?' she asked when he could hear her.

'No, but it will be if you go on like that.'

'Well, isn't it my money you wanted to marry me for?'

'It's funny,' he said, 'I thought it was. And I can see it's a completely different proposition—'

'You mean you *don't* want to?'

'Stop pouncing! No, I think I *do* want to, and I'm only saying 'think' because we're back at the dreary old problem of what to do with me to get me earning some money. Clearly I can't marry you without a job. You'd have to get one, too.'

'Any minute now you'll suggest that we both go *trudging* off to Harrods every morning to earn our married livings.'

This made him angry, as something of the sort had just begun to cross his mind. He shifted nearer the table in order to reach the bottle as she went on, 'Rush hour every morning and evening—worn to the bone, both of us and nasty little married crush hour every Friday—or is it Saturday?—night. Besides, we could never go anywhere decent—our holidays would be too short. Surely you can see?'

He took another drink and said, 'Why did you stay here then?'

'Because I wanted some money and then, even when I found you hadn't got any much, I was sorry for you.'

'Well, I started by wanting *your* money, and now I'm sorry for *you*.'

'What on earth for? *Are* you?'

'Yes I am!'

'No need to shout! I just wanted to know. And do you honestly think you love me?'

'Considering how awful you're being without putting me off, I must.'

She poured them both large drinks.

'Well I don't love you,' she said calmly. 'Sorry, but that's that. And before you can start telling me that I might get to, I'd better tell you that it isn't just you—it's anybody. I just never get to care enough. I used to think it mattered and tried awfully hard with people, but now I know I'll never change so I don't bother.'

She twisted in the chair and leaned forward over the table with one of her sudden, but entirely controlled, movements, and began cutting up some more limes. He thought of her during the last few days—and nights.

'You seemed to me to have been bothering with me.'

She looked up from the lime cutting. 'It is the easiest way not to be rude to people, really, isn't it? Of course I didn't want to hurt your feelings.'

'What do you think you're doing *now*?'

'*You're* making me have to do that—*probing* away and trying to change everything. And I warn you,' she added, 'tequila often makes people madly quarrelsome, so you'd better be careful.'

Before he could reply, the telephone rang, and seeing that she seemed eager to answer it, he felt determined to thwart her. This was easy, as the instrument was on the floor by the fireplace, much nearer to him, but he hadn't realized that she'd left a tray on the rug at the end of the sofa until he'd stepped into and tripped over a bowl of braised celery. 'For God's sake!' he said just after he'd picked up the receiver: she seemed bent on humiliating him; there seemed to be no end to her horrible, appalling behaviour...

'Darling—it's me.' It was May, sounding apprehensive and miles away. 'Oliver? Was that you sounding so angry just now?'

'Not with you, though.'

'If you've got people I—'

'Nobody who matters,' he said with what felt like vicious smoothness.

'Oh well. Because I don't want to interrupt you—'

'You're not. What is it?' It must be something: she regarded even toll calls rather like brandy—only to be indulged in in an emergency.

Ginny had got up and was clearing away the remains of dinner except for the tray he had trod upon. The moment she opened the sitting-room door, thin far-off howls could be heard from Millie shut up in the spare room above.

' ... so extraordinary—I felt quite frightened.' May was saying. The line now seemed to be crossed, because from even farther away a woman's voice said, ' ... all over the back stairs—so Tuesday would be no good.' Her voice faded suddenly and Oliver quickly asked, 'What frightened you?'

'I told you, darling; but it's so unlike him that I expect it's just because I don't feel too good anyway that I'm imagining it.'

' ... five miles there *and* five miles back and I've never known her finish what's on her plate—' and another voice, astonishingly like the first said, 'No good suggesting anything to *you* on a Wednesday —' both voices agreed that it wouldn't be. Millie howled again and Ginny hissed, 'Shall I let her *out*?'

'Do what you like,' Oliver shouted—into the telephone by mistake.

'Darling, you're obviously having a party and I wouldn't have rung you but I've never felt like this before—'

'Like what? I'm sorry, but I didn't hear the beginning part—'

'So frightened. Somehow, it's the most awful house to be alone in, so I wondered whether you could possibly—'

'Where's Herbert?'

'I *told* you, darling—he's gone *storming* off in the car. So *could* you—just for tonight?'

At this moment, the other voices broke in; a crossed line, they said with muted umbrage: it was funny how some people listened to other people's conversations ... May started to apologize; triumphant barking could be heard from Millie, and Ginny came to lean

233

against the architrave of the open door in a Petrouchka-like attitude.
A wave of retrospective humiliation swept over Oliver at the sight
of her.

'I can't possibly come down tonight; I've got appalling 'flu,' he
said more loudly than anybody else who was talking. There was
silence for a moment. Then May said:

'Of course you shouldn't dream of moving then, darling. But
would you mind very much if I caught the last train up and came
to you?'

Panic assailed him. Except for feeling that she mustn't come—not
now of all times, anyway—he was paralysed. If she came, he *knew*
that everything with Ginny would go wrong, and what's more
she'd *see* it go wrong. The crossed-line voice was now saying that
it was the *second* Friday in every month that she went to Mr Work-
sop.

'No,' said Oliver; 'don't do that: not tonight, anyway. Look, I'll
ring you in the morning when things are a bit more settled. How
would that be?' he added when there was no reply and then May
—she sounded miles away again—said she didn't know; she expected it would be all right.

'It's hopeless on this line, anyhow,' Oliver said trying to sound
bluff and calm instead of guilty and panic-stricken.

'Goodbye, darling. It was nice to hear your voice.'

'Goodbye.' He put down the receiver and ostensibly glared at
Ginny who was now sitting astride Millie.

'That was your mother you couldn't be bothered with, wasn't it?'

He ignored this. 'You *can't* have meant what you said just now.'

'I bet I did, but what was it?'

'About not—about simply not hurting my feelings in bed—about
not caring about me, in fact.'

'Oh that. Mmm. 'Fraid you're wrong.'

'Women can't pretend to that extent; it's an absurd exagger-
ation—just because you don't want—' but she interrupted him:

'They can pretend and most of them do. And most of them get
away with it. You can always get away with it, in fact, except in
one situation.'

234

'And what's that?' He thought he was speaking calmly and merely folded his arms to stop himself shaking.

Ginny had got off Millie now and was back in her original leaning position in the doorway. 'If the man is really, honestly, completely in love with you, you couldn't cheat,' she said, 'it wouldn't work and you wouldn't want to anyway. There'd be no need.' Her voice went back to what it usually was. 'But oh brother—it's the way to find out whether a man loves you. It's the—big—infallible test. It always works.'

'You mean you pretend, and if he doesn't catch on it means he doesn't love you?'

She gave a little nod, and then slid slowly down with her back-bone against the frame until she was sitting on the floor. Then she said again, 'It always works.'

Whether it was her pretty, clownish clothes, or her disconsolate position, or feeling that she meant what she said—and more, that what she said meant something—he didn't know, but he had suddenly a quite different feeling about her; as though she was Elizabeth, or a child, or somebody in some way poor who needed affection and protection and pity ...

'Ginny, now you've said all this, couldn't we try again—'

'Oh don't say *that*! Let's both have another drink quickly before I have to tell you something else.' She sprang effortlessly to her feet and dodged round him to the tequila table. When she'd helped herself, she said, 'The test, you see, is that the other person doesn't know they're being tested. If they knew, then all that would happen is that we'd both be cheating.'

'But if you found someone who passed the test—would you marry them?'

'Oh that. I don't know. I never have found anyone and it's a private rule not to cheat about the test.'

'But surely—that's the point of the test, isn't it? That you'd marry them if they passed?'

She took another glass of neat tequila and then threw her head back to squeeze drops of lime juice into her mouth. At last, she said,

'If you swear—I mean seriously swear—not to tell anyone, I'll tell you something.'

'All right.'

'No—seriously.'

'I am serious,' he said—sounding merely peevish as people do when pressed on this point.

'I couldn't marry you—or anyone. I *am* married.'

He stared at her while she composedly selected and lit one of her small cigars. When, eventually, he said, '*What?*' she went on as though she had always been going to: 'My father fixed it when I was fourteen. He disapproved of my mother's morals, you see: she got sort of custody of me and he was afraid I'd get like her. Whenever she "knows" any man in the Old Testament sense for more than a few months she *always* marries them: my father says that she is incurably middle-class in this way, so he decided to queer my pitch in that direction which what with the money *and* my mother has been a godsend.'

'Who are you married to?'

'Oh—some boring old man on my father's estate. He's about a hundred years older than me so my father said he'd probably die about when I got sensible. I only saw him that once. But my father keeps an eye on him, of course.'

'I'm glad to hear that.'

'You're rotten at sarcasm. You mean, you're shocked. You're British to the backbone—except for about an eggcupful of Scots blood I'm not British at all. My father's hacienda is about the size of Ireland.' She thought for a moment: 'Well—perhaps not the size of Northern and Southern Ireland—just Eire.'

'So what? There's no point in showing off about that now. I'm clearly not going to profit by it.'

That made her laugh. 'Good for you. I wasn't showing off. What I meant was that on his land my father is a kind of king. He can do what he likes. But he's *not* been beastly to José at all. I promise. He gave him a house and enough land to grow food for his huge family and he more or less bought José a much younger and prettier woman than he'd ever have got on his own. Of course he made

Ginny

José mark a document saying he'd always leave me alone and had no claims on me and all that. But I promise you he likes Lola and she's all right because he's got more of everything than anyone else she might have taken up with—'

'But supposing they want to get married!'

'Oh Oliver! They wouldn't want to do that! It's far too expensive—hardly anyone does. Extraordinary the way you *harp* on marriage! I warn you, you'd better not meet my mother, she's taken to marrying people younger and younger than she is and she's just about got to your age—'

'I don't care about your mother!'

'Well I often think that I'm tremendously like her so I bet you're well out of me. Look—if I'm going tonight, I simply must pack.'

'*Are* you going tonight?'

'It's too depressing staying after one of these conversations, I find.'

'You do, do you,' said Oliver hopelessly, but she had already vanished upstairs. In a messy, multi-horrible way he'd never felt worse in his life. The whole evening had been a bit like being at the wrong (receiving) end of some major character's revelations in a play of Shaw's. It wasn't that his heart was broken, exactly; there was little or no good clean misery about it: he felt angry, sad, disgruntled, shocked (he called that astounded) a bit miserable, a bit humiliated, rather anxious, considerably depressed, slightly overwhelmed: his pride was hit, his self-confidence dented ...

'What will you do if you never meet someone who passes the test?' he asked when she staggered down with the smallest black and white suitcase.

'Never marry,' she answered with such weary practice that he had to go on:

'Am I *exactly* like everybody else you've ever met?'

'Not abso*lutely exactly* like everybody I've ever met.'

Which was really only half withdrawing the barb—and twisting it to boot.

He brought all her other cases down at once, partly not to prolong the agony, and partly to show her, but she didn't seem to notice and he broke a banister. 'My taxi should be there,' was all she said. She had changed out of her Pierrot clothes and was back in the mustard coat.

He stared stupidly at her: the whole thing was getting worse than a play and more like some boring—and fairly bad—dream.

'I ordered it while I was packing, silly.'

'Where are you going?'

She was trying to open the front door and did not reply.

'Claridges', I bet.'

And when she did not say anything to that, he seized her by her spiky little shoulders. 'It wasn't true about the money, was it?'

'Oh—Oliver!'

'What about the other things?' He shook her slightly. 'The being married and not caring about anyone—all that?'

'Oh Oliver! You are a fool! It wouldn't matter, would it, whether it was true or not. The point is I've *told* you. Even *you* ought to be able to understand *that*.' The bell rang and in surprise, he released her. As she opened the door, she said, 'I honestly think you are one of the dimmest people I've ever known.' A lightning, feathery kiss on the side of his chin and that was that. Helplessly, he watched the taxi drive away (she didn't look back or wave). In the house the stairs smelled of her rich rose scent, there was more washing up than the kitchen would hold and Millie was guiltily cracking goose bones. One of the dimmest people she'd ever known. He went slowly up the scented stairs in search of the tequila.

THREE

···⟡···

AN OLD DEVIL

THE reason that the colonel had 'stormed off', as May had put it to Oliver, was that he had mistakenly thought all day that it was Tuesday. The naked, incontrovertible truth had dawned only when—long after dark—there was still no sign of the dogs' weekly (and inadequate) consignment of horse-meat. The moment he started to complain about this—which of course he did to May, there being no one else to complain to—she told him that it had come yesterday. 'It always comes on Tuesdays,' she had added.

'I know it does. And it hasn't come today. That's what I've been trying to say.'

'It's in the fridge.'

'Why didn't you simply say it had come then? No need to make a damned mystery of it.'

'Herbert, don't be absurd! Of course I'm not making a mystery. It came yesterday, like it always does, and naturally I didn't rush to tell you. I couldn't have; you were out.'

'How do you mean 'like it always does'? You said just now it always came on Tuesdays.'

'I did! It does!'

'You don't mean to tell me it's Wednesday!'

'Of course it's Wednesday.'

He would not believe her until he had looked up a radio programme for Wednesday and tested that it was actually in progress. And even then he didn't seem pleased: rather more furious than ever, in fact. He became suddenly panicky about the time and wouldn't believe her about *that*, either: just snapped at her.

'Are you going out?'

'Of course I'm going out. Why on earth else do you think it matters what blasted day it is?'

She said nothing to this, but eventually tracked him down—or up—to his dressing-room where she found him fumbling irritably with his ties. It was half past seven: fear—now familiar—at being left alone in the house with her evening pains coming on induced her to make one of those gestures which are vaguely in a self-preserving direction but none the less more often cause damage. 'Herbert, I really think you might tell me more what you are doing. I really think it's a bit much to be left suddenly at this time of night. Just because you've forgotten something.'

'You do, do you?'

'Well, *yes.* I mean—you didn't even believe me just now about what day it was. And then you sound as though it was all my fault.'

'I never said it was your blasted fault—'

But she had fatally interrupted, 'Couldn't I come with you?'

Of course she couldn't. And not only could she not come, but why on earth had she asked? Was he to have no vestige of privacy—have every little thing he did—or wanted to do—or, as in most cases *had* to do—interfered with, probed into? It was time she realized that he gave up far more of his life to her than most husbands did to most wives, but it was his personal and bitter experience that if you gave any woman an inch she asked for an ell. By now he had changed his tie, brushed his hair, arranged a new pocket-handkerchief and apparently whipped himself into a state of such general indignation that it would have been hopeless for her to attempt an answer to any specific charge. He decided that he wanted to see how much money there was in his wallet but not, of course, in front of her, so he sent her off to his den to look for his car keys. But she had hardly got down the stairs before he called out that he had found them (nine pounds ten and his cheque book). Then, because he really couldn't face her again, he shouted, 'Off now: shan't be late,' and scarpered down the back stairs. He was almost smiling as he let himself out. A bit of an old devil, that's what he was ...

May found it very difficult to be angry. She was not an unemotional woman, she simply found *anger* difficult; perhaps confused would be a better word for her feelings round about being angry. To begin with she so often felt that any unfortunate state of affairs was the result of something she had done (and since Dr Sedum, *been*): to go on with, she could far too often see the other person's point of view. It was therefore almost impossible for her to fix upon the reason for or object of anger. Being told to find Herbert's keys at once made her forget why he wanted them, and not finding them before he did made her feel (very faintly) guilty and inferior. As she heard one of the many back doors slam behind Herbert, her main feeling was of desolation. 'It was too bad of him' was as far as she could get about her husband leaving her without warning and for no reason at the beginning of yet another long winter evening. She decided to bolt the back door after Herbert before she began thinking about any of it. But by the time she had done this (the back door was at the farthest possible point from Herbert's study) her mind was too full of the emptiness of the house to sustain what had seemed like a straightforward state of indignation with her husband.

Her feet seemed to make too much noise on the uncarpeted passages, and the varnished pine floors had an institutional and discomfortingly unfurnished air that in turn gave the house the feeling of being barely, even uncertainly inhabited. She paused in the kitchen, but the thought of supper made her feel queasy and tired. This was not what Claude felt about it: and he rammed her thoroughly with all his firm and furry bulk until it was clear what his requirements must be. She fed him and heated herself some milk while he ate. When the milk was hot, she longed for a little whisky to put in it: the chances were that Herbert would have locked up the drink but perhaps it was worth going to look. Claude accompanied her as he never slept in the kitchen in winter if he could help it. She was glad of his company through the creaking baize doors that swung and creaked so long after one had passed them and decided that if there *was* any whisky she would shut them both in Herbert's study with as many electric fires as possible.

There *was* a small drop: it was so small that he hadn't bothered to lock it up. Unexpectedly, there being some, and it being so little, started to make her feel angry with Herbert again. It really was monstrous that he should go off as he had done, without warning, to goodness knows where leaving her entirely alone in this awful house that she had really come to hate. And if she hated it so much, why on earth had she let Herbert bludgeon her into buying it? Why wasn't she living in Lincoln Street with Oliver—leading entirely his own life, of course, but *there*? The whisky wouldn't be locked up *there*. She had got used to far too much: had been taking bad things for granted which must surely be even worse than taking good ones ...

Claude, who had been sitting on her lap, tried once more to like milk with whisky in it, but the filthy taste was too much for him. He shook his head violently, and beads of hot whisky-milk flew from his chin and whiskers and landed all over the place. He was going to have to wash his face to get rid of the smell, and as he could never manage this unless he was on a really firm base, he jumped heavily off May's lap to the floor where he found that her legs were taking up all the hot room in front of the fire. 'How affectionate he is,' she thought as he butted impotently against her until she made room for him. She wasn't entirely alone while Claude was about. It didn't seem to make much difference moving her feet from the fire to make room for him, as she couldn't feel them anyway. It must be a very cold night. This made her remember that the fire was not on in the bedroom, which would be icy, and then she began thinking of the awful trek upstairs, feeling for and turning on the half-a-dozen light switches—and then, without warning, she began to feel frightened. She was almost at once too much afraid to consider what she was frightened of: she simply knew that she did not want to have to make the journey upstairs and down again; did not even really want to have to leave the comparatively small and bright room. This was when she telephoned Oliver. While talking to him she managed to discover and thence to explain that in fact Herbert going off in this sudden manner had frightened her; she couldn't very well just say that it was the house, but Oliver sounded very busy and there were some other people talking so she wasn't sure whether he heard properly or not. Then he said he had 'flu and then something else he said made it clear to her that he didn't really want her. She knew she was going to cry, so she said something pointless and sensible to put an end to the conversation in time. Crying left her feeling rather sick, but, she told herself, relieved in her mind. The whole thing showed what a beginner she must be about the League, because she tried several times to think of higher and better things and didn't in the least succeed. But she *did* remember afterwards that something had been said about making use of what material was to hand, and clearly Herbert came under that heading. She had *married* him, after all. Why? She had to think very hard about him to recall the first impression he made upon her ... Chelsea Flower Show—the last day. Marvellous weather, too hot, in fact, to march about in one's best clothes; but they had met wearing them, both in search of a good shrub rose to buy when the show closed. The circumstances weren't the point: what had he been *like*? Very frank and straight-forward: simple, in a way, but chivalrous: obviously, she had thought, a man who liked women: he had a keen way of looking at you as though he was interested because he immediately under-stood you so well. He had been modestly reticent about himself—he didn't want to bore her etc.—but he had been an awfully good listener and it happened that at that time she particularly needed one. Oliver had just come down from Oxford; not, as she had fondly hoped, with a brilliant degree and a dedicated determination about his mission in life, but with a Second, the general reputation for not having done a stroke of work and the expressed intention of enjoying himself. This was when he needed a father, when even uncles, she had felt, might have stiffened up his moral fibre, but alas, there were no uncles. Clifford had had a sister but she had never married: she herself simply did not know a single man of approx-imately her own age except her lawyer and her dentist, neither of whom she had felt would be really right for dealing with Oliver. So this large, military-looking, interested and courteous stranger was an open blessing. They had had dinner together, at the end of which she felt better about Oliver than she had for months (they had spent most of dinner over him, neither Alice nor Elizabeth proving to have the sheer staying power as a topic of conversation that Oliver seemed to have).

In the end (when they had got to Grand Marnier and coffee) the colonel—as she already thought of him—had leaned forward and said how much he admired the gallant way in which she had for years shouldered burdens clearly meant for men. When she explained how much easier everything had become since Aunt Edith in Canada had died, he said money be damned, excuse his French, it in no way lessened her *moral* responsibilities. And May, who had never really thought of relations with her children in those terms, instantly began to worry about *why* she hadn't, since this kind and upright gentleman seemed to do so. What she now should do was stop worrying about her son, realize that he was—to all intents and purposes—grown-up, and start to live her own life a bit more. Get out, make new friends—enjoy herself. At the time she had simply agreed with this agreeable advice: afterwards she had interpreted it. What he had really meant—only he was far too kind to say so— was that in spite of all her secret vows about it, she had imperceptibly become a possessive and stultifying mother: living her life vicariously through her wretched children. This was wrong and at all costs must stop at once. With her new friend, the costs did not seem to be at all high. They started to spend every Saturday together: Kew, Richmond, the river-boats to Greenwich, Queen Mary's Rose Garden in Regent's Park, Hampstead Heath, and then invariably home to tea or drinks and supper at Lincoln Street. Quite soon, she had realized that Herbert was not a monied man and she had used the utmost delicacy to avoid his having to pay for things...

One thing she realized about her life was that through some initial piece of cowardice (masked, at the time as not wanting to hurt other people's feelings), she kept on landing herself in awkward situations. The present predicament was really due to her having given in over buying Monks' Close in the first place. Now, having got it, she wanted to leave it to the League in her will and Herbert wanted her to leave it to him. Really, the fairest thing to do would be to sell the place and leave or give them half each of the money.

In the case of the League she would give it to them: in the case of Herbert they could buy some small but comfortable place to live in that would suit whoever outlived the other. Darling Elizabeth seemed to have married someone with almost too many houses, and Oliver, of course, should have Lincoln Street. It all seemed so simple when she thought of it by herself. In one way this solution got easier as time went by, because, as Herbert had predicted it would, the house was steadily increasing in value. Agents wrote to her—not often, but regularly—asking whether she would consider putting the house on the market, and the last sum quoted by them (Herbert always made them do that) was the astronomical one of twenty-two thousand pounds. *Surely* enough to go round? Yes, but plans of this sort, or indeed any sort, did not take into account the possibility of her dying before she had accomplished them. Herbert was also right about making a will. She must not dally any longer, and whatever he might feel she could not now go back on her promise to Dr Sedum. If she died, the League would get everything: otherwise, she would share it out. Tomorrow morning she would ring Mr Hardcastle and get him to post her the will to sign.

A sound outside—a car in the drive?—and some of her fears returned; it was horrible to feel nervous in one's own house. She decided to pull herself yet further together; to go and make her bed-time Horlicks and take it straight up with her. Claude could easily be got to come too as he adored Horlicks and benefited from her hot-water bottle.

Upstairs—Herbert insisted on the windows always being open—the bedroom was as dankly cold as a railway station in an east wind, and loneliness overcame her. Elizabeth, in Jamaica, was unspeakably far away. She decided to ring Alice, who after all would be far the most likely to explain that her father often rushed out in the evenings (whenever Herbert had seemed to do anything eccentric, Alice had been in the habit of saying that he was often, or even always, like that). But Leslie answered the telephone: sounding, May thought, as though he was a little drunk. Alice was in the nursing home, he said; she'd got pneumonia and lost the baby, but she was perfectly all right. May sent shocked and affectionate messages, but she wasn't sure if Leslie took them in: he kept saying, 'Well, I'll tell her you phoned,' in a sort of heavy, final way and then not putting down the receiver so she said goodbye firmly, to stop the conversation. Poor Alice! She was the only person May had ever met about whom she felt continuously protective. She would write to her tomorrow morning. Claude had drunk the first half inch of Horlicks, but hating cold rooms even more than he liked hot milky drinks he had got right into bed in order to be next to the hot-water bottle. She got into bed with him and composed herself for sleep by remembering Herbert as he was when she first met him. His frank kindness: his simplicity: many people with these old-fashioned virtues were sometimes the weeniest bit boring ...

* * *

' ... look at me like that, I feel as though you've known me for years.'

'I wish I had.'

'That's a nice thing to say.'

'Not nice, m'dear: true.'

'Some trifle? Or would you prefer the cheese board?'

'Which are you going to have?'

'Well—I shouldn't really, but tonight I'm going to spoil myself. A little trifle. I ought to watch my figure really.'

'Nonsense! A little of what you fancy, eh?'

'That's what my husband always said! *I'll* watch your figure, Myrtle, he said, *you* enjoy yourself. What about you? Two trifles, please, Ramon.'

They were the last in the dining-room, and their table, if not the best, was the most secluded. The tables round them had already been laid for breakfast; the Muzak, like the Tyrolean sconces, had been turned low: they sat before the unearthly cheeriness of a Magicoal which cast endless speedy reflections upon the horse-brasses each side of the huge brick fireplace. Myrtle Hanger-Davies owned the hotel: at least, she had inherited it from her husband, Dennis, who had clearly died from obvious forms of over-indulgence at the early age of fifty-six. Myrtle had been much younger than he when she married him and although they had been married for some time before he died (last September) there was no reason to suppose that she had caught him up. She had spent dinner telling the colonel these and other salient facts, and, frankly, she had not enjoyed herself so much for years. The great question was whether she should continue to run the hotel, or whether she should sell up and go abroad — possibly to run something or possibly just to retire. What she had felt was that on the one hand, she did not want to feel lonely, as she might in somewhere like Majorca with nothing to do, but on the other hand, she'd seen a lot of human nature. She sighed. The colonel expected that she had and agreed that it was something of the devil and the deep blue sea. The trifles arrived, and Ramon, who was certainly trained in some things, had brought a jug of Bird's custard *and* a jug of cream. Myrtle had quite a lot of both, and so did the colonel.

'When in doubt always do nothing, Dennis used to say. What do you think of that? As a maxim?'

'Lot of old-fashioned truth there —'

'Excuse me one moment — what will you have? With your coffee, I mean.'

He decided on Drambuie and she a Tia Maria. The conversation came to a halt while Ramon was getting these things. The colonel gazed at her. She was blonde and very well covered, both of which he liked: tonight she wore a tight electric-blue woollen dress with a high neck, so she was well covered in that way too. At her shoulder she wore a poodle brooch that was made of real diamonds with ruby eyes. Her hair had been done that day and so had her nails — it was a damn good thing he hadn't gone on thinking it was Tuesday ...

' ... look at me like that, what are you thinking?'

He laughed challengingly and said, 'You'd be surprised.'

'Would I really?' she asked hoping not.

'I was wondering if you'd ever been to Portugal.'

'Never!' she said. He certainly wasn't predictable — you never knew what he would say next.

He gazed at her a moment in silence, 'Ah well,' he said in the end.

247

A little blazing shiver began at the bottom of her spine and travelled right up to the back of her neck. At this moment, Ramon returned with the liqueurs and coffee. When he had gone, she raised her Tia Maria and said, 'What shall we drink to—a Merry Christmas, or a Happy New Year?'

He picked up his glass,

'Let's start with a Merry Christmas.'

* * *

John had been watching Elizabeth watching a humming bird. The bird was feeding from a bottle of honey and water. It was so small, and so amazing in colour, that even when it poised itself to siphon up the nectar she could hardly believe that it was really *there*. The expression on her face was serious: she was almost frowning with attention and pleasure. It was Christmas Eve; the sun was beginning to drop like a huge, round, red-hot stone into the sea, palm trees were turning darker than shadows and the mosquitoes had not yet started their night assault. The humming bird left; Elizabeth, who had been sitting on her heels, linked her hands behind her neck and stretched—in the middle of which she became aware of John.

'Did you see?'

'Yes.'

'Only feathers are that colour—or those colours, I suppose you'd have to say. Flowers aren't; jewels aren't.'

'Silk?' he suggested.

'It tries to be. Doesn't work, though, because there's always too much of it.'

'Butterflies,' he said, sitting beside her.

'Of course.'

'And tropical fish.'

'That's one of the things I like best about you.'

He waited.

'How you go into things. There are far too many things that a good many men don't think it it worth talking about.'

'Is that so?' One of the things he noted with amusement was the way in which her generalizations about men proliferated as her confidence grew about their marriage.

'Yes. A lot of men would think it was silly to discuss humming birds at all. A lot of men—'she stopped as she saw his face.

'I married you for your experience, Mrs Cole. It was a woman of the world I was after—'

Here the telephone rang which it all too often did. The only way in which John could leave England for so long was by letting people telephone him whenever they felt like it. He had explained this at the beginning, and she was very good and always read a book while he was talking which meant that she neither fidgeted nor listened. When he was finished he saw that she was starting *Bleak House* which he knew she had read.

'It's the fog,' she said looking up as he bent to kiss her. 'The contrast to here is so terrific.'

'It must be. Now. What would you like to do this evening? A terrifically vulgar man has asked us to a party—'

'What kind of party?'

'The kind that starts off very pompous with too much of everything and ends with people getting thrown into the swimming pool.'

'What else might we do?'

'We might go to Negril and have a hot-fish beach picnic.'

'Can't we do both things?'

'We'll do anything you like, my darling.'

'Don't you care at *all* what you do?'

'Not if I'm with you.'

The sun was almost touching the sea: the palm trees, relaxing against the sky, were black and silhouettes.

'I can't ever have been in love before,' he said, 'because I know I've never felt like this. And I'm pretty sure it's what people always do when they're in love. I wouldn't have known before; but I do now.'

She waited, wanting to see if it was the same.

'*You* know. My God, I *hope* you know. It's finding that you're very simple: that you don't need anything at all except the presence of the person. That scrambled eggs, or going to bed early, or it raining the whole day, are all enhancements: anything at all can make you think you are happier than you were before. It's feeling that everybody else must be better than you thought, and that whatever they are you mustn't be against them because perhaps somehow, they've missed it—'

'It *is* the same for everybody,' she said. 'I mean—you couldn't stop thinking of enhancements, but basically it's the same.'

The sun was sliding down out of sight. 'It looks as though there was a sort of slot for it—just beyond the sea and before the sky begins.'

In the end, they didn't go anywhere, but stayed by their own pool, and drank Daiquiris and swam and had supper and talked, as John later remarked, as though they had known each other all their lives but hadn't met for a year.

'We might as well be in a basement in Fulham Road.'

'Oh no we mightn't. There'd be no oxygen and you'd have too many clothes on.'

She was wearing one of his shirts over her bathing dress.

'God, money, sex, how to bring up children, birth control, democracy, education, socialism, looking after animals and things, boarding schools, homosexuality, good names for boys, how much we *agree* about things—oh dear, I've just thought—'

'What?'

'We've never had a serious quarrel! Do you realize that?'

'Nor we have. Do you want one, particularly?'

'Oh *no*! Of course I don't! I was just thinking how awful it would be when we do.'

He was bending down to lift her off the sofa.

'Perhaps we shall just not find the time,' he said.

FOUR

⚜

CHRISTMAS EVE

TEN days after his pleasant little meal with Mrs Hanger-Davies it was Christmas Eve, and from first thing in the morning, nothing seemed to go right. To begin with he woke up with indigestion— or something that felt damn like it. He'd taken a couple of Alka Seltzers with his morning tea but before they'd had a chance to work, May had started nagging him about the house—they'd-have-to-get-rid-of-it-it-was-far-too-large-for-them stuff. It was some time before he realized that she was serious: even shouting at her didn't seem to shut her up. Then, when he'd slipped out for a quick drink at the pub, he'd suddenly had a feeling that he ought to ring Myrtle: funny—he really had a sixth sense or something. She said she was so glad he'd phoned, because all his talk about Portugal (he'd only mentioned it for God's sake, he hadn't talked about it at all) anyway, she had said that all his talk about Portugal had given her ideas. She was going on a cruise to the Canary Islands. When? Next week. A *cruise* of all things. Everybody knew what occurred to middle-aged widows on *them*. He liked a lot of time to arrange things in—he hated being rushed—but that was what was happening to him, and just when he wasn't feeling up to scratch. Having told Myrtle three or four times what a splendid idea he thought the cruise was, he asked whether he might pop in for a spot of tea. Had he really got time for that on Christmas *Eve*? Myrtle had always understood that that was when most gentlemen did their shopping. Had she now? (Damn good thing she'd reminded him.) Well, from this point of view, at least, he'd like her to know that he was no gentleman. He'd laughed a good deal when he said this to be on the safe side. He'd rung off and rang May to say that he wouldn't be

251

back for lunch because he'd suddenly remembered his Christmas shopping. That put the lid on it. He'd go to London and kill two birds with one stone: pop into the lawyer (he'd written to Mr Pinkney asking him to prepare an appropriate version of his will—recently signed with a flourish in the presence of Mr Pinkney—for his wife to sign): then he'd have a spot of lunch at the club, then he'd nip along to Selfridge's where they often had bundles of slightly imperfect handkerchiefs at decent down-to-earth prices—back to Waterloo—train to West Byfleet (Myrtle's nearest station); Myrtle—and then May. Bit of a marathon, especially when he wasn't feeling quite the thing in the first place. Still—he was never a man to shirk his duty, which was what he called anything that he wanted to do enough to decide to do it. He headed the Wolseley towards West Byfleet; it would be madness to take the car to London on Christmas Eve.

It was madness to try and get about London at *all*: there were far too many people milling about all over the station, far too many children and parcels—you couldn't move without falling over them—and there was such a mob on the stairs to the Underground that he decided to walk to the Strand and Mr Pinkney's office. It was bitterly cold and the sky looked as though there might very well be snow later. He paused on Waterloo Bridge because walking seemed to have a bad effect upon his indigestion—he'd been walking fast to try and keep the cold out. The river looked damn bleak: they said nowadays that there was no need for a man to go down three times before he drowned, he'd be dead anyway by then from the effluent. He couldn't for the life of him understand somebody throwing themselves off a bridge in any case, but then suicide had never been in his line.

At the lawyer's it was very tiresome. Mr Pinkney was engaged they said: he had someone with him. When he objected to this, they asked whether he had an appointment. Of course not; he'd come all this way simply to pick up some papers that Mr Pinkney should have ready for him. They went away again and after what seemed a positive aeon came back and said would he like to wait just a few more minutes, Mr Pinkney *would* like to see him. Eventually Mr Pinkney did. He was full of breezy bonhomie, which meant, the colonel knew, that he was not going to do what he had been asked. So as soon as they had finished agreeing about the possibility of there being snow, he fixed Mr Pinkney with his frankest look and said he'd simply no idea that one was supposed to make an appointment when one was just going to pick up some papers: then before Mr Pinkney could reply, he added that of course when he came to think of it, he could see that chaps like Mr Pinkney had to organize their lives pretty carefully—it was damn foolish of him not to have realized that before. Mr Pinkney said well, there it was.

He'd happened to be in London for a spot of Christmas shopping —Mr Pinkney doubtless knew what store the ladies set by Christmas—and so his wife asked him to pick up her will ... His voice died away and he leaned slightly forward in his chair in order to fix Mr Pinkney more firmly with his simple, expectant gaze.

Mr Pinkney also leaned forward and cleared his throat very gently. Possibly the colonel didn't understand that generally speaking affairs of this nature could not be conducted in this manner. But the colonel did not look as though he understood what Mr Pinkney meant. What Mr Pinkney *meant* was that if Mrs Browne-Lacey wished to make a will, it was up to her to communicate personally with him or any other lawyer whom she wished to direct in the matter. Mrs Browne-Lacey had not been to see Mr Pinkney—

His wife was far from well. Not up to doing her own Christmas shopping in fact. Besides, like most sensible women, she expected her husband to deal with all that sort of thing—

Perhaps she would care to write to Mr Pinkney with instructions—

She wouldn't have sent *him* to fetch the papers if she'd wanted to write—she wasn't *well*: he was only trying to save her any extra trouble—

Mr Pinkney entirely appreciated the colonel's attitude, but he was afraid that in this particular matter he really was unable to act without personal instructions. He leaned back in his chair rather firmly, as one closing this interview.

It seemed to him quite amazing—all they wanted to do was leave things to each other—that so simple a matter should be made so complicated. No doubt Mr Pinkney had some expert, technical reason for feeling as he did, but for the life of him, he couldn't see what it could be.

Mr Pinkney sighed; if they weren't interrupted he might well be let in for trying to explain to the old boy. But luckily (though late) Miss Scantling came in with the stock bogus message (used on relatively few clients, it was true, but on them with jaw-aching regularity).

'Your call to Rome is waiting.'

Mr Pinkney started to his feet. Forgive him, but he must take that call. Perhaps Colonel Browne-Lacey would discuss matters with his wife and let him know after the holiday what was required. Mr Pinkney would be happy to go down to Surrey if Mrs Browne-Lacey wished. The colonel must excuse him—all the compliments of the season ...

The air was raw, and seemed colder after the stuffy warmth of Mr Pinkney's office. The colonel's thoughts for the first few minutes in the Strand were positively murderous. Damn the man! Pompous, pretentious, pedantic, pettifogging little cog in the wheel. It was people like Mr Pinkney who were responsible for the decline of this country. Bureaucratic bores, intent on some letter of a minor law at the expense of getting anything whatever done ...

Lunch would be heartening. He'd get a bus in the Strand to his club. He got the bus all right: simply because the traffic was solid: you could step on to a bus any time, and people were constantly doing this and stepping off again. After ten minutes of being stationary and crawling forward the odd yard, he got off too and walked. One certainly got on faster walking, but still, not fast enough. It was half past one by the time he reached his club only to find that the luncheon room was full. He enjoyed his first drink, however, but after two more his indigestion seemed worse. At least, funnily enough, draining his glass and suddenly remembering Pinkney leaning back in his chair, he had the extraordinary sensation of something slamming against his rib cage, his gullet, the back of his throat or the top of the front of his head—a kind of weak banging that hurt and was very bad for him without making any vital difference... Afterwards he felt distant and relaxed; as though something momentous had happened that nobody else could possibly understand—like his heart stopping and his blood changing direction, a difficult and dangerous thing to do. It was not easy to put the glass on the table and he couldn't even think clearly about it not being easy. He'd simply got too much on his plate. A bit later when he'd almost had a doze, and they'd told him they had a table for him, he summed it all up. Filthy weather, Christmas, bureaucrats, the wilful unpredictability of women—he'd got to simplify things somewhat. His spirits rose at the sight of the menu when Doris finally brought it to him: it was nearly two and he was starving. He decided upon hare soup, grilled sole and treacle tart. Henry came over, and the colonel told him he was busy today and how about half a bottle of his usual, and Henry smiled admiringly at the colonel's acumen and everything seemed all right for a minute or two.

But when it came, he didn't really enjoy his lunch; left most of the soup to leave room for the sole, but then found he didn't seem to fancy the sole. He felt tired, somehow, and he'd clean forgotten what treacle tart did to his dentures, so he had a drop of coffee, signed his bill and made off. Getting to Selfridge's was so bad he nearly gave up, but by the time he felt like that he'd shouldered and tramped three-quarters of his way there, and he couldn't think of anything else to get, or, come to that, anywhere else to get it.

He had a bit of luck in Selfridge's. They were selling small, white handkerchiefs with a nice bit of lace on them and embroidered initials in bundles of a dozen. This was when he realized that both their names began with M—a considerable saving. He bought a bundle and got the girl to divide them into two lots of six and then to wrap them up fairly well in flat boxes with robins on them. He was in and out of the shop like a dose of salts. It then took him—he timed it—nearly an hour to reach Waterloo. Nothing but queues when he got there: he couldn't even buy a platform ticket because the machines he went to had all run out or broken down or something. So then of course he had to go back to the bottom of the ordinary ticket queue again. He just caught a train, and that meant standing in the draughty corridor for the whole journey next to a man, who, as he planned to tell Myrtle, was definitely not using Amplex: also, he hadn't brought his muffler, and had the uneasy feeling that he was getting a stiff neck. He sometimes wondered whether he took enough care of himself.

The Wolseley wouldn't start—at least, not until he had totally lost his temper, got out the handle and had a go at turning her over. Icy gusts of station air eddied unerringly round the gap between his socks and his trousers as he bent despairingly over the machine, at the same time as he felt trickles of sweat edge their way from behind his ears to the top of his collar. He was late for Myrtle already, and what on earth was he to do if this infernal engine wouldn't start? Just then it did—gave a convulsive heave in a forward direction (he'd left it in gear) and died again. But it *had* started.

All the way to the Monkey Puzzle Hotel he tried to think out what he was going to say to Myrtle, but he was driving along a road he didn't know at all well and he was worried about being late— for the second time running with her. Also, the snag about rehearsing conversations was that people—women, at any rate—simply did not say whatever it was you'd planned they should say; so the whole thing was thrown out pretty well from the start.

He was certainly right about things getting thrown out. When he got to the Monkey Puzzle, first he was told that Mrs Hanger-Davies was not in, had gone to hospital or some such gibberish: then he was told—none of the blasted servants spoke decent English —that Madame-very-work-not-see-at-all stuff. He brushed aside the feller who said all that; he was a little chap and fell against a huge wreath of real holly that stood on an easel in the entrance hall—in fact he was such a little runt, that he nearly fell *through* it. The colonel couldn't help seeing the funny side of that. He pushed open the door to Myrtle's private sitting-room-cum-office without ceremony and went in.

She was there, of course, but in the middle of some interminable telephone call. She looked upset and abstracted and not even specially glad to see him.

It was minutes after he had tip-toed with an elaborate pantomime of not disturbing her that she stopped her monotonous performance of listening for a long time and then saying how sorry she was and then listening again. Then it turned out that the chef—cook chap— had dropped dead that afternoon—heart, or something.

'It was his poor wife I was talking to. Poor thing; two kids *and* she's a foreigner. He was only forty-six, she says. Really—I seem to be haunted by it: first Dennis and now Antonio: you can't help wondering who the third will be. There's no rhyme or reason to it *and* the holiday coming on and all. He was only halfway through the turkeys and they say there's going to be snow.' She blew her nose for rather a long time—ending up by wringing the end of it while she was still blowing which the colonel found a bit much.

'It sounds as though a nice cup of tea would do us both good,' he suggested hopefully; there was no sign of any other refreshment.

'Out of the question—for me, anyway, I'm afraid. I must be off to the kitchens. I could have a tray sent through to the residents' lounge if you're very keen.'

'Oh, come—surely you could spare a few minutes m'dear. It's Christmas *Eve*, after all.'

But she had got to her feet and was tucking her handkerchief in the pocket of her emerald green cardigan. 'You wouldn't realize as you've never been in the business, but it's just be*cause* of the holiday that I must keep on the go. I've spent all afternoon trying the agencies for a temporary but of course they've got nobody and they close early, and then it took me a long time to get hold of his poor wife, and we're nearly full right through over next week-end and one way and another I just don't know which way to turn.'

Controlling his rage he asked about the cruise.

'Oh I cancelled that first thing. I couldn't possibly go away now for ages. If I do get a replacement for Antonio I'll have to break them in, and if I don't, the cooking will have to be done by yours truly. Is that for me? How nice; I'm always short of hankies. I'll keep it till tomorrow to open. Shall I ask them to bring you some tea in the lounge?'

But he said he thought he would be getting along, he mustn't be too late. They wished each other a Merry Christmas and he stumped out to his car that had had ample time to get freezing cold again.

In the car he nearly cried: well—actual tears came to his eyes. Damn it all! He'd keyed himself up all *day* for this meeting with Myrtle: he'd planned that it should be important—cosy, intimate, but definitely epoch-making. Just as she seemed to like recalling how funny that they should have met in the same railway carriage three weeks running, she was to have remembered tea on Christmas Eve ... Well, she wasn't off on her cruise: one had to count one's blessings. On the cold, slow journey back to Monks' Close he tried to do this, and Alice, his only daughter, came suddenly—and for the first time since she had left home—into his mind. She had always been an attentive housekeeper; warm room, hot meal, no-questions-asked type of thing. An admirable stopgap, that was what Alice had always been, and for the first time, here he was, going to have to manage everything without her.

* * *

Alice had spent the afternoon having a rest on her bed as Mrs Mount had insisted she should. She and Leslie were spending Christmas with his parents: it was one of those large plans that Alice didn't think about too much when it was first mooted and then realized later that the reason she hadn't was that she would have dreaded it so much. Ever since her miscarriage—and that seemed weeks ago now—she had found it very difficult to care about anything. This was not, as Leslie and his mother seemed to think, because she was so heart-broken at losing the baby—she wasn't and hadn't been that in the least. She'd wondered when she woke up the first night in the nursing home whether she'd lost someone she might have been able to talk to, but the thought had simply crossed her mind and left no wake. Probably not, was the answer she had given herself at the time. What she had found unnerving was how much everybody else seemed to expect her to feel, and what a lot they seemed to know about it. She'd spent ages listening to the various things that Leslie, Mrs Mount and Rosemary told her she was feeling. When they weren't there she simply lay either staring at the ceiling or with her eyes shut. She'd had pneumonia as well as the miscarriage, and for a few days people hadn't talked so much—had just brought flowers, which she had liked. The nurses had been very kind all the time; they kept telling her how she was *going* to feel, but they did not commiserate or describe any similar experience. She was a very good patient, they told her, and she certainly never complained or asked for anything, but this was only because there was nothing she wanted. It was not until she was more or less over the pneumonia that she began to notice that there was something wrong with her—that she was, or had become, a sort of gap or void. She did not mind being like that very much, but she felt that everybody else would mind if they noticed, and she became increasingly afraid that they might. With them her face ached with trying to smile and respond generally, and when she was alone she found herself listening—to see if anyone was there—to see whether she could catch herself out existing, or not existing, as the case might be.

Alice had always found communication with anyone difficult, although up until now she had been able to talk to herself. But now there was the sort of silence inside her, as though it was too dark to see at all, and there had been a heavy fall of snow so that all ordinary sounds of people had ceased, some general and complete eclipse of the senses that would be mysterious and awful if one had left any sense working that could know that. She did still seem to have, albeit precariously, some small, critical stronghold that intermittently sent out a series of S.O.S.s of a disapproving nature. The results of these were useless. On one occasion, the chaplain looked in on her during his rounds and asked if there was anything he could do for her, and had only halfway withdrawn his head from round her door before she had said yes. When he was sitting down, his initial expression of alarm fading to goodwill, she tried very hard to tell him about this non-existence feeling and ended by asking him what he thought it meant. He had replied, after not much hesitation, that it was clearly a case of body being so debilitated that mind—he let alone spirit—could not function properly, if at all. She would feel miles better, he said, when she had recovered from the effects of the antibiotics and benefited from whatever tonic he was sure she was getting. When she was up—a bit of a change—the sea, perhaps, and she would be a new woman. He'd pop in again before she left them, he had added when on his feet, which he was sure would be *soon*. The next time, she had asked her doctor whether people who had had rather bad miscarriages and pneumonia often felt that they did not exist. Of course they didn't he had answered at once: it was all in her mind: women often felt run-down and nervy after a miscarriage and that set them imagining all kinds of things about themselves. There was nothing the matter with her; she must simply not give way to hysteria. He had no doubt that she'd be pregnant again in no time and Bob's your uncle. She gave up after that.

So here she was, in the Mounts' spare room having a rest so that she would be all right for their party that evening. Mrs Mount had been cooking and/or assembling food for days: Rosemary had asked several men and Sandra was having her best friend; a number of Mount relations were attending—they would be thirty-eight in all. Alice had never been good at parties (in fact she'd been to very few), but the Mounts' parties were the worst she'd ever tried to be good at. Everybody seemed to know everybody else extremely well: there was a great deal of public badinage, and when—as experience had awfully taught her it invariably was—this was directed at her, she was struck dumb, paralysed, utterly done for. There were always too many people for the room: the large dining-room table loaded with food took up a good third of it. It was also very hot, as Mrs Mount imported fires and put them all over the place so that the room was alive with scorching culs-de-sac and perfectly airless. None the less, Mounts and Mount guests managed to eat and drink and think of things to say to one another for hours and hours, and Alice, as a quasi-Mount, was in agony. Sometimes, late in the evening, they played terrible games that drew attention to people and, she felt, particularly to her: 'games' being a kind of cynical synonym for torture. The worst feature of these social nightmares was the feeling that everybody was enjoying themselves except her. It seemed so unfair: like being colour blind or tone deaf or not being able to smell or something. 'Relax!' people would cry; 'not to *worry!*' 'She's shy,' someone would inevitably, but publicly, confide—as though she was, not tone, but stone, deaf. The last, awful thing that Alice had noticed about the Mount parties was that they were all exactly the same. Since knowing and marrying Leslie, she had been subject to several and she could not find anything different at all about any of them. After hours of refusing more and more food (people always pressed refreshments upon you if you didn't talk much) and trying desperately to talk at all; escaping sometimes to 'powder her nose'—really to go somewhere where she could open a window and breathe—she would return to find the hard core of the party plotting some awful game where you were sure to have to stand up in front of everyone and pretend to be somebody or do something while everyone else shrieked with laughter at how funny you were and how badly you were doing it. She had begged, first the family generally, and finally Leslie, to let her off this particular part of the festivities, but they wouldn't: Mrs Mount took the view that the less Alice wanted to play games the more good it would do her to play them, and Leslie always said that he simply didn't understand what she was talking about. He always said that. At this point it occurred to her to wonder whether she got on worse—or less—with Leslie than with any of the rest of the Mounts simply because she saw so much more of him? Because really things had reached a point where even half hours in the nursing home with Leslie had been a peculiar ordeal. At least Rosemary and Mrs Mount did most of the talking: but Leslie expected her in this, as in most else, to be like his mother and sister. Some part of her had been making kind of emergency allowances for how everything seemed to her—being in the nursing home, staying at Mount Royal as the house was unlaughingly called—but now, considering Leslie, she inevitably thought of their bungalow and going back there alone with Leslie to live. For a few moments she thought carefully about each room there; the black glass and black Formica in the bathroom that showed every mark, even water looked shocking on them, the bleak prettiness of their bedroom (at any moment now, marital relations were to be resumed, according to both the doctor and Leslie: it was like

some ghastly weather forecast), the sitting-room or lounge that
never, whatever she did in it, seemed to be inhabited, seemed just
to tolerate pieces of furniture, and sometimes people as well, being
there: it was actually filled to the brim with Mount wedding
presents—the cocktail cabinet (Mr and Mrs Mount), the coffee
table (Rosemary), the corner cupboard (Aunt Lottie), the black
arm-chairs bought with the Albert Mounts' cheque and the beetroot-
coloured rug that Leslie's best friend's mother had made for them;
and finally, the spare room—Leslie still called it his study—that
Elizabeth had actually stayed a night in with Claude... 'I do know
something—because of loving him,' she thought gratefully. She
thought of the windswept and scarred piece of ground that was to
become a neat little garden (no shade for years, because there were
no proper trees on the whole estate,) and then she simply thought,
'I must put a stop to it—all of it,' and the next moment she was out
of bed and dressing quietly and sensibly in her warmest clothes. She
packed her small suitcase with a nightdress, her kimono, some
slippers and her sponge bag. All the time she felt not the slightest
excitement or fear; nor did she think about what she was doing—
she simply got on with doing it. Her purse contained only fifteen
shillings, but then in the wallet was the five pound note that May
had given her on her wedding day—her very own money, and
enough. Getting out of the house was easy: everybody was shopping
or at work excepting Sandra, and she was immersed in a bubble
bath with Rosemary's transistor going full blast. The danger was
meeting any Mount returning, not so much just outside the house,
as she could hide in the laurel bushes, but in the street itself. It was
five o'clock and the lamps were lit: they would recognize her easily
if they saw her from a car or a cab. She turned down the street
away from the main road; it would be better to walk round the
block. It was all quite easy, really, and in fact, suddenly got even
easier. A cab set down a woman laden with shopping bags: the
driver was pleased to pick up a fare at once and take her to the
station. In the cab it occurred to her that she had left no letter, no
message, nothing. Would they, would Leslie, perhaps, wonder
what had become of her? They would think she was mad; but

would they actually *mind* her disappearance? Not awfully, she hoped;
she didn't want to cause them any trouble. By the time she reached
the station she had decided that she had been quite right to leave no
note; if she had, and they had found it at all soon, it was just possible
that Leslie would have come to the railway station in search of her.
This thought unnerved her so much, that after she had bought her
ticket to London, she hid in the Ladies until the train came in. She
would write a letter from Lincoln Street.

* * *

The only good thing that happened to May on Christmas Eve was
that she got a telephone call from Elizabeth—all the way from
Round Hill, Jamaica. It came through in the afternoon while Mrs
Green was still there, and she, having, just that minute, witnessed
May's will, was very pleased: events of this kind were what she
went out to work for.

'Yes—it is really me,' Elizabeth was saying.

'Oh—darling, how lovely.'

'How are you?'

'I'm fine,' May lied; what else could one possibly say? It didn't
matter anyhow, it was each other's voices they were after, not what
either of them thought or said about anything. Mrs Green was going
round the den shutting the narrow, gothic windows with the utmost
meaning, although May couldn't think why.

'How's Jamaica?'

'It's almost more like one imagines than I thought it possibly
could be. Tremendously beautiful and worrying. Is Oliver spending
Christmas with you?'

'No, darling—he doesn't seem able to make it. He seems rather
low. Depressed,' she added: the full luxury of talking to her
daughter was beginning to penetrate: she knew she would remember everything they said all day. 'How is John?'

'Well, he's very well: only his daughter is threatening to come
out here and she never seems to have a good effect upon anyone.
That's the only thing. How is Herbert?'

'He's fine,' May lied again. What could she say about him? Pride, unhappiness, years of protecting Elizabeth and months of not wanting to be possessive or get in her way stopped her crying out, 'He's awful! He's turned into a quite different person. I think he even hates *me* some of the time. I'm miserable and a lot of the time I feel so ill I think I'm going to die.' None of this came out: there was simply a short, and, Mrs Green thought, an unbelievably expensive silence. At *last* Mrs Browne-Lacey was behaving like a lady: sitting about and wasting other people's money in unusual ways.

'When are you coming back?' It would be lovely to know that; something to look forward to.

'I don't know. Well, I do, really. By the end of January, anyhow. Did you know I was having a baby?'

'Oh *good*. When?'

'May.'

'Yes?'

'I'm *having* it in May you idiot.'

And just as May was thinking that in that case, she must have been having the baby for quite a long time, Elizabeth said, 'What I most wanted to say was, I'm sorry I sort of got married behind your back: it wasn't exactly not wanting you to be there—' her voice tailed off.

May said, 'Darling, that's *quite* all right—of course.' Indeed it was far more than all right, she thought, after they had said goodbye. Both of them knew perfectly well why Elizabeth had behaved in this way; what they had both needed was for it to be made clear that the exclusion had nothing really to do with Elizabeth not wanting her mother. No need to go further.

Mrs Green was simply waiting about in the hall outside the den.

'I shut the windows because of the noise from the birds,' she said, 'as soon as I realized where your call come from.' She waited, expecting news.

'Elizabeth is having a baby,' May said happily. 'Isn't that lovely?'

'Oh madam!'

But that was all about the day that *was* lovely. Mrs Green went just before lunch. May then realized that she had not bought

enough bread to make bread sauce for the chicken that she and
Herbert were to celebrate Christmas with. This meant walking to
the end of the drive and half a mile to the crossroads for the bus into
the nearest place to shop. It was extraordinarily cold: people kept
looking at the still, congested sky and prophesying snow. She was
frozen by the time she caught the bus, and never got warm again
that day. The only bread left in the shop was the much advertised
pre-sliced Sorbo rubber so she bought one or two other things to
make the whole journey feel more worthwhile. Then she longed
for some tea or coffee before waiting for the bus back, but the only
place had a queue of people waiting for a table, there was only one
bus back, and she had to give it up. It was nearly dark by the time
the bus set her down, and she plodded back along the road, up the
drive, her exhaustion tinged with slight, persistent, humiliating
fear. The dogs barked on her return: they had no discrimination,
and were, in any case, bored to death. She knew that the first thing
would be to feed them.

One way and another, by the time Herbert returned—much
later than she had thought he possibly would—she was feeling
thoroughly overdone and worked up, and longing for a cosy drink
and chat.

She knew Herbert was in a bad temper before she even saw him,
as he did not call out, 'Here we are, m'dear; all present and correct.'
He didn't call out at all, but she heard him crashing about in his den,
swearing in that peculiarly savage way that alarmed her enough to
make interrupting him a minor ordeal.

'Why the devil didn't you light a fire in here?'

She had forgotten. At least, it hadn't been worth lighting before
she went shopping because it would simply have gone out. And
since she'd been back she'd had so much—

'Give me a box of matches.' He fumbled angrily with shiny,
purple hands.

She had turned on the bigger electric fire just before lunch—

'I can see that. I'm not a complete fool. It may be easier for you
to use the electricity in this irresponsible manner, but it costs far
more than lighting a good, old-fashioned fire.'

'Really, Herbert, I told you I had to go *out*.'

'What on earth did you have to do that for?'

'And anyway, good, old-fashioned fires have to be cleaned out and re-laid. They're not necessarily cheaper—just nicer in some ways. Let's have a drink—'

'What are we having for dinner?'

'Well—I didn't know what you'd feel like—'

He sat slowly back on his heels. While he turned his head slowly towards her as though he had a stiff neck and it was painful to look at her.

'Didn't know what I'd feel like,' he echoed, 'I see. So I come back frozen to the marrow after slaving away all day to a cold room and no food at all—in order to have the pleasure of choosing which tin you will open—'

Here without either meaning to or being able to help it, she burst into tears. At once everything got better. While she was crying and explaining, more or less incoherently, that it wasn't just tins, she'd laid the fire specially to save Mrs Green—they'd run out of bread and what with waiting for the bus both ways you couldn't leave the fire and she was sorry she was such a hopeless housekeeper but she felt so rotten—he, making loud clucking noises, had helped her into (his!) chair and put her poor feet that she couldn't feel on to a footstool and found her a paper handkerchief and a cigarette and said that what they both needed was a stiff drink. So while she worked the bellows on the reluctant fire, he fetched glasses, unlocked his cupboard, and for once gave her a whisky that was quite dark brown. He put her Christmas present ostentatiously on top of his roll-top desk and she told him about the little mixed grill she had planned for them. They listened to the seven-thirty news and then, just as he was getting himself a second drink and she was talking of going to the kitchen, the pains began. They had never been so bad: appalling stomach cramps that doubled her up and made her sweat with pain, until she knew that she must vomit somehow or other. He supported her upstairs, put her in the bathroom and when, gasping, retching minutes later, she was fairly sure she had finished, he practically carried her to bed. He said he would fill her a hot-water bottle and call the doctor (the only telephone was in his den). She lay for what seemed a long time, shivering and sweating in bed: the nausea was dying down, and she felt thirsty and frightened She knew she ought to undress, but felt too weak to make the attempt. The question 'What *is the matter* with me?' recurred urgently in her mind and perhaps what frightened her most was finding that she was afraid to think at all of an answer. It was awful feeling this kind of fright, and at the same time feeling too tired to bear it: she cried a little and couldn't find a handkerchief and snuffled quietly against the sheet. She tried to think what Dr Sedum would say to her in these horrible and despairing circumstances, but nothing either useful or comforting came to her mind. It was cowardly to be frightened like this: but she mustn't make too much fuss or Herbert might get fed up with her, and she was utterly dependent upon him. 'Like this, at any rate,' she thought. Her teeth were chattering and she felt clammy and squalid. She could hear Herbert's measured tread on the stairs and then in the passage and tried to smile at him when he came in with the hot-water bottle.

'Not much of a Christmas Eve.'

'Can't be helped. Here you are, old girl.'

'I'm dreadfully thirsty.'

'Always is after one's been sick.'

'Could you get me a glass of water? Oh—and what did the doctor say?'

He was tucking the eiderdown round her legs and did not immediately reply.

'Herbert?'

'What? Of course I'll get you some water.' He went off to the bathroom and seemed a long time there.

'Don't drink too much at once or you'll have it up again.'

'What did the doctor say?' she asked again when she had had a few sips.

'Said I was to put you to bed, keep you warm, and he'll be along first thing in the morning.'

'Not tonight?'

But he repeated, 'First thing in the morning.'

'Herbert, I don't want to fuss, but I think I *am* rather ill.'

'If you must know, it's my fault for giving you such a stiff whisky. A drink like that on an empty stomach—I'm prepared to bet you didn't have a proper lunch, did you now? Thought not. A drink like that on any empty stomach, and yours has been in a delicate state lately—see what I mean?'

He had been fidgeting with things on the bedside table, now he straightened himself and passed a hand over his hair which she knew he did when he was embarrassed.

'I think we ought to get you into bed. Do you want me to—er—?'

'No thank you darling, I'm sure I can manage.' She wasn't at all sure, but she didn't want to embarrass him, besides she felt so squalid and miserable after being so sick that she wouldn't really want anyone to help her.

'Right. I'll pop down and make your hot drink.'

'Did the doctor say whether—'

'Yes, yes, he recommended it. Settle your stomach and warm you up. I'll have one with you.'

As he was leaving the room she called, 'If you see Claude, his food's on the top shelf in the larder. I couldn't find him anywhere earlier when I did the dogs. He must be ravenous.'

'Right.'

'And Herbert?'

She had wanted to tell him how kind he was being, but he had already gone. After a moment or two, she sat up and slowly pulled her jersey off over her head, but this simply made her feel so cold that she could not face taking off any more clothes. She reached for her bed-jacket, and then her woollen dressing-gown. When they were both on, she felt warmer, but more tired, and lay down to have a little rest until Herbert came up with her drink. He had had nothing to eat, poor dear, so she hoped he was getting himself something.

She became awake quite suddenly: one moment her head was on the block and the guillotine knife was coming down with its inexorable force, and the next moment her eyes were open, the alarm clock was ticking away and she was herself, in bed with the bedside lamp on. She remembered that she had been ill, and that Herbert was fetching her a drink—she must have dozed off. As she sat up, she realized that she still felt pretty awful, and looked to see whether she had any water left.

Then she got a bad shock. The alarm clock said twenty to four. She found herself staring, wondering how on earth it could say that— that would be—that meant that she had been asleep for *hours*! She was still wearing her dressing-gown. Except for the clock ticking, the room was very quiet—much of it shadowy with only one lamp on, but it looked as though her door was ajar. Herbert might have brought up her hot milk, found her asleep and not liked to disturb her. Then where was the milk? Herbert might have brought up her drink, found her asleep and taken it away again. But then where was Herbert? Herbert might have brought up her hot milk, found her asleep and not liked to disturb her *so* he had taken the drink and gone to sleep in another room. He'd left the door ajar in case she needed him. This final conclusion seemed sensible and likely, and she wondered why it did not make her feel less anxious, but it didn't. She did not want to go and look in all the rooms for Herbert in case when she found him she woke him up, which she knew would make him very cross indeed. But on the other hand, she did need to know that he was *there*—where he was, she meant, of course. It would be too awful if he had just got tired of her being ill and simply gone off somewhere as he had been doing rather a lot lately. Other considerations took over. Her stomach, which felt as though it had been repeatedly kicked, warned her that another attack of diarrhoea was imminent; she'd have to get up. She got to the bathroom all right, but it was horribly cold there, and she found that she had to walk very slowly because the ground seemed feathery and uneven as though she was walking in a dream. This feeling was increased when she pulled aside the passage curtain and looked out on to the drive and lawn and shrubs. It had been snowing heavily: everything was thick with it, and even in the dark, luminous. Very large flakes were still slowly slipping down and casually coming to rest. It crossed her mind that she was actually dreaming. In a dream she would go—no, float—downstairs to something amazing.

Obviously it wasn't a dream; none the less she was going down-stairs, that was the thing to do. She pulled her dressing-gown up round her throat, clutched the banisters with one hand and started down.

She went straight to Herbert's study because she saw that the light was on there. It was one of those glaring lights, a naked bulb topped by a shallow glass shade—it did nothing to soften, let alone conceal what she found.

Herbert was dead. He seemed to have opened a window just before he died as his hand was still clenched upon the casement catch, and he lay with this arm, its shoulder, and his head upon it, half out of the window. It looked a very odd position, but then she realized that in fact he was jammed there; as he had fallen, the width of his shoulders had stuck in the narrow window frame. The rest of him was sprawled over the low stone window seat and the floor. Snow had fallen against the open casement window and his head and clung there, making his white hair look like dirty ivory, and he was so cold to touch that she knew he was dead. She noticed all this without feeling anything, but it seemed to her that everything was happening so slowly, like people said about films, and things that for all she knew she might have run into the room, seen all this and any minute now would give a shriek—it was just that she hadn't got to the shriek. She never got to it. There was more to notice in the same slow, minute and passionless manner. The fire had gone out, but in the hearth lay a document—stiff paper, red ribbon and seal—that she recognized as the will that had arrived from Mr Hardcastle and been witnessed by Mrs Green—this, no yesterday, morning. The paper had been slightly burned—quite burned at one corner—and it lay just below the grate as though where it had ceased to burn it had dropped from the fire. She tried to remember where she had left the will. Elizabeth had telephoned just after Mrs Green had done her bit on it, and she had put it on top of Herbert's bureau to dry while talking to Elizabeth. Then, she had forgotten it. On the edge of the bookshelf by the top of the bureau was a wide tumbler about a third full of what looked like Horlicks. Milk was spattered about the shelf and even as far as the bureau, and she knew what that meant. Oliver had suggested giving Claude milk goggles for Christmas as he seemed to blind himself with spray when engaged upon drinking. It was Claude who had had the Horlicks. She tasted it but it was not at all nice cold, and was anyway no good for quenching thirst. By the Horlicks were her cigarettes and she took one and lit it. It reassured, at the same time as faintly nauseating her. The room was icy. Even the telephone felt cold to touch. She dialled the operator but there was no more or different sound. She tried two or three times but nothing happened: the line, she decided, was dead. Like Herbert. The cigarette was making her feel very sick. Herbert was *dead*. He must have had a heart attack or stroke, or something like that, and had been trying to get some air and she had been too far away to help him. She felt she ought to try and get him out of the window because it looked so uncomfortable, but when she tried to pull him in by the shoulders he did not move at all—was quite horribly rigid. So she simply brushed the snow off him, and that was when she saw the marks of Claude's paws on his collar. She stopped bothering with the snow after she had uncovered the part of Herbert's face that had been shrouded by it. His eyes were open and his expression made her feel uncomfortable to the point of fear. He looked as though he had been stopped in the middle of some violent resentment, and that, in turn, made her feel that at any moment his resentment might suddenly resume ...

She was frightfully thirsty. Whatever she ought to do—and she had not thought what that might be—she needed to drink something first, and she decided to make some tea. She must have got very cold without noticing, as one of her feet seemed to have gone to sleep; when she started to walk she simply could not feel where the floor was, and so, in fact, she literally stumbled over Claude.

He lay just by the swing baize door to the kitchen quarters, and he, too, was dead. He was not stiff but his fur had that impersonal feel to it that was retrospectively unnerving. Poor Claude! As she was getting to her feet, she saw the pool of vomit. She turned on another passage light: all along the passage near the wall were the marks of Claude's final misery. He must have come in through the open study window, drunk the Horlicks—

What she thought then was so monstrous that she felt the distinct urge to lose consciousness—in vain. It was as if she had suddenly looked behind her and caught the glimpse of a hideous cloven foot in the door: her mind made some frenzied but too faint resistance and then fell back against the force of some horrid explanatory and voluble crowd. The Horlicks had been made for her. She had been feeling very ill. A whisky had also been made for her earlier. For months, drinks of various kinds had been made for her. She had been so ill this evening that she had thought she was going to die. Claude was dead. Her children were away. She had been mysteriously ill for ages. He had had two other wives. They had both died. He had made her buy this house and had changed from seeming to care deeply for her to seeming sometimes actually to hate her. If she had drunk the Horlicks she would be lying dead. She might have been very sick, but she would still have died. An agony of horror that anyone in the world could be like that; she did not feel personal about it: simply, she would never have believed that there could be such a person unless it had been proved—as it now seemed to be— in relation to her. Claude must have suffered, she now knew, great pain before he died instead of her. She knelt down again to take him up in her arms: Alice had loved him and he deserved proper obsequies. (Alice!) But he had watched her, afraid, in pain, knowing all the time what was to become of her, indeed, arranging her eventual death—for what? She stumbled with Claude in her arms to the kitchen where she laid him in the cardboard box in which he had often slept. His eyes were open: they were going dull and she tried to shut them, but they would not stay. She put on a kettle and began to make tea without thinking at all. She would drink the tea very slowly, and time would pass, and in the end it would be morning and the doctor would come ...

After the tea she got up from the kitchen table: if the doctor was coming (but perhaps, that, too, had been a lie?) there were things she must do. It meant going back into the study, and she discovered that she dreaded this. It was as though she was more afraid of the stiff, wicked thing jammed in the window than she had ever been of the living creature whose cover had been that of being a bit of a bore — but none the less a straightforward, kindly man… There were things she *must* do.

So, shivering, wretchedly ill (she paid another visit to a freezing lavatory) she none the less carefully put away her will (he must have read it and had a fit of rage at its contents) and then dealt with the tumbler of Horlicks. When she tipped it away, she saw that there seemed to be a good deal of sediment in the bottom of the glass and that was when she wondered weakly what poison he had used. She washed out the tumbler very carefully, wondering whether she was going to die in any case, or whether she had been sick enough to escape. She would also have to bury Claude. Everything took ages because she could hardly walk. She opened the heavy front door: the snow had stopped, but it lay about five inches deep in the drive and that meant that there would be drifts. In any case, she found that under the snow the ground was iron-hard from previous frost and that she could not dig it with the study coal shovel. This made her cry, and once she had begun, she could not stop at all.

She wanted everything to be tidied away before the doctor came: she did not want poor, gentle Alice to have to know what her father had been. This idea — that had occurred when she had been putting Claude in the box — had grown to the exclusion of any other, and she kept explaining to herself why it would be terrible for Alice to have her father posthumously dubbed a murderer. She might realize that her *own* mother had probably been poisoned: 'slowly fading health' which was how that poor lady's demise had been mentioned had now an ominous sound to it. And then there was her stepmother, whose mysterious ailments had also culminated in death. If Alice were told anything, she could hardly fail to guess a great deal more; more, certainly, May felt, than she should bear. So of course it was awful that the ground should be so hard. Indeed, after a rest in the kitchen (she had turned out the light and shut the door of Herbert's study) she put on a coat over her dressing gown and carried Claude out for a second attempt. And this was where, at six in the morning, Alice had found her.

FIVE

···⚬···

OLIVER AND ELIZABETH

T H E call came through at five in the morning on Christmas Day, and to Elizabeth it seemed hardly to have finished one ring before John had turned on the weak and yellow electric light and was propped up in bed on one elbow listening to the operator.

'Yes,' he was saying; and then, after a pause, 'I said—I accept the call.'

She thought then from his voice that it was Jennifer, and moments later, when his look of speculative affection dissolved to a courteous blank and he settled down to listening she knew. No good going on sleeping, or even pretending to sleep.

After a very long time, John said, 'It certainly sounds like rather a muddle.' There was another pause while he listened. Then he said: 'Oh *no*! Why? You really ought to know why by now. We've come all this way in *order* to be by ourselves. Honeymoons aren't usually attended by close members of the family. I realize that. Yes—you told me.' He listened to another long speech. 'Well—we'll have to see. Wait a minute.' He groped for a pencil. 'Next time, you might work out the hours before you call.' He wrote something down. 'All right all right. I was simply telling you. Yes—I'll see to it.' He put down the receiver and turned to Elizabeth. 'Oh dear, oh damn. That was Jennifer.'

'Yes.'

'She has contracted some sort of alliance with someone who sounds like a *joke*—they're so awful.'

'Is she in love with him?'

'Love?' He looked startled. Then he said, 'She's only known him ten days; he's married and he's just got through a cure. He's also a Catholic so he really is married—'

274

'Goodness.'

'She is also pregnant—she says.'

'How can she be, if she's only known him ten days?'

He shrugged. 'Some sort of remote lack of control. But why does she have to come here?'

'She's *not* coming here!'

'That's what she rang up about.'

Elizabeth threw herself back on her pillow in mock horror to conceal the real kind.

'She's bringing him with her.'

'How long for?' she asked much later when they were having breakfast.

'Nothing was said about that.'

'When, then?'

'This afternoon. I'm meeting them at the airport.'

'I don't want you to.' She was trying to sound sulky because she was frightened.

'Darling, don't be silly.'

She burst into tears which faintly shocked both of them. He thought of course she was pregnant; she wondered why on earth she should seem to hate Jennifer so much. After a few seconds in-effective struggle, she rushed off the terrace into the house. He, in turn, sat battling with the murmuring pangs of guilt that had become noticeable, like indigestion, when her tears had brought his attention up against them. In the end, finding he could do nothing about himself, he went to comfort her.

She was sitting on the edge of the bath, sternly combing her hair.

'You asked me last night whether I cared at *all* what I did. Remember?'

She went on combing her hair. 'You said, "not if I'm with *you*."'

'That's right.'

He took the comb out of her hand and threw it on her dressing-table. 'I want *you* to feel like that,' he said and took her hands. 'I want you to feel that you could have 'flu or break your leg or embark upon an evening or a week with some of the world's greatest bores, or be shipwrecked or anything awful you can think

275

of, and that you'd feel all right about any of those things because you were with me. The only thing *I* couldn't bear would be to be without you.'

'The only thing *I* couldn't bear.'

'So however awful Jennifer is—and I expect she'll be that one way or another—she won't make any real difference to us. See?'

'I warn you,' he remarked when he had finished signing the letters the secretary brought in before lunch, 'I warn you that all this engagement business is probably just a bid for my exclusive attention. And I'll have to go through the motions of considering the match and advising her against it. *That'll* mean a few heart to heart talks.'

'I'll come with you to the airport?' she suggested after lunch.

'No—it'll be bakingly hot, and you went to bed far too late last night. Have your siesta and I'll come back and wake you up with tea.'

But he never did come back because on his way home from the airport the car went at a great speed into a bus that was travelling in the opposite direction, and thence through some fencing into a small ravine. The bus driver said that he thought the car was completely out of control, but the whole thing happened on a corner and so quickly that it was difficult to know for certain. The police said that the steering was locked and that an inner tube had blown, and that either or both of these things could have caused the accident. John, who was alone in the car, died almost at once, but nobody in the bus was seriously hurt.

*   *   *

It was Oliver who fetched her from Jamaica. By the time he got there the worst of the arrangements were over or had been made: the lawyer and accountant had flown out and gone back, the inquest was done, reporters dealt with—even the packing was finished. Oliver arrived one morning and took her back to London that afternoon: she did not want to stay; the sun was out too much, she said. There was only one road to Montego Bay and the airport and so they passed the ravine with its broken fence. She asked the driver to stop the car, and got out, and Oliver knew that she did not mean him to come too. When she came back, she said, 'She made him go to the airport for nothing. Didn't bother to call and say she'd changed her mind—just sent a cable letter that afternoon. I wish I could stop thinking about any of that.'

He did not know what to say. She seemed to him to be either stunned or oddly restless—as when for instance, she completely repacked a suitcase in the plane. But everything about her—even the restlessness—seemed to be stiffened with a kind of dignity that he had not known she possessed. She slept in the aeroplane and woke with tears on her face, but she went away at once and came back without a sign of them. He could not help feeling slightly afraid of her and hated himself for this feeling, because it could be no use at all to her. When they were being given dinner and she was pretending to eat, he asked her where she wanted to go, and she said at once the house in the country.

'Not ghastly old Monks' Close!'

'No: John's house.'

'Do you want me to come with you?'

'Of course I do.'

McNaughton unexpectedly met them at the airport. As soon as they had been cleared by Customs, there he was immediately. She clearly had not known he would be there: she called his name, and took his hand in both of hers and for a second he saw a look of such desolation on both their faces as though exactly the same thing had hurt them in the same way at the same moment, and then she—his sister—stopped it, said things, made them do things with the luggage and get through the next few minutes somehow.

They spent the night in an hotel at her request, and the next day, Oliver drove them down to the house in the country in the same white car that she had been given in France. On the way, he told her about May, and Herbert, and Alice, ending with the extraordinary and awful time he had had with Alice, when she had poured out all her terrible suspicions.

'Never known Alice talk so much,' he said—seeing that he had really caught her attention. 'You know how she doesn't seem able to tell you anything that she wants you to know? Well, this time she couldn't stop. She walked out on Leslie, planning to go back to the old Close, but she caught a rather late train from Bristol so she tried to spend the night at Lincoln Street, poor little thing. I was out. It was an appalling night, so off she went to Waterloo and caught some sort of milk train or whatever they're called because she was afraid she hadn't got enough money for an hotel. When she got to the station it was nearly five, of course no cabs so she walks— through snowdrifts and all. And when she got there, she found him dead, and poor darling May weeping with a torch and a coal shovel in the garden because she couldn't bury Claude.'

'What had he died of?'

'Herbert? Rage, I should think. But the thing is—you were right about him.' She was silent, and he was afraid that he'd lost her again. 'Because what do you think Claude died of?'

She shook her head.

'Arsenic, my dear: a hell of a lot of it. Meant for May. That's what I mean. He was such a screaming bore, I didn't think he could be wicked as well—but that's what he was. A monster. Alice said her mother *and* her stepmother. She took poor old Claude to be analysed because she was so worried about May. She thinks May doesn't know and it would kill her to find out.'

'What does May think?'

'She thinks Alice doesn't know, and it would kill her to find out. That's why she was trying to bury Claude.'

'Poor May! Poor Alice!'

'Well—in a way. But they've decided to look after each other— because they feel each other have had such an awful time. So they're going to live in Lincoln Street and go to frightful meetings where nobody can say what they mean because they don't mean anything. It suits Alice because it makes her feel more like other people, and it suits May because it makes her feel worse than everyone else which is what she feels is right.'

She asked more questions about her mother; indeed, the subject lasted them almost until they arrived. He knew when they were approaching the house, because she fell silent except for telling him which way to go, which was not the quickest way, she said, but the way she had come before. The morning had been grey and overcast, but as they drove through a beech wood the road became a lattice-work of shadows and sunlight, and the bare trees ahead turned fox-coloured. Then they were out of the wood and a few minutes later she told him to stop. 'That's the house,' she said. 'Will you come with me now?'

They walked through a wicket gate across a field towards the house which was set on a terrace above them. There was a black painted door which she opened to present them with a flight of steps. They walked slowly and in silence up the steps, past a little thorny hedge where she stopped a moment, and then on to the house itself. At the dining-room windows he saw that the round table was laid for two. Elizabeth was ahead of him now, walking round a corner of the house which had bare snaky branches growing round its windows. When he joined her, she was standing in front of a conservatory, its windows misted so that one could not see clearly inside. She tried the door and it opened. Standing on the black and white floor in a huge tub was a camellia growing up to the roof, twelve, fourteen feet high and encrusted with flowers and buds of pale red flowers. She shut the door behind them and said: 'He promised that my best Christmas present would be here,' and then she made a sound articulate only of sheer misery that ended, 'Oh Oliver! What shall I *do*? How do I bear it,' and stretched out her hands blindly to find him.

Much later, when she had finished crying, for that time, she said some of the things that she had to say once—to someone. 'It's the first time I do something—anything—that I last did with John that's so difficult. I keep on making myself do them—in a way to spoil things—to try and make things I remember with him *un*holy, and then, even that seems wrong and feeble. Do you know what I mean?'

'Yes,' he said—really trying to. But nothing had ever happened to him, he knew, that could even approach making him feel as she was feeling, and as he wondered whether it ever would, he noticed a pang of humble envy.

'It changes,' he said. 'Time changes people always whether they like it or not. You've got that baby to have and bring up. And if you go on wearing that black velvet mac, you'll end up looking exactly like an outsize mole,' and was rewarded by the first, watery smile. But she said:

'I feel like black. I know now why people wear it. But after I've had the baby, I won't, of course. Babies prefer yellow or red.'

'Shall I stay with you—till you have it, anyway? Not happily ever after or anything, but just as a sort of stopgap?'

'It's what people usually are to each other, isn't it,' he went on after she had agreed and he'd thought that she might be going to cry again. 'Except for people properly in love, of course,' he added out of kindness to her feelings. 'And I can't imagine being that.'

'Of *course* you will. I've had mine, but *you* will.'

They looked at each other in a way that they had always done whenever each had thought the other wrong or stupid ('she'll find another love; of *course* she will'), and both were aware of the familiar state of affectionate challenge that on this single occasion neither had the slightest intention of taking up.